Friends
with
Benefits

Friends
with
Benefits

A Novel

Marisa Kanter

CELADON
BOOKS

NEW YORK

FRIENDS WITH BENEFITS. Copyright © 2025 by Marisa Kanter. All rights reserved. Printed in the United States of America. For information, address Celadon Books, a division of Macmillan Publishers, 120 Broadway, New York, NY 10271.

www.celadonbooks.com

Designed by Michelle McMillian

Library of Congress Cataloging-in-Publication Data

Names: Kanter, Marisa, author.
Title: Friends with benefits : a novel / Marisa Kanter.
Description: First U.S. edition. | New York : Celadon Books, 2025.
Identifiers: LCCN 2024047955 | ISBN 9781250358899 (trade paperback) | ISBN 9781250358905 (ebook)
Subjects: LCGFT: Romance fiction. | Novels.
Classification: LCC PS3611.A5498 F75 2025 | DDC 813/.6—dc23/eng/20241023
LC record available at https://lccn.loc.gov/2024047955

Our books may be purchased in bulk for promotional, educational, or business use. Please contact your local bookseller or the Macmillan Corporate and Premium Sales Department at 1-800-221-7945, extension 5442, or by email at MacmillanSpecialMarkets@macmillan.com.

First U.S. Edition: 2025

10 9 8 7 6 5 4 3 2 1

this one's for me

Author's Note

While *Friends with Benefits* is fun and romantic, please note that there are sensitive topics, including medical gaslighting, health anxiety, mentioned death/illness of a parent, parental neglect, and the realities of living with chronic pain. Please be gentle with yourself and take care while reading.

Friends
with
Benefits

1

Evelyn Bloom knows she isn't famous, but it still stings when press photographers lower their cameras the moment she and her sister step onto the red carpet outside the Dolby Theatre. She'd paid for an Uber Black from Pasadena to Hollywood and those thirty-three minutes in a BMW X7 cost as much as the monthly payment on Phoebe. So the least she could get is a photo of her stepping out of the black SUV with the Getty Images watermark stamped across her face. Phoebe is a ten-year-old Mazda CX-3 that she loves with her whole heart, but Imogen called it *too embarrassing for the occasion.*

Now inside the theater, Evie's phone vibrates with the Uber receipt.

She winces.

Imogen.

Evie follows her to the line for the bathroom, grateful to Imogen for escorting her without even asking. Living with a chronic illness that fucks with your GI tract, for Evie, means a mandatory bathroom stop before any major event. Sometimes two. Just in case. Jules, her therapist, would ask Evie to interrogate if it's Crohn's or the anxiety of a Crohn's flare that triggers this. Does it matter? Evie doesn't think so.

"How are you feeling?" Imogen asks, examining her lipstick in a compact as the line moves at a glacial pace.

A bit nauseous, if she's being honest. "Fine."

"I, for one, am kind of obsessed with being the plus-one tonight."

From Uber Black requests to being on a first-name basis with the theater's security team, Imogen Bloom knows how to navigate a premiere. She works in casting for an unscripted series and networks her ass off, attending premieres and galas and wherever her boss sends her to recruit C-list celebrities and influencers. But Imogen is off duty tonight. She's here with Evie.

For Evie.

"Gen?"

Imogen spins 180 degrees and squeals. "Portia? Oh my God, you look incredible."

Portia Devereaux, a supporting cast member in *Ginger*—the film premiering here tonight—is one of the few reality television contestants who successfully pivoted to a film career. Imogen discovered them when she was a wide-eyed baby intern in the casting department for *Big Brother*, and Portia's success on the show directly led to a full-time job offer for Imogen upon graduating from UCLA.

"Working?" Portia assumes.

Imogen shakes her head, blond curls bouncing around her shoulders as she loops her arm through Evie's. "Nope! Evie is one of the Foley artists who worked on *Ginger*."

Portia's eyes meet hers. "Amazing."

Evie's natural instinct is to downplay what a major deal this is. "I interned for the studio during post. Right place, right time."

Imogen rolls her eyes. "Annaliese had a scheduling conflict, so Evie stepped in and did the Foley for *Ginger*. She learned the dances in an afternoon and—"

A stall door swings open, and Evie's next in line, so she bolts, desperate to remove herself from the conversation before the obvious next question: *What are you working on now?* Because this night is a total fluke. Evie Bloom is not a working Foley artist. Yet. She spends her days working for a media conglomerate, editing podcasts for former reality dating show contestants turned influencers.

It's not a dream job, but the benefits are good.

Done in the bathroom, she exits the stall and washes her hands next to Zendaya, who says, "Excuse me," as she reaches across her for a paper towel and it takes every ounce of restraint for Evie not to blurt out *I love you*. Well. Even if tonight isn't a turning point that marks the beginning of a long and successful career, at least Zendaya spoke to her.

"Ev. *Zendaya spoke to you,*" Imogen says as they take their seats in the mezzanine.

Evie knew that a biopic about Ginger Rogers was going to be a big deal—big-budget movies about Old Hollywood are certified Oscar porn. But it's one thing to know it and another to see the caliber of celebrities that showed up to the premiere.

"I just. I cannot believe that *the* Zendaya Maree Stoermer Coleman is going to hear my talented sister dance," Imogen says.

"And she won't even know it."

It's the truth. She's not the star of the movie. No. Evie Bloom is not the face. She's every step on concrete, on linoleum, on carpet. She's the cadence of Ginger's movements— the buoyant beat that accompanies running into the arms of any one of her five husbands, the jump of joy when she lands her first film, the crisp, clean shuffles that define her as a tap legend. All the sounds that make a movie magic.

In *Ginger*, Evie is a part of that magic.

Not the face, but the feet.

She *loves* that magic.

Evie inherited her fascination with sound from Grandma Pep, the beloved host and executive producer of *Some Pep in Your Step*, a local radio show that featured anyone with an interesting "happy-making" story. Peppy Bloom was on the air for over thirty-five years. Some of Evie's most formative childhood memories are summer days in the studio with her grandmother, where she asked the audio engineers endless questions and absorbed so many lessons on how to tell a story not just with words but with sounds.

It was one of Grandma Pep's stories that directly led to her becoming a storyteller with sounds herself. One blistering summer day, she went with her grandmother to interview a team of Foley artists who worked on the Paramount lot. Evie was nine and watched with wide-eyed wonder as these people explained to Grandma Pep that their jobs were to create the sound effects that make a movie—and they used the most unexpected objects. She learned that a celery stick can mimic the sound of a broken bone, that gloves with paper clips on the fingertips are adequate dog paws, that a hand in a jar of mayonnaise is a kiss.

They create the sounds that breathe life into a film, Grandma Pep explained as her audio engineer recorded a Foley demo for the segment. Evie's mind near exploded watching them use a bathtub to create the sounds of a boat cutting through water. She remembers that day so vividly—the smell of mayonnaise, the *snap* of celery, the awe of it all. Afterward, her ears started paying extra close attention at the movies, trying to guess the truth behind the sounds she heard.

Eighteen years later, Evie is seated among the stars at a premiere for a film that *she* breathed life into.

Well.

In the mezzanine above the stars.

Imogen's elbow nudges her. "It's still pretty early. You should be out there mingling!"

"I hate mingling."

"*Evie.*"

Imogen has always made it look so easy—mingling, networking, any word that can be defined as speaking to strangers. Evie loves everything about the work that is being a Foley artist, but she really hates the *people-ing* of it all, the reality that opportunities depend on it. An incredible portfolio is useless if no one will take the time to listen to it. Objectively, Imogen is right. She should be mingling.

Of course, she doesn't tell her sister this.

Or admit that she doesn't know why small talk is so easy for Imogen yet so impossible for her.

Instead, she sticks out her tongue.

Imogen mirrors the expression, then continues, "Portia is chill. They're also blowing up in a major way, and I set up the intro and . . . you totally flopped."

"We were in the bathroom, Gen."

"So?"

"It didn't exactly seem like the time to pitch myself."

"Maybe not, but you didn't have to downplay your contribution to *Ginger* either."

Evie didn't downplay anything. It was true, what she said to Portia, that the opportunity was a happenstance of right place, right time. Annaliese Fallon, who stars as Ginger, was meant to dub herself—to come into the Foley studio and record her dances in sync with video. Just like any other sound effect, adding the taps in postproduction guarantees a crisper, cleaner sound and allows more control to the mixers in charge of layering all the sounds together. But then a scheduling conflict sent Annaliese to her next role, on Broadway, earlier than anticipated, so she never had the chance to record the dances that she'd flawlessly executed on-screen.

And the studio was fucked.

Ross Snyder, Evie's boss, scrambled in frantic search of a solution. Put tap shoes on his hands and winged it. The taps were in sync but wrong. A shuffle that should have been a scuffle, a flap that should have been a ball change. To the untrained ear of the general public, Ross's hand taps would suffice. But this was a love letter to Ginger Rogers. A movie for dancers.

And Evie's first dream, before Grandma Pep had spectacularly shattered the illusion of sound, was dance.

I'm a dancer, she told Ross, her voice small and palatable. *I can do it.*

Ross cocked an eyebrow, skeptical.

Ross is an asshole.

Give me the tapes and a day.

Ross sighed, conceding that he had nothing to lose.

Evie didn't tell Ross that she *was* a dancer, past tense, or that she'd have to tear her closet apart to find the worn BLOCHs that she hadn't put on since high school. She didn't tell Ross that she wasn't sure if her weakened ankle could handle the choreography. Nope. When Ross Snyder looked up at Evie with tap shoes for hands, Evie saw an opportunity—to prove her worth, to get a Foley credit in a major theatrical release, to dance again.

She took it.

Of course she did.

She learned the choreography and perfected it until her feet bled.

After the recording session, her calves burned. Her ankle screamed *enough*. And Evie loved every minute of that day. She is so drawn to Foley because of the physicality, the musicality, the rhythm required. Being in the studio, Evie is almost a dancer again, and it felt incredible to actually dance, to be Ginger's feet.

Thank fucking God, Ross said when Evie played back her work for him.

It's the closest she ever got to a thank-you from Ross Snyder.

"Well. I tried," Imogen says with a shrug, then pulls out her phone and starts typing, her eyebrows rising in the amused expression that is for one person only. "It's Sloane, asking if I need anything from Costco and . . . since when are we *Costco people?* How did this happen?"

"You moved in together after three months like a sapphic cliché, Gen. Of *course* you're Costco people."

Imogen flips her off. "Valid."

Evie laughs, then reaches for her phone after it vibrates with a new text:

You're Ginger tonight. I'm so proud of you, Evelyn.

It squeezes her heart, those nine words from her best friend.

"Theo?" Imogen assumes.

Evie nods.

"I sort of feel bad. He would've been a better plus-one." She checks her teeth one final time for lipstick. "Just in terms of, like, appreciating the dance of it all. I would say sorry for calling dibs as your blood, but I'm not. So."

Evie snorts. "You're a great date. And anyway, it's a school night."

Theo Cohen—*Mr.* Cohen—would never be out past 10:00 p.m. on a school night. He has twenty children that he's responsible for in the morning, teaching the next generation multiplication and assigning book reports and doing experiments to learn about weather systems that don't exist in Southern California.

"Bitch, I *knew* you invited him first."

Evie laughs because of course her extra ticket was Imogen's first, always, forever.

But she's just too easy to mess with.

Anyway, Evie will watch *Ginger* with Theo from the comfort of her couch when it's on Netflix next week—when they can rewind and rewatch and analyze the dance routines like they're seventeen again, in search of inspiration for their next duet. If it's even good. Evie's feet had to be approved by so many sets of ears—Ross's, the sound mixer's, the music supervisor's, the director's, Annaliese Fallon's. Still, she must approve her work with her own ears before she allows the person whose opinion she cares about most in this world to listen, too.

She rereads Theo's text, then tucks her phone into her clutch as the lights dim and the Metro-Goldwyn-Mayer lion roars. Evie's feet are the opening beat. Ginger is rehearsing one of her routines with Fred Astaire in *Swing Time*. Annaliese Fallon looks incredible. Evie sounds incredible. And for the next two hours, she's lost in the beautiful, intricate sound design. Sound is taken for granted, but Evie loves the art, the science, the *magic* of shaping an audience's experience through what is not seen but heard. It's kind of blowing her mind, that every time the music starts and the dancing begins, everyone is seeing Annaliese but hearing her. Evie's art and talent are an integral part of this movie.

It's an indescribable feeling.

It is purpose.

A sort of fulfillment that is notably absent when she opens Pro Tools every day and works on the latest podcast for the reality dating show *Ever After*. She loves these podcasts as a listener—their smart, feminist, intersectional takes on a franchise that refuses to progress beyond the patriarchal foundation upon which it's built. But spending forty-plus hours a week in front of a screen editing them?

It. Is. Torture.

Evie isn't meant to sit in front of a computer screen.

She's meant to move.

"Evie," Imogen whispers, dabbing a tissue to her eyes as the credits start to roll. "Holy shit."

Evie squeezes Imogen's hand.

"I felt you," she continues. "Like, I closed my eyes and we were at a competition again."

Imogen danced, too, following in her big sister's tap shoes. But she danced for the fun of it, for the costumes, for the unrequited crushes she always had on other dancers. Dance never became Imogen's identity. It was simply a thing she did, not who she was.

Dance is who Evie was.

Until she wasn't.

Until she *couldn't*.

Evie and Imogen stay glued in their seats for the credits to see the name *Evelyn Bloom* under the Foley department. It's the credit that Evie believes will jump-start her career, the credit she listed on the union application that's currently pending. If approved, she can begin to take on more work. In the union, she'll be paid guaranteed minimums and not be lowballed as most early-career freelancers are. In the union, she'll have health benefits that will free her from the Pro Tools life. Benefits that cover the appointments, the screenings, the medications necessary to manage her chronic illness.

The credits roll.

Evie waits to see her name.

Waits.

And waits.

And—

"What the fuck?" Imogen snarls at the credit.

Foley artist: Ross Snyder

As quickly as it appears, it's gone, and Evie's eyes sting as if she's been slapped. She knows Ross is an asshole, but she thought he was at least an asshole with integrity. But of course, he's just another man in the industry more than happy to take credit for a woman's work. She bled for *Ginger*. She deserved this credit.

She needed it.

Her union application is going to be rejected without it.

Evie's stomach cramps, a dull pain shooting through her lower abdomen, reminding her that the dream that felt so close to possible just two hours ago is once again very much not.

"Ev—"

"Can we go home?"

Ross just ... erased her from *Ginger*. Tonight was supposed to be good. Working for Ross Snyder was the worst six months of Evie's life, but tonight was meant to be proof that his exploiting her passion for unpaid labor was worth it.

Evie exits the theater biting the inside of her cheek so she doesn't burst into furious tears.

Fuck Ross.

Fuck passions.

Fuck.

This.

2

M r. Cohen's winner pick didn't even make the jury!"

Theo Cohen's fourth graders erupt in *oohs* and giggle at his humiliating loss. Every day, he's humbled by a scathing drag delivered by one of his students—be it the way he walks, the color of his shirt, or the total embarrassment of losing your *Survivor* winner pick pre-jury.

Theo covers his ears. "Milo! Spoilers!"

"It's okay, Mr. Cohen," Jeremiah says. "We voted for an amendment to the spoiler rule."

Theo raises a single eyebrow. "Oh?"

"Yep!" Sierra confirms, with a chipped neon-pink nail polish thumbs-up.

Milo stands, his chair screeching against the floor. "The twenty-four-hour Spoiler Embargo may be lifted if Mr. Cohen's winner pick is eliminated."

Milo then marches over to Theo's desk to hand him the amendment, handwritten and signed by the entire class. *Embargo* was a challenge vocab word last week. Milo genuinely did spoil last night's episode for Theo, but he's way too proud that his kids just correctly used *embargo* in a sentence to care. Integrating his favorite television show into his curriculum has made Mr. Cohen *cool*. The teacher every fourth grader crosses their fingers and wishes for at Foothill Elementary. Kids live for the challenges. Theo has a collection of *Survivor* puzzles in his classroom—color pattern, unscramble the phrase, 3D, and, of course, the iconic slide puzzle.

Every Friday starts with a *Survivor* recap and a puzzle.

Theo reads the amendment, his expression serious.

Minor spoilers are worth the collective joy his students take in calling him a loser.

"Fair enough."

Theo pins the amendment to the corkboard hanging on the wall above his desk, alongside the rules for participating in *Survivor* Fridays and the list with each kid's winner pick. Successfully select who wins after the first episode and receive either a homework pass or five extra points on the weekly vocabulary quiz. If his winner pick is eliminated pre-jury, the finale party becomes an ice cream party.

Theo chooses a likely pre-jury boot with intention, to give his kids an ice cream party.

It's been great for classroom management, *Survivor* Fridays with Mr. Cohen. It keeps the kids on track, looking forward to the puzzles and strategy chats at the end of the week. Theo can make any concept relate back to the show—the science behind some of the physical challenges, the character arcs and storytelling over the course of the season, the complicated history of the filming locations and challenging the show's appropriation of Indigenous culture. During his first year teaching, Ms. Connors spoke to Theo about *appropriation* being a challenge vocab word after a parent complained that *politics have no place in the classroom.* He now makes it a point to use it as the challenge word on the first vocabulary quiz of the year.

It's the easiest way to immediately identify the Problem Parents.

In college, Theo took Classroom Management, a semester-long unit dedicated to tips and tricks for managing problem students—the disruptors who pull focus and derail a lesson with an off-topic comment or an ill-timed fart joke. But Theo learned real quick that nine times out of ten, kids are not the problem. It's the parents who derail a lesson with a call to Ms. Connors, who question his independent reading list, who discredit him because he's one of the youngest teachers at Foothill.

Parents are the worst part of the job.

Easily.

But the kids are worth it.

Theo crosses his name off the *Survivor* board, and everyone cheers. "Okay! You've had your laugh, so it's time for mine. Who's ready to learn how to multiply some fractions?"

"Are you going to sing?" Annabelle asks.

"You know it."

Cue a collective groan.

They'll complain about Mr. Cohen's songs. Call him cringe or corny. But he'll sing a song about multiplying fractions to the tune of "Let It Go" and it will stick. Even if they mock him, they will have *multiply, multiply, the numerators to-ge-ther* stuck in their heads until the end of time. Or at least until the statewide cumulative exam. His mom taught him that. She had a song for everything, and Theo can still hear her singing them. It's in these moments, when he's introducing a new concept via song, that he feels closest to her.

After a somewhat successful lesson, Theo's students line up two-by-two for gym class. Handing them over to Ms. Walsh begins forty-five minutes of quiet. Usually. It's his prep period, meant for setting up for the afternoon, for grading Play-Doh dioramas of endangered species, for Clorox disinfecting the surfaces of his classroom. Sometimes, Juniper Delgado, a third-grade teacher whose kids are in art class when his are in gym, will knock on his door and they'll do some grading together to a compilation of Seth Meyers monologues. Most of the time, he's listening to a *Survivor* recap podcast, oscillating between photocopying enough worksheets for the rest of the week and texting his best friend, Evelyn Bloom.

But today?

Today, his precious prep time is booked with the principal of Foothill Elementary.

Theo knocks on the office door. "Ms. Connors—"

"Veronica," Ms. Connors corrects with a soft chuckle.

Veronica Connors has been the principal at Foothill Elementary since Theo was a student at this same school. It doesn't matter how many times she insists on being called *Veronica*—she will never not be Ms. Connors to him. This applies to any educator Theo knew as a student at Foothill. It's weird, the shift in perspective from student to colleague.

Theo's positive he'll never get used to it.

"Veronica," he repeats, then takes a seat in one of the chairs in front of her desk.

Her eyes shift from her desktop to meet his. "How are you, Theo?"

"Good."

"What's on the agenda?"

"I just wanted to share a proposal I put together for a class trip to the Griffith Observatory."

Her brow furrows. "You know the fourth graders go to Kidspace."

Kidspace is a rite of passage for a Pasadena kid—be it via a field trip, a birthday party, or a weekend activity. It's not a terrible place for a kid to spend a day, with its three and a half acres of indoor and outdoor tactile exhibits. It's just, well, *basic*, as Annabelle would (and did!) say. While the museum is technically for the under-tens, Theo's kids feel too old, too *been there, done that*, for it to be the fourth-grade field trip. He remembers that feeling, once a Foothill fourth grader himself. So every year, he proposes an alternative field trip for his kids.

Theo clears his throat. "I know. But with the focus on earth science and space in the curriculum, we believe that the observatory would be a more educationally enriching experience for the students."

It's a more eloquent response than *But Kidspace is basic*.

"We?"

"The fourth-grade teachers all agree Kidspace is a bit, um, basic."

Theo swallows.

Shit.

Ms. Connors—*Veronica*—sighs. "I'm sorry, Theo. Kidspace gives us a generous discount for our annual field trip and we just do not have room in the budget for anything extra this year, with the third graders going to the zoo."

"What?"

"Juniper made a compelling case. If we cannot educate the kids on the problematic truths of the Gold Rush without parents up my ass . . . then we may as well just take them to the zoo."

Theo is stunned. The annual third-grade field trip is to a historical reenactment of the Gold Rush. It's a complex with architecture that emulates 1800s Americana, where the kids have a blast digging for gold nuggets, completely oblivious to the brutal displacement of Indigenous people during this period. The historical center vaguely glosses over its ugly truths. How American of it. Theo isn't upset that the third graders of Foothill Elementary will no longer be exposed to history that's ignorant at best and racist at worst.

But.

He pitched the zoo last year.

"Juniper's husband is a veterinarian for the LA Zoo, you know. He's going to take the kids on a behind-the-scenes tour and let them feed giraffes. Really make them feel special."

He knows.

Last year, Theo asked Juniper if Joey, her then-fiancé, would be down to give his kids a tour of the zoo if his proposal was approved. He shared his pitch with her. Theo always shares his pitches with Juniper. As the only twentysomething teachers at Foothill, he believed they had aligning interests.

He believed they were friends.

Theo gives Ms. Connors a terse nod.

"I'm sorry," Ms. Connors says, apathy in her voice. "Maybe next year?"

It's her annual refrain.

It's also Theo's cue to get out. He pushes his chair back and stands, exiting Ms. Connors's office with ten minutes of his prep period remaining. Theo has two options. He can knock on Juniper's door and ask, *What the hell?* He doesn't begrudge this win for her kids, but allies aren't supposed to backstab each other. Now he has to figure out how to explain to his kids that an afternoon at Kidspace is just as cool as *feeding fucking giraffes.*

There's no way to explain that.

He already sees Annabelle's eye roll.

As the mere concept of confrontation makes Theo want to melt into the floor and disappear Wicked Witch of the West–style, he goes with the second option. Doing nothing.

Soft.

Theo hears Jacob Cohen's voice in response to his inaction, but his dad's brand of toxic masculinity is a particular trauma that he unpacks with Brian, his therapist, every Tuesday at four. So he pushes that voice, that word, away and Clorox wipes the desks, the smartboard, the pencil sharpener, before he returns to the gym to retrieve his kids. After gym, it's snack and silent reading time. Theo has a basket of single-serving prepackaged snacks at his desk so that no kid will be snack-less. He makes sure to have gluten-free options for Kaia and Tyler. Over his desktop, he watches his kids silently snacking and reading books selected from the class library. Currently, they're drawn to the classics—the Percy Jackson series and *Diary of a Wimpy Kid.* Also anything by Kelly Yang or Jason Reynolds. Theo's classroom library is curated, like his snack collection, with his own funds. He can do snacks and books.

He can't self-fund a whole field trip.

Theo observes his kids reading and snacking on carrot sticks and Goldfish and can't believe that this is his life—still living in his hometown, now teaching at the elementary school he attended.

He's a *townie.*

Somewhere in the multiverse, Theo Cohen is an activist, working with a New York City nonprofit to reform curricu-lums nationwide. He takes his plans to Washington. Fights for accessibility to technology, for free breakfasts and lunches, for the quality of one's education not to depend on the zip code in which one lives.

In that universe, he isn't in the classroom.

Theo kind of loves his classroom—the bright-colored drawings tacked onto walls, the beanbag corner he set up so the kids can be comfortable during movies, the library he curated with books he loved as a kid and books he loves as an adult who teaches kids. He loves Maude, the guinea pig that Evelyn bought for his class during his first year teaching who is somehow still alive. He loves the memories of his mom that are in this room.

In this school.

Lori Cohen was a second-grade teacher at Foothill Elementary for more than thirty-five years. On Theo's desk are side-by-side first-day-of-school photos. His first day of kindergarten and his first day as Mr. Cohen. One features a toothless grin. Both feature Lori's arms wrapped around him, so proud. Of course, he sometimes wonders what Multiverse Theo's life is like—the Theo who works on progressive education reform, the Theo who lives in a closet-size apartment in Manhattan, the Theo who still has a mom . . .

"Mr. Cohen?"

His name is an inquisitive whisper.

Theo looks up from his computer. "What's up, Kaia?"

"What does *reverent* mean?"

She points to the word in her copy of *The Lightning Thief.* Kaia O'Connell takes silent reading seriously—both the silent and the reading. If she doesn't understand a word, she will always ask Theo before she moves on to the next chapter. He defines *reverent* and Kaia returns to her seat to write it down. She has a whole notebook full of new words and Theo's definitions. Kaia can look it up in the dictionary or on one of the class iPads after silent reading time, but Theo is always encouraging his kids to ask for help.

He wishes more adults encouraged him to ask for help.

Theo's eyes return to his screen, where there is a new email in his inbox.

Subject: this new math is INCONCEIVABLE

He coughs to cover up his snort at the not-at-all covert subject line from Evelyn, aka mommingismylife@gmail.com. She believes it's a genius way to contact him at work. He keeps his phone locked in his desk while his kids are in the room because if they can't have devices out, neither can he. What started out as a system for emergencies has devolved into his best friend spamming his inbox with subject lines from the point of view of a disgruntled parent. Subtle, Evelyn Bloom is not.

Theo opens the email.

can we watch at mine tonight? also . . . you may need to talk me out of committing arson.
just kidding.
OR AM I!!

The more momager the subject line, the more unhinged the message. *Survivor* Wednesday is on Thursday this week, as Evelyn spent last night attending her first movie premiere— and they never watch without each other. Even in college, they watched together from opposite coasts, Theo from his NYU dorm and Evelyn from her UCLA one. She splurged on a VPN so they could watch together on East Coast time. It was a whole thing.

Theo types a response.

Sure. Warning: I have been spoiled.

p.s. if you're so worried about my emails being screened,

you maybe shouldn't threaten to commit a felony?

(she's kidding!)

Evelyn answers immediately:

I'M KIDDING.

omg THEODORE. you checked reddit?

Theo replies:

Milo.

Not even a cough can suppress the laugh that escapes at Evelyn's response—what a butt! deduct ten points from his diorama project. at least. It's a disruptor. Silent reading time is over, and not only that, but Theo now must explain what's so funny. These kids don't let him get away with anything. It's the start of a chaotic afternoon—Tyler steals Emerson's favorite marker. Annabelle bursts into tears when she sees a *check mark* on last night's homework, not the check plus that she expects out of herself. Kaia asks if Pluto is still a planet. Milo says, *Pluto is a dog, Kaia.*

By the time it's a quarter to three, Theo is exhausted.

Jeremiah raises his hand. "My cousin Lola says that Mrs. Delgado is taking her class to the zoo this year."

"Who is Mrs. Delgado?" Milo asks.

"*Ms. Garcia*," Annabelle says, like *duh.* "She got married, so she's Mrs. Delgado now."

"That's so patriarchy of her," Sierra says.

"Are we going to the zoo?" Kaia asks.

Theo shakes his head. "We're going to Kidspace."

He braces himself for the collective groans, and his kids don't let him down.

"Kidspace is for babies!"

"Mr. Cohen. I had my birthday party there in, like, *first grade*."

"We never got to go to the zoo!"

"That's not fair!"

It's hard for Theo to calm his students down, to assure them that Kidspace will be a great time. They're right. He won't gaslight them into thinking that a museum they've already visited multiple times in their nine short years of life is better than a day at the zoo—or a visit to a planetarium. He just lets them vent and groan until the bell rings and bus numbers are called. Milo is right, it *isn't* fair. And Theo doesn't want this to be a teachable *life isn't fair* moment for his kids. They'll learn that—if they haven't already—on their own.

He just wants them to stare up in wonder at the stars.

As the classroom empties and Mr. Cohen becomes Theo once more, he makes a promise to himself that this year somehow, some way, his kids will see the stars.

3

Evie sips on matzo ball soup as Jeff Probst extinguishes the flame of Theo's winner pick with a dimpled smirk.

"Milo is such a little shit," she says.

"I know. But he used *embargo* correctly in a sentence."

She hears the pride in his voice and thinks that school would've been a more bearable place if there had been more teachers like Mr. Cohen.

After the eliminated castaway's inspirational final words, Theo stands and makes his way to the kitchen for seconds. The entire bungalow smells like Lori Cohen's matzo ball soup, like their childhood. Theo makes it upon request. It's one of the few meals that's guaranteed to soothe her stomach when she's having a Not Great Pain Day. She's in remission. For now. But stress can trigger a flare. Rage can, too. Evie is stressed *and* pissed. A terrible combination for her body, despite being in clinical remission for five years—her longest stretch of *for now* since her diagnosis a decade ago. It's the forever qualifier with chronic illness. For now. Her case is classified as mild. For now. Her diet and the medication administered by infusion every eight weeks keep the inflammation in her colon at bay. For now.

It used to make her so angry.

It *still* makes her anxious.

But right now, the soup helps, even if it doesn't quite taste the same as when Lori made it.

Does it ever?

Theo sinks into the opposite end of the worn jade patent-leather couch. "Do you want to talk about it?"

Fuck Ross!! is the only text that Evie sent Theo about *Ginger*.

Besides the arson threat she sent to his work email in a moment of impulsive fury.

She places her soup mug on a coaster and turns up the heating pad resting across her stomach. "I have to withdraw my application."

Theo's eyebrows scrunch together. "What?"

"I don't qualify."

Without a credit on a union project, Evie's application to IATSE—the International Alliance of Theatrical Stage Employees—is null and void. After everything she put herself through for that film. Evie didn't just bleed, she *danced*. Learned complex choreography and let herself love it again. Not the all-consuming love that defined her adolescence, but a quiet *maybe I don't have to let go of this part of me* love. It was the first time she dared to let dance back into her heart since she fell. Two months before graduating high school, Evie tumbled out of Theo's arms, her ankle buckling coming out of a simple lift at her last competition. An accident that not only shattered the future she had imagined for herself, but also led to a diagnosis that explained it all—the fall, the bone-deep exhaustion, the pain that she'd become so used to living with. In the decade since her diagnosis, she's grieved the reality that audiences will never watch her dance again. In therapy, she's felt all her furious feelings that a joint had to fracture—that *her body had to break*—in order for her pain to be taken seriously. Accepted the reality that even with physical therapy, *even in remission from Crohn's,* her ankle will never be strong enough to dance at the level she once did.

But it felt incredible, being Ginger Rogers. Though no one saw her dance again, they *heard* her. It's not recognition that she requires. Evie knows no one sits through the credits.

But damn it, she needed that credit.

"Shit," Theo says.

"Ross would've done the Foley with tap shoes on his hands if it weren't for me."

She sighs, impulsive fury fading until she just feels deflated and defeated about the whole thing. Maybe it's a sign. She's meant to edit together unsolicited relationship advice from Amber B. and Tiffany P. and any influencer who wakes up one day and decides to start a podcast. She's good at her job. She *likes* Amber B. and Tiffany P.—their commentary is smart and their notes for the edit are spot-on and they don't pop the mic. It's just not her passion. Maybe that's okay.

Maybe a job can be just that.

A job.

"I'm sorry, Evelyn," Theo says.

He's the only person, besides her grandparents, who calls her by her full name. Even when she started going by Evie in sixth grade and had to correct the pronunciation of teachers a many on the first day of school (EH-vee, *not* EE-vee), she never corrected him or asked him to make the switch when she entered her Evie era. Evelyn is for family, and Theo is family.

"When he promised me a credit, I believed him. It's so embarrassing, Theodore."

Theo's name is not Theodore.

It's just Theo.

But she is Evelyn to him and he is Theodore to her.

"Is there not anything you can do?"

"As an unpaid intern?"

Theo has no response. He knows as well as she does that in this situation, she's powerless. After a beat, he shifts to face her. "It's bullshit. Ross is a dick. But there will be more opportunities. Better projects."

Evie knows this is true, objectively, but damn it, she wasn't supposed to hustle and freelance and lose any more sleep pursuing this path than she already has. Maybe there will be more movies or television shows or video games to break out her career as a full-time Foley artist.

But *Ginger* was supposed to be *the* break.

Evie is allowed to mourn the reality that it isn't.

Theo is not allowed to brush her feelings off.

"Do you know any arsonists?"

"Evelyn."

"Still kidding."

In this moment, she misses Lori so much. Theo's mom would've at least humored the arsonist in Evie before rubbing her back and letting her cry, assuring her that her feelings are valid. She'd make matzo ball soup and they'd watch Tom Hanks and Meg Ryan fall in love again and again. Lori Cohen was more of a mom to Evie than her actual mom, who's very much alive and off gallivanting around Europe with her husband, Jean-Paul, and their six-year-old daughter, Margot. Naomi Deleve-Laurent's new family. She's currently somewhere that begins with the letter *M*. Marseille? Mykonos? Evie doesn't know and, quite frankly, doesn't care.

Theo cleans the kitchen.

As he ladles leftover soup into Tupperware, Evie lets it go, him brushing off her feelings in pursuit of a solution. Pep and Mo's bungalow is an open floor plan, so she just has to shift her position on the couch to watch him move as comfortably in her grandparents' kitchen as if it were his own. Theo grew up baking challah and folding hamantaschen in this kitchen alongside her and Imogen and their grandparents.

Evie lent Theo her grandparents, and in return, he gave her a mom.

"How's Gen liking Culver?" Theo asks.

"She's so in love. I miss her so much."

"You just saw her yesterday."

"For the first time in a week."

Imogen moved out three months ago, left the Pasadena bungalow and moved into a condo on the west side with Sloane. Evie reacted as if there were an ocean between them and not just the 110. It's the same difference. She now has to drive through downtown to see her sister. Evie has ghosted many a Hinge date due to this impractical commute. Maybe she's left her soulmate on read. If so, LA traffic is entirely to blame. If someone lives off the 405 or the 10? It'll never work.

Evie and Imogen had lived together in Pep and Mo's bungalow since Gen graduated from UCLA. *You can be indefinite house sitters*, they pitched, after telling their grandchildren that they'd spent a small fortune on an RV and were off to glamp their way across the continental United States. *Someone has to keep the plants alive*, Mo, tender to a prizewinning tomato garden, had said. So optimistic, Evie's grandfather was. Imogen drowned the poor tomatoes that first summer the Bloom sisters lived alone, together.

Evie assumed she would be here for a year, max.

It's been three years house-sitting the quaint craftsman-style bungalow built in 1919 and purchased by Pep and Mo for a steal in 1973. Once wine tipsy and wallowing over their zillennial reality, Evie and Imogen looked up the bungalow on Zillow, their eyes bulging out of their sockets at the seven-digit Zestimate. They laughed, then burst into tears at proof of what they already knew to be true—they will never be able to afford property in LA County.

Three years in the bungalow.

Three months without Imogen.

The silence has been incredibly unsettling. Evie has never been the best at being alone, so Theo has been spending more nights at the bungalow than in his own apartment, a two-bedroom off Del Mar he shares with two college acquaintances turned friends, Pranav Singh and Micah Solomon. Theo's place is okay in small doses, but it's too much people-ing and a guaranteed allergic reaction to Puck, Pranav and Micah's feral cat.

The bungalow is comfortable.

Safe.

Cat-free.

Theo returns to the living room with a pint of Talenti Cold Brew Coffee gelato (dairy-free), two spoons, and a pair of thick wool socks for Evie's always-freezing feet. She puts on the socks—pink with llamas—and asks Theo how the whole field trip proposal went. Not great. He tells her about the zoo and the backstabber.

"They say you can never trust a Juniper," Evie says, mouth full of gelato as she opens her email to check if Amber B.'s notes on the transcription of the latest episode of *After Ever After* have landed in her inbox. As a product of hustle culture, she is never not plugged in.

"Who are *they?*"

"Me. Right now—"

Her face scrunches at a nonsensical subject line in her inbox.

Subject: NEXT IN FOLEY application status

She refreshes her inbox to confirm that she's not imagining it. Next in Foley is a ten-month fellowship for nonunion, up-and-coming Foley artists, to work and learn under the mentorship of some of the best in the business. It promises two guaranteed credits on union projects, the ticket to the benefits that Evie so desperately requires in order to work in this world full-time. Next in Foley is a prestigious, incredible opportunity.

It's an opportunity to which Evie never applied for three valid reasons:

The hours are full-time.

The pay is shit.

There are no benefits.

"*Imogen,*" Evie hisses at her screen before showing it to Theo.

Her sister would've had access to her computer, to the folder with the reel that Evie cut together to send to prospective employers and freelance clients. Imogen is the sister whose head lives in the clouds because Evie's the one who keeps them both tethered to reality. She says shit like *Let your passions lead you forward* and *means* it because if she stumbles along the way,

Evie is always there to pick her up, to be the practical sister so Imogen doesn't have to be.

Evie is so pissed that this email exists.

But damn it, she wants to know if she's good enough to get in.

So of course, she opens it.

"Holy shit."

She reads it more than once, more than twice, more than three times. Her eyes then meet Theo's, who looks at her as though he's waiting for an explanation that she can't give. She can't speak, so she throws her phone at him, wordless. His expression attempts to remain neutral as he reads, but the corners of his lips turn up (a betrayal!) as he processes words she has already memorized.

Well, the first line.

Evelyn Bloom,

Congratulations, you have been selected to join NEXT IN FOLEY as a fellow in our upcoming cohort, studying under the mentorship of Golden Reel Award winner Sadie Silverman.

It's validating and heartbreaking. Evie wipes at the angry tears that run down her cheeks. Shit. This is why she never applied to Next in Foley, why she told Imogen that she would never apply. Now that she's not only been accepted but has the opportunity to work with a Foley artist who she admires the hell out of, she wants it so bad.

And there's just no way.

She crunched the numbers once, to see if it would be possible, but the premiums on healthcare in the open market *plus* the increase in out-of-pocket costs of the medications that keep her in remission would bankrupt her before the program was over.

Imogen knows this.

Theo's frown is surprised. "You're not happy."

She shakes her head. "I can't do it. Gen *knew this*, but she forged my application anyway."

"Evelyn." Theo runs a hand through disheveled dark brown curls, his thick Eugene Levy–esque eyebrows knitted together with concern. "What if—"

The front door of the bungalow swings open and crashes against the wall with a loud *bang*.

Theo jumps to his feet.

"Gen?" Evie shouts, a hopeful guess because she's the only person besides herself and Theo with a key, and also it would be so satisfying to chew out her sister in real time. "You scared the shit out of us!"

Silence.

Then, footsteps.

"Shit." Evie stands, her brain shifting from being pissed at her sister to worst-case scenario as depicted in every true-crime podcast she listens to like the basic white girl she is. She grabs a frying pan off the counter and holds it like a baseball bat, channeling her inner Rapunzel. *Tangled* was a formative film. Theo reaches for the bulk bag of matzo meal and ducks behind the island, reaching for Evie's hand to pull her down to hide with him.

Evie is somehow, impossibly, both terrified and amused. "What exactly is the plan? Bludgeon the intruders with a bag of matzo meal?"

"Shut up. I panicked," Theo whispers.

Outside, a car door slams.

Are nighttime intruders usually so *loud?*

"What do we do?"

"Call nine-one-one?"

"My phone is on the couch."

Theo pats his pockets. "Mine too. Shit."

"Go get it," Evie says.

"Me?"

"Take this."

She holds out the frying pan and he gives her a *look.* "Seriously?"

"What? It's more useful than your panic weapon of choice."

"I'm not—"

Evie reaches for the bag of matzo meal in an attempt to rip it out of Theo's grip and arm him with the pan, but he's holding on to that bag as if his life depends on it, and it *rips,* matzo meal flying and covering the cabinets, the floor, *them.* It coats their clothes, goes up their noses, settles in their hair. It's going to be a wild sight for the coroner to see at the crime scene, two best friends whose final moments were covered in matzo meal and—

"We're *baaaaaack,*" Grandpa Mo's baritone sings from the front door.

"Ev? Sweets?" Grandma Pep's distinctive alto shouts as if it's not almost 10:00 p.m. on a Thursday and their neighbors aren't asleep.

Oh.

Evie's adrenaline-sped heart returns to a normal rate. Her eyes meet Theo's. Matzo meal is in his eyelashes. "Grandma?" She stands, brushing off her sweats and ignoring Pep's expression. "What are you doing here?"

"What am I doing in my own home?" Pep sasses, a hand on her hip.

"Hello, Theo," Mo says to a Theo who's laughing on the floor.

"Do we even want to know?" Pep asks, assessing the mess that is her kitchen and her granddaughter.

Theo stands. "Your unexpected entrance sounded like a break-in."

Mo snorts. "In this neighborhood?"

Pep laughs and pulls Evie into a hug. She smells like Estée Lauder perfume, the scent still so comforting. "Sorry we scared you, Sweets."

"I missed you so much."

"Us too, Evelyn," Grandpa Mo says with a tender squeeze of her shoulder.

"Are you back?" Theo asks.

Mo shakes his head. "No, son. This is just a pit stop to slumber and, um, share some news."

Evie pulls out of her grandmother's embrace. "News? Are you okay?"

Grandma Pep and Grandpa Mo are active, their minds sharp. Still, they're approaching eighty, so Evie's brain jumps to the worst conclusion. Someone is sick. Neither one *looks* sick, but neither does Evie. Neither did Lori until—

"It's nothing like that, Sweets," Pep says.

Her shoulders sag with relief. "Okay. So what is it?"

"Why don't we all take a seat," Mo suggests, gesturing toward the living room.

So . . . this isn't health-related news, but it *is* sit-down news? Evie's stomach lurches, braces for the bad. "Mo. Whatever it is, just say it. *Please.*"

Her grandfather sighs. "We're back because . . ." Mo swallows and scratches his beard. "Someone made an offer on the house, Evelyn."

"We wanted to tell you in person," Pep adds.

Evie blinks.

Reels.

"Since when is it for sale?"

Of all the reasons that her grandparents could be back, she never would have thought it's because they're selling the bungalow. House-sitting is temporary, but the bungalow is supposed to be forever. Evie assumed that one day *she'd* purchase it from them. Keep it in the family and make it hers, for real. She can't imagine living anywhere else.

"It's an offer we can't refuse," Mo says.

"I'm sorry," Pep says. "It all happened so fast. Our Realtor advised we jump on it."

"With Genny out and settled, the timing felt right," Mo adds.

It is a casual dagger to her heart.

"When?" she asks.

Grandma Pep winces, so the answer is soon.

"We close in a month."

Okay.

A month, at least, gives Evie time to grieve, to process, to apartment hunt.

"But you need to be out for repairs by the end of next week."

Shit.

Evie's nose wrinkles, combating the panic tears threatening to surface. "You really could've called."

"It was only just finalized this morning, Sweets." Her grandmother applies gentle pressure to Evie's shoulders, which have risen so high they nearly brush her earlobes. It does little to ease the tension. "A few offers fell through in escrow. We didn't want to needlessly worry you."

What the fuck is *escrow*? Evie is going to be sick. She retreats for the bathroom and hurls semi-digested matzo meal and her heart into the toilet, then moans, "What the fuck is this day?" to herself. Emotional whiplash makes her queasy. Shit really does happen in threes. First *Ginger*, then Next in Foley, now *this*? Out by the end of next week? What will she do? Where will she live?

"Hey." Theo's knuckles rap on the door, his tenor soft with concern. "Are you okay?"

"No."

"Stupid question. This is a lot, but we'll figure it out. Okay?"

We.

Theo is here.

You are not alone.

Evie whispers this to herself again and again. Tries to forget that she has proven time and time again that she is a person who is easy to leave. She was five when Dr. David Bloom, an archaeologist, left for an excavation in Argentina. Chose his research over his daughters. Just twelve when Naomi took a beat in New York, where she met Jean-Paul. Chose a man over her daughters. It's been only a year since Hanna took a production job in Atlanta, ending a three-year relationship and breaking Evie's heart.

Everyone leaves, often sooner rather than later.

But Theo is the only person who left because she pushed him away, to New York, toward his dream. He's also the only person who came back—and she's terrified that any day he's going to wake up and *poof* back to his dream life.

"I already miss it," Evie says.

"I know."

She doesn't have her dream life, but at least she came home every day to a place she loved.

Loved.

She's already thinking about the bungalow in past tense—like how she thinks about dance, about Hanna, about her parents. She *used* to dance. She *was* in love. Her parents *left*. Now? She *loved* this bungalow. She winces over this latest shift from present to past, another end of an era. Evelyn Bloom has always hated endings.

But *oof*, are they extra brutal when there's no way to see them coming.

STELLA HOFFMAN'S DANCE ACADEMY, THIRD GRADE

Evie

Evie is just eight years old when she enters Stella Hoffman's Dance Academy for the first time, her heart in her throat.

"Don't be bashful, Evelyn," Grandma Pep says, coaxing her to come out of hiding, to step out from the safety of being shielded by her grandmother's legs and make eye contact with a stranger. "Miss Stella is a friend."

Bashful.

It's Grandma Pep's word for her, but she doesn't know how to articulate that it's more intense than that. She doesn't yet have the language, the vocabulary, to describe the terror she feels at the mere *idea* of speaking to a stranger. It will be a decade until she has a diagnosis, has medication, has coping mechanisms to deal with the social anxiety that debilitates her in this moment.

"Hi, Evelyn!" Miss Stella speaks in the melodic cadence of a Disney princess. She squats down so that she's eye level with Evie, who absorbs every detail—platinum-blond hair in a perfect ballet bun, neon-green nails, pale pink tights that match her own. "I'm so excited to have you in my class."

"She's excited to be here," Grandma Pep says.

No. She's not.

It's confusing, her anxiety. She asked to take dance classes. She wants to be a ballerina. When she turns the music up, up, up and dances around her bedroom, her brain is so quiet. She isn't being mean to herself for misspelling a difficult word on a spelling quiz, isn't scared to go to school, isn't worried that her mommy is going to disappear again. Dance allows Evie to be in her body and gives her a break from her brain. But she didn't consider until this moment that these classes would mean talking to people, dancing in front of people. Now confronted with this reality, her brain screams, *No, no, no.*

Brains are so weird.

How can she both want something so bad and not want it at all?

"Go on, Sweets."

She hugs her grandmother's knees goodbye, then steps out of her pink Crocs and follows Miss Stella into the studio that's already filled with tiny dancers sitting in friend clusters. In the center of one of these clusters is a boy—the only boy—with curly brown hair. His laugh is pure joy.

Just try.

She reaches into her tote bag for her brand-new ballet slippers, then stuffs the bag in an empty cubby along the wall as Miss Stella tells everyone to get on a dot. Evie doesn't understand what this means until she processes the evenly spaced neon stickers dotting scuffed wood floors. She stands on the pink dot closest to the door.

"You're on my dot," someone in a purple tutu says in a tone that very much implies that this isn't okay, prompting Evie to surrender her dot. It's probably safer to wait until everyone claims one.

The boy waves her over with a one-dimple smile. "This spot's open."

So she stands on the dot next to him, toes touching the highlighter-yellow sticker.

"Is this your first class?" he asks.

She nods, wordless.

"Obviously it's your first class at *Miss Stella's*, but is it, like, your first dance class *ever?*"

She nods again.

Purple Tutu butts in. "Wait. Do you even know what a plié is?"

Evie shakes her head, wordless.

"*Wow.*"

"So, that's Caro," the boy says as Purple Tutu skips back to her dot. "Don't worry. Miss Stella is the best. What's your name?"

"Evelyn," she says.

"Ev-e-lyn," he repeats, enunciating each syllable. "I'm Theo."

"Like Theodore?"

Purple Tutu, Caro, now back on her dot, laughs. "*Ew*, no. Just Theo."

Evie feels her cheeks get hot at the sound of collective laughter. This is why it's safer not to speak, because it's better than saying the wrong thing. Somehow, she always says the wrong thing. Even worse than feeling her red-hot embarrassment, she can *see* it in the mirrored wall, her face turning into a tomato.

Don't cry.

But then the boy, *Theo*, says, "You can call me Theodore."

Her eyes meet his.

She tries it out, clueless in this moment that her life has just changed. "Okay, Theodore."

"I think I like Theodore."

His nose crinkles when he smiles at her, dissolving her anxiety just as Miss Stella turns on the music. Evie remembers every detail of that first dance class—warming up to *The Lizzie McGuire Movie* soundtrack, learning her first sixteen counts of choreography, realizing that she could dance in front of, *with*, other people. She remembers Theo's one-dimple smile, his nose crinkle, his kindness. She remembers not saying another word to him that day, giving him nothing more than a tiny wave goodbye.

She remembers obsessing over their interaction for the rest of the night.

Him saying, *I think I like Theodore.*

And her last thought before drifting off into a dreamscape being *I think I like Theodore, too.*

4

"This is *endless*."

Theo and Evelyn are in the middle of packing up the bungalow's office–slash–guest room when she flings herself onto the taupe suede futon, her Snoopy slipper–clad feet dangling off the armless end. Shoulder-length blond hair falls in front of her face, obscuring her forest-green eyes.

"You really don't have to subject yourself to this, Theodore," Evelyn continues. "It's not your fault I'm a low-key hoarder."

He raises an eyebrow. "*Low-key?*"

She flips him off, then stands and declares it's time for a bubble tea break and exits the room without asking him what he wants. She doesn't have to. Alone, he returns to the boxes. Theo has spent the weekend helping Evelyn pack up nearly two decades of memories—their entire childhood, adolescence, early adulthood—into cardboard boxes. Pep and Mo's bungalow has been a second home to Theo, a place that always felt warm and safe, even more so after his mom's diagnosis. Colorectal cancer. Stage three. At home, Theo had to be okay, strong, *a man*. He was fourteen. A kid. But that didn't matter to Jacob, his dad, who drilled those words into Theo over and over during the two years of treatments that spanned between Lori's diagnosis and initial remission. At home, Theo felt nothing at all. Emotions were for the bungalow, where he could feel his feelings without judgment. So losing this space?

It's a lot to process.

Theo doesn't process.

He's too busy packing, taping, and labeling boxes:

BOOKS

TCHTOCHKES

BLANKETS

So many blankets—all crocheted by Evelyn in various colors, patterns, and textures. Theo has lost count of how many blankets he's folded. Just when he thinks he's pulled the last one from the closet, another one appears. He folds and boxes and folds and boxes blanket after blanket while his favorite *Survivor* podcasters recap the most recent episode in his ears. A necessary distraction. Without gameplay analysis to keep him grounded, Theo would surely be losing his shit over some of these blankets. A blue-and-white checkerboard one that Evelyn was proud enough of upon completion to gift to his mom. A soft sage blanket that his mom started after she relapsed and Evelyn finished after she—

Theo pauses the podcast.

Wipes his eyes and forces himself to finish the thought.

—*died.*

After she died.

It's been five years since her relapse and grief still bowls him over. Sometimes the trigger is obvious—Tom Hanks's voice, any Dolly Parton song, a sage blanket. Other times, it hits him out of nowhere. Earlier this week, it was a perfectly ordinary day at school until Milo, a struggling speller, got a perfect score on a quiz using a memory trick that Theo learned from his mom back when *he* was a struggling speller and he just . . . wanted so badly to call her. Random moments like those are the worst, because that's when Theo must sit with the truth that it's never going away, this grief—and it's always going to hurt. He has to be able to move through it. With Milo's breakthrough, he sat with the grief as he slapped a Buzz Lightyear sticker on top of the quiz, then continued grading. In the case of the soft sage blanket that is still in his hands, he will fold it and box it and move on to the next blanket because sometimes it's just easier to do than to feel.

Theo resumes the podcast.

Folds.

Boxes grief with the soft sage blanket.

And moves on.

Twenty minutes later, Evelyn returns with a lavender oat milk boba tea for herself and a peach green tea with mango pearls for him. Then she settles next to him and wraps some ceramic tchotchkes from the bookshelf. A cow, a crepe, a teacup. Her phone vibrates and she glances at the screen, her shoulders sagging before showing Theo. It's a listing for a one bedroom in Lamanda Park, the area of Pasadena where he grew up: $2,100 a month.

"*Fuck.*"

"Who does Pasadena think she is? If Pep and Mo sold this place to a developer who's just going to flip it into an Airbnb, I swear—" Evelyn cuts herself off and pinches the bridge of her nose. "Sorry. I'm spiraling and also just really sad."

"I know," Theo says, unsure how to begin to articulate how much the bungalow means to him, too.

He doesn't have to.

When Evelyn looks at him, her eyes glassy, he knows she knows.

"Also? Crashing with Gen is going to be so awkward. She still won't apologize."

Of course she won't. She can't exactly apologize for something she didn't do. Theo tapes shut a boxful of blankets as he considers how to respond because he knows full well that Gen doesn't owe Evelyn an apology for submitting her portfolio to Next in Foley. *He* does. It's been a week since she received her acceptance email, but she's been in housing crisis mode. It's the first time she's brought it back up. Theo has meant to bring it up himself, but he didn't expect her initial reaction to be so hostile. Seeing the look on her face when she read that email, he knew that he'd overstepped. Crossed a boundary.

Still, he owes her the truth.

"Ev—"

"And she has the audacity to act like she has no clue what I'm talking about! It's a bit much, even for Gen—"

"It wasn't Gen."

Silence.

Her eyes meet his. "Seriously?"

Theo nods. "I'm sorry."

She hurls a throw pillow at him. "What the actual fuck?"

"I'm sorry!" he repeats, catching the pillow before it topples his tea. Her aim is shit. "Everything about that fellowship is meant for you and . . . I guess I just thought you weren't applying out of fear? I didn't read the small print or even consider that the program wouldn't include health insurance."

"It doesn't really matter what you thought, Theodore. *I said no.*"

"I know."

Months earlier, when he encouraged her to apply, he heard her *say* that word, but he remembered the first time she described being in a Foley studio to him. *In a way, it's kind of like dancing and . . . I don't know? I didn't expect that to feel so good?* She'd confided this over FaceTime, from their dorms on opposite coasts, her words tumbling out fast in excitement and her eyes sparkling with a passion he hadn't witnessed since *dancer* was her identity. Their identity. And in the seven years since that conversation, Evelyn has worked so hard, done countless unpaid and underpaid internships, built a portfolio.

And, sure, he heard her say no. But he never considered that she *meant* it.

"I am so mad at you."

"I know."

Angry tears slide down her cheeks and it makes his chest tighten, a physical pain. Evelyn said no and he . . . just ignored it. Of course she's pissed. Theo didn't listen, opting instead to submit the application, as if he knew what was best for her. It's something his father would do—something he did—all the time, whether it was signing off on clinical trials for his mom or submitting applications to colleges that Theo had no interest in attending. *I just want you to have every opportunity,* he'd say. *Is that so wrong?* Always, his dad would ask for forgiveness, not permission.

"I want it." Evelyn's admission is soft, and it cracks him in half. "So bad. How am I supposed to keep mindlessly editing podcasts now?"

"Okay. Then let's figure it out. What if—?"

"Theo."

He winces. *Theo.* Another indication of how massively he screwed up.

Evelyn stands and presses the heels of her hands to her swollen eyes. "I need a beat."

She then exits the room, ending the conversation and making it clear that there's nothing to figure out—at least not with him. Evelyn leaves Theo sitting with the nauseating realization that applying to Next in Foley on her behalf was *textbook* Jacob Cohen behavior. He can't fix this. Can't go back in time and undo what he's done. But he *can* finish folding these blankets. So he turns toward the mountain of them (seriously, how are there still so many goddamn blankets?), then packs up the rest of the memories into boxes and exits the bungalow without saying goodbye.

Theo makes a pit stop at Trader Joe's on his way home, where he picks up an avocado, a carton of almond milk, cashew butter, whole wheat wraps, dried mango, maple-flavored almonds, honey-infused goat cheese, a week's worth of vegetarian dinners from the freezer aisle, two bags of Impossible chicken nuggets, and a tub of dark chocolate peanut butter cups. He only meant to restock on almond milk, but he blacked out the moment the sliding doors opened, later returning to his car perplexed because he hates goat cheese and *shit*—was he that distracted?

Yes.

At home, he unloads the groceries to find not one but *two* varieties of goat cheese: honey and jalapeño.

He sniffs them.

Ugh.

Theo stickers each cheese with a yellow dot—the visual signal to his roommates that this is cheese for all, please eat it!—and sticks it in the deli drawer. He labels his food, then retreats to his room to grade math quizzes. Once finished, Theo removes himself from his desk and the grading to find Micah and Pranav playing *Super Smash Bros.* in the living room, Puck asleep on Pranav's lap, unfazed as Pranav-as-Young-Link spin attacks Micah-as-Pikachu off the stage. Despite having played *Super Smash Bros.* countless times with the guys, Theo has no idea how that just happened. Pranav curses under his breath, then sets the parameters for the next round, his eyes fixated on the screen.

"Hey."

Micah looks at Theo. "Want in?"

"Sure."

He picks up a controller, selects Kirby, sinks into a beanbag chair, and tries to relax into the game. He cannot. *Super Smash Bros.* stresses him out. It's too overstimulating—he never knows where to focus on the screen or which buttons to press in the most strategic order. He attempts a sneak attack on Micah that results in him launching Kirby off a cliff. Theo's personal gaming preferences tend to be of the *Animal Crossing* and *Sims* variety—soothing and single-player.

"Have you had a chance to look over the lease renewal?" Theo asks as Kirby resurrects themself on the screen.

Pranav pauses the game. "About that . . ."

Instead of finishing his sentence, Pranav opts for a long sip from a can of LaCroix. Theo's eyes shift from one roommate to the other. Micah's left eyebrow is twitching. Both are avoiding eye contact with Theo—but also with each other. *Shit. Did Pranav and Micah break up? Again?* Pranav and Micah are codependent and chaotic and have an annual "we're too young to be Domestic Gays" panic. But the breakup never lasts longer than a week, because despite their drama, they *love* being Domestic Gays.

Micah runs a hand through longer-on-the-top ginger hair, his Adam's apple bobbing. "The thing is—"

"We fell in love with a condo in WeHo," Pranav confesses.

Theo blinks. "What?"

"It all happened so fast," Micah says.

Theo doesn't understand how it's happening at all. Pranav works in program strategy at Netflix. Micah is a PhD student at Caltech. These are people he commiserated with about inflation and the housing market and how screwed up it is that they can only afford to live here because of one another. How the fuck are they buying a condo in West Hollywood?

"It's time to fully embrace our domestic truth," Micah adds.

"And have a ten-minute commute. But we didn't mean to blindside you," Pranav says, as if that even matters. "Our first two offers fell through, so—"

Whatever the end of that sentence is, Theo doesn't hear it. Offers? Plural? He short-circuits. Currently, Theo has enough money in his checking account to cover rent, groceries, and the luxury that is his Peloton membership . . . amassing the savings to be in a position to be able to make *an* offer on any property in LA County is unfathomable. Being a renter for the foreseeable future is his reality. And that's fine. Theo likes his job. He's content. Or he was, before learning that he's hemorrhaging roommates and . . . he needs to think. Retreat to his spreadsheets. Crunch numbers. This unit is rent-controlled and it would suck to lose it and—

Theo is spiraling.

He resumes the game.

Detaches.

"Cool."

"Cool," Micah repeats.

"You're pissed," Pranav says.

"Truth bomb?" Micah asks. Theo's nod is terse, but it's enough permission for Micah to continue. "Since Imogen moved out of the bungalow, we sort of assumed it was only a matter of time until you moved in with Evie?"

"Why the fuck would you assume that?"

Pranav's laughter scrapes against Theo's skull. "Seriously?"

"You're never here," Micah says.

Theo smashes the controller keys in no particular order and somehow his Kirby shoves Pranav's Young Link off the cliff. It's incredibly satisfying. Victorious, he stands and drops the controller onto the beanbag. "Well. I'm sorry to inform you that Evelyn's grandparents just sold the bungalow. She's sort of in her own housing crisis."

Micah and Pranav exchange a look before Pranav turns to Theo with a smirk. "You're welcome."

"What?"

"Sounds to me like you need a roommate and Evie needs a room."

Oh.

Theo's brain had jumped straight to panic mode, not even pausing to consider such an obvious solution. Ask Evelyn to live here. It's not as if they're not constantly together anyway. As roommates, their chill nights in can be even lazier. It could be so good, in theory. So why does thinking too much about the reality of living with his best friend, of seeing his favorite person with morning bedhead, of hearing her shuffle around the apartment in those ridiculous slippers make him so . . . nervous?

"Perfect." Micah fluffs his hair again, the strawberry tint of his cheeks fading with relief. "I wanted to tell you—"

"Micah."

"—but Pranav wanted to keep it hush until it was a done deal." He reaches for Pranav's hand and twines their fingers together. "Asshole."

Micah's tone is loving, adoring. Pranav's pupils are heart-eye emojis. It's disgusting how cute they are, Theo's roommates. Ex-roommates. And it *is* an asshole move, this lack of notice. Theo should state this.

Instead, he lets them off easy. "It's the end of an era."

Five years ago, Theo didn't know what to expect when he responded to Pranav's post in an alumni Facebook Group. Open bedroom in Pasadena. $800/mo plus utilities. Comes with two chill roommates who adhere to a strict cleaning schedule and one less chill (but perfect) cat. What started as a roommate-ship of convenience with Pranav Singh and Micah Solomon has evolved into actual friendship, forever bonded by a reverence for pineapple on pizza, an obsession with *Lost*, and a traumatic bedbug incident.

Theo exits the living room to process their imminent departure and the possibility of Evelyn taking their place. He reaches for his phone to text her. But he can't. She needs a beat. Meaning she'll text him when she's ready to talk. It's an established boundary he won't cross, not even when he has some major news—and a major proposal—for her. Instead, he pulls up the lease and reworks his budget, relieved that he can (barely) afford to split the rent two ways instead of three, relieved that he doesn't have to let this spacious rent-controlled apartment go—

Except.

As he skims over the lease agreement, he notices a stipulation.

Each tenant must provide proof that their monthly salary is at least three times the rent.

Three times?

Each?

Maybe . . . it's not an enforced stipulation?

Theo bolts from his desk. "Micah? Pranav? Is there a guarantor attached to our lease?"

"My parents," Micah says, so casual, so oblivious, so privileged. "We never would've been approved for this place otherwise."

"Right."

Theo's brain reverts to panic. Of course. Nothing is that easy. For a moment, he believed that he could fix Evelyn's housing crisis.

But actually, *shit*, now he's in one, too.

5

Evie tours eleven apartments in three days and on a scale of one to soul-crushing, apartment hunting in LA is right up there with the balance of her medical bills. About $1,700 a month will get her either AC *or* a refrigerator. In those three days, she blew through an entire tank of gas driving to various listings across the city, a total waste of time because the decent ones already had multiple applications in process and the still-available ones had weird stains on the walls and roaches in the sinks. There was one spot in Palms, near Imogen, that seemed promising—hardwood floors, natural light, a fridge—until she found a bloody T-shirt in the shower. She and Imogen ran without so much as a goodbye to the broker because *holy shit* did they just tour a crime scene? Is their DNA now all over a crime scene?

After this minor trauma, they're in stop-and-go traffic on the 110, still processing the Palms Incident, not processing that they're en route to say goodbye to the bungalow for real, when Imogen asks, "Are you going to call Theo?"

Evie shrugs, easing up on the brake pedal just to crawl a few inches forward.

"Let me rephrase," her sister amends. "*Call Theo*. Did he do something stupid? Yes! Were his intentions sweet? Yes! Are you going to forgive him? Of course! He should be there to say goodbye."

Imogen is right.

Of course she'll forgive Theo.

But right now? She still wants to be furious. Evie hasn't even had a chance to unpack her complicated feelings about Next in Foley with Jules, who's off this week because therapists need vacations, too. Evie needs Jules. Because Theo crossed every friendship boundary. She said no. She *meant* no. And yet the tiniest part of her loves that he knows her well enough to see right through this specific no. Evie isn't sure what this means, but being mad at Theo is pretty much the worst feeling in the world. Sometimes, she wishes her best friend wasn't so nice. It'd be way easier to stay furious if he radiated just a smidge of righteous asshole energy. But Theo apologized profusely, took accountability, and gave her the beat she needed that resulted in three harrowing days of apartment hunting.

So.

Evie listens to her sister.

Theo answers on the first ring. "Hey."

"I'm still mad at you," she says, despite the relief she can hear in that one-syllable *hey* cracking her resolve to remain furious. "But Gen and I are about to turn over the keys to Pep and Mo and . . ."

She leaves the sentence unfinished, because *she is mad at him, damn it*, and not willing to say how she feels—that it wouldn't feel right, saying goodbye to the bungalow without him. But it's the truth. How many hours did they spend in that space—as kids doing homework together on the hideous mushroom rug in the living room during the ninety minutes between school and dance, as dancers rehearsing duets in the spare room with mirrored closet doors in the final hours before a competition, as adults watching *Survivor* together every week?

A lot.

"What's your ETA?" Theo asks.

"Fifteen minutes."

"I'll be there."

They pull into the driveway fifteen minutes later, and there he is, wrapped in a Peppy Bloom embrace on the front porch—and whatever anger remained dissolves in real time, neutralized by his simple act of showing up for her. She cuts the engine and pushes her car door open, not at all ready to say goodbye. Imogen squeezes her hand after they exit. Theo's eyes meet hers as Pep greets her and Imogen with hugs at the bottom of the porch steps.

"It's a lot, isn't it? Goodbye."

"Sure is."

Evie pulls away from her grandmother's embrace, fishing for keys that sank to the bottom of her tote bag. Once retrieved, a ballet slipper charm imprints her palm as she removes the key that has belonged to her since she was ten, the key that has meant *home* since she was twelve. Imogen mirrors her, as little sisters so often do. Placing the keys in their grandmother's palm, Evie has never felt more untethered because she is someone who clings to roots. Stability. Someone who is content to stay. Imogen hugs Theo hello, then pushes the front door open, disappearing into a house that's no longer home for a final walk-through.

Evie is still.

Pep's calloused thumb reaches toward her to brush a tear from her cheek. "It's just a place, Evelyn."

"I know."

Mo approaches, tentatively, holding an envelope out to Evie. "Don't argue."

Inside is a wrinkled check made out to her for five thousand dollars.

Her eyes widen. "Grandpa—"

"Don't. It's for emotional damages," he attempts to joke, but when Mo's eyes meet hers, his expression is serious. "Ev. We're aware that we put you in a shit situation by asking you to move with no notice. A situation that you have handled with so much grace and maturity. So you're going to let us help you. Are we clear?"

Evie nods.

Mo squeezes her shoulder. "Good."

Peppy Bloom and Mo Goldberg put their retirement plans on hold fifteen years ago, when Naomi left her daughters on the bungalow steps in the pouring rain. *I love you so much, my tiny dancers, but I need a beat,* Naomi had said, squatting to be eye level with a ten-year-old Imogen. Evie remembers not feeling fear or abandonment, only grateful that the rare downpour hid her angry tears. At least her father was a consistent, expected absence. Naomi was much more unpredictable. Burned out on being a mom, she'd often leave Evie and Imogen with their father's parents for extended beats.

Most times, Naomi would be gone for a week.

Two, tops. Not that time.

So Pep and Mo made a home for the Bloom sisters in every way their parents weren't capable of doing. Cared for them in all the ways Naomi and David couldn't. Evie has accepted more than enough help from Pep and Mo over these last fifteen years.

She refuses to take even a penny of their retirement money, but for now she'll slip the check into her back pocket because it's easier than arguing.

And she'll rip it to pieces the moment they drive away.

"Where to next?" Theo asks.

"Tahoe," Pep says, her eyes sparkling with anticipation. "We've never been, if you can believe it."

Evie laughs. "I can."

Her grandparents were never the best at understanding the concept of a vacation. Pep had her radio show and Mo bounced around from studio to studio, overseeing the set construction for various films and television shows. Sometimes, the work meant traveling. But never—at least in the first twenty-four years of Evie's life—had her grandparents traveled to *travel*, until Pep put down the mic three years ago.

"It turns out there's a whole world outside of LA County," Mo teases.

Pep shrugs. "Who knew?"

Mo's nose crinkles when he smiles at Pep, an expression that single-handedly assures Evie that love is real. Her grandparents are coming up on forty years together. Pep was a single mother to a ten-year-old David when she stumbled onto one of Mo's sets on the Paramount lot. Before her radio career bloomed, she was a sound editor for the studio, nursing a crush on a set designer. *Need some help?* she asked in her best (terrible) transatlantic accent. Mo, focused on the flower details he was painting on a gazebo, didn't register the question, her *presence*, until she dropped the schtick and used her actual voice. Pep helped him put the finishing touches on the gazebo—or delayed him, depending on who is telling the story. After, Mo asked her how she felt about food. *I eat*, Pep said with a laugh.

Forty years later, it's how he still asks her if she's hungry.

They're adorable, her grandparents. Still so in love, though they never married. Perhaps *because* they never married. Failed first marriages and messy divorces had dulled their desire to tether themselves together with a piece of paper. Evie doesn't just respect the hell out of their love; it's a love that she wants for herself.

"Tahoe is unreal," Theo says.

Evie nods. "You're going to love it."

"Sure hope so! Ready to hit the road?" Mo asks.

"I left something in the van for Evelyn," Pep says as she makes her way toward the RV parked on the street. "Come on, Sweets."

Evie follows her grandmother down the driveway and up the steps into the decked-out mobile retirement home. Pep and Mo truly pulled out all the stops, hiring an interior designer to gut and renovate the RV, installing quartz countertops, Smeg appliances, and a Klipsch sound system—an aesthetic that screams, *There will be no roughing it in the woods on our adventures.* Pep sits on the cream leather couch and pats the empty cushion next to her. Evie takes a seat, prepared for a story and wondering what recipe or tchotchke or vintage accessory will be gifted to her before this goodbye.

Pep reaches for a box on the quartz countertop. "From one audiophile to another."

She takes the box from her grandmother, feels the weight of it in her hands and . . . *is it?*

She opens it.

It is.

Inside the box is a vintage RCA 77-DX. A microphone. Not just any microphone, but the one that her grandmother recorded with during the thirty-year run of *Some Pep in Your*

Step. It's Peppy Bloom's most prized possession, a symbol of the trailblazer she is and everything Evie wants to be. She swallows a lump in her throat because it's so much, Pep letting go of the mic and passing it on to her.

"Genny may have mentioned the fellowship," Pep says, her voice lowering in tone to something serious. "I wish I heard the exciting news from *you*."

Evie shrugs. "I can't do it."

"Why is that?"

Of course, Imogen left that part out. "No benefits."

"Ah."

Her expression shifts to instant understanding. Growing up, it was Pep who'd been Evie's most fierce advocate, the adult who *believed her*. Pep who obtained legal guardianship in order to put her granddaughters on her union health insurance. Pep who took Evie to *so many doctors*. Her adolescence was one sterile office after another, a paper gown chafing her skin as the doctor-of-the-month pressed on her tender, bloated stomach, then went over her normal (*always* normal) lab results and attributed her pain to stress, to anxiety, to Naomi. *That gut-brain connection is a powerful one!* After she fell, the on-call trauma attending did a thorough workup, ordering imaging for the obvious injuries and bloodwork based on her accounts of the ever-present pain and accompanying fatigue that threw her balance off in the first place. She didn't know in that moment that this would be the beginning of receiving an answer with so many questions, that she would soon have validation that her pain wasn't in her head, that Pep and Mo would be so supportive emotionally—and financially— through numerous trial-and-error treatments until a combination of luck and medical alchemy got her into remission.

Evie doesn't know, cannot *fathom*, the cumulative cost.

Pep won't tell her.

She still struggles to accept this gift, that she's merely swimming in medical debt and not drowning in it. Because Crohn's is expensive to manage even in remission, even with insurance—requiring biologic medications, biannual colonoscopies, and so much bloodwork that she's on a first-name basis with the phlebotomists at her local lab. It is not dramatic to say that Evie's quality of life depends on the quality of her health insurance.

So.

She can't do the fellowship.

It's that simple.

"Their loss," Pep says, wrapping an arm around Evie and giving her shoulder a gentle squeeze. "Yours, too. I'm sorry, Sweets."

She leans into her grandmother's embrace, always appreciative that Pep has never pushed or gaslit her into believing that anything is possible. Some things are not possible for her. At eighteen, the metal in her reconstructed ankle took dance from her, a Broadway-bound future no longer possible. Now a dream fellowship isn't possible. Not because of Crohn's disease, but because of America and its fucked-up employer-based healthcare system.

"It's bullshit."

Pep nods. "It is."

That validation is a loop in her head as she, her sister, and her best friend watch Pep and Mo drive away from the bungalow that meant home. *It is. It is. It is.* Evie feels the weight—the legacy—of Pep's microphone in her hands. It *is* bullshit, but turning down a fellowship is not giving up on a career. Determination blooms in the pit of her stomach, a desperate *need* to be worthy of this gift that penetrates her jaded core.

Imogen blows a raspberry at the three missed call notifications that glow on her screen. "I need to hop on a few calls."

"On a Saturday?"

"Don't ask." Imogen sighs, then turns toward Theo. "It'll take an hour or so to get home right now. Can I take them from your place? My boss is overstimulated by café noise."

"Course."

His apartment is just ten minutes down the road. Once Imogen is settled on a beanbag at Theo's and connected to Wi-Fi, a curious Puck looking over her shoulder, Theo's eyes meet Evie's and she locks in on his brown irises. "So. What now?"

What now?

Evie will keep apartment hunting.

Continue to freelance.

Diversify her portfolio.

Even—ugh—*network.*

But first?

"Afters."

Their spot is open, a red metal picnic table and bench in the back corner of the parking lot of what used to be a gas station and is now the best place to get ice cream in Pasadena. Gas station ice cream isn't something Evie knew she needed until it existed, though the vintage Texaco pumps exist solely to create an aesthetic. Afters—said gas station ice cream institution— opened their junior year and became a post-dance tradition of sorts for them, a reward after long Wednesday nights at Stella Hoffman's Dance Academy.

"Afters after?" Theo asked during a break from learning new choreography, pushing back sweat-drenched curls that stuck to his forehead before kneeling to retie his tap shoes.

Evie focused on rolling out calves that screamed at her with a tennis ball. "Sure."

"Sweet."

He held out a hand. Evie took it and ignored the arm attached to it, the flex of his biceps as he pulled her to her feet. She let go, then turned her attention to Stella's choreography. Or tried to. She kept starting early, on the down beat, and cursed under her breath with each false start. She looked over at her partner and caught him scratching the back of his neck, the hem of his shirt riding up to reveal a light trail of hair starting at the bottom of his belly button. Evie swallowed. *Fuck.* Theo was hot.

So what?

He was also *Theo.*

Fifteen attempts later, Stella instructed them to take off their tap shoes and run "Someone Like You," because, as she so bluntly put it, Evie needed a win. Evie cursed under her breath. Sure, she could dance that routine in her sleep, but tap was safer. Less touching. Hand-holding at most. Contemporary was complicated lifts, his hands on her hips, their tangled limbs. Choreography that used to not faze Evie at all and now very much did. But she let the music take her to another place and in those 122 seconds, Evie could let herself love him like that. For the performance.

Obviously.

Because he was *Theo.*

If he were anybody else, by then she would've leaned into the attraction, the impulsive feelings. Evie *loved* kissing— boys, girls, everyone. Loved the brief bliss of feeling wanted by boys, girls, everyone. But she didn't love the complicated af- ter, jumping ship as soon as the vibe shifted away from casual and toward the potential of something more, of getting hurt, of being left. Theo—their friendship—was too important to risk.

So she squashed the crush, the lust, the whatever she was beginning to feel, and four hours of dancing concluded with ice cream and sharing a pair of headphones to watch the newest episode of *Survivor* on Theo's phone. The following week, Evie was the one who asked, "Afters after?" and it's been their thing ever since. The chill of the dry Southern California air paired with the chill of dairy-free mint chip a necessary cooldown after hours in the studio, a necessary reminder that whatever was happening to Evie's heart inside the studio would stay inside the studio.

In the decade since, Afters has become the space Evie goes to reset.

She and Theo need a reset.

So they order their dairy-free mint chip in a cup and ube brownie in a cone and sit at their picnic table. Evie comments on the weather, how hot it still is for mid-October, as she scrapes the perfect scoop with a bamboo spoon. Fresh mint on her tongue is a sweet respite from the heat, from her grief. The bungalow is gone. Pep and Mo are gone. But at least after a shit day, there's always Afters.

Theo looks at her. "Evelyn, I'm—"

Evie cuts him off, reaching across the table to take his cone and smush the tenth, twentieth, *millionth* sorry right back into his face in sticky-sweet ice cream form, and only when his nose, mouth, and chin are purple does she say, "I know."

His purple mouth quirks. "I deserved that."

"I know."

Then she hands him some napkins.

He takes them.

And they reset the same way they always do—with Theo

handing her an earbud and them watching *Survivor* on his phone. After the episode, Evie recounts her harrowing week of apartment hunting and the bloody T-shirt.

"It's brutal out there," she laments, crushing a now-empty ice cream cup in her hand. "Never give up your lease."

Theo snorts. "I think I have to. Micah and Pranav closed on a condo in WeHo."

"What?" Evie's eyes widen at information that could solve at least one of her problems.

"How they swung that is a mystery to—"

"I'll take it."

He hasn't offered. But it's *Theo*. After a week on Imogen's couch, Evie could tear up at just the idea of a bedroom. With a door. In this moment, she's more than relieved to let Theo be the solution to her housing crisis. She is *not* a damsel in distress, but her bank account is very distressed by the prospect of shelling out more than half her monthly income to rent an apartment without a necessity—a *renter's right*—as basic as a fridge.

"I wish it were that simple."

"It's not?"

"I had that thought, too, so I spoke with Sal. My landlord. He informed me that we're not eligible to take over the lease, like, financially."

Not eligible financially? What? They're both adults with full-time jobs. W-2 jobs. Salaried jobs. She's aware that neither of their chosen paths has provided them with the financial stability of padded savings accounts and stock market portfolios. But they're fine.

Evie's brow creases, confused. "I thought the unit was rent-controlled?"

"There's a stipulation in the lease that, sans a guarantor,

each tenant must provide proof that their monthly salary is at least three times the rent."

Evie does the calculation once, twice, three times, triple-checking her mental math because the number she gets every time is obscene. *"Each?"*

Theo nods.

"You're sure?"

"Unfortunately."

"Fuck."

"I know. Micah's parents were on the lease, so it's never been an issue."

Evie doesn't have a financial safety net. Her father literally fled the country, working on an excavation site in Argentina and pretending his six-figure student loan debt disappeared . . . so his credit is presumably in the toilet. Naomi has money. Well. Jean-Paul has money. But she'd rather take the Palms apartment where someone was probably definitely murdered than ask her mother for help. Theo asking his dad is as much of a nonstarter as Evie calling Naomi.

So.

Pep and Mo's crumpled check is still in her back pocket. Evie supposes she could call her grandparents, but that feels more like a last resort than a viable option. They've already done so much—*too much*—to help her out. She wants a worry-free retirement for them. Doesn't want to burden them with her financial woes.

"Sal is giving me until the end of the week to figure some-thing out, but unless we rob a bank or one of us wins the lottery . . ."

Theo lets the sentence trail off as he scrolls through the rental agreement on his phone. Evie can almost hear him thinking, just two words bouncing around in his skull in a loop. *Fix this, fix this, fix this.* It's Theo's best worst quality, his desire to be a fixer. Because some things can't be fixed—not her ankle, not her diagnosis, and not the bullshit terms of this lease.

"What are we going to do?" Evie asks.

We.

In moments like these, she's here to remind him not to be so in his head, that they can problem-solve together. He fixates on the lease, his expression unreadable at first, but a moment later it relaxes into his signature smirk—and just as she can hear his brain working, she can also *see* the moment a solution clicks into place.

"There's a way that we can qualify to renew my lease."

She arches a single eyebrow. "Without committing a felony?"

"It's a . . . let's call it a loophole. A brilliant one, actually."

"I'm listening."

When Theo looks up, she resists the urge to inform him that he still has a bit of ice cream on his face, the purple ube in his dimple adding a touch of levity to this moment. A rogue curl falls in front of eyes that meet hers and Evie is starting to believe that *loophole* is a generous descriptor for whatever he's about to suggest. It's going to be a felony. A misdemeanor at minimum. Theo pushes his hair out of his eyes and flashes her an ube dimple grin, and Evie braces herself, wondering what it says about her that she would rob a bank for him, if he asked.

She opens her mouth to say this.

To assure Theo that she'd do anything for him, if he asked.

She doesn't. Thankfully. Because his brilliant loophole solution? It's the one thing—the *only* thing—that she'll never, *ever* do.

"Marry me, Evelyn."

6

Theo braces for the impact of those three words that tumbled out of his mouth like a revelation. He watches as her face expresses an entire spectrum of emotion in real time, morphing from wide eyes to furrowed forehead lines, her lips pursed together until she can no longer contain the laughter that escapes in the form of a snort-cackle that makes him so anxious. Not to take back the proposal, but to clarify it. He can't. At least, not while Evelyn continues to snort-cackle (*snackle?*). She plucks a napkin from the dispenser between them and leans forward to wipe his cheek. Purple ice cream streaks the napkin.

"I'm sorry," she snackle-cries. "For a second, I thought you were serious."

"Hear me out," Theo says.

Evelyn crumples the napkin. "You're serious?"

In the beat of silence that follows, Theo considers leaning into the joke that Evelyn so badly wants this to be. It's not too late to laugh off his very serious proposal like he's still the ten-year-old kid who wrinkled his nose any time an adult in their lives referred to Evelyn as his girlfriend.

But.

It's a solution.

"I am."

"Theodore."

He holds his phone out to show Evelyn the paragraph that inspired him. "We can combine our income to meet the minimum salary threshold if we're married."

"Seriously?" she asks, and he watches her read and reread that single paragraph until her tiny forehead vein protrudes. "So our financial status is sufficient, so long as we change our relationship status? That's bullshit. *No*. No *way*."

"Ouch," Theo mutters, clutching his heart. "Don't let me down *too* easy."

Evelyn kicks his shin, then winces. "Sorry," she whispers, caressing the toe that just smashed into his leg. "It's a loaded question."

His eyes meet hers. "I know."

They were twelve when Naomi left her daughters to "find herself." Just kids when Evelyn fell apart in his arms at the end of the recital her mother had missed. Over the years, Theo has listened to Evelyn wax poetic about how marriage—the institution—benefits men more than women. She'd recite studies and statistics about how many people exist in unhappy marriages because the patriarchy sells a false narrative, a fantasy—and the reality, to quote teen Evelyn, *fucking blows*.

"I won't do it," she'd declared just a year ago, after she turned down Hanna's proposal—and Hanna responded by accepting a job offer in Atlanta. Reeling from the breakup, Evelyn asked Theo to spend a weekend in Big Bear. "I love her, but I can't marry her," she confessed as the two of them stared up at a sky so magical it almost made the blisters he could feel forming from the six-mile hike worth it. "Naomi jumped into marriage and, like, became a wife. David's wife. At twenty-six, her identity was so wrapped up in him, and then he left her, left us . . . and then she left us. I'm working with Jules on not being so angry about it. Naomi leaving, remarrying, tethering herself to someone else because it was such a great idea the first time around. She never learns. But I did . . . and I love Han, I want to be with her. But I won't marry her. I refuse to legally bind my heart to someone who could just wake up one day and leave."

In the darkness illuminated only by the stars, Evelyn Bloom vowed that she would never marry. Then she fell asleep on his shoulder and his heart cracked in half listening to her snore. Once upon a time he wanted it all—marriage, a family, a white-picket-fence cliché of a life.

But he'd let go of that fantasy of a life with Evelyn long ago.

They'd woken up covered in mosquito bites. On the miserable hike back to her car, she referred to them as *platonic soulmates* and he only felt relieved that they'd never crossed the invisible boundary between friendship and something more, that the universe intervened in a truly dramatic fashion every time he walked that line like a tightrope.

Because she truly is his happy place.

In the most platonic-soulmate way.

Marry me, Evelyn.

Of course he understands her visceral reaction to his question that he didn't even phrase as a question. It's a loaded ask for him, too, because regardless of his own issues with his father, he can't deny the truth that his parents were in real, proper love. Lori's death destroyed Jacob, caused him to push, push, push his grief away, his memories of life Before Cancer, his son who needed him. Now? Theo's anxious just thinking about that white-picket-fence cliché of a life, overwhelmed at the thought of opening his heart enough to anyone because, really, is the temporary joy worth the inevitable pain? Theo isn't sure who he's more afraid to be in these hypothetical situations . . . the person who dies or the person left behind.

But.

This isn't a proposal to build a cliché of a life. It's also not a trap. Rather, it's a proposal for two platonic soulmates to game an economy that makes it way too hard to build *any* kind of life. It's a temporary freedom. In more ways than just being a short-term solution for their housing crisis.

Finally, Evelyn says, "I'll call Pep in the morning. I hate to ask them, but getting married just to keep an apartment is kind of insane."

"Maybe," he concedes with a shrug. "But have I ever told you that I have excellent benefits?"

She rolls her eyes, but he sees the moment it *clicks* for her. The flicker of possibility in her expression indicating that she understands exactly what he's offering. "Theodore—"

"You could take the fellowship."

"Oh."

Oh?

"Did you already say no?"

"No."

Theo's eyebrows knit together because he knows she wants this. She told him as much, before she knew that he forged the application that secured her spot. Theo can't un-make that decision, but he can address the reason why she didn't apply in the first place and it feels just as important as the apartment situation. Maybe more important, because Theo also fucked up her first dream, shattered her future as a dancer with a single irreversible mistake.

But.

This is a fixable mistake. He removes his wallet from his pocket and pulls out his insurance card. He hands the piece of plastic to Evelyn and watches her eyes widen upon taking in just the minimal information that the card provides—his in-network deductible, out-of-pocket maximum, and copays.

"Are you trying to seduce me?"

Theo swallows, his Adam's apple bobbing. "Is it working?"

"It's not . . . *not* working? Shit. I've never seen a deductible so glorious," she admits, handing his insurance card back to him. "What's your coinsurance situation?"

Theo frowns. "Coinsurance?"

"How much does your insurance cover after you hit your deductible?"

"Um." Is this a trick question? "Assuming it's in-network . . . all of it?"

"Shut the fuck up."

"Is that not how insurance works?"

Evelyn looks at him like that's *not* how insurance works. It's how his works. Theo should know. Who knows how much money he'd spend without it—on EKGs that assure him that *no*, he's not having a heart attack, on CT scans that do not diagnose him with a brain aneurysm, on bloodwork that always comes back normal. Every visit is justified. Because once he hits that glorious deductible, the most he pays to quiet his brain is a ten-dollar copay for the office visit. It's always temporary, that quiet, but seeing doctors and running tests provide the reassurance he needs to keep functioning.

"Your premiums must be ridiculous."

Sixty bucks, taken out of each biweekly paycheck. "Not really."

"Can I see your EOB?"

Theo opens the healthcare app on his phone and clicks on the link to his plan's Explanation of Benefits. Evelyn reads and scrolls and reads and scrolls past preventative care, past testing and imaging, to hospital care, and then to prescription coverage. Care and medication that she needs. Evelyn attempts to keep her expression neutral, but Theo knows her too well and notes every subtle reaction—the twitch of her lip, the flare of her nostrils, the ever-so-slight widening of her eyes.

"I—" she begins, then pauses. "Theodore. Insurance like this would change my entire life."

Theo smiles. "Yeah?"

Evelyn hands his phone back to him and he registers the tears pooling in her lash lines. "I can't."

"Ev—"

"I love you so much for the offer, but you don't want this with me."

"It's my idea."

"It's not necessary. I'm positive Pep and Mo will agree to cosign the lease."

He shakes his head and waves away those words. "You want to live together?"

Evelyn nods.

"Then stop overthinking this. Marry me. Accept the fellowship."

She runs a hand through her hair and exhales a shaky laugh. "I'm kind of spinning out."

"You don't have to," Theo insists. "It's just a signature on a piece of paper that would buy us some time to breathe."

"Just a signature," she repeats, bemused.

He nods. "We keep my apartment. You take the dream job and become a working Foley artist. Once you're in the union, which, correct me if I'm wrong, also has excellent benefits, we'll sign another piece of paper and return to our regular platonic-soulmate life."

"You're serious."

"Incredibly."

"Theodore."

"What? It's a great idea. Unless you're secretly in love with me . . ." His eyes widen. "Holy shit. You're secretly in love with me."

"Head over heels," she deadpans.

"Knew it."

Then they're laughing. Well, he's laughing and she's snackle-ing. It always feels so good, his ability to say the exact right thing to get Evelyn out of her head. Once their laughter sub-sides, she stands and shoots her ice cream cup into the trash can nearest to their table. "Can I take a beat to process?"

That isn't a no.

"Sure."

"Cool."

"I'd be a fantastic husband."

Evelyn's nose scrunches. "I know."

Theo ignores the sincerity in her tone that doesn't match her expression. "Sal needs an answer by the end of the week."

She nods. "You mentioned that."

Theo needs to swing by Ralphs to pick up produce for the week. Evelyn needs to retrieve Gen from his apartment, so she circles around to the other side of the table where he's still seated and wraps her arms around his neck in a goodbye hug, before whispering, "I'd be a terrible wife."

He looks at her, mimicking her expression. "I know."

She lets go of him, then shoves his shoulder. "Asshole."

Theo laughs. "Text me when you're at Gen's?"

"Sure."

"I'll do a grocery run and be home before you're even through downtown," Theo says. "This life could be yours, too. Just marry me, Evelyn."

She removes keys from her tote bag. "I do miss Pasadena."

"So come home, then."

Evelyn's expression turns serious, those words disarming enough to render her speechless. Theo worries it's too much. Way too earnest. But he's trying to sell a plan that doesn't just provide another year of housing security for them but also gives her the security she needs to pursue her art.

Theo can do this for her.

She can let him do this for her.

"Okay."

Theo's eyebrows rise, as this is the shortest beat to ever beat. "Okay?"

"*Yes.*"

His heart hammers in his chest, thrashes wildly against his rib cage at the one-syllable answer to his question that changes nothing. *It changes nothing.* Theo can marry his best friend and *it can mean nothing* outside the benefits—health insurance, a Foley fellowship, a retained apartment.

"Assuming it would be low-key," Evelyn adds.

"Super low-key! Really, no one even needs to know."

"Gen needs to know."

"Only Gen needs to know."

"Pep and Mo, too," Evelyn adds, then nods once and it's firm. Decisive. "Okay."

Theo googles *same day marriage LA county how* in that order because what even are words and starts a shared to-do list because lists are logical, lists are calculated, just like this decision. It's a straightforward process. Go to the LA County Registrar-Recorder/County Clerk office (*not* city hall) with a photo ID, bring a witness, pay a fee, sign some papers, and . . . that's it.

"I have a half day on Wednesday," Theo says. Well, technically his kids do, but he'll be free from the afternoon of professional development by two o'clock, enough time to make it to the closest office, even in traffic. "It's probably our best shot of making it during the week."

Her eyes meet his. "As long as we make it home in time for *Survivor*."

Home.

We.

Theo ignores whatever that sentence is doing to his heart. "Of course."

Evelyn breaks the eye contact, her attention shifting to a screen aglow with notifications. Gen has blown up her phone in a truly dramatic fashion that has her off to retrieve her sister and return to the west side, but not before standing and saying goodbye with one more hug. "Are we seriously doing this?"

"It's just a piece of paper," Theo repeats. "Nothing will change."

"We're getting married so I can quit my full-time job for a minimum-wage fellowship."

"Yeah."

"That's kind of a monumental change."

"It is." Theo nods. "I meant with us. Nothing will change. I promise."

Evelyn rolls her eyes, then takes a step out of the embrace. "That I'm not worried about, Theodore."

It's not until the headlights of her car turn on and he watches Evelyn pull out of the parking lot that Theo dares to acknowledge—then promptly swallow—the truth that his insistence, no, *promise*, that nothing will change was possibly more for himself than it was for her.

AFTERS AFTER, JUNIOR YEAR

Theo

Everything changes his junior year, and it is so incredibly inconvenient, being in love with his best friend. He first felt it, the flutter of a crush, their first day back in the studio after summer break. Evelyn had just returned from a summer-long dance intensive with blue hair cut short, a tattoo on her rib cage, and a girlfriend. Talia. When she peeled off her tank top during the break, exposing a cluster of music notes just below her sports bra, Theo short-circuited.

Hot.

Evelyn is hot.

"Tattoo?"

She pushed her bangs—also new—out of her face with a headband. "It's the opening notes of 'Vienna.'"

Billy Joel.

Her favorite song.

Also—or, perhaps, even because—his mom's favorite song.

"How?"

Evelyn showed Theo another new acquisition from her summer without him, a piece of plastic with her face on it and a false identity next to it. "Talia knows someone."

"Oh."

Tattoo? Oh? Had a summer apart fucked with his brain chemistry, rendered him no longer capable of speaking to his best friend in more than one-word sentences? *Pull it together.* Did he miss her? Yes. Did he love her? Of course. *But not like that.* In the bathroom, he splashed water on his face until his heart calmed down. Then Evelyn took his hands in hers, guided them to her hips and talked him through new choreography that wasn't theirs yet but would've been, could've been, had he not been distracted by how little she was wearing, by blue hair skimming her collarbone, by *that fucking tattoo* to learn any of it.

Such a cliché Theo Cohen had become.

Six months later, Evelyn is blue hair no more, her relationship with Talia is no more, but that flutter is ever present. It's a soft whisper in his ear when he watches her dance, a quiet yelp when her freezing feet press against his warm skin during a movie night at the bungalow, a punch in the stomach when she stops by his house after school with a lavender latte, Lori's favorite, just because. Currently, it's the laugh that accompanies listening to Evelyn butcher the lyrics of "Ribs" as she drives them from the dance studio to Afters. She finds street parking and doesn't cut the engine of Pep's 2008 Honda Accord until the song reaches its climax and fades to a soft conclusion.

"I'll order for us," Evelyn says, walking ahead to the window.

Theo claims a picnic table and sets up *Survivor* on his phone and wonders, as he so often does, would it really be so terrible to acknowledge this all-consuming flutter? To ask if she feels it too? What if she says no?

What if she says *yes?*

He isn't sure if he's ready for either answer, so he doesn't ask.

Theo never asks.

Instead, he leans into his attraction to anyone, *everyone* else. Always, it is physical. Casual. A summer fling with Nicolette Moore, a rising senior who wrangled elementary school kiddos alongside Theo, both student teachers at SHDA's dance camp. Late nights kissing Yaz Gonzales, his AP Bio lab partner, in the back of her orange Nissan Murano until their lips were swollen. Maya Jones, a sophomore in jazz company with him, asked him to homecoming. Violet Parker, the junior class president, invited him to the winter formal. Girls, *plural*, liked him, and he isn't sure when it happened, when being a male dancer became *cool*—but who is he to question this rebrand?

Evelyn slides into the bench across from him, and when he looks up from his phone, he doesn't find his usual—two scoops of ube brownie in a cup with a cone on top. In front of him is an aluminum tray with maybe the equivalent of those two scoops in compostable sample cups arranged to spell a one-word question:

PROM?

Theo is so thrown by this question—by *Evelyn* asking this question. "Prom?"

Whatever his reaction is, he knows it's wrong by the way her cheeks tint pink before she says, "It's dumb. I know. But I already bought a dress and . . . we should go! As friends, obviously. It could be fun? Unless . . ." Her eyes meet his and see the answer to the question she hasn't even asked. "Caro?"

He picks up a taste of ube brownie, the tail of the question mark, and nods.

"I told you."

"She literally just asked today. After the littles left."

Theo student teaches with Caroline Shapiro-Huang every Wednesday before his studio time with Evelyn. He takes a city bus to the studio straight from school and hangs out with tiny dancers between the ages of six and ten, leading warm-ups and tying tap shoes alongside Caro—a former dance friend, current real friend, suddenly *cute* friend. Caro's dad has Hodgkin's lymphoma and it's nice talking to someone who gets it, but also *not* talking to someone who gets it.

Not that Evelyn doesn't get it.

She loves Lori, too.

But she can't—*won't*—speak the worst possible outcomes out loud.

What if her doctors missed something?

What if it comes back?

What if she dies?

Caro's dark sense of humor about it all is disarming. So is her melodic laugh, her obsession with *I Love Lucy*, how she has a silly nickname for every tiny dancer. Goose. Joker. Roo. Stella pays student teachers in the form of a generous tuition discount, but it's so *fun*, just being around Caro and the kids, that Theo would honestly do it for free if he didn't need the discounts because cancer is expensive.

"Was it at least this cute?" Evelyn asks, then reaches for one of the ube brownie samples and throws it back like a shot.

"What?"

She takes another. "The promposal?"

Theo shrugs. "She just asked."

In the parking lot, they confirmed plans to hang out later tonight, like they have been every week for the past month. She honked at him after he walked away, toward the studio, toward the next two hours with Evelyn, and he turned to find Caro hanging out the window of her Ford Bronco and shouting a question at him across the parking lot.

Do you have a prom date?

His response, *Do I?*, triggered her super-specific laugh.

You do now.

Evelyn nods. "Cool."

She has almost finished the *P.* Unsure what to say next, Theo swallows and opts to hand her an earbud. She takes it and they watch *Survivor* in silence. Is she watching it? Theo's not. He's stuck on the promposal written in his favorite ice cream flavor that she's currently scarfing down one letter at a time, so confused because she seems disappointed, so confused because he *likes* that she's disappointed . . . and does that mean that he should've said no to Caro? Is this Evelyn's way of asking him if he feels the flutter, too? Because the answer is *yes.*

Yes.

Yes.

Yes.

Evelyn pauses *Survivor* before Jeff even snuffs a torch and he wonders if this is it, the moment that two best friends acknowledge whatever this energy is between them and everything changes. But then she stands and he barely registers that she looks especially pale in the lamplight glow of Afters before she hurls into the trash can and the timing of this random Evelyn vom is impeccable, truly. Theo holds her hair back while she hurls, the once-blue tips now faded teal, and not even watching her vomit his favorite ice cream squashes the flutter. Concern creases his forehead because it's been happening more often, the vomiting. So even when she insists that she's fine after, as she always does, Theo drives her to the bungalow, where they watch *The Lizzie McGuire Movie* until she falls asleep on his shoulder.

It's not too late to still hang out with Caro.

Theo cancels on Caro.

7

"Happy Wednesday!" says Evie's boss, soon to be ex-boss, Katia Belafonte, executive producer of *After Ever After.* "How are you?"

Evie's eye twitches. "Great."

"Great!"

They're the first two in the weekly pitch meeting, a video call that Evie takes from Imogen's couch, her laptop propped on a stack of books. During a moment of awkward silence, Katia tucks a rogue strand of her otherwise sleek onyx bob behind her ear and by the time it occurs to Evie to ask her how *she* is, more faces populate her screen. Cohosts Amber B. and Tiffany P. Outreach and booking manager Claudia Cho. Graphic designer Saskia Evans. Just six people are responsible for producing the dating show recap podcast. Soon to be five, after she quits. Once this salary, combined with Theo's salary, secures his apartment.

If she quits.

Evie has no clue *how* to quit.

I quit.

Her pulse spikes just thinking those two words. How? She's a twenty-seven-year-old adult who's in therapy, who's doing the work. Yet she's still the little girl who walked into Miss Stella's class all those years ago, so terrified by something she wants, by articulating that want.

First, to dance.

Now, to quit.

At least she has a few weeks to figure out how to quash the panic that swells her throat every time she even *thinks* about quitting because she's not a person who leaves—not places, not people, not even a job. After participating in hellos and small talk, Evie turns her camera off. She takes her laptop to the couch, lies down, closes her eyes, and tries to stay present. She truly does. Why? It doesn't matter. Five years of her life that included surviving three rounds of layoffs, two promotions, and an acquisition that opened an antitrust case against her employer are ending.

It's not just quitting that scares her, but what it means.

Accepting the fellowship.

Marrying Theo.

Any attempt at active listening is over the moment her phone lights up with an email.

Subject: marriage license (holy shit)

As someone from the analytics department (Gerri? Kerry?) joins the call to go over last season's engagement metrics, her anxiety about quitting becomes second to the memory she's spent the last three days attempting to rebury.

The memory Theo unknowingly excavated with those three words.

Marry me, Evelyn.

She's no longer on Imogen's couch. She's lying in a king-size bed in a tiny Airbnb nestled in the Santa Barbara mountains, tangled in butter-soft satin sheets, tangled in Hanna, who's still asleep. Evie watches her chest rise and fall, absorbing every detail of this moment—the silk bonnet with little strawberries protecting her curls, the drool on her pillow, the way her gold septum piercing reflects the light. She watches in awe of their present and reminisces about their beginning. Sophomore year. UCLA. Hanna Greene, bursting through the door of A History of Cinema ten minutes late like a sexy tornado. Evie, taking in her every detail—her ombré blue box braids, the small mole under her left eye, her choice to wear socks with Tevas. Hanna, twisting in her chair after choosing the seat in front of Evie.

"Do you have a pencil?"

"Yes."

Evie handed over her only pencil, distracted by the septum piercing.

For two years she ignored her crush, until they were on the set of a senior thesis together. Hanna, a grip. Evie, a boom operator. After a 2:00 a.m. wrap, Hanna asked her if she wanted a milkshake. "Yes," she lied, instead of telling Hanna that dairy messes with her stomach. They went to Lulu's, the twenty-four-hour diner on campus, where Evie opted to sip on a root beer while they whispered their biggest, scariest dreams out loud and laughed until the sun came up. Their first kiss tasted like a root beer float.

"Come back to mine?" Hanna asked against her mouth, Evie's back pressed against Lulu's brick façade.

She replied without hesitation. "Yes."

"I have a job lined up in Atlanta," Hanna confessed the following morning. "I'm not looking for anything serious."

Lucky for Hanna, neither was Evie. So their beginning was a situationship with a defined end date. Easy, casual, perfect. After graduation, Hanna left. Evie stayed. But the following year, Hanna returned to LA, showed up at the bungalow with a lavender latte, and what started as a senior-year situationship became a three-year relationship.

Evie's first *real* relationship.

Hanna's eyelids flutter as she rolls onto her side and burrows into Evie. Hanna, a script coordinator for a network procedural, planned this getaway during the brief hiatus between seasons. Both live in LA, separated by up to an hour-long commute. For now. It's their three-year anniversary and Evie's ready to live with Hanna, ready to really begin their life together.

Hanna drapes her leg over Evie's thigh, her knee pressing into her full bladder. Evie untangles herself, in need of the bathroom, then searches Hanna's overnight bag in need of toothpaste. Her fingers brush against velvet and the sensation is an electric shock of panic. *No.* Her hand wraps around a small velvet box. *No.* She removes it from Hanna's bag and it's exactly what she thinks it is. *No.* She opens the box. *No.* A simple solitaire diamond set in gold sparkles in the morning sun.

No.

"Ev?"

Hanna's morning voice sounds like sex.

Evie's knees feel liquid.

Hanna presses her palms against the mattress to sit up and reaches for clear-frame glasses on the nightstand. Seeing the ring box in Evie's hand, she laughs. "Shit."

"I needed toothpaste."

"Come here, Ev."

"I need to use the bathroom."

She locks the bathroom door behind her and squeezes her eyes shut. Evie's just twenty-six, the same age her parents were when they got married, and though she's certain she doesn't want to follow in their footsteps, it terrifies her how easy it would be to say yes.

It's always been so easy to say that word to Hanna.

Yes.

Too easy to lose herself in the fantasy.

Yes.

Like Naomi did.

Yes.

Like Evie swore she would *never* do. She *won't.* Hanna is unfazed by the amount of time she spends in the bathroom. When Evie opens the door, Hanna isn't on one knee. She's standing at the end of the bed, ring in hand, looking so goddamn good in an oversized Paramore T-shirt that barely covers her ass and the strawberry bonnet that fully covers her hair.

"I had a whole thing planned, but fuck it. I love you so much. Marry me, Ev?"

No.

No.

No—

"Ev? Is that doable?"

Evie is jolted out of the memory, Amber B.'s direct address reminding her she's somehow still in a work meeting.

She unmutes herself. "Super doable."

"You're the best," Tiffany P. says.

A message notification pops up on her screen.

Saskia.

Saskia E. (they/she): ummm . . . u good?
Evie B. (she/her): . . . do i even WANT to know what
I just agreed to?
Saskia is typing . . .

Saskia stops typing.
A moment later, Evie's phone vibrates with a text from Saskia.

sass evans
bitch?? u just OK'd weekly bonus podcasts like it was
nbd??
10:31 A.M.

DID I?
10:32 A.M.

NO
10:32 A.M.

gif of Michael Scott screaming no
10:32 A.M.

this is why u can't sleep thru these calls!!
10:33 A.M.

or this is why they WANT me to sleep through them . . . !
10:34 A.M.

touché
10:35 A.M.

Evie reads that last message in Saskia's voice.
Toosh.
She first heard their Australian accent say—shout—*toosh*

in a crowded Midtown bar last year while visiting the New York office, where Saskia is based. Now Saskia and Evie are work besties bonded by the super specific ability to recall any Best Picture film if prompted by a random year (1942? *How Green Was My Valley.* 2011? *The King's Speech.* 1984? *Terms of Endearment*), the shared trauma of surviving multiple layoffs and an acquisition, and the casual sex that happens whenever they're on the same coast. They first hooked up after her relationship with Hanna imploded, and it's so nice, how not-complicated Saskia is.

Wait.

If I marry Theo, can I still hook up with Saskia?

Yes, she reasons, because nothing will change.

Theo promised.

And he's the only person in her life who doesn't make a promise unless he can keep it. It's why, outside his life-changing benefits, she agreed to this ridiculous arrangement. Also because a past version of herself *would* accept a request as absurd as doubling her output. She has medical debt, student loans, so many bills. She needs the money, the benefits, the stability. And at least she likes her colleagues, likes putting her degree and expertise to use, likes that eighty percent of the time she works in her pajamas.

It could be so much worse, she would've rationalized just a week ago.

Evie has always been good at rationalizing.

"So. Off to . . . where, exactly?" Evie asks after Theo slides into the passenger seat of Phoebe outside Foothill Elementary. "I keep wanting to say city hall even though I know that's wrong."

"LA County Registrar-Recorder/County Clerk office is a mouthful." Theo unbuttons the sleeves of his light blue dress shirt, rolling them up to his elbows to expose toned forearms that she absolutely never notices. "But actually . . ."

His knee bounces, a nervous habit. Evie's mind races with possibilities, the first and most obvious one being that he changed his mind, that he doesn't want to go through with this. Even though it was his idea. Evie isn't sure how she feels. Relieved? Disappointed? Resigned?

". . . can we swing by the house first?"

"Really?"

Theo nods. "I need to pick up something."

"Oh."

It's so unexpected, Theo's request, that it doesn't even make Evie's top ten list of possibilities. *The house* refers to his childhood home, a Spanish-style ranch in Lamanda Park, where his father still lives. Theo avoids it. Uses language that distances himself from it. *The* house. Not *his* house. Evie doesn't avoid it. Every Sunday morning, she swings by with Lucky Boy breakfast burritos—a weekly routine that started shortly after Lori's death. In the beginning, Jacob told Evie to fuck off and slammed the door in her face. She left the burrito on the porch. But she kept coming back. Eventually, he let her in.

First, they just ate together in silence.

Then they watched old episodes of *Monk*, *Cold Case*, whatever was on cable television.

He didn't mention Lori by name for two years.

But now?

He cooks for her, and they talk. Every Sunday, Jacob asks about Theo. Afterward, Theo always asks how Jacob is doing. *Call him*, she nudges gently. As far as she knows, he hasn't. Sometimes it pisses her off that she's still the intermediary between Theo and Jacob. How they live in the same city but may as well be on opposite sides of the planet. She knows it was never great, their relationship. She saw how Jacob tried to mold Theo into a version of himself, a successful commercial real estate developer. She knows that it wasn't easy for Theo to have a father who, on a fundamental level, didn't understand him. Losing Lori only further drove a wedge between them, and it's just so sad how broken they are—because Jacob Cohen may be flawed but at least he's *here*.

At least he cares enough to try.

Five minutes after Theo's out-of-character request, Evie pulls over at the curb in front of the house and puts Phoebe in park. Jacob isn't home. His silver Buick isn't in the driveway. It's intentional, the timing. She understands what this means. "Is this a rescue mission?"

Rescue missions happened regularly after Lori died.

Evie and Theo sneaking into the house to retrieve artifacts, memories of her.

Theo nods. "Mom's rings."

Evie short-circuits, her heart leaping into her throat. "What?"

"We don't have rings. What couple shows up to get married without rings, Evelyn?"

Theo says this simply, like it's so obvious, before he's out of the car and heading toward the house and *no, no, no*. It's a valid point. Needing rings. But there's a T.J. Maxx down the street. The idea of Theo sliding Lori's ring onto her finger? Of carrying such an important piece of her around? *No*. It's way too much. Evie wants a ring that's as fake as this marriage.

It needs to be fake.

She follows him into the house to tell him this, but he doesn't even make it beyond the front door.

"Fuck," he whispers.

Evie is used to the state of the house—the stench of weed,

the dust that covers the furniture, the lack of available surface area. Piles of papers stacked on tables, outerwear draped over every kitchen chair, boxes filled with miscellaneous trinkets, collections of vintage dishware, comic books, Beanie Babies.

It's hard to let things go, Jacob once told her over Sunday morning breakfast burritos.

Evie's hand finds Theo's, their fingers interlacing.

She squeezes.

Because it's a lot.

Theo squeezes back, then lets go. Pinches the bridge of his nose and breathes. "Let's start upstairs. I'll take their bedroom. You check mine?"

Theo saying *their bedroom* cracks her heart in half. "Okay. But Theodore? I can't . . . her rings . . ." She hears the emotion in her voice but doesn't want him to be the one comforting her so she swallows it. Refuses to allow her eyes to water. "I'll rescue them with you. But I don't want . . . I *can't*. You should save them. For a real proposal."

Theo's eyes meet hers.

He scratches his neck. Then says, so softly, "I think she'd like it? You holding on to them in the meantime."

And what is she supposed to say to that?

She doesn't say anything. Isn't even given a chance to be-cause, once again, Theo's gone, those words propelling him beyond the front hall, toward his parents' bedroom in the back of the house. Evie follows him, splitting off at his bed-room door, another room that's less a memory of childhood and more a storage closet for a hoarder. It's all Lori's—her clothes, her books, her baking supplies. Only a shelf of tro-phies and plaques, relics from their competitive dance past, are recognizably *Theo*. She opens drawers and sifts through boxes—*endless* boxes—as she tears apart the room, unsure if she wants to laugh or cry because the last time she came in contact with an engagement ring?

It broke her heart.

"Any luck?" Theo asks, standing under the doorframe.

"No."

"Me either." He rakes a frustrated hand through his hair, then crosses the threshold to sit on the edge of the bed. "She tried to give them to me. Toward the end. But I was in so much denial I couldn't, and now who knows where they are? If Jacob even knows where they are?"

She moves a box of baking sheets to the floor to sit next to him. "Theodore. We'll find the rings. Maybe not today, but that's okay! We don't need them to get married. It's not—"

"You're getting married?"

Jacob's voice scares the shit out of them, as does his presence in Theo's room. He's business semicasual, dressed in slacks a size too large because he hasn't put back on the grief weight loss and refuses to buy new clothes. Evie hears a hint of joy in the question that's impossible to process.

Theo stands. "You're here."

"In my own home?" Jacob snorts. "Where the fuck else would I be?"

Theo winces. "Hi, Dad."

"Answer my question."

"I don't know where else—"

"No, the first question." Jacob's expression softens, his eyes shifting to meet hers. "Evelyn, are you marrying my son?"

Then, Jacob Cohen smiles.

He smiles.

And Evie's brain breaks.

It's the only explanation for what happens next, for the way her limbs take on a life of their own. She stands and loops her arm through Theo's, then rests her head on his shoulder like it's the most natural thing in the world because Jacob smiled for the first time in literal years and if this marriage is going to give her a shot at her dream career maybe it can also give Theo a chance to repair his relationship with his dad.

So.

Evie speaks before her brain can stop her.

"Yes," she says, beaming at Jacob, then beaming at Theo. "I am."

8

Yes, I am.

Theo's reeling from those three words and how easily they tumbled out of Evelyn's mouth. How effortlessly she explained the situation, the timing, the urgency to his father. How she conveniently left out the tiny (major!) detail that they're doing this because they love each other, not because they're *in* love with each other. Key distinction. As Evelyn drives toward the government building that's not city hall, he attempts to process it all from the back seat. Jacob is in the passenger seat, a spot he occupies without protest.

"I am positive that Lori is losing her shit up there," Jacob says, the corners of his mouth lifting in a sad smile.

Theo's positive he's losing his shit *back here*.

"I wish she was here," Evelyn says.

"She is," Jacob says.

Theo feels the weight of the bamboo ring box in his pocket, his stomach doing somersaults as Evelyn merges onto Arroyo Seco Parkway. He leans against the window, presses his cheek to the glass, and closes his eyes, the only instant remedy for the carsickness he's always dealt with on this roller coaster of a freeway. Focuses on breathing through the nausea and his quiet rage because Jacob doesn't deserve to be here. Not just due to the physical absence from his life since Lori died. Even in the Before Cancer timeline, he'd never been present. But. He is now. Theo hates acknowledging the complicated truth that this, Jacob's presence, his ability to willingly—no, *enthusiastically*—hand over the rings, matters to him. He doesn't.

Instead, he observes Evelyn and Jacob's dynamic, their easy back-and-forth, while fuming over the fact that he's been relegated to the back seat, like a child, *on his wedding day.*

No.

On the day that he's signing a legal document so he doesn't lose his apartment and so his favorite person can pursue a dream career.

That's a mouthful, though.

So wedding day it is.

Forty minutes later, Imogen greets them outside Not City Hall, a brick building in South LA so nondescript that Evelyn completely misses the parking lot and gets stuck in a fifteen-minute traffic jam trying to loop around one block.

"Genny Bloom!" Jacob says, then hugs her and it's bizarre, seeing his father act like an actual person.

"Mr. Cohen?" Imogen says, then mouths, *What the fuck?* in Theo and Evelyn's direction, still in Jacob's embrace. Theo can only respond with a useless shrug. "Hi! It's so wonderful to see you."

Jacob snorts as he lets go of Gen, then goes to open the door. "It's not because I was invited."

Theo hears the edge in Jacob's tone and chooses to move toward the blast of cool indoor air, to get in line. Chooses to ignore it even though there's something hilarious about the idea that Theo owes him an invitation, that he owes his father anything at all.

Gen laughs, interpreting the dig as a lighthearted quip. "If it makes you feel better, I'm only invited because they needed a witness."

"Eloping just felt right for us," Evelyn says.

Is that what they're calling it now? Theo can't keep up.

"Did it?" Jacob asks.

"We wanted it to be a surprise," she adds.

At this Jacob *does* laugh. "As if this is a shocking development!"

Then he beelines for the bathroom, still laughing. Even if Jacob's assessment of his relationship with Evelyn is basic and boring and based on the outdated (not to mention heteronormative) assumption that two people of different genders cannot be friends, Theo has to swallow emotion that he doesn't even know how to articulate because he can't remember the last time he heard his dad laugh.

No one dares to speak until Jacob is gone.

"Okay. What's happening?" Gen asks.

It's the first time Jacob's been out of earshot since Evelyn threw herself into Theo's arms. "I'm just as clueless, Gen."

Evelyn shrugs. "Theo wanted Lori's rings. We got them. But now Jacob assumes that this, *we* are real."

"And that's necessary because . . ." Gen starts.

"No way would he have handed them over if he knew the truth," Evelyn says.

Theo frowns. "You don't know that."

"Theodore."

She's right.

He knows she's right.

"Also," she continues, "if this makes him happy, would it be so bad to . . . I don't know? Let him be happy?"

His heart cracks in half. "Evelyn. He's going to tell everyone."

"I know."

"This is quite the pivot from only Gen and your grandparents needing to know."

"I know."

Theo isn't sure Evelyn fully understands what she's saying. It's one thing to sign a paper that says they're married and another thing to actively pretend to *be* married. And to do it for Jacob? To be an anchor for a man who has been emotionally unavailable for pretty much the entirety of his life? It feels all kinds of fucked-up to let Evelyn do that for him. For *them*. Theo knows he's just as much the reason. Somehow, Evelyn still believes in the bullshit fantasy that Jacob Cohen is capable of being more than who he has always been.

Theo's a realist.

But.

Jacob smiled.

Jacob laughed.

Jacob is still his dad.

Gen nods. "You're in love. Got it! Will pivot accordingly."

The line moves at a glacial pace and the attempts at small talk upon Jacob's return from the bathroom are painful. Gen keeps Jacob engaged in conversation because if there's one thing Imogen Bloom cannot handle, it's an awkward silence. She asks him if he's watched anything good lately, and Theo learns that Jacob is extremely into cooking competition shows. The more intense (read: abusive) the environment, the better. It's so much easier for Jacob Cohen to show Gen the Instagram account he made to follow his favorite chefs than to ask his son a question as simple as *How's this school year going?* But Theo supposes it's also easier for him to let Gen entertain his dad than to ask him a question as simple as *How've you been?*

So.

Finally, they are summoned to fill out the paperwork. His pulse spikes with each signature required on the very official marriage license application. Is this the wedding, elopement, whatever that he pictured for himself? Not at all. He imagined an outdoor ceremony at the Huntington, a chuppah made of flowers, Lori seated in the front row during the ceremony.

So, really, it was never going to be what he imagined.

"Hey. You good?" Evelyn asks, her voice low.

It's the first time he looks at her, *really* looks at her since she picked him up from school. He's been fixated on everything but her—the rings, Jacob, not vomiting in her car, the paperwork. Eyes lined in metallic gold meet his and Theo blinks stupidly at the vision that is Evelyn Bloom. Her hair is tied back in a bun. Not a ballet bun, but a messy one, her too-long bangs swept to the side. He recognizes the earrings she chose, simple gold hoops that were a high school graduation gift from his mom. He blinks away the emotion, eyes shifting to full lips coated in clear gloss. Suddenly, Theo doesn't know where to look—at her shoulders, where the tie straps of her dress are secured with two perfect bows, at the wildflower print with its plunging neckline and fabric that skims her hips, that accentuates the outline of her ass—

Theo swallows hard.

Fuck.

She's his best friend. She is so gorgeous.

Both things can be—*are*—true.

"I'm good. You look beautiful," Theo says. "Objectively."

She laughs. "You look objectively beautiful, too."

They return the paperwork, then wait to be called by a county clerk. Seated in the waiting room, Evelyn slides her hand into his. It's confusing because it's something she would do even if no one was watching, thanks to a friendship that blossomed out of a dance partnership. Meaning they've never shied away from physical touch. As friends. Her feet propped up on his lap. His head on her shoulder. Their hands, constantly entwined. Her freezing fingers squeeze his and . . . is she pretending? What is and isn't okay in the name of pretending?

Theo isn't sure.

He never planned on pretending.

He can't pretend.

"Dad, I—"

Jacob cuts him off. "You don't have to apologize. I get it. Your mom and me? We almost eloped, too."

"What?"

"Nearly got married on a beach in Cabo, just Lor and me."

"Seriously?"

Jacob nods. "I had to talk your mother out of uninviting Aunt Mae after a minor altercation over the menu. Wedding planning is a goddamn nightmare."

Theo has no clue at what point during the last five years defined by grief Jacob started talking about Lori again, but it will never not be an electric shock to the system. Hearing him say *Lor*. Jacob still referring to them as a *we*. A unit. It breaks his brain, even though Theo knows—he *knows*—that letting Jacob Cohen back in, even a little bit, will be a massive disappointment. It always is. Because people don't change.

But . . .

What if they do?

What if he can?

It's the faintest whisper of a thought, just loud enough that Theo keeps his mouth shut while Jacob rambles and reminisces until a clerk calls their names.

"Cohen and Bloom?"

They stand.

Jacob clears his throat. "You know we've always thought of you as a daughter, Ev—"

Evelyn wraps her arms around Jacob's neck and Theo feels some kind of way watching that embrace. He presses the heels of his hands into his eyes, quick, before his dad can see him emoting, before he can be told to *stop*. He knows that she has breakfast with Jacob every Sunday. But knowing that his dad is more of a presence in Evelyn's life than his own and seeing it are two different things, and while this wall, this boundary, between father and son is more than necessary, it still really hurts.

He'll never say that.

Or show it.

Evelyn wipes the single tear on her cheek with the pad of her thumb, then takes his hand and they follow the clerk, a short Black woman with a fade, pink cat-eye glasses, and matching lipstick who introduces herself as Tanya. She leads them into the ceremony room: four white walls, a wooden podium, and a single canvas hanging on the wall with the quote *You have my whole heart for my whole life* written in calligraphy. Theo wants to laugh. He wants to cry. *He wants his mom.*

"Good afternoon! We're gathered here today—"

Once Tanya begins, everything moves so fast. Theo doesn't hear a single word of the canned nonreligious ceremony they preselected, hyperfixated on Evelyn's hands in his, squeezing so hard he's positive her nails have left marks in his skin. He's not the most devout Jew, but the customs matter to him and it's a bummer that the ceremony options were either any sect of Christianity or nothing at all. He doesn't know the Sheva Brachot from memory, so he says the Shema to himself because that blessing is at the top of the call sheet for pretty much any and every service.

Evelyn lets go of his hands and she has, in fact, imprinted on him.

"I didn't prepare anything," she says, and it takes him a moment to catch up with what's happening, that Tanya must've asked if they wrote their own vows. "I'm, um, not the best when it comes to words or, like, feeling my feelings out loud. But. If there's any time to speak in clichés, I'm pretty sure it's when you're marrying your best friend. How lucky am I?"

Theo denies, denies, denies the way those words make him feel.

Tells himself she's just speaking facts.

He's her best friend.

And she's marrying him.

He attempts to match her fact for fact when it's his turn to speak. "You're my person, Evelyn. You have been since we were eight years old and you stepped foot into Miss Stella's dance studio. I just . . . I had to know you. And every day, I am so glad I do. Know you. I'd do literally anything for you, and I'm so excited to keep doing life with you."

Every word is a fact.

An objective truth.

Someone sniffles.

Fuck, why is *Gen* crying?

At least Evelyn isn't. Her smile is wide and Theo is able to finally relax, just in time for the ring exchange. Evelyn's eyes bulge, like this is the first time she considered that he, too, would need a ring. But Theo's prepared for this. He pulls two boxes from his pocket, handing a cheap basic band he purchased online for himself to Evelyn, who visibly relaxes. He hangs on to the priceless one that he would've torn the house apart in search of, a vintage Victorian-style ring with intricate engraved botanical details around the delicate gold band.

Theo repeats every line of the ring exchange, from *with this ring, I thee wed* to *until death do us part*, then slides the ring onto her finger. It was Bubbe Ruth's before it was Lori's, and now it's Evelyn's, and he knows that she isn't his forever in a romantic sense but she is in literally every other sense. He will always be doing life with her, so it just makes sense for her to be the one to hold on to it.

For that to be enough.

It's then Evelyn's turn to place a ring on his finger, and he doesn't hate the way it feels.

"I now pronounce you husband and wife," Tanya declares. "You may kiss your spouse."

Their eyes meet. Theo's expression is meant to convey that this doesn't have to be a *kiss* because speaking from experience, kissing her is so damn dangerous. But before he can even process what's happening, Evelyn presses her body flush against his, wrapping her arms around his neck and pulling his lips to hers, initiating it.

Their third kiss.

The first time, they were thirteen, just children, awkward and anxious to get their firsts out of the way. It was too wet and so weird and both vowed to never do that again, a vow they kept for an entire decade. Until it happened again. Theo had just turned twenty-three, Lori had just died, and they were both so tangled up in each other's grief that it sort of, oops, just happened.

Theo and Evelyn laugh about the first kiss.

They never mention the second one.

In the aftermath, both pretended that they were too intoxicated to remember—but of course Theo remembers. It's more than muscle memory, it's mastered choreography, the way his body reacts to hers, pulling her closer, despite his brain screaming at him to *stop*. He tells his brain to shut up, but then it reminds him that Jacob is here, and he honestly needed that reminder. Theo absolutely cannot go feral on his best friend *in front of his estranged father*.

But he doesn't stop kissing her.

Why should he? It's their third kiss. And just like the first two, it doesn't count.

It's not real.

9

E vie hauls the last of the cardboard boxes that contain her life into the empty bedroom in Theo's apartment. Her bedroom.

In their apartment.

Evie's still getting used to that—calling it *theirs*.

She places the final box on top of the stack in the corner of the room, winded from multiple treks up and down the steps that lead to and from Theo's second-story unit. Their unit. Evie wipes the sweat from her eyebrows, the back of her neck, between her thighs. She then turns on the window AC and sticks her face directly in front of it, closing her eyes and letting the cool air shock her system, allowing herself a minute to catch her breath. It's been ten days since Evie married her best friend, a week since their apartment application was approved, and five days since she gave notice at her job. Next week, she'll say goodbye to a podcast she started working on straight out of undergrad and to a team of people who, besides Saskia, she'll likely never speak to again. Once she's on the other side of this job, she'll have a week to unpack and decompress before she starts working under Sadie Silverman. Her hero.

It's all been A Lot.

Evie places her hand over her fluttering heart, not sure of the source of its overreaction—whether she can blame moving heavy boxes in the heat or the reality that this room is *hers*, that she lives here.

With Theo.

The boxes, she decides.

It has to be.

Sure, Evie's life has changed in these first ten days of marriage. But so far, true to his word, nothing about her relationship with Theo has. His vows did not burrow their way into her heart. When his tongue slid into her mouth, it did not alter her brain chemistry because she already knew that Theo is a fantastic kisser. Objectively. They spent their wedding night watching *Survivor*. He cooked vegan enchiladas. She helped clean the kitchen, then drove back to Gen's because the apartment wouldn't be theirs until Micah and Pranav moved out the following weekend.

At the time, another week and a half on Gen's couch felt like an eternity.

"Evelyn?" Theo's voice enters the room. "You okay?"

"Overheating," she says.

"Same."

Theo joins her, stands at Evie's side, and though her eyes are still closed, she feels his left arm press against her right, an indication that he, too, is hinged forward so his face is next to hers. He still smells like mint and eucalyptus and their adolescence. This is exactly how afternoons practicing new choreography in the bungalow would conclude, with the fan speed set as high as possible, with the temperature as low as it could go, with Evie and Theo almost cheek to cheek, their breath ragged, their hearts pounding in unison. This position? It brings Evie back to being sixteen, to the height of her crush, her lust, all the unruly feelings she vomited into a trash can after the most embarrassing promposal to ever promposal. To imagining their ragged breath, their tangled limbs, in an entirely different context . . .

Evie swallows.

Stands straight.

Theo is still bent over, shirtless, and seemingly on the verge of making out with the AC. Her eyes follow the planes and contours of his back—from his sculpted deltoids to the sharp jut of his shoulder blades, down the curve of his spine. He relaxes into a forward fold, drawing her eyes to the tattoo on his left bicep. *Slow down, you're doing fine.* Billy Joel. A lyric from "Vienna." The same song tattooed on her ribs. Theo then stands and pushes matted curls off his forehead, that tattooed bicep flexing. *Hot*, she thinks. *Theo is hot.* Evie finds it better to acknowledge it, the attraction, the occasional filthy thought that comes with it, than to deny it. He's her best friend. Her platonic soulmate.

But she has *eyes*.

"Do we need to make any more trips?"

Evie blinks, then shakes her head. "That's everything."

Silence—*stillness*—settles between them. Evie and Theo have been in a state of motion, propelled by to-do lists and logistics and cardboard boxes. But that's everything. There's nothing left to do. They can stand still. Be married. Whatever that even means.

Theo swallows. "Cool. Well. I'm going to shower, then start dinner."

"Can I help?"

"I am perfectly capable of taking a shower, Evelyn."

She shoves his shoulder, ignores his teasing smirk. "With *dinner.*"

Theo laughs, waving her offer away as he exits the room. "Please don't."

Fair enough.

Evie falls backward onto the queen mattress on the floor in the middle of the room, relieved that she doesn't have to pretend she wants to cook, or even *can* cook. Theo cooks. Evie eats, then cleans. *Please don't.* Another assurance that nothing has changed. She could use a shower as well, so she stands and peels herself out of the tank top and bike shorts that are stuck to her skin, unzips the duffel bag that contains her toiletries, and enters her en suite bathroom. Honestly, the bathroom situation in this unit couldn't be more ideal, something always top of mind when choosing a place to live. This apartment has two full bathrooms, one in the hallway off the kitchen, the other in the primary bedroom. Initially, she insisted that Theo be the one to move into the much more spacious room that Micah and Pranav once occupied.

She knew he wouldn't.

Evie twists the faucet and keeps the water just shy of warm, then steps into the cool porcelain tub, grateful for the privacy as her mind wanders down the hall, to Theo in the shower, to a scenario where she is *helping him shower*, lathering his chest with eucalyptus soap, because as Jules constantly reiterates in therapy, Evie's thoughts are just *thoughts*. She's allowed them.

It's not like she'd ever act on them.

After, she emerges from her room in a tank top with a built-in bra and basketball shorts, her laptop tucked under her arm. In the kitchen, Nighttime Theo, *Glasses* Theo, is sautéing vegetables on the stove. Tomatoes. Red onion. Yellow pepper. Evie takes a seat on a barstool at the island, reaching for a diced pepper and popping it in her mouth.

"Is a vegan pasta primavera okay?"

Is that okay?

"More than okay, Theodore."

"Good, because I already made the sauce."

Dinners without Theo are basic and boring and safe—tofu over rice, a spinach and tomato omelet, maybe lemon chicken from the Trader Joe's freezer section and a baked sweet potato if she's feeling fancy. After her Crohn's diagnosis, food became exhausting. After some trial and error via a low-FODMAP elimination diet, she learned what foods triggered symptoms and stuck to a handful of simple, tried-and-true recipes, not having the energy or patience to branch out, refusing to invest any more time thinking about food.

But Theo likes to cook.

Believes the time invested in preparing a meal is worthwhile.

Knows the list of foods that are incompatible with Evie's body.

She watches the ease with which he moves through the kitchen, tossing a dish towel over his shoulder as he sautés. Thirsty, she stands and opens the fridge stocked with every Evie Bloom staple—almond milk with a hint of honey, Tofutti cream cheese, and even her favorite brand of cashew-based yogurt. In remission, her diet is less restrictive than during a flare, but dairy is, sadly, always a firm *no*. This morning, she nearly teared up seeing a fucking *yogurt* because it just . . . it means so much, that he cooks for her, that he fills a fridge with things she can eat, that she's able to actually enjoy food because of him.

She pulls two pamplemousse LaCroixs from the fridge, placing one on the counter next to the stove for him, knowing he won't pop the tab until he's done cooking.

"Thanks."

Evie returns to her seat and opens her laptop, the web browser still on IKEA. Since Pep and Mo refused to accept rent while Evie occupied the bungalow, she was able to save. Not *a lot*—there were still so many medical bills and student loan payments—but enough to take a risk on a low-paying fellowship.

Enough, she thought, for furniture.

Her eyes widen.

Then she slams her laptop shut, overwhelmed by the number of choices on her screen and the *cost* of each choice.

Theo strains the pasta. "Furniture Panic?"

"Furniture Panic," Evie confirms.

Theo plates the dishes at the counter, then presents them on the island, the closest thing to a kitchen table in their apartment. Two barstools are among the few pieces of furniture that survived the Purge—also known as Micah and Pranav taking all the furniture that rightfully belonged to them. Other survivors include a set of beanbags, a struggling calathea, a fifty-inch flat-screen television mounted on the wall, and all Theo's fancy kitchen shit. Theo doesn't own a real couch—just every hyperspecific cooking gadget, from an avocado slicer to a tofu press.

"Maybe we should take some of the bungalow furniture," Theo suggests gently. "For now. It's just sitting in storage anyway."

"No." Evie shakes her head, unable to explain how wrong that feels. As much as she loved the bungalow, she doesn't want the apartment to feel like Bungalow 2.0, doesn't want reminders of the place she lost in this new space that she'll eventually lose, too.

"I get it."

With Theo, Evie rarely has to explain.

"Unrelated to Furniture Panic..." She takes a bite of cooked onion coated in the cashew-based primavera sauce, and it's so delicious she almost weeps. "Um. There's no good lead-in to this so ... I'm just going to say it. Jacob posted a photo of us online."

His jaw hangs. "He did not."

Evie opens Facebook and shows him the picture she had no idea Jacob took, too distracted by Theo's hands on the small of her back, by the stubble on Theo's cheeks scraping her palms, by the mutual face sucking. She watches him process it—the *Congrats to the happy couple!* caption, the number of comments, the *thumbs-up* in the corner of a photo way too hot for a Facebook feed.

"Fuuuuuck," Theo hisses, taking the phone and scrolling through the comments.

"My mom saw this. He hasn't posted since ..." Evie doesn't finish that sentence. "I didn't think."

Theo removes his glasses and drags his hands down his face. "*He* doesn't think. Are you okay? Have your parents ..."

"Reached out?" Evie snorts. "Nope."

David doesn't believe in social media as a concept, which just feels like an easy out to not keep in better touch with his children. But Naomi? She hearted Jacob's photo this morning. Evie felt so stupid scrolling through the list of names, checking to see if her mother's was among them. Pathetic for wondering if this news would be worthy of a phone call. More hurt than she'll ever admit that nope, it wasn't.

"I'm sorry, Evelyn."

She shrugs.

Chews.

Swallows.

And moves on.

"I don't have the heart to tell Jacob to take it down, but at least we can untag ourselves and scrub the evidence."

"Scrub the evidence," Theo repeats.

Evie nods, her expression serious. "If that photo is tied to our social media it has the power to, like, *ruin* sex for the duration of our marriage."

Theo chokes. "*Evelyn.*"

"What? I'm serious! People—generally speaking, of course—do not choose to bang married people."

"Well. You should've thought about that before you mounted me in front of my dad."

"Theodore."

He snorts, then concedes that she's probably right about scrubbing the entirely fake but positively incriminating face sucking and immediately locks himself out of his account due to too many password attempts. He had to download the app first. Theo hasn't had Facebook on his phone since undergrad. Really, he should be thanking her. She's salvaging his—*their*—sex life.

Speaking of.

"While we're on the topic, we should probably establish some rules, like, for bringing people back to the apartment. Right?" When Theo doesn't respond right away, just stares at her, bemused, she continues. "Sock on the door is cliché but effective. I'm also happy to vacate the premises when you bring a lady friend home. Just give me a heads-up."

"A lady friend?"

Evie scrunches her nose, as if that'll mask her blush that's something fierce. "I can just stay with Gen."

His eyes sparkle with amusement, like this is funny. It annoys Evie. She's trying to have a serious conversation. It's not like they don't talk about sex, as if they're incapable of it. Theo knows Evie hooks up with Saskia every time they're in LA. Evie knows Theo never sleeps with anyone more than three times because of attachment issues that he won't deny. Sex has never been off the table, in a conversational sense. Evie likes that they're so open about it. She's never felt any kind of way about Theo's sex life.

But in all fairness, she was never living with him.

"Within reason, obviously," she continues. "I mean, I can't stay with Gen *every* night. So."

"Evelyn."

"Theodore."

"How much sex do you think I'm having?"

She swallows. "Um. A lot."

Once again, Theo laughs, like this conversation is so hilarious. "You won't be at Gen's every night."

"Good. Because I'm happy to go. Just not every night."

Theo nods. "Cool. Noted."

She holds eye contact for a moment, then lets the subject circle back to furniture while they finish dinner, a back-and-forth debate that amounts to an IKEA date in their calendar. It's in hers as *HELL* because Evie's certain that if hell is real, it's the Burbank IKEA. Theo has quizzes on plant structure to finish grading. Evie insists that she'll clean, that she's happy to, so he retreats to his room and she scrubs the ceramic pasta pot until her fingers prune, reading way too much into that entire conversation because her anxiety manifests in overanalyzing every social interaction, the moments where she sounds like an absolute idiot always on max volume.

But not with Theo.

Never with Theo.

Yet currently with Theo.

She moves on to loading the dishwasher.

I can just stay with Gen. By trying not to make things weird . . . did she make things weird? She doesn't know. She *does* know that she'd rather stick her hand in a jar of mayonnaise every day for the rest of her life than hear the real, *actual* sounds that come out of Theo during sex. If she heard them, lips on skin, hands on ass, his frustrated groan—

Glass shatters on the floor.

Evie looks down helplessly at the cup that slipped out of her hand.

Fuck.

THEO'S HOUSE, SEVENTH GRADE

Evie

"You're off, Theodore."

Theo's eyebrows knit together in confusion. "I really don't think—"

Evie restarts the song, Coldplay's "Viva la Vida," her index finger smashing against the play button on his boom box with more force than necessary because she doesn't want to talk to him right now. She doesn't want to be here, with him, around him, at all. Nope! But if she didn't spend this Sunday rehearsing with Theo, like every other Sunday since fourth grade, she'd need to offer an explanation she isn't willing to give. An explanation she's not sure she even understands. Every time they make eye contact in the hallway and he looks the other way, it literally feels like her guts are being ripped out of her stomach. Theo is supposed to be her safe space. He's the only person who knows the truth about her living situation. Evie tells everyone that she's been staying with her grandparents because her mom has "a gig in New York." In reality, she has no clue where her mother is. It's been six months since Naomi took a beat. Six months since Evie has slept through the night. Imogen kicks her in the shin in her sleep because, even though they have their own rooms in the bungalow, her sister cannot—will not—sleep alone. Unconscious Imogen wraps her limbs around Evie, as if she's terrified that if she doesn't hold on tight, her sister will leave her, too. How can a person, a *mom*, claim to love them . . . then leave them so easily? Evie has a perma-bruise on her left shin. That is love. *Staying* is love.

She thought Naomi loved her.

She thought *Theo* loved her.

Now, in his backyard, when it's just them, she can almost believe it. When they're alone, Theo is himself. At school? He's someone small, someone who follows Connor and Matt and the Four Square Jerks around like they walk on water.

It's so frustrating.

Theo abandoning her again and again and again.

He executes the combination of taps with precision.

Still, Evie cuts the music. "Again."

Theo exhales, pushing his curls off his forehead. "Okay. I *know* I got it that time—"

She presses play, then joins him on the bamboo tap mat covering a section of the deck. Her back to him, Evie channels her annoyance, hurt, *rage* into the choreography, articulating every step and launching into a double pirouette with way too much momentum, crashing into Theo.

They both go down.

She lands on top of him, her heart smashing into his.

He looks up at her. "Are we okay?"

Her smile is sour. "Great."

She rolls away from him, pulling her knees into her chest and wrapping her arms around them to recalibrate, to focus on her breathing like Grandpa Mo taught her after her first panic attack, to *not cry*. It's their first year of middle school, the first year they've attended the same school. Evie was so excited. It's so stupid. It's not like she even needs Theo. Evie has friends. Caro, Gracie, and Iris at dance. Lola, Jamie, and the Allisons at school. But Theo is her best friend. Or so she thought. Maybe she's wrong. Maybe they've always just been *dance* friends.

Ugh.

It's all so embarrassing.

"I think we're off, Evelyn."

"*Evie*," she snaps, digging her nails into her kneecaps.

He frowns.

Then scoots a few inches closer. "What's wrong?"

Seriously?

"You're kind of a butt, Theodore."

"Me? I know the combination. You keep making me start over for *no reason*."

Evie's nostrils flare, her stomach twisting and cramping. She winces, tears prickling her lash line that have nothing to do with Theo Cohen being a massive butt and everything to do with her period. Maybe. Probably. She doesn't keep track, even though her grandmother bought her a small appointment calendar and a pad of stickers for that very purpose. She tried for a few months but doesn't see the point.

It's always a surprise.

Everything that hurts is always a surprise.

Period cramps.

Naomi.

Theo.

"*Ev*." Theo's eyes widen with concern, cutting her name at the first safe syllable. "Talk to me."

"You're my best friend," she admits.

"You're mine."

"I'm *not*. At school . . . you act like I don't exist."

Theo's cheeks redden. "I just—Connor and Matt *suck*, okay?"

"If Connor and Matt aren't evolved enough to know that people of different genders can be friends, how is that our problem?"

"I don't want them to, like, harass you."

"How noble of you, Theodore."

"I'm serious! Unless you, like, want everyone to think we're dating, we can't be school friends."

Evie laughs. "So what if people think we're dating?"

"We're not."

"Right. But why do you care if they *think* that? Why do you care so much about what the Four Square Jerks think at all?"

"The Four Square Jerks?"

"Matt and Connor's crew."

"Am I a Four Square Jerk?"

"Lately!" Evie stands, so over this conversation. "Can we just run the routine again from the first chorus so I can go home?"

She flinches.

It's the third time she's referred to the bungalow as *home*.

She presses play.

"I'm sorry," Theo says, standing and moving toward her, then pausing the music. "I don't want to be a Four Square Jerk. It's just . . . Connor and Matt made sixth grade suck so bad and they *leave me alone now*. School is easier, pretending to be friends with them."

Evie softens.

She knows Theo has been bullied because he's a boy who loves to dance.

"You're my best friend," she repeats. "But I want to be school friends, too."

Theo's quiet as she removes her tap shoes and packs up, so ready to call her grandmother and ask to be picked up early. So hoping Theo will ask her to stay. She wants him to choose her over the Four Square Jerks. But she doesn't want him to be bullied by the Four Square Jerks because his best friend is a girl.

Also?

It bothers her, Theo seeming weirded out by the idea of them dating. Why is this bothering her? Does she want to be more than Theo's best friend? She doesn't think she likes Theo like that. But how does she know? He's her favorite person. Maybe that means they're supposed to be more than friends? She isn't sure. It's all so confusing. She loves Theo. But does she want to kiss him? She's thought about it. Has he thought about kissing *her*?

Now she can't stop thinking about it.

One step away from her dramatic exit, she pivots. "Maybe I want to be more than friends."

"What?"

Evie's cheeks are on fire, but she doubles down. "I don't know. If people at school are going to assume either way . . . we might as well figure it out ourselves? I mean. Think about it. Like. If we were to, say, I don't know, kiss, we'll know for sure that we're supposed to be just friends instead of, like, wondering—"

"You *wonder*?"

Evie shrugs. "Don't act like you *don't*. It's not a big deal."

She isn't sure how their fight devolved from calling Theo a Four Square Jerk to an admission that she's thought about kissing him . . . but whatever! Evie's here now. Her eyes meet his. They're the same height. His cheeks are on fire. Evie *knew* it. Theo has wondered, too.

"I've never kissed anyone before."

"Me either," Evie admits. "Can I?"

Theo nods, so she leans in and presses her mouth to his, against lips that are somehow, impossibly, both dry and wet. Neither move. Or breathe. She's kissing Theo. This is kissing? Huh. *It's weird*, she decides. Kissing is weird. Kissing Theo? Super weird.

But maybe . . . not bad weird?

She pulls away.

Theo's expression is undecipherable. "That was—"

"Weird."

"Weird," Theo repeats, cheeks still pink.

She can't decipher his expression, if this kiss was good weird or bad weird or just *weird* weird. Embarrassment slams against Evie's diaphragm. She's so full of it. Of course she needs Theo. As a friend. Naomi left and he knows why and the last thing she wants is for there to be any variety of weird between the two of them.

"Want to run it again?" she asks, deflecting.

"Sure."

Relieved, Evie reties her tap shoes, then together they run through the tap routine once more, not missing a single step, completely in sync. Afterward, she turns toward him because she can't let it go without asking, without confirming.

"Just friends?"

Theo nods. "Definitely just friends."

Evie throws her arms around him and buries her face into the crook of his neck, so ready to bury the weirdness of that kiss and so relieved to have her best friend back.

10

It's Halloween and Theo is teaching the state capitals dressed as Woody from *Toy Story* when it happens.

He points to Wyoming.

Milo, who is Super Mario today, raises a white-gloved hand.

Milo, who ran up to Theo and Evelyn at IKEA last night twenty minutes into them debating the aesthetic merits of various kitchen tables. Milo, whose mom, Natalia, used to babysit Theo. Whose grandmother was Lori's best friend. Who witnessed Natalia congratulate them, his face scrunched in initial confusion. Milo, who is a spoiler of *Survivor*. A terrible gossip.

Milo, who's currently the only volunteer.

Theo calls on him.

He has no choice.

Milo adjusts the mustache stuck above his lip, then asks, "Why didn't you tell us that you got married, Mr. Theodore?"

Cue his classroom exploding in commotion.

Doctor Barbie (Annabelle) gasps. "*What?*"

"Someone seriously married *you?*" Miles Morales (Tyler) shouts.

"*OMG, OMG, OMG,*" Ariel (Kaia) squeals.

He can't say he didn't see it coming, but the separation of his professional and personal life was nice while it lasted.

"Unfortunately, 'why didn't you tell us that you got married, Mr. Theodore' is *not* the capital of Wyoming."

Milo rolls his eyes. "Cheyenne."

Theo nods and Milo rises from his chair to choose a sticker. Fourth graders are incredibly motivated by stickers. Shit, Theo is still motivated by stickers. It's not a check that signifies the completion of a task on his to-do list, it's a sticker. Milo chooses Stitch frothing at the mouth. A respectable choice.

"Why aren't you wearing a ring?" Wednesday Addams (Sierra) asks.

"*Because,*" Milo begins, now standing before the class. "He didn't want us to know. Obviously."

Annabelle scrunches her nose. "That's really weird, Mr. Theodore."

This whole Mr. Theodore era? It's one thousand percent Evelyn's fault, for calling him that at IKEA. *Theodore! I had no clue that your Milo . . . is Natalia's Milo!* As soon as Milo giggled, Theo knew. One casual Friday, he wore red high-top Converse sneakers. Milo had the class calling him *Mr. Clown* for an entire week. Kids are brutal. But Mr. Clown learned a valuable lesson—their ruthlessness was heightened by a reaction and validated by the laughter of their peers. So. He doesn't love being called Mr. Theodore, but he acts unbothered. Refers to *himself* as Mr. Theodore. Because if he's in on the joke? It's no longer funny.

"Deception!" Jeremiah, the Luigi to Milo's Mario, yells.

Kaia nods. "I am *aghast*."

"What's her name?" Sierra asks.

"*Their* name," Annabelle corrects. "Don't assume, Sierra."

Theo has a choice to make. He can raise a stern eyebrow and tell his kids if they don't get through all fifty states now, he'll have no choice but to make up the lesson during *Survivor* Friday. Or he can leverage their interest that borders on entitlement to information about his personal life to get through the lesson. *Survivor* Friday is his favorite part of the week. He doesn't want to reteach the capitals when they could be doing the color block puzzle.

Is it even a choice?

Theo blasts "1985" by Bowling for Soup.

Sierra covers her ears. "Mr. Cohen!"

"What did we do to deserve *this*?" Kaia whines.

Jeremiah groans. "I just got this song *un*-stuck."

"Here's my offer," Theo says, after cutting the music. "If we can name all fifty capitals before lunch, I'll spill the details that, for whatever reason, you want to know."

Annabelle scoffs. "*Whatever reason*?"

"This is *major*, Mr. Theodore!" Kaia says.

"So do we have a deal?" Theo asks.

Silence.

He restarts the music.

"Fine!"

"Deal!"

"*Whatever*."

Theo laughs. "Great. Now, who can tell me the capital of South Dakota?"

They get through the entire country with ten minutes to spare. Ten minutes is almost too much time to allot to this.

It never ceases to amuse him, what motivates his students. A deal is a deal, so Theo calls on raised hands and answers any reasonable question about his so-called marriage.

Her name.

Evie.

How they met.

At Miss Stella's dance school.

Why he didn't tell them.

It didn't exactly seem relevant to the curriculum.

If she watches *Survivor*, too.

Of course.

By lunchtime, Theo is exhausted. He Clorox wipes his desk, then collapses into his chair, removes his cowboy hat, and unwraps his avocado sandwich, more than ready for twenty blissful minutes of solitude. Until today, school has been the place where he still feels the most himself. At home, he tries to be himself. Except now he can't fall asleep without watching an episode of *Love Island* with Evelyn. He wakes up to her voice either humming or singing "Here Comes the Sun" to her plants. It raises his resting heart rate, a data point that he records daily. At first, the spike concerned him. He almost made an appointment with his cardiologist. Instead, he told Brian at his next therapy session, who asked if he had any other symptoms—chest pain, shortness of breath, heartburn. *No.*

It's just the song.

Evelyn singing.

So he supposes it's still concerning, that spike.

Theo pinches the bridge of his nose, inserts earbuds, and plays "1985" to clear his head. He doesn't even get through the entire song before there's a knock on his door, then Ms. Connors's head poking in. "Theo? Do you have a moment?"

He removes his earbuds, sitting up a little straighter. "Course."

"I heard that congratulations are in order?"

Milo works fast.

Theo shrugs.

"So nonchalant." Ms. Connors laughs, entering his classroom, and it takes his eyes a moment to adjust to the colorful chaos of her flowy rainbow pants and T-shirt that says HOCUS FOCUS. She takes a seat at the student desk closest to his and crosses her ankles. "Well, congratulations! Everyone is just thrilled for you. Though . . . I can't say we're not the tiniest bit surprised. I mean. We didn't even know you had a girlfriend."

He laughs. "It's not like anyone ever asked."

It comes off defensive.

Ms. Connors's eyebrows crinkle.

Then soften.

"You're right. I'm sorry."

"Oh."

It catches him off guard, the apology.

He has no idea how much he appreciates one until it happens. Because five years into his career at Foothill Elementary, Theo still isn't seen as a colleague. He's Mrs. Cohen's son. The kid who was *not* a pleasure to have a class. He's not an idiot. Theo knows he's a nepo baby. Knows that Lori outed his big dream to reform education policy out of pride, but also knows that's the reason why everyone keeps him at arm's length. They think he has one foot out the door. They don't see the effort Theo makes to empower his students and meet them where they are. They don't browse his highly curated (and self-funded) library. Or believe that Theo is meant to be in the classroom.

But Theo loves his job.

He's damn good at it, too.

"We care about you, Theo. We're a family, here at Foothill."

Theo nods, wondering if Ms. Connors is speaking on behalf of the entire faculty or using the royal *we*. Who's to say? It doesn't matter. If they are, in fact, a family, then he's the baby. Not taken seriously. A nuisance. Naïve. *Fuck that.* Theo doesn't need a work family. He needs field trip proposals to be approved, smaller class sizes, and an annual supplies budget.

Of course, he's not going to actually say that.

"Thanks, Ms. Connors."

"Veronica."

"Veronica."

"I mean it. I truly am sorry if you've felt isolated or excluded in any way. The first few years as an educator are tough under any circumstances. Yours . . . I just need you to know that you're doing great, okay? Parents are happy. The kids love you. Your mom would be so proud."

Theo's eyes sting. "I appreciate that."

He swallows the emotion before any tears fall, Jacob's voice a loop in his head.

Weak.

Weak.

Weak.

"Enjoy the rest of your lunch, Theo." Ms. Connors stands and heads toward the door, but pauses and pivots to face him before she exits. "Out of curiosity . . . do you play pickleball?"

Theo doesn't sport.

He does, however, read the monthly staff newsletter.

"I dabble," he lies.

"We're down a team for next weekend's tournament," Ms. Connors says, referring to the faculty pickleball league she runs. "Louisa is out. Sprained ankle. Such a shame. We can't run a tournament with eleven teams."

"That's too bad."

"It is."

Theo doesn't know what else to say, so he takes a bite of his sandwich . . .

"Does your wife also dabble?"

. . . and promptly chokes on it, coughing up a piece of crust that went down his windpipe. *Wife*. Theo's smartwatch alerts him of his elevated heart rate. Ms. Connors waits for the coughing fit to end. Waits for an answer. Theo hopes she perceives his nod as enthusiastic amid his active choking. Evelyn will probably be pissed. She dabbles in pickleball as much as Theo does.

But.

An invitation to Ms. Connors's pickleball tournament? It *matters*. Juniper got one last year . . . and now her kids are going to the zoo.

"She does," he confirms once the coughing fit subsides.

"Remind me of her name?"

He doesn't recall telling Ms. Connors her name. "Evie."

"Would you and Evie have any interest in being our twelfth team?"

"I'd have to check with her, of course—"

"Excellent! You're a lifesaver."

"I'm—"

"Also, I've been thinking about your class's field trip. Maybe you're right about Kidspace. Let's chat next week?"

Then Ms. Connors is gone, heels *click, click, clicking* down the hallway before Theo has a chance to respond. Minutes later, she sends over the roster that's made up of eleven staff members and their spouses. Without quite meaning to, Theo committed himself and Evelyn to the Foothill Elementary Faculty Pickleball Tournament. He needs to buy ... rackets? Paddles? Also, it's not lost on him that every member of the pickleball league is married. It can't be a coincidence that Ms. Connors only invited Theo because he's married now, too. But as a cis white man, he isn't exactly the demographic to scream discrimination. So he's participating in a pickleball tournament in exchange for ... a field trip? Maybe?

Is this extortion?

It's not ... *not* extortion.

Fuck.

Theo needs to learn how to play pickleball.

He comes home to a semiassembled bookcase.

"Shit. You're *home?*"

Theo snorts. "Hello to you, too."

Evelyn is sitting, legs crisscrossed, in the middle of the living room floor, surrounded by screws and pegs and shelves, the assembly instructions for a Billy bookcase in her hands. She's still in her pajamas, pink satin shorts paired with an old NYU sweatshirt. His sweatshirt. Theo swallows, then steps over a particleboard shelf and sets his thermos on the counter, narrowly avoiding being impaled by a screw in the process.

"How is it already four?" Evelyn groans, eyes lifting from the instructions to meet his. Still dressed as a toy cowboy, he braces for teasing that doesn't come. "I meant to finish this hours ago ... then got derailed."

"What happened?"

"My old insurance was billed for my last infusion, resulting in a *cute* bill."

She gestures to the statement on the coffee table and Theo's eyes bulge at its total. "*Jesus.*"

"I called the infusion center before the appointment, they scanned my new insurance card at the appointment, yet still I spent three hours on the phone with the billing department this afternoon to fix someone else's mistake. It's fine. The claim is being resubmitted. But dealing with this shit? It's so exhausting."

Theo's nostrils flare.

He remembers the hours Lori spent on the phone, the back-and-forth between billing departments and insurance, the delay of her treatment plan because of a denial. Because you can't just be sick in this country. You must also argue, appeal, *beg* for insurance to approve and cover lifesaving screenings and treatments. Lori needed a colonoscopy years before her doctor ordered one. *You're too young for cancer! It's just IBS. Have you tried eliminating dairy? Gluten? Every major food group?* By the time her symptoms progressed to the point where the scope became medically necessary . . . they learned that she was, in fact, not too young for cancer. And it had spread to her lymph nodes.

It's more than exhausting.

It's infuriating.

"It's bullshit," he says.

"I know. I was supposed to build a bookcase today."

"We still can."

Theo cannot fix the entire healthcare system, but he can build a bookcase. He removes his cow-print vest and yellow button-up, then sits on the floor next to Evelyn and starts inserting pegs into the shelves, not needing the instruction manual. In undergrad, he had a whole TaskRabbit moment. Manhattan is expensive.

Basically, Theo can build a Billy bookcase in his sleep.

Evelyn doesn't resist the help, just passes him a screwdriver, her fingers brushing against his. Then she pushes up the sleeves of his sweatshirt, exposing the sound wave tattoo across her right forearm. It's the intro of Peppy Bloom's radio show. Her fourth tattoo. After Pep went on-air for the last time, Theo drove Evelyn to a tattoo shop in Santa Monica because Iris Cameron, once a student of Miss Stella's, is the only nonmedical professional that Evelyn trusts to stab her repeatedly with a needle. Theo once called Evelyn's tattoos etchings for the people she loves. She corrected him. *Not love, Theodore. Trust.* His eyes linger on the sound wave. He glitches. Fuck. This is why he tries to avoid them. The music notes on her rib cage. The lavender sprig on her left triceps for Gen. The bee on her ankle for Mo. This sound wave.

It's safer.

To avert his eyes.

To not obsess over her tattoos.

To not feel some kind of way that there isn't one for him.

"How was school?" she asks.

His eyes shift away from the ink on her skin. "The kids call me *Mr. Theodore* now."

"Shut up."

"I'm serious."

She laughs. "I'm sorry, but that's kind of incredible."

"Evelyn."

"What? It could be worse, Mr. Clown."

She bumps her shoulder against his. *I love you.* It's in these moments, when Evelyn is teasing him—*literally calling him a clown*—that the three words he's become an expert at downplaying surface as a thought bubble in his brain. It used to scare the shit out of him, but now he accepts it. He loves her.

Of course he does. Why shouldn't he think that her silliness is adorable, want to burn down and rebuild healthcare in America for her, obsess over her tattoos?

Theo can love his best friend.

He's not *in* love with her.

"Ms. Connors knows."

Evelyn nods. "Okay."

"I should probably start wearing the ring to school."

Her eyebrow twitches. "Okay."

"I . . . also signed us up for a couples pickleball tournament."

"What?"

He recounts the entire interaction as he nails the back of the bookcase to the assembled frame—explains that he didn't mean to, it sort of just happened, really he was extorted. Evelyn relocates to one of the beanbag chairs, her expression shifting from initial annoyance to amusement listening to him overexplain the simple truth that his boss asked him to do something that's absolutely not in his job description and he couldn't say no.

"Only if you're up for it. Obviously."

"Yeah. I'll do it . . . if you come to breakfast on Sunday."

His pulse spikes. "Evelyn."

Every Sunday, she's gone before he even wakes. On those quiet mornings, Theo laces up his sneakers, blasts the next *Survivor* podcast in his queue, and runs. After Lori's diagnosis, Theo would run until it hurt, until he was bent over and retching because physical pain could be *felt*. Now he has Brian. Still, he runs every Sunday, a ten-mile loop that takes him right past his childhood home during Evelyn's breakfasts with Jacob. He's thought about stopping. Knocking. He never does. Instead, he picks up speed and doesn't slow down until he's home.

"That's my offer."

Her eye contact?

It's challenging.

He does a cost-benefit analysis, then sighs. "Okay."

A pickleball partnership solidified, they stand and flip their finished bookcase upright, positioning it against an empty wall in the living room, then break for dinner. Afterward, she populates the shelves with their books, semialive plants, and framed photographs. So many photos. Tiny Evelyn and Imogen in matching tutus. Theo's bar mitzvah. Evelyn, ten or eleven, wearing giant headphones, behind a sound mixer at Pep's recording booth. Theo, eight, and Lori on the spinning teacups at Disneyland. Evelyn and Theo, fourteen, cheesing after the tap duet that earned them first place at a regional competition. Them, seventeen, unironically practicing the *Dirty Dancing* lift. Evelyn, twenty-four, cheeks flushed and lips turned down in a pout post-hike. Theo, twenty-six, cheeks flushed and lips turned up at a karaoke bar in Koreatown.

"What?" Evelyn's looking at him, nose scrunched, as if trying to decipher his reaction. "Is it too much?"

He shakes his head, any lingering feelings about their deal dissolving in real time. "No! These are awesome."

"I thought they'd make the space more . . . I don't know. Homey?"

Theo takes in these candid but curated moments of their history, ignoring any feelings about the noticeable gap in their timeline as he looks over at her in his sweatshirt, then asks, "Are there more?"

Evelyn's smile is small. She disappears to her room, returning a moment later with a stack of prints. They spend the rest of the evening in the beanbag chairs, their shoulders pressed together, choosing the most ridiculous photos from their life to display in their apartment. Their home. Evelyn holding up a chocolate chip cookie the size of her face. Theo's freaked-out reaction to an eagle landing on his head at the San Diego Zoo. Them, at Miss Stella's, seeing who can hold a headstand the longest.

Theo remembers hating it, Evelyn always sticking a camera in his face.

Now?

He thinks it's pretty awesome that these exist.

Also. Does she really not know that he used to be so in love with her? Does she not see how many times the camera caught him looking at her with goddamn hearts in his eyes? It's just . . . so obvious to him. A part of him wants to acknowledge it. Laugh at it. But he stays quiet as she continues to sift through the photos, Theo looking increasingly lovesick in each one.

When Evelyn gets to the end of the stack, she stands. "Question."

"Answer."

Theo braces himself.

She sees it, too.

That stupid look on your face.

In the photos.

"Pickleball. Is it just, like . . . tennis with paddles?"

Theo laughs, ignoring a feeling that can only be described as relief, then shrugs helplessly. "I have no clue."

11

I've got a large vanilla latte with oat milk for *EE*-vie."

Her name is written on the cup in black Sharpie.

EEVVIE.

It's never not surprising, a barista's ability to mess up a four-letter name. Eve. Evvie. Evey. Eevie. And that's just *this week*. Evie grabs a handful of sugar packets on her way out the door. Sadie Silverman—Evie's mentor—doesn't do liquid sweetener. She prefers the texture of sugar granules in her coffee. Evie doesn't (read: shouldn't) drink coffee, so yesterday, she asked Theo to make his the Sadie Silverman way. If marrying her wasn't testament enough that he would do anything for her . . . nearly choking to death on his latte à la Sadie definitely confirmed this.

Her coffee order is among the many reasons why one should never meet one's heroes.

Back in Phoebe, Evie places Sadie's latte in a cup holder and checks the time. She has ten minutes to drive the two miles from Romancing the Bean to the Burbank soundstage where Sadie Silverman is currently contracted to record Foley for the live-action remake of Disney's *Chicken Little*. Evie wants to know . . . who asked for that. In theory, she should be early. In the reality that's LA traffic, she'll be at least five minutes late. Sadie Silverman won't care. Evie will hand Sadie Silverman her latte, and the moment the cup with her butchered name on it leaves her hand, she will become invisible. Seriously. Latte à la Sadie tethers Evie to her human form. It's her only purpose as a fellow—besides *observe*—and maybe her expectations were too high.

Of Next in Foley.

Of Sadie Silverman.

On Monday, the first two words Sadie Silverman said to her were *You are?*

Evie Bloom, she'd said, then added as soon as it was clear that her name meant nothing to Sadie Silverman. *Your fellow.*

Sadie Silverman blinked. *Right, of course!*

Then she uttered her basic yet unhinged coffee order, along with a soy matcha for Charlie—her mixer in the sound booth with a salt-and-pepper beard and heterochromia—and sent Evie to Romancing the Bean, the only coffee shop within a five-mile radius Sadie Silverman trusts. By Wednesday, she learned that latte à la Sadie is a daily ask. So today, Thursday, she opts to preempt the ask by showing up to the studio with it already in hand. Maybe Sadie Silverman will see this as taking initiative.

Maybe *this* coffee will be a breakthrough in their non-relationship.

Driving down Magnolia, the newest Olivia Rodrigo single blasting through Phoebe's speakers, Evie sees zero flaws in this logic until a red Tesla makes an unprotected left out of a residential street, cutting her off as if it is entitled to.

She slams the breaks.

Screams, "Fucking fuck!"

Evie doesn't hit the Tesla.

But half of latte à la Sadie is in her lap.

Do not cry.

Do.

Not.

Cry.

But she can't stop the stressed, pissed-off tears from falling down her cheeks for the remainder of her drive. She pulls up to the studio gate and flashes her badge, then parks and wipes off smudged mascara. Her stomach cramps and *fuck* the gut-brain connection. Evie would sever it herself if she could. Phone in hand, she calls Theo to curse out the Tesla. He doesn't answer. Of course he doesn't. It's 9:00 a.m. on a school day.

It's fine.

She doesn't need it.

Theo's comfort.

Evie runs to the bathroom, where she remains until her stomach settles and her eyes depuff. Then she reapplies mascara before heading into the studio, half-empty cup in hand.

"I'm so sorry," she says, in lieu of a greeting as she approaches Sadie Silverman, who is securing block heels that she's not even five feet in when standing. She's dressed in billowy black pants and a white T-shirt, her gray-at-the-roots hair pulled back in a messy bun. "A Tesla cut me off."

Without a word, Sadie Silverman takes the cup from her, pours two sugar packets into it, then downs *half a large latte* like it's a tequila shot.

It's equal parts terrifying and impressive.

"*Teslas,*" Sadie Silverman mutters, crushing the empty cup in her hands. "I needed this, thank you. It's been a day."

"Is there anything I can do?"

She shakes her head. "Charlie can show you how the mixer works."

"I—"

—*know how a mixer works.*

She cuts herself off, because Sadie Silverman has moved on, sifting through a box of carpet swatches. Evie's shoulders sag in defeat as she exits the studio and enters the mixing room. Charlie Crosby greets her with a sympathetic nod, sipping on his soy matcha. "Chicken feet."

Evie blinks. "What?"

"She's never recorded Foley for an anthropomorphic chicken before and the studio keeps asking for revisions on the steps. First pass, too chicken. Second pass, too human. What the fuck does an anthropomorphic chicken even sound like?" Charlie gives her a look. "Execs says they'll know when they hear it."

"Seems reasonable," Evie deadpans. "Today you're supposed to teach me how to operate that"—she points to the mixer, the same mixer she recorded *After Ever After* on— "sound thingy."

Charlie snorts. "Well, Evie. This here *sound thingy* is called a *mixer.*"

They laugh. Evie and Charlie appreciate each other's sense of humor. Charlie appreciates that Evie knows how to operate a mixer and has an ear for the nuances of sound. Evie appreciates that Charlie not only pronounces her name correctly, but also read her résumé and asked genuine questions about her hopes and dreams. In just four days, she's developed a rapport with Sadie Silverman's mixer that she should be developing with Sadie Silverman herself. At lunch on Tuesday, she learned his story. Charlie has been in the business for thirty years, starting as a boom mic operator before transitioning to postproduction. He met Sadie Silverman at a queer bar in West Hollywood before Evie was born, and the two, quote (from Charlie!), "bisexual babies" grew into one of the most sought-after Foley duos in the industry.

"Sadie is incredible," Charlie says, his eyes sparkling with admiration. "Just guarded. Give her time. Or expedite it by bringing her some chicken feet."

After a morning in the mixing room with Charlie, observing Sadie Silverman record Anna Kendrick's footsteps for an upcoming thriller, she spends the afternoon running around Burbank in search of chicken feet. Charlie doesn't provide any direction. It's super helpful. After rummaging through her own personal prop bag she keeps in her trunk, Evie ends up back on Magnolia, browsing the thrift stores that line both sides of the street for any shoes or tchotchkes that could mimic the sound of chicken steps.

"Any luck?" Charlie asks upon her return to the studio with an afternoon latte à la Sadie, an extra-large with extra sugar packets to make up for that morning.

"Nope."

"Next time, kid."

Charlie Crosby is the only man of a certain age who can pull off calling Evie *kid* in a way that is neither condescending nor creepy. It's weirdly comforting. Evie is certain that her father issues definitely do not play into this dynamic she's developed with Charlie—who's a single dad, who has photos of his two teenage daughters on his desk, who makes sure to leave the studio by 5:00 p.m. and not one minute later to get home to them. As Evie imagines a childhood with a dad like Charlie, Sadie Silverman enters the mixing room after an entire day of stepping in sync (*so* much of the job is footsteps!). "How'd she do?"

"A natural," Charlie says.

Sadie Silverman nods.

Pivots.

Then exits.

"Give her time," Charlie repeats.

Evie tosses her backpack over her shoulder and nods. "See you tomorrow, Charlie."

"And how is that husband of yours?"

Evie's laughter is buoyant, light, *breezy*. Grandma Pep is relentless.

Also, terrible at FaceTime.

Currently, she's speaking to her grandmother's chin. "Theo is good. We miss you."

"We miss you, too."

"EVELYN," Grandpa Mo bellows, off-screen, in the driver's seat of the RV. "I HAD NOTHING TO DO WITH THE PACKAGE."

"*Mo.*" The phone hovers high enough that Pep is now a chin and a lower lip. "Did it arrive, Sweets? The package? The tracking code glitched. As you're well aware, technology hates me."

Evie flips her camera to show the unopened package on her nightstand. "I have the package."

"Wait for Theo to open it."

"Grandma."

"It's a wedding gift."

"*Grandma.*"

Evie called Pep and Mo two days after she married Theo,

the moment they indicated they were back on the grid after their Tahoe escapades. She was transparent with her grand-parents about the situation. Evie needed health insurance to take the fellowship. Theo has great health insurance. That's it.

Sounds practical, Mo said.

Pep chuckled. *Okay, Sweets.*

She was more than prepared for Pep's reaction.

Her grandmother believes that Evie and Theo are "end-game," a term that Evie taught her while binge-watching *Gilmore Girls* together for the first time. A massive mistake. What started as an offhand comment, one that she effectively muted during her Hanna and his Caro years, became a constant re-frain once she was single, as they were both single and, quote, "barreling toward thirty" (they're twenty-seven!).

So.

Peppy Bloom is goddamned delighted by this development.

Her laughter is one of Evie's favorite sounds. "You're welcome. Anyhoo, talk sound to me before I lose you!" Her grandpar-ents are on the road again, approaching the California-Oregon border. Service on rural roads is super spotty. "How's your first—"

The bottom half of Pep's face is frozen on Evie's screen.

She's gone.

Evie sighs and peels off her clothes before face-planting onto her bed and *ugh*ing into her pillow. As much as she wanted to vent to her grandmother, a not-so-small part of her is relieved she doesn't have to admit that so far, being Sadie Silverman's fellow is not a dream. How naïve was she to think that this fellowship would be different from any of her past experiences? *Give her time.* Evie's time is valuable, too. And she's exhausted. Her bones are tired and this fatigue infuriates her and terrifies her. If she's *this* exhausted without stepping foot in the studio . . . can she even do this? Can her body handle it? Or is this just going to end in another shattering heartbreak?

She points and flexes her toes.

Feels the dull ache that radiates from her right ankle.

A joint movable due to metal.

Evie's processed this injury, the screws connecting bones together, the loss of dance in her life. But the thing about grief—whether it's over a person, a place, a passion—is that it never ends. Not really. She acknowledges it in the SHIT TO UNPACK WITH JULES note in her phone, then reaches for the package on her night table for a distraction, ignoring Pep's request.

Wait for Theo.

She opens the box.

It . . . is filled with sex toys.

Handcuffs.

Nipple clamps.

Rope.

Lube.

Dildos.

An entire—according to the packaging—*all kink-clusive* toy box with a note that simply says *Love, Grandma* . . . and it's not until she reads that signature that she loses it. Laughs so hard tears stream down her face at the most Peppy Bloom gift. She took Evie to Romantix on her eighteenth birthday and helped her pick out her first vibrator, taught both her granddaughters that their pleasure mattered, wears a T-shirt that says *Pro O*.

Evie snaps a photo of the box and sends it to Gen.

Imogen Bloom
fucking GRANDMA
5:57 P.M.

!!!
5:57 P.M.

i'm 💀
5:57 P.M.

                 she really said?? have you considered BONDAGE?
                                        5:58 P.M.

i love her so much
5:58 P.M.

. . . also have you?
5:58 P.M.

                                   with THEO?
                                        5:59 P.M.

um
6:00 P.M.

no
6:00 P.M.

but let's unpack why your brain went there
6:00 P.M.

"So for dinner—"

Evie is so fixated on her phone, on her back-and-forth with

Gen, that she doesn't even register Theo's voice, its proximity to her, or that she's not wearing pants.

"—I'm thinking . . . *fuck, Evelyn.*"

Evie drops her phone and jumps to her feet, unsure if she's more mortified by the fact that her best friend is speaking directly to her extremely exposed ass or that the fabric that is (barely) covering said ass has tiny corgis printed on it. She reaches for the nearest pair of sweatpants tossed haphazardly on her bedroom floor. "Sorry!"

"I . . . the door was open."

"I know. My bad. Today sucked, Theodore. I failed to figure out what Chicken Little's footsteps sound like and Pep sent us a kink box and it is so *hot* in here—" Evie cuts off her babbling, tying the drawstring on her cotton joggers. "I'm sorry that pants were not a priority."

Theo's eyebrows rise. "A what box?"

Evie waves at the package.

Pulls out a silk mask, a whip . . . and a butt plug.

"*Fuck,*" Theo hisses, his eyebrows knitting together as she drops the butt plug in his palm. "How am I ever going to make eye contact with Pep again?"

She twirls a strand of anal beads around her index finger. "She's relentless. But also an icon?"

"Does she really think we would . . . use this stuff?"

We.

We.

We.

"Are you kink-shaming my grandmother, Theodore?"

"Evelyn."

"*Oh.* You're a butt plug virgin."

"*Evelyn.*"

"What about this?"

Evie holds a stroker up to one eye like it's a telescope and she's having way too much fun with this. Flustering Theo. She's been open to a whole spectrum of sexual experiences. Cannot deny that light bondage of the handcuff variety is such a turn-on. Will absolutely deny that the revelation that she's more experienced with toys is not *not* a turn-on. Theo is probably a traditionalist when it comes to fucking. Hands. Mouth. Tongue.

She drops the toy back into the box.

Swallows hard.

Now Theo's the one who looks amused. "Are you finished?"

Nope.

Evie nods and returns everything to the box, closing it up, and after a debate about the storage location ("They're your sex toys, too, Theodore!"), she folds and stores the box on the top shelf of her closet. She stands on her tiptoes, pushing the box as far out of reach as she can, pushing the *desire* that it stirred within her as far away as possible.

Until Theo says, so casual. "So. Corgis?"

Her skin is on fire. Cheeks, neck, chest. "What? They're adorable."

Theo nods slowly. Evie's eyes refuse to meet his, instead focusing on the jut of his chin, the faintest hint of stubble along his jaw, what it would feel like to brush her fingers across—

She blinks.

When her eyes open they're locked with his dilated pupils behind round tortoiseshell frames, pulled up by a magnetic force she can't resist.

Theo says, "They are."

Fuck. She feels those two words right between her legs. Tomorrow, Evie will blame exhaustion for the way her brain short-circuits. Not for the undeniable *attraction* she feels in this moment, but for allowing the thought bubble to even enter her brain that maybe Theo is attracted to her, too. It's *Theo.* Why is she so flustered?

You're horny.

Duh.

It's not Theo.

It's that Evie hasn't had sex since ... well, since before she signed a marriage license.

"Anyway! Dinner. Veggie burgers cool?"

Evie nods. "Great."

"Cool."

It's the *I need to get laid, stat* epiphany that allows Evie to laugh it off, to revert back to herself. "Didn't know you were a corgi guy, Theodore."

"Me either," Theo says simply, then shuts the door on his way out.

Evie locks the door behind him and blasts music so loud she feels the bass reverberating in her bones, then reaches for the vibrator inside the velvet bag in her night table drawer and denies, denies, denies the attraction in the privacy of her own bedroom, where she is absolutely not imagining her best friend, her *husband's*, hands, mouth, tongue between her legs.

12

Evelyn's legs in a tennis skirt are a problem.

She's knelt on the pickleball court, lathering SPF onto her exposed legs. It's 8:00 a.m., an hour before the tournament is set to begin, because she wants to practice on a real court before their first match. In the nine days since accepting Ms. Connors's invitation to the Foothill Elementary Faculty Pickleball Tournament, Theo and Evelyn have been studying the rules, watching serving tutorials, and listening to the most popular pickleball podcasters. Last night, they stayed up until 1:00 a.m. volleying a wiffle ball back and forth across their living room, using their recently thrifted couch as a makeshift net, then agreed to an early arrival today because it isn't in their nature to half-ass anything. Not when the alternative is winning.

But.

Winning requires focus.

On the game.

Theo is focused on something else entirely, sipping water as his eyes—safely hidden behind tinted aviators—fixate on the flex of Evelyn's calf muscles, on the way her hands move in methodical circles up, up, up each leg, on their refusal to miss even a millimeter of skin. Satisfied, Evelyn stands, then lifts and folds over the hem of her tank top so as not to sunscreen stain it while she protects the sliver of midriff exposed to the sun and it's so hot. Sun protection. Evelyn.

"Get my back?" she asks, handing him the tube of sunscreen and pivoting.

Theo wordlessly applies sunscreen to the back of her delts, her traps, her upper lats exposed by the halter top that's his new favorite shirt because it gives him an excuse to touch her. His eyes shift down to that skirt—that *skirt*—wondering what tiny animal print is covering her ass today. It's another problem, his inability to stop thinking about his best friend in goddamn corgi panties. Theo swallows. Hard. Pulls his eyes back up as his hands linger on her shoulders, massaging out a knot and when she lets out a soft moan . . .

Fuck.

He lets go.

"Thanks."

Evelyn takes the sunscreen back, swipes an extra layer of protection over his prone-to-burning nose, then jogs across the court to drop the tube in her duffel bag—completely, thankfully, oblivious to the effect that she has on him. She props one foot on the bench next to her and reties neon pink shoelaces. Theo's aware that he's still staring at her, that he has been since the moment they stepped onto the court, that he cannot stop—

"Theo?"

His eyes shift toward the voice that pulls focus from Evelyn, a voice spoken from lips that taste like strawberry ChapStick. Her red hair is not chaos curls splayed on a hotel pillow, but two perfect braids cascading down her back. Theo glitches, seeing this woman on a pickleball court in Pasadena. So entirely out of context. Her aquamarine eyes flicker to the gold band on his finger and he catches the furrow of her brow, the question in it, before her expression resets to neutral indifference.

"Violet?"

"You know my sister, Cohen?"

That voice belongs to Juniper Delgado. Theo's closest teacher friend, turned zoo proposal thief, now nemesis. She smiles at him, a sincere one because, of course, Juniper doesn't know she's been demoted from friend to nemesis. Of course, he's only actually beefing with her in his head.

He blinks.

Sister?

"We met at EdCon," Violet says, then turns to Theo. "What . . . three, four years ago?"

"Four," Theo confirms.

Met is the lite, elementary-school-teacher-appropriate way of saying *hooked up* at the educational conference Theo attends on behalf of Foothill Elementary. Every summer, he spends the first week of August at a conference center in Santa Ana attending curriculum workshops and debating policy and reading legislation, and he loves his kids—he *does*—but that week surrounded by educators who are just as passionate about making the system better as he is? It's always so restorative. As is—*was*—casual sex with Violet Garcia, a former fourth-grade teacher, now vice principal in Long Beach.

"Small world," Juniper says.

"Are you here for the tournament?" Theo asks.

A stupid question, considering Juniper and Violet are in matching pink tracksuits.

"Agatha is in labor. Joey's assisting with the birth," Juniper explains.

Cool.

Violet is only here because *an elephant is giving birth.*

"Congratulations?" Violet asks, eyes once again on the ring, that single word a challenge because the last first week of August is a recent memory. Just three months ago, she texted Theo her room number and he showed up with veggie pizza and a six-pack of Blue Moon. He hears the question mark. *Have I been screwing a married man?*

Theo stuffs his hands in his pockets. "Thanks."

Juniper smiles at him and either he's reading way too much into Violet's energy or Juniper is choosing to ignore it. "Newlywed looks good on you, Cohen."

"I think so, too. Hey, Juniper."

Evelyn is back at his side, looping her arm through his.

"Ev, this is Juniper's sister. Violet," Theo says, gently squeezing her freezing fingers because she knows about his initial, ridiculous puppy-dog crush. Even helped him craft the texts that Violet ultimately left on read four years ago after he returned from EdCon not at all ready for a commitment, but all-in on a gorgeous (and, more important, *safe*) distraction.

Yes, that Violet.

Be nice.

Evelyn lets go of his hand, holding it out to Violet. "Evie. His wife."

Violet wraps her perfectly manicured hand around Evelyn's, whose nails are chipped blue and bitten down to the quick, and everything in Theo's conflict-averse core screams *run.* Really, is sucking up to his boss worth *this*?

"Veronica roped you into the tournament, too?" Juniper asks, still oblivious.

Theo nods.

"Cool."

"How long have you been a pickler?" Violet asks.

"Oh, it's—"

Evelyn bumps his hip with hers, effectively silencing him. "We don't give intel to the competition, Theodore."

Violet points at Theo with her paddle. "Okay, don't tell me. *Show me.*"

Theo flushes, that rasp, the *innuendo*, taking him back to that hotel room in Santa Ana. "Actually—"

Evelyn cuts Theo off. "You're on."

Juniper and Violet laugh, clueless as to how serious Evelyn is right now. Only Theo sees the tiny wrinkle between her eyebrows, feels the intensity radiating from her skin, hears the competitive edge in her voice. It's more confident than she has any right to be. The same fearless tone she'd have in the dance studio before leaping into a new stunt, so sure that Theo would catch her. After extended held eye contact with Violet, Evelyn pivots and claims a quadrant of the court, gripping her right ankle for a standing quad stretch—and because Theo's watching her, always watching her—he clocks her almost imperceptible wince. It activates an internal alarm, a visceral panic, that screams:

Pain.

Evelyn is in pain.

He jogs over to her because *nope.*

Theo will not be responsible for his best friend's pain.

Again.

"Don't," she says.

"Your ankle—"

"—is just a little stiff, but otherwise fine."

Her tone is sharp, her words defensive. It snaps him out

of the irrational panic, and Theo backs off, raising his arms in retreat. Because no one knows Evelyn's body—its limits—better than she does. It's an established boundary since her diagnosis. Theo can express concern . . . but he must listen to her, must believe her when she's in pain and when she is not. Most of the time, he does. Believe her. Sometimes, though? Right now? Anxiety wins. He drops his shaking hands to his sides. Checks his pulse: 144. *Shit.*

He closes his eyes.

Takes slow, intentional breaths.

And because his eyes are closed, he doesn't see it coming. Lips—holy fuck, *Evelyn's* lips—pressing against his jaw in a soft but firm kiss that lights his skin on fire. Her teeth tease him, grazing along his jawbone until her mouth is millimeters from his. It's enough to make him forget where he is, who's watching, his own name. A past, younger, reckless version of himself wants to lean into this moment. Smash his lips into hers and pretend that it's real. Admit how much he wants this to be real.

But he isn't that Theo.

And it isn't real.

So he pulls back.

Asks, "What was that for?"

Evelyn looks at him.

Past him.

Then shrugs innocently. "I just wanted to."

Evelyn and Theo got pickled.

Definition?

They suck. Didn't score a single point in the practice game played against Juniper and Violet, who shouted nonsense phrases at them after every rally—

What an unfortunate falafel!

Smash!

Did you see that tweener?

Evelyn full-on sprinted away from the court when Violet screamed "Scorpion!" at the top of her lungs only to learn that a scorpion is not just a predatory arachnid but also the name of the shot Violet had just executed. Overall, Theo and Evelyn's instincts are good. It's the execution that's lacking. It doesn't help that he can still feel her teeth on his skin. Or the *sting* on his right butt cheek every time Evelyn swats him with the paddle. Theo keeps hitting the ball out of bounds. She keeps fouling by stepping into the kitchen. Both lack a total awareness of their bodies and how they relate to each other within the boundaries of the court.

It's a mess.

Evelyn hasn't stopped laughing, her cheeks flushed from exertion as they rehydrate and lick their wounds before his colleagues begin to arrive for the tournament.

"We . . . really thought we had a shot."

"Speak for yourself."

"Next time, less falafeling."

"Next time, pretend we're home and stay out of the kitchen."

She shoves his shoulder, and the *snackle* she emits—that ridiculous sound—makes his heart flutter. That sound? It's worth the humiliating defeat. Even at the hand of his nemesis and his fuck buddy who still look like Greek goddesses and . . . how? Theo's shirt is sweat-drenched. Evelyn's face is the color of a tomato. Juniper and Violet didn't even break a sweat.

"Good luck in the tournament, *Theodore*," Violet says.

"You need it," Juniper teases.

"Kick rocks, Juniper," Evelyn snaps.

Juniper's eyes widen.

Evelyn's narrow.

"*Bitch*," she mutters under her breath once the sisters are out of earshot.

"Was that really necessary?"

"You know I don't fuck with Juniper."

"She's not so bad."

"She wronged you."

Evelyn's voice is low, serious, *fierce*.

"Is this still about the zoo? I can't fault her for advocating for her kids. Also? She didn't do anything to you."

She shakes her head. "That's not how we work."

I could kiss her.

"Also?" she continues. "Violet kept aiming for your crotch. She's pissed. Can't blame her. I, too, would be if I thought I banged a married man."

"*Evelyn*."

She laughs, enjoying this.

"Theo? You made it!"

He turns toward the voice that belongs to none other than Veronica Connors. His boss. Her entourage of doting colleagues surround her, duffel bags slung over their shoulders. Mary Pendergast. Diane Silver. Shana Jones. Corrine Baptiste. Wendi Simmons. All teachers. Well. Wendi is the school's psychologist. All faculty.

All picklers.

Theo stands. "Hi, Ms. Connors."

"*Veronica*," she says, unable to get it through her head that Theo is incapable of calling his elementary school princi-pal by her first name. "You must be Evie!" Evelyn stands, and

Ms. Connors, hit by something he can only describe as *over-whelm*, throws her arms around her. "I didn't put it together, but of course! You're Lori's Evelyn."

"Oh. I suppose I am."

In Ms. Connors's embrace, Evelyn looks at Theo like she could cry. Theo feels like he could cry. He senses his colleagues' eyes on him, feels the awkwardness that emanates from people uncomfortable with grief. Which is, honestly, most people. He's never prepared for these moments, for people casually mentioning his mom. Every time, it feels like that person is picking off a scab. Every time, it leaves a fresh wound.

"It's so wonderful to meet you!" Ms. Connors says.

Evelyn smiles. "You, too, Veronica. I'm looking forward to dinking with you."

Ms. Connors laughs, loud (because even his boss is a twelve-year-old), then squeezes Evelyn's arm tenderly. They exchange pleasantries and a few jokes at Theo's expense before Ms. Connors assigns them a bracket number and a court. He feels the entourage watching them. Mary, Diane, and Shana. Second-grade teachers. Lori's best friends. Theo waves. Diane waves back. Shana averts her eyes. Mary looks a little teary. And it throws him—more than the jaw kiss, more than even Violet.

He turns toward Evelyn to comment on this, but before he says a word, she mutters, "You've got to be kidding me."

Juniper and Violet have also been assigned to their court. At the net, *Juniper* apologizes to *Evelyn*. Violet wins the coin toss. Chooses first serve and the shady side of the court. Then yells "Kick rocks!" as she sends the ball toward Evelyn, who returns it in earnest and Theo sees her mouth form a perfect O when it lands in bounds, initiating a volley that she returns once, twice, three times . . . until Juniper faults, the ball landing in the net.

Evelyn drops her paddle and throws her arms around him. "Holy shit! *We scored.*"

Theo laughs. "We did not."

In pickleball, only the serving team can score.

"Then I shall rephrase. They didn't score!"

I could kiss her.

He thinks it, again, the moment their eyes meet. Justifies it. Everyone is watching. Is this not a situation to rebrand from the teacher his colleagues still see as their student? Be the image of a doting husband by kissing his wife? Marriage (and Louisa's sprained ankle) got him into the pickleball tournament. Already, Ms. Connors put a meeting on his calendar Monday morning to discuss the planetarium. Being believable . . . could mean being taken *seriously*, which could lead to more invitations, more opportunities.

For the children.

Obviously.

His logic brain grasps at straws, refusing to admit that if he kisses Evelyn right now it will be for one reason and one reason only.

Because he wants to.

She lets go before he can make up his mind, skipping to her side of the court to get into position. Theo, off-kilter from the adrenaline, from the body contact, from the *desire* that's becoming harder by the millisecond to control, botches the return when Juniper serves. Evelyn nails it. Does she run on vengeance? Theo is mystified as the game progresses and, well, they're not great, but they are less pathetic than they were an hour ago. Twenty minutes later, the score is 9–7. Somehow, impossibly, they're only down by two and Theo is officially delusional enough to believe that not only can they even the score—they can *win*.

Evelyn serves.

Violet returns.

The ball flies toward the center line, within reach. Theo hustles, at full speed, toward it, sure that it's his rally.

Only so is Evelyn.

They collide.

Just like last time, Theo is two beats behind.

He can't catch her.

She goes down.

Hard.

And he's seventeen again. They're no longer on a pickleball court, but in a ballroom in Anaheim, at their final dance competition. Evelyn's on the ground, unable to stand on her own. Because of *him*. Theo's pulse pounds in his eardrums. He doesn't remember screaming her name or running to her or dropping on his knees at her side. What brings him back to now is the crimson on asphalt. Blood. It gushes from both of her knees, where skin used to exist. *Fuck.* What if her ankle got reinjured? What if she needs PT again? What if she has to quit the fellowship in order to properly heal? What if he has to take her to the hospital and she catches a virus that her immunocompromised body can't fight off and this results in a flare-up? Over *pickleball*? How is this happening again? Didn't Theo learn *anything*?

"Ev? Are you okay? I'm so sorry. *Fuck*."

Theo can't *breathe*.

He's choking on his heart.

Then there's a hand on his chest. Sometimes, Theo swears that the pressure of her hand is the only thing that has kept his heart inside his chest cavity for almost twenty-eight years. At ten, when stuck on a section of jazz choreography a week before the recital. At twelve, when on the verge of failing sixth-grade math. At fourteen, when his mom uttered the word *cancer*. At eighteen, when he was terrified that going to New York would be a huge mistake. At twenty-two, when the cancer came back. At twenty-three, the moment he became a person without a mom.

"Hey," Evelyn says, her voice so soft it hurts. "*Theo*. I didn't land on it. *Look*." She points and flexes her bad ankle, then rolls it in both directions. "I'm okay. I mean, my knees sting like a bitch. But I'm okay. Okay? Breathe."

He covers her hand with his, and they stay like that, tethered together, until his heart calms down and his rational brain regains consciousness. *She's fine. I'm fine. We're fine.* He lets go of her hand. Runs his fingers through his hair, then bends down to scoop Evelyn into his arms and carry her to his car, conceding the game. Obviously. Theo sits her in the trunk of his hatchback Nissan Versa and cleans up her wounds with the first-aid kit in his trunk. Checks her vitals. Checks *his* vitals. Memorizes his own—141/89—to record in his health log.

"I'm sorry," Evelyn says.

"What?"

"We could've won! But then I got overzealous and ran into the brick wall that is *you* and—"

"Evelyn. If you think I care about the game right now . . ." His voice trails off as he wraps gauze around her knee. "I don't."

"Okay."

They're quiet while he wraps the other knee, then the swollen, bloodied knuckles of her hand that kissed asphalt. Once she's settled in the passenger seat of his car, he jogs back to the court to let Ms. Connors know that they're going to head out.

On their way home, Evelyn speaks first. "I'm sorry about Violet."

"Ev."

"What?"

"Stop. Please."

Theo cannot bear it, Evelyn apologizing when she's the one in pain. Those were her first two words to him a decade ago, when she woke up from the surgery that meant she'd never dance again—at least not at a competitive, professional level. *I'm sorry.* Because they didn't place in a regional dance competition. Because she fell. No. Because Theo, so wrapped up in his feelings to the point of distraction, didn't catch her. It's his fault. He's *furious* with himself. He swore nothing would change, only for this marriage to reignite feelings that cannot differentiate between fact and fiction and he's so mortified, so ashamed that those stupid, reckless feelings hurt her.

Again.

THE BUNGALOW, THE SUMMER BEFORE
HIGH SCHOOL

Theo

They're fourteen the first time Theo almost confesses three words to Evelyn that have the potential to change everything.

I like you.

He's at the bungalow, lying next to her on the cool linoleum floor of the shed that Mo, a carpenter, finished and converted into a dance space for them. They're recovering from a contemporary routine to a bummer of a Sondheim ballad: "Send in the Clowns." Theo *hates* clowns. Theo feels like a clown. Staring up at the whirring ceiling fan, their chests heaving exhausted breaths in unison, those three words punctuate every thought. *I like you.* He tilts his head toward her. *I like you.* Her cheeks are flushed, a sheen of sweat coating her upper lip. *I like you.* It becomes all-consuming, the impulse to say those words out loud.

I like you.

I like you.

I like you.

"Again."

Evelyn stands, then reaches both hands out to him,

completely oblivious. From pinkie to thumb, each nail is a different color—cerulean, lavender, mauve, sunshine, and mint—because without polish she'll bite them until they bleed. He takes those colorful fingers and she pulls him to his feet. He anticipates the release, but she just shifts her grip, pressing her palms against his and twining their fingers together.

"We have to tap into the *emotion* of the song," Evelyn says, her voice soft and serious. "You need to pretend you're in love with me, Theodore."

His brow furrows.

Her lips split into a smile, a laugh bubbling up from her throat because it's ridiculous, obviously, the idea of him being in love with her. In reality, his furrowed brow is a reflex because . . . *seriously?* He almost says it. But then she lets go of his hands and jetés across the shed to the stereo, restarts the song, and launches herself into his arms. It's their first duet with choreographed lifts. At first the pressure stressed him out. He started lifting weights, using the garage that Jacob converted into a home gym, considering his protein intake. Now? Theo loves lifts. He loves that every biceps curl, chest press, and protein shake consumed in the name of dance gets to be a *fuck you* to his dad. He loves the challenge of learning a new lift and the trust required to execute it.

He loves that they have that.

The song ends.

Theo and Evelyn are frozen in the final embrace, her legs wrapped around his torso.

It's so much.

I like you so much.

"Better. Again?"

She places her hands on his shoulders to dismount,

but before she can jeté away to restart the song once more, Theo reaches for her wrist. Her eyes meet his, wordless. It's so quiet, the only sound the syncopated thrashing of their hearts, and maybe what Theo's about to say will change everything. But . . . maybe it won't. It's not like they're not already a hyphenate—at home, at school, at dance. *Evie-and-Theo*. It's not like they don't already spend pretty much all their free time together. It's not like they don't already love each other.

Theo swallows.

I like you so much.

He's going to say it, because he *has* to say it, because not saying it physically *hurts*.

"Ev? I—"

A knock on the door separates them and sends him backward, the admission caught in his throat.

"Kiddos?" Mo's head pops in. "Time to wrap it up. Theo, your parents are waiting inside."

Theo frowns. *Parents? Plural?* Mo disappears before he can ask for clarification because Jacob has never accompanied Lori to pick him up from a dance rehearsal at the bungalow. It's Tuesday. Jacob should be at the office, or touring properties, or doing whatever he does to *be a provider*. Theo must've misheard. He chugs water, then stuffs the bottle in his duffel bag, unsure if he's frustrated or grateful for Mo's interruption. Evelyn switches out the CD in the stereo and they cool down to *Fearless*, stretching out their fatigued muscles before exiting the studio shed.

"I felt it that last time," Evelyn says.

"Hmm?"

"Love," she admits with a casual shrug. "It's easy. Pretending."

"Pretending," Theo echoes like an idiot as she walks ahead of him.

He sees Jacob's black BMW in the driveway. He didn't mishear. His dad is here. At the bungalow. Why is he here? On a Tuesday? At all? Theo follows Evelyn through the patio slider that connects to the kitchen, tapping his fingers against his thigh. Inside, his parents are sitting on the living room couch. Their mouths are moving, but he's unable to make out the words. A teakettle whistles on the stove. Pep pours boiling water into three mugs. Biscotti is arranged on a serving platter. What is happening? Evelyn seems just as mystified. Her eyes shift back and forth from the biscotti to the tea, then up to Pep.

"Grandma?"

Pep doesn't make eye contact, just drops a spoon in each mug. "Hey, Sweets! Bring out the biscotti?"

Evelyn frowns.

Doesn't move.

Theo picks up the tray. "I got it."

It all blurs in slow motion, everything that happens next. Peppermint tea. Jacob's stoic expression. A tray of stale biscotti. Lori's nose scrunches as she pats the empty couch cushion next to her and says, "There's something you need to know, both of you, and it'll be so much easier to just say it once."

Theo's pulse spikes. Her nose scrunch. Theo makes the same face when he's trying not to cry. *Bubbe died. Or Zeyde. Or we're moving to the west side. Or Naomi is taking Evelyn away.*

Or.

Or.

Or . . .

He doesn't see it coming, the three words that change everything.

"I have cancer."

"What?"

Lori and Jacob are speaking words at Theo but it's too much medical jargon. *Colorectal cancer. Stage three.* His brain can't process the news, but his body feels every word. *Chemo.* His palms start sweating. *Bowel resection.* His chest tightens. *Treatment starts tomorrow.* He can't breathe. *My prognosis.* Theo doesn't remember standing up or leaving the room in the middle of his mom sharing her *cancer prognosis* or retreating to the studio shed. He just remembers the panic clawing at his throat. Choking him, as Jacob enters the studio shed. Remembers pressing the heels of his hands to his swollen lids to avoid eye contact with his dad.

Remembers Jacob's admission. "I'm terrified, too."

"Dad—"

"Whatever you're feeling? Feel it here, then *leave it here.*" Jacob squats down so he's eye level, then places an awkward hand on Theo's shoulder. "We'll get through this as a family, but you have to be strong. Her prognosis is good. So we're going to be positive. Okay?"

Jacob's voice is *thick.*

On the verge of choked up.

Cry.

Theo remembers thinking it.

How desperately he wanted to see his father cry.

"Okay?"

"Okay."

Jacob squeezes his shoulder, then stands. "I'll give you a moment to pull yourself together, son."

He remembers biting down on his lip so hard it bled.

The taste of metal on his tongue.

Jacob repeating, "We'll get through this."

Nodding as if he's capable of pulling himself together as his father exits . . . only to fall apart all over again because he's not strong, because he's in shock, *because his mom has cancer*.

Cancer.

Cancer.

Cancer.

"Theodore?"

He doesn't remember Evelyn entering the studio shed—just the soft, tentative way she says his name and the gentle pressure of her hand on his chest. His heart hammering against her hand. Jacob's voice is in his head. *You have to be strong.* He remembers feeling so embarrassed that she saw him like that. So relieved that he didn't spill his guts all over the studio shed floor. Theo jerks back, away from her, because it's too much, her touching him like that. It's impossible to be strong when his heart is in her hand.

He remembers pushing, pushing, pushing.

"I'm fine."

"It's okay if you're not. I'm not."

"You're not?"

"I love her, too."

"It's not the same."

"I didn't mean—"

"She's my mom, Evelyn. *Mine*."

He remembers watching her expression as she registers the verbal blow—morphing from stunned, to pained, to *angry*. Knowing the precise combination of words that would hurt and saying them anyway because is that not strength? Lashing out, allowing emotions to manifest in anger? He remembers just wanting her to go away. Feeling so scared and lonely once she did. Then pulling himself together, swallowing the emotion—every emotion—until he didn't feel anything at all.

13

Evie holds back Imogen's hair as she vomits rainbow sprinkles and churros into a Main Street, U.S.A., trash bin.

"I can do the teacups, I said," Imogen moans. "It'll be different this year, I said."

"Always the optimist."

"It's my best quality."

"Bested by motion sickness again, Gen?"

Theo appears at Evie's side with a blue Gatorade because he's been around long enough to know that despite Imogen's best efforts, she'll always face the consequences of the spinning teacups. Evie didn't have to ask. Theo just knows her little sister's post-vom electrolytes of choice. She ignores the way this act of care tugs at her heart as Imogen raises her middle finger in their direction, then stands tall and adjusts her mouse ears.

"Fuck off."

Theo holds out the Gatorade. "You're welcome."

"Thank you."

Imogen takes the bottle, chugs half of it, then skips toward

Big Thunder Mountain. Evie and Theo trail behind, just as they always do, during their annual pilgrimage to Disneyland. It's where Evie and Imogen have spent every Thanksgiving since Evie obtained her driver's license and built up the courage to brave the I-5. Because on this day, the Bloom sisters are not interested in eating turkey, or watching grown men give each other concussions, or celebrating genocide. No. What they're interested in is riding all the rides until one of them (Imogen) pukes. It's Theo's fifth pilgrimage. He began tagging along after Lori died. Imogen invited him, a gesture that cemented what Evie already knew to be true. Theo is more than her best friend.

He's family.

She could've used that reminder before she dragged her teeth along his jaw like a feral animal. *Ugh.* It's been weeks since she jumped him on a pickleball court, an impulsive moment that stirred up something dangerous. Weeks. Yet every sensation from that day is etched into Evie.

Her tongue on his skin.

Crashing.

Falling.

Bleeding.

Instead of processing that instinct to touch him in front of Violet—the *possessiveness*—she avoids, avoids, avoids. For Evie, the back half of November highlights included mid-to-disappointing episodes of *Survivor*, not itching off the gnarly scabs on her knees, and a conversation confirming that Sadie Silverman does, in fact, know her name. She's still buzzing from the breakthrough she had with her mentor yesterday before they parted ways for the holiday. It was lunch. Evie had just offered Charlie the dill pickle that came with her chicken salad sandwich from Arnie's when Sadie Silverman entered the mixing room, her eyes fixed on Charlie, her expression indecipherable.

I watched Ginger.

Evie gasped.

A piece of celery lodged in her windpipe.

Sadie Silverman pivoted toward a coughing Evie and asked, *That . . . the dancing? It was you?*

Still hacking up a lung, Evie could only nod.

Ross is a limp dick. Do you want to accompany me to a spotting session on Monday?

It's a major upgrade from being the Coffee Bitch and wistfully observing Sadie Silverman work while separated by a glass window. During a spotting session, the director, sound editor, music editor, and Foley artists watch a locked cut of the visuals and catalog the needed special effects, music cues, and Foley sounds. It's a chance to network, learn, and prove that she's worth being taken seriously, that she can be trusted to work on real assignments. Union assignments. And shouldn't *that* be her focus—on making the most out of every opportunity, on securing credits, on reapplying to IATSE as soon as possible? Once that happens, she can file for divorce. Evie can have her best friend back.

"Evelyn?"

His voice pulls her from the memory. "Hmm?"

"I think we have to accept it."

Theo needs to be more specific, because her mind goes only to things that are impossible to accept. Marriage is blurring the boundary that's kept him in the friend zone. Gives her an excuse to act on the attraction that she's been quietly acknowledging for . . . what, a decade? Only three times has she dared to acknowledge it out loud. At seventeen, when Theo rejected her promposal. At nineteen, when she spent her entire savings on a flight to New York. At twenty-three, the night of Lori's shiva. Every time? It's been a huge mistake. So. No. She will not accept it, if the *it* in question has anything to do with whatever her lips on his jaw may have unleashed.

"What?"

"Gen is a Disney Adult."

She laughs, feeling relieved and ridiculous all at once. "Did we not already know this?"

"Knowing something isn't the same as accepting it."

Theo's tenor is breezy, but his eyes are fixed ahead, likely searching for the nearest snack stand because he doesn't do roller coasters. Evie attempts to let his words—their implication—fade with the wind as she removes her nutmeg sweater. If Imogen's delusion is that she can overcome the teacups, hers is that autumn exists in Southern California. She applies sunscreen onto her bare shoulders. Theo offers to hold on to her backpack and she hands it over and shocks herself when their fingers brush in the transfer. Evie swallows, then walks toward the coaster solo, attempting to navigate around THE HENDERSON FAMILY, a mob of neon orange T-shirts clustered in front of the Big Thunder Mountain entrance, while convincing herself that the sun, this *heat*, is the reason for her flushed cheeks. But. Theo's right.

Knowing something is absolutely not the same as accepting it.

Because she knows that she likes it.

Her mouth on Theo.

His mouth on her.

But she'll *never* accept it.

Imogen, already in line, waves her over, and she weaves awkwardly through the queue to reunite with her sister. Imogen's eyes are fixated on her phone, likely checking wait times in the Disneyland app.

"Sorry," Evie says. "I got swept up in a neon-orange riptide."

"The Hendersons? Oh. I assumed you and Theodore ditched me to scandalize Mr. Toad," Imogen teases, eyes not shifting from her screen. "Did you see Aunt Mir's email?"

Imogen slaps her phone into Evie's palm.

Subject: avia's b'nai mitzvah

It's a visceral reaction, the flip of Evie's stomach that precedes nausea. She tries to recall the last time she saw Avia Deleve-Gomez. Remembers it was here, in this very park. Miri and Mateo traveled from the Upper West Side to the Happiest Place on Earth for Avia's sixth birthday. Evie, twenty and spending her summer at the bungalow, drove to Anaheim, desperate to catch up with Naomi's younger sister. Desperate for any connection to Naomi.

So desperate, she agreed to take Avia on the teacups—who then vomited all over her vintage combat boots. Motion sickness. It runs in the family. Then she learned through the aunt she barely knew that Naomi was *summering in Cannes* with Jean-Paul. Evie excused herself to dry-heave in a public bathroom before fleeing the premises to crochet blankets with and be comforted by the person who she sometimes pretended was her mom.

Lori.

Evie scans the email for the date.

Early January.

Six weeks from now.

"You're thinking about it," Imogen says, voice flat.

"What?"

"Going."

"You're not?"

"No."

Evie hands Imogen's phone back as they near the front of the line, then pulls out her own to confirm that the email is in her inbox, too. Forwarded with a note. *We miss you.* Evie swallows a lump in her throat. Miri stays in touch. Sends birthday cards and the occasional surface-level text. So she knew it was coming, this invitation. And she always intended to say no. But—

"How many?"

A cast member cuts off her minor spiral, directing Evie and Imogen to dots to stand on until their train arrives. It's not until they're on the ride and going up, up, up in darkness toward the light that her sister speaks again.

"Even if I wanted to subject myself to that, I can't really dip into savings right now. For the flight. Sloane wants to move back to Denver."

"Oh."

Oh.

Evie grips the lap bar, her big sister brain activating on their ascent to the apex and natural light. "I'm sorry, Genny. Breakups *suck.*"

"Where exactly did you hear that we're breaking up?"

"You're going to try to make long-distance work?"

"No." Imogen shakes her head and Evie's stomach drops before *they* drop, understanding rattling her before her sister says, confirms, "I'm going, too."

"You're moving to Denver."

Evie exits Big Thunder Mountain nauseous, though from the coaster or this news she's not sure.

"I am."

"*Why?*"

"Sloane hates LA and I love Sloane. So." Imogen shrugs, then makes a pit stop for a churro on their way to meet back up with Theo. "It was easy. Saying yes."

"What about your job?"

"Half my team is remote," Imogen says. "It's not an issue. At least until I figure out what's next."

"What's *next?*"

"Yeah. Remember how into ceramics I was in high school? Maybe I'll explore that. There's a lesbian-owned pottery studio in the mountains outside Denver that looks like an idyllic dreamscape. I can sign up for classes, then apply for an apprenticeship. Maybe barista in the meantime! I don't know! But it's fun to dream about it . . . which feels like a sign? LA is all I've ever known. You know?"

"So you're just going to . . ." Evie swallows. *Leave me.* ". . . uproot your entire life for someone you've been dating for less than a year?"

Imogen's expression hardens. "I knew you were going to be like this."

"Be like what?"

"A buzzkill."

"It's my job."

"Except it's *not.*" Imogen storms ahead, biting aggressively into the churro. "It's really not."

"Someone has to be logical."

She pivots, then swallows. "Love isn't logical. I *love* Sloane. I'm pretty sure I want to marry her. Eventually! And you know what I'll do? I'll *propose.* Not come up with some bullshit reasons to marry the person I love."

"What does that mean?"

Imogen laughs. "Come *on*."

"Fuck off, Gen."

Where is this coming from? She's used to it from Pep. Not Imogen. *Never* Imogen. It cuts deep because Imogen knows—she *knows*—how true those words once were. Every time Evie misread a moment and considered crossing the line from friendship into something more, Imogen was the one who comforted her in the aftermath. She knows who Theo is to Evie. Who he's not.

"Sorry." Imogen throws up her arms, cinnamon sugar churro dust flying. "I'm sorry. Can we not fight today? *Please*."

Evie's expression softens.

She has so many questions, so many *feelings* about Imogen's news, but she swallows them because she knows in her bones that her little sister spilled the news today, here, *at Disneyland*, to have an out. No fighting on Thanksgiving. A Bloom sister rule. So she lets it go.

Besides, Imogen is in love for now.

Her lease isn't up for six months.

"I'm sorry I'm a buzzkill."

Imogen snorts. "You're not."

They reunite with Theo, who's waiting under an awning with a chocolate-covered Mickey Mouse ice cream that's melting faster than he can consume it. When he licks his fingers clean, Evie averts her eyes. Imogen's eyebrows rise. *Bitch*.

Theo, oblivious to their entire wordless conversation, says, "I added us to the virtual queue for *Dr. Strange in the Hundred Acre Wood*."

Imogen's eyes snap toward his. "Holy shit. You *got in*?"

Theo frowns at his phone, then shows his screen to Gen. "I think so?"

Evie's grateful for the subject change, until an hour or so

later, when she learns against her will that this is part of the next phase of the MCU. Musical crossovers. It's a fever dream, the entire production. Imogen loves it. "According to Jo, a Broadway transfer is, like, inevitable," she says.

Jo, better known as @johanna_ever_after, is Imogen's favorite Disney influencer.

Theo's eyebrows rise. He mouths. *Disney Adult.*

Evie stifles a laugh. He's right. Her sister is a Disney Adult. Evie loves Imogen's unapologetic enthusiasm for the things that bring her joy. Imogen gushes over the power ballad between Dr. Strange and Eeyore, then speed walks ahead toward a gift shop that's dropping a limited-edition *Dr. Strange in the Hundred Acre Wood: The Musical* pin. Evie and Theo follow, continuing to go wherever Imogen leads. Evie attempts to keep up—with the pace, the conversation—until she feels fatigue from the heat, from her *feelings*, seep into her bones. A reminder that this tradition takes a toll on her body. A promise that she'll spend tomorrow horizontal. She pushes sweaty bangs off her forehead. Puts one foot in front of the other. Fades. It's a classic feature of Evie's particular brand of Crohn's. Being fine until she's not.

"Theo?"

He doesn't ask what she needs.

Just squats low enough for her to climb onto his back and it is instant relief, being off her feet.

Her mouth hovers in front of his ear. "Thanks."

"Always."

Imogen burns out by 2:00 p.m.—right on schedule—then sleeps through the entire ride back to Pasadena. Theo drives. As soon as Imogen starts to snore, Evie's cue that it is safe to speak, she word vomits her sister's news and every complicated fucked-up feeling about it.

"It's just so . . . *Imogen* to jump into something so reckless so soon."

Theo shrugs. "I think it's brave."

"You're supposed to be on my side."

"There are sides?"

Instead of responding, she opens Instagram. It's a mistake. The first photo she sees is a post from Naomi's account of Margot, her sister, in a blue Burberry peacoat, skipping through Central Park, with a caption that reads, *tons to be thankful for #burberrykidsxbluey*. Margot looks so much like Imogen at that age it hurts. Strawberry-blond curls. Piercing blue eyes. Evie is so angry. So incredibly jealous.

It's fierce, irrational.

Naomi is not a good mother.

Evie *knows* this.

But it's just like Theo says, knowing isn't accepting.

A memory surfaces. Thanksgiving. She's eight. Imogen is six, the exact age Margot is now. Evie doesn't remember what they were arguing about. Her and Gen. Barbies? A stolen shirt? The TV remote? Does it matter? She rarely remembers the trigger, just the reaction. *Why are you doing this to me?* Their dad was on a research trip in Nicaragua. Unreachable. Naomi locked herself in her bathroom. Unreachable. Evie pounded on the door. Begged Naomi to come out, tears streaming down her cheeks. Smoke alarms sounded. Downstairs, Imogen tried to salvage the charred turkey. But it was too heavy. The turkey. The ceramic Dutch oven that held it. Evie heard a scream, a shatter. Silence. Then the soft *click* of a lock. Naomi exited the bathroom. Evie followed her downstairs. Pled. *I'm sorry, I'm sorry, I'm sorry.* Her mother took in the mess, the disaster, the catastrophe that she created, said, *I need a beat*, then plucked her keys off the table. There was no one to call—their dad was a continent away, their grandparents in Atlanta, where Mo was contracted to build sets for a popular zombie show. So Evie cleaned up the mess. Kept Imogen fed and distracted until Naomi returned two days later with Barbies, with candy, with empty promises.

At eight, Evie already knew not to trust Naomi's promises.

Imogen has a crescent moon scar on her left wrist from where ceramic burned her skin. In the rearview mirror, she watches her sister's chest rise and fall, so proud of them for reclaiming this day and creating memories that aren't completely fucked. Could this be their last Disney Thanksgiving? It hurts too much to think that far ahead, to consider what it means if her sister really, truly puts an entire mountain range between them.

"That's Margot?"

Stopped in traffic on I-5, Theo's eyes shifted to her screen.

"Yeah."

"She's getting big."

Evie has the opposite reaction to the photo.

She thinks, *Margot is so little.*

Was she ever that little? She doesn't remember ever feeling little. Not with Imogen on her heels and Naomi's emotions to manage. She fixates on the photo. Margot is smiling so wide her nose scrunches. Is it real? Or has Margot—a child, a *baby*—already learned that their mother's mood is dependent on that smile, that Naomi's love is conditional? If Evie thinks about Margot too much it physically hurts, so she exits Instagram and opens Aunt Miriam's email and rereads it. Naomi could be there. But also . . . *Margot* could be there.

Evie could see her baby sister.

"Aunt Mir sent an invitation to Avia's b'nai mitzvah."

"Avia's *twelve*?"

"I know."

"When is it?"

"January."

"Do you want to go?"

She bites her lip. "Naomi could be there."

"I hope she is." There's an edge to his voice. "It's about time she faces what a massive mistake she made."

Evie's laugh is hollow. She chews the inside of her cheek, *hard*, the hidden pain of a blooming canker sore preferable to any visible signs of pain. Theo's words hit a tender spot, but she refuses to let anyone, even him, see how raw the abandonment still feels. It's pathetic.

"Naomi doesn't make mistakes."

Theo's jaw tenses, his knuckles white against the steering wheel. "You want to go."

She shouldn't.

But.

Aunt Mir wrote, *We miss you*. Margot might be there. Combined, those two reasons are enough for her to want to put the date in her calendar, want to book a flight, want to show up for what little family she has.

"Do you have a plus-one?" Theo asks.

"I do, but—"

"Great. When is it?"

"It's in New York."

"I assumed."

Evie would never ask, but of course Theo would never make her ask. Doesn't even make her verbalize the *why* that is pulling her toward RSVPing *yes*. He just promises that if this is something she wants to do, he's in. It slows down the speed of her heart, even if there's something terrifying about the thought of herself and Theo together in New York again for the first time since she confused her abandonment issues and missing him for something more.

Imogen's voice echoes in her head. *Come on.*

It's fine.

She has six weeks to prepare.

"Thanks, Theodore."

"Always."

Evie RVSPs before she can change her mind, then squeezes her eyes shut and surrenders to the fatigue in her bones, safe and scared and so exhausted.

14

Theo is woken by the assault of cold air on his bare chest, the song "Wake Up" by Hilary Duff blasting through his Bluetooth speakers. He groans, palming the mattress for the duvet to cover his skin, to cover his *ears*. Unable to locate the warmth, his eyes open and—*shit*. Evelyn is standing over him, his duvet in her hand. It's going to smell like lavender vanilla now. Like her. She's dressed in jeans and a gray sweater. She looks so cozy. Half-asleep Theo wants to pull her toward him, wants to splay his ice fingers across her torso, nestle into her, and fall back to sleep. Instead, his palms sink into the mattress as he sits up and blinks the sleep out of his eyes, considering which offense is the worst.

The cold.

Evelyn's face.

Hilary Duff.

"*Evelyn*." Theo reaches for the pullover crumpled in a ball next to his bed. "What did I do to deserve this?"

"We're late," she says.

Fuuuuuck.

Did Theo really, for one second, believe she forgot that in exchange for participating in a pickleball tournament, he promised to join her for breakfast with his dad? No. But after two breakfast-less Sundays passed . . . he definitely hoped. Evelyn slept in until noon the morning after the Pickleball Incident. Theo woke up to a text from Jacob. Evelyn ok? It splintered his heart, the concern in that question. He leapt out of bed to check on her but didn't dare enter her room unannounced, just pressed his ear to the door, her soft snoring enough to crack his heart fully in half. Jacob canceled breakfast the following week. He had, quote, *A Thing*. No, Evelyn didn't elaborate. No, Theo didn't ask.

"*Theodore.*"

Glasses on, Evelyn's features sharpen into focus.

Her brow, furrowed.

Her lips, a devastating pout.

Her finger, jamming into the volume button on her phone.

"I'm up." Theo covers his ears. "*Fuck.* I'm up!"

Silence.

"Ten minutes," she says, then pivots. "I'll be in the car."

Bossy.

Theo groans. Relishes the silence, then runs a frustrated hand through his pillow-matted curls, exhausted because he was up until 3:00 a.m. finishing midyear report cards. His students are a blast, but the endless paperwork and admin and parent complaints are soul draining. And the short holiday week has been a *week.*

Monday, Ms. Connors pushed back their meeting about the planetarium *again.*

Tuesday, Annabelle vomited in *front* of the trash.

Wednesday, Jeremiah's mother expressed concern over graphic novels being included on the winter independent reading list. He owes her an email but needs to simmer first, because how he wants to respond will probably (definitely) get him fired. Jeremiah, a reluctant reader, loves graphic novels. Why is that a problem? Theo wants his students to engage with stories, to fall in love with stories, in whatever medium is most accessible to them.

Thursday, he spent Thanksgiving in Disneyland, swallowing his irrational fear of Mickey Mouse. Is it irrational? Or is a five-foot-tall anthropomorphic mouse not, objectively, terrifying?

Yesterday was Lori's birthday.

So.

He really just wants to sleep in.

Instead, Theo stands and pulls on the nearest pair of jeans, which are wrinkled from being crumpled on the floor because his laundry situation is borderline desperate. He promised breakfast. He did not promise to put effort into said breakfast. It's pointless, to try for Jacob Cohen.

To care.

Ten minutes later—as he's brushing his teeth—his speakers become a torture device once more, this time the clip with the disastrous run of *la la la*s from *Raise Your Voice*. Evelyn exploited her pickleball-related injury with a Hilary Duff marathon and subjected Theo to that marathon. He's still paying the price. Ever since the tournament, she's been a specific combination of distant and hostile. It came up in therapy this week. Brian wondered if Theo asked Evelyn about this energy. Theo doesn't need to ask. He knows. There's a distinct before and after. Pickleball. Before and after Theo put her in a position that almost reinjured her. For what?

"Was that necessary?" Theo asks, sliding into the passenger seat.

"You're here. So."

But why?

He wants to ask, but the question would come out choked, strangled—and besides, does he even know what he's asking? Why is *this* her condition? Why did he agree? Why does she still believe that his father is capable of being more than exactly who he is? If anyone should understand the particular pain of being failed by a parent, isn't it Evelyn? Why does a small part of him dare to hope that this time, *this time*, Jacob will prove him wrong?

He doesn't ask.

Jacob opens the front door before they're even out of the car, as if he's been waiting for them. Her. Two things strike Theo: the tenderness in his father's eyes when they land on Evelyn and his complete lack of facial hair. Clean-shaven Jacob is jarring. It's like looking at himself with an age filter—his curls grayer, the lines in his face carved deeper. But he's the carbon copy of his father only in appearance.

"It's been a minute," Evelyn says in lieu of hello, crossing the threshold into the house.

It's that easy for her.

Not Theo. He's stuck, his feet glued to the concrete stoop and hating how much he wants *this*—breakfast with his dad, with his *wife*—to be real. How the simplest of desires can be the most complicated, feel the most impossible. Once he steps in it's only a matter of time before the illusion is shattered, before he feels like a loser for even pretending at all.

Jacob clears his throat. "Theo."

He looks into the mirror, at his future face. "Dad."

Jacob opens the door a tad wider and despite his better judgment, Theo takes the step inside that feels more like a leap. It's tidier than last time—the papers in neat piles, the wood surfaces dusted, an old photo of their family of three hung up above the fireplace. He blinks at the image of Baby Theo looking straight at the camera, of Lori's eyes on Theo, of Jacob fixated on Lori.

"What's on the menu this week?" Evelyn asks.

Her question pulls Theo's eyes from the photo and his nose toward the scent of cinnamon sweetness.

"I've got a spinach and mushroom frittata in the oven," Jacob says, sitting and sagging into the worn leather La-Z-Boy in the living room. In response, they sit opposite him on the couch. "Cinnamon apple scones are cooling on the stove. I used vegan butter this week. You've been warned."

Evelyn's nose scrunches. "Thank you."

Theo's quiet, processing.

Jacob is baking again?

Attempting vegan pastries?

Jealous.

You are jealous.

"Don't thank me yet, kid." Jacob chuckles—the *fuck?*—before his eyes land on the scabs that run along the knuckles of her right hand. "Who did you punch and what did they do to deserve it?"

Evelyn snorts, then shakes her head. "Bad fall."

"Not because of Theo again, I hope."

Jacob says this so casual, so matter-of-fact. Theo tenses and lets the accusation sting, more ashamed than upset as Evelyn loops her right arm through his and presses their palms together. His fingers brush the rough, jagged skin. *My fault. My fault. My fault.*

Theo knows it.

Jacob knows it.

Evelyn can admit it.

But she just asks, "When has Theo ever let me fall?"

Oh.

He braces for the comeback, unprepared for the guttural *hmph*, the rise and fall of Jacob's (equally Eugene Levy–esque) eyebrows, the changing of the subject entirely. "And how's the fellowship? Has Sadie Silverman grasped yet that you know what a fucking mixer does?"

"I think so?"

Evelyn releases his hand, basking in Jacob's attention, and that ugly jealous feeling reignites as she shares updates Theo already knows and Jacob listens. Asks follow-up questions. Is attentive. He doesn't love her relationship with his dad, but he really hates witnessing it, hates even more how much he wants it for himself. Theo is supposed to not care.

Not *want.*

But accept.

"And you, Theo?" Jacob's eyes shift to him. "How's . . . school?"

His jaw tenses, burned too many times to be tempted to bask. "Good."

"Good."

The oven beeps.

Jacob stands. "Frittata's ready."

His dad cannot escape fast enough.

"He's baking?" Theo asks, as soon as Jacob is out of earshot.

"He's *chefing,* Theodore."

Theo knows that his father is capable in the kitchen, denies that maybe he himself is capable *because* of Jacob. Theo's memories in the kitchen are so vague, so entirely incompatible with the rest of his childhood that he sometimes wonders if he made them up. Images resurface. Kneading dough together, the gentle pressure of his father's hands over his. Waking up to the sound of the stand mixer at 2:00 a.m. Each of them licking batter straight off a beater. Feeling *close*.

"Did you know he wanted to be a pastry chef?"

Theo shakes his head, but if his memories are true, it doesn't surprise him.

"He applied to the Culinary Institute of America," Evelyn continues. "Got in, too . . . but his father wouldn't let him go. Told him that men didn't belong in a kitchen and encouraged him to pursue a business degree, to follow him into real estate, to be a provider. He listened. How messed up is that?"

Theo blinks. "How do you know this?"

"We talk."

"Right."

"It makes me wonder who he would be. You know?"

"No."

"It's context."

Context that, if anything, illuminates exactly who Jacob Cohen is.

A coward.

The frittata is delicious, the scones even better, and it's infuriating. Unlike Evelyn, Theo doesn't want to wonder if Jacob Cohen, the pastry chef, would've been a different sort of dad. Supportive. Nurturing. Not a sexist asshole. What's the point of wondering? It's not who he is. Theo swallows his fury with each bite of his father's food in pointed, indignant silence. Allows Evelyn to be the one to carry the conversation, to ask questions, to care.

"How was last week?" Evelyn asks.

"Macarons are not for the faint of heart."

It turns out, Jacob's *thing* last weekend was a master class with a *Great British Bake Off* winner. He shows them the photo he took, holding up his sad, deflated macarons next to a white woman in chef garb, whose blond hair is graying at the roots. Theo recognizes the woman. *Bake Off* is one of his comfort shows. It reminds him of his mom.

Evelyn laughs. "You tried?"

"Silvie says I have potential."

"Silvie?"

Theo surprises himself with the sound of his own voice, but who the fuck is *Silvie*?

No one named Silvie has ever won *Bake Off*.

"My . . . erm . . . I started going to a grief group?" Jacob admits. "Silvie leads it."

Theo's eyebrows rise. "Oh."

"It's helped."

Theo thought his father's admission was going to be that he's dating, that Silvie is his girlfriend. But this? It's almost worse. It's a messed-up thing to think . . . for this to be Theo's reaction to his father seeking help. But. Why now? Theo tried to nudge his father toward grief counselors, toward therapists. Back when he cared. His therapist told him not to push. Said that Jacob would have to want it for himself. He's right. Theo knows it's irrational, childlike even, to want Jacob to do something, to do anything, to try, for *him*.

But it still hurts.

He controls his emotions, then takes them out on the dishes, unable to sit in uncomfortable silence when Evelyn excuses herself to use the bathroom. Theo scrubs away the remnants of breakfast on the plates, watches the crumbs wash down the sink.

Jacob sets empty plates on the counter next to him. "You know, we're more alike than you think."

As hard as he works to be nothing like his father, there's a whisper of truth in those words.

Both father and son are at ease in a kitchen.

Both left cheeks dimple when they smile.

Both settled in their path instead of chasing after more.

Theo's eyes shift from the dishes. "Yeah?"

Jacob nods, then says, voice low, "We both fell for women who deserve better."

"You think I don't know that?"

He hates himself the moment those words leave his lips, that he gave his father the exact reaction he provoked. Hot water scalds his knuckles. Theo feels the burn on his skin, in his chest. He drops the plate, and it clatters against stainless steel. Not even a grief-counseled, *pastry chefing* Jacob Cohen can stop himself from speaking words that he knows will hurt.

"Don't fuck it up. Be the man she deserves."

"I—"

"Theodore?" Evelyn's voice cuts him off, thankfully. "Ready to go home?"

Theo can't escape fast enough. He says goodbye to his father with a curt nod, then watches Evelyn give him a stiff hug, the earlier warmth evaporated. Jacob asks if they're still on for next week. He's making croissants. She nods, then grabs Theo's hand and leads him out the door, away from awkward words, away from painful memories, away from the house that stopped feeling like a home the moment his mother took her last breath within those walls.

"I'm sorry," Evelyn says as soon as they're in the car, as soon as it's safe to feel.

Theo, seeing tears in her eyes, immediately softens. "It's fine."

"It's not," she insists, her voice fierce, *angry.* "You're right. Jacob's stuff, his context . . . it's not an excuse. And me pushing this breakfast on you is because of my own stuff, which is, like, also not an excuse. I thought . . . I'm so sorry."

"Ev. It's okay."

"*No.*" Tears fall down her cheeks, and his instinct is to reach toward her, to wipe them away. He doesn't. "I see it. Okay? I *see* it. But the baking, the group therapy . . . I thought it'd be good for you to just see that he's trying? But he's not. At least not with you. I'm the actual worst."

"I promise you're not."

Evelyn shakes her head, then is quiet for the short drive home, not speaking again until she parks and cuts the engine.

"I hope you don't believe him."

"What?"

"You're not Jacob. And someday? Whoever she is? You deserve her." She shifts, pressing both her palms gently against his cheeks and he's not sure if she's freezing or if he's on fire. His eyes meet hers. "Theodore. Listen. *You deserve her.* It. Love. A real marriage."

Theo swallows.

Not her.

You.

You.

You.

He nods against her palms, the safest course of action. Lies. Ignores the frantic flutter of his heart when she lets go and heads inside. Ignores the truth that his father is right about one thing and one thing only. He doesn't and has never deserved Evelyn Bloom.

15

"F*uck* me," Evie moans midchew.

"Isn't it obscene?"

Yes, the amount of scallion tofu schmear between the freshest, most perfect bagel *is* obscene. Yes, the detour to Tompkins Square Bagels, Theo's favorite bagel spot in the East Village, was—despite her initial reluctance—a good decision. Yes, the hour-long train ride from JFK into Manhattan (even though they're staying in Bushwick) and trekking her suitcase through slush was worth it.

She swallows, then nods. "I am wrecked."

Theo giggles.

Giggles.

Her hanger fades, and after another bite, she's giggling, too. Why? She has no clue. Red-eye flights are awful. Airplane bathrooms are a crime against humanity. But right now, she's eating a god-tier quality bagel. In the East Village. With Theo. Who can't stop giggling. Who's so disarming when he's wearing his glasses. Who she's *married to*. It's all so absurd. The last time they were both in New York she was nineteen. Evie's been back a handful of times but has always made a point to keep the city at a distance. Stayed at depressing chain hotels in Midtown. Met up with Saskia at whatever overpriced bar her feet could carry her to. Refused to attempt the subway, to explore, to fall. So in the week leading up to this bagel, she's been on edge, unsure how it would feel to be back in a city she almost had, with the person she almost had it with.

And.

Well, Evie feels so much.

So many exhausted, delirious feelings.

Instead of acknowledging any one of them, she snaps a silly selfie with the bagel and sends it to Saskia.

"Gen?"

"Sass."

"Oh."

Since leaving *After Ever After*, her friendship with Saskia has devolved from daily texts and reviewing whatever they watched over the weekend in memes to an Instagram like, a TikTok link, the occasional DM. Still, Evie is almost positive that if she texts a ?, Saskia will drop a pin to a brunch spot. Evie will wear something tasteful but slutty. Knee-high boots required. Saskia will be ten minutes late and arrive like a tornado, their caramel curls windswept, cheeks as rosy as their lips. Evie will sip on an overpriced matcha and they'll exchange life updates. *I married Theo for his health insurance. It's the only reason I was able to take the fellowship.* And it'll feel good, to state it plainly. Necessary. *Good on you*, Saskia will say. They'll split the bill, then Saskia will excuse themself to use the bathroom. Five minutes later, Evie will join them.

And it'll feel good.

Her lips on Saskia's skin.

Their tongue between her legs.

Necessary.

"Did you text Eli?" she asks.

"No."

"You should!" What's meant to be a gentle nudge comes out way too enthusiastic. "I mean. I was thinking of seeing if Sass wanted to meet for brunch. So."

She may as well have said, *Why don't you go get coffee with a friend while I fuck my former coworker?*

Theo doesn't react. He just finishes his bagel, crumples the foil, and licks cream cheese from his fingers, then says, "Maybe I'll text Caro."

"Yeah?"

Evie knows that Caroline Shapiro-Huang lives in Harlem. A law student at Barnard, per Instagram. She also knows that Caro is his Saskia. They were never serious, not like Evie and Hanna's relationship. Except. Caro was *also* Theo's prom date, the person who reminded him of home during undergrad, his longest situationship.

Theo's mouth quirks. "It'd be nice to catch up."

Translation: *I can get laid, too.*

And why shouldn't he? Get laid, too. Really, she should want this for them. Because the last time her tongue tasted skin it was his, the last time lips kissed her they belonged to him, the last time she touched herself she came to images of Theo's mouth between her thighs. She needs a factory reset to deprogram the way her body reacts to him. She needs space to remind her body, her brain, to *not go there*. Because of course it's easy. Living with Theo. Coming home to Theo. Being with Theo.

This marriage is messing with her head.

It's not real.

She doesn't *want* it to be real. Evie blew up her relationship with Hanna, who she loved, *who loved her*, because she didn't want to be married. Ever. She lost Hanna. She won't lose Theo, too. Won't ruin their friendship for the potential of something more when she knows he's someone who sees marriage in his future. It's not fair to him—to either of them, really.

He's her platonic soulmate.

Platonic.

Theo stands, pulls a beanie over his ears, and tosses her duffel over his shoulder. She bundles up, then follows him to the L, dragging her suitcase. Its wheels leave an imprint. Evie isn't used to it. The wet *slosh* of her steps. Walking in shoes with no tread. Cold that whistles with a *bite* and stings her nose. Theo points out meaningful locations on their way to the train—his first apartment, the independent movie theater that screens foreign films, the elementary school where he student-taught. Evie is mesmerized by the shape of his breath, the warmth in his voice, the shift in his posture. He points to a building where he once saw children selling apples from their kitchen window, the stupidest smile on his face.

She's never seen this Theo before.

Almost *vibrating.*

In the science of sound, there's the phenomenon of resonance. It happens when an object or system is subjected to an external force or vibration that matches its natural frequency. What's wild is that when this happens, it absorbs energy from the external force and starts vibrating with a larger amplitude. And Evie thinks, for the first time in her life, that she's witnessing this phenomenon in a person. Theo's natural frequency matches New York.

New York amplifies him.

"Do you ever think about moving back?" she asks as the train approaches.

Evie doesn't hear his answer.

Just screeching brakes.

Theo still has people in the city, so they take the train to Bushwick to crash with one of them. Dev Kumar, who lived with Theo in an apartment-style suite during their freshman year at NYU. The roommate she did *not* hook up with the one and only time she visited. Really! That was Topher. Now Dev is a general surgery resident at New York-Presbyterian. He's at the hospital, so he left a key in a lockbox attached to a window grate outside. Evie assumes that his life is like an episode of *Grey's Anatomy*. Dev's apartment is small but tidy, with a laminate floor and gray walls and stainless-steel appliances. A space that would be described in a listing as "gut renovated." The second bedroom is big enough to fit a sleeper sofa that pulls out into a double bed and a Peloton that doubles as a drying rack.

Evie removes her shoes, then her socks, which are soaked through. She questions every decision that led to numb toes, so terrified that being here is a mistake, but still hopeful she'll be happy that she showed up anyway. She can't wait to tell Jules. Ask, *Is this growth?* Jules will laugh. So. Even if this entire weekend is a major disappointment . . . at least it will be a great therapy topic that isn't about Theo. Unlike the last three.

Four.

Five.

Ugh.

Evie unzips her suitcase, then immediately forgets why she unzipped her suitcase.

"Evelyn?"

She blinks. "Hmm?"

"When are we supposed to be at the synagogue?"

"Shabbat starts at five."

Avia's ascent into adulthood begins with the candle lighting at the evening Shabbat service, followed by an oneg hosted by Miriam and Mateo. It's optional, but Evie didn't suffer through an overnight flight not to attend any and every event that includes free food. It's only noon, so they have time to chill. Adjust. Evie still has time to prepare for this imminent family reunion and the nonzero chance that Naomi will be there.

But first?

Her limbs need contact with a soft surface, immediately.

"Want to watch the next episode of *Love Island*?" Theo asks.

Evie almost blurts, *I love you*. Instead, she rummages through her suitcase for sweatpants, a T-shirt, and her toiletry bag before retreating to the bathroom because travel clothes have always seen shit that clean sheets don't deserve. Dev left a stack of folded towels on the vanity, *fluffy* towels, so she opts for a quick shower to wash away the stale airplane scent from her skin. When she returns to their room, Theo's asleep on top of the duvet, dressed in clean joggers and a half-zip, *Love Island* paused on his laptop. Evie swallows. His presence on the bed accentuates how *small* it is.

Still, her bones scream, *Horizontal! Now!*

She listens.

Lies next to him.

When Evie gently removes his askew glasses, he stirs. "I'll take the couch tonight."

"Theodore." *Couch* is a generous descriptor for the two-seater futon in the living room. She pictures his scrunched, contorted limbs unable to find a comfortable position. Even in his sleep, Theo's thinking about her comfort at the expense of his own. It's ridiculous. Evie rolls her eyes. "Don't be weird."

"I'm not," Theo mumbles.

She smirks.

"*This* is weird," he continues.

"Hmm?"

"Weird that it's not weird, you know?"

Evie watches his chest rise and fall with each breath and her sleepy brain is back in Jacob's kitchen, hearing words not meant for her ears. Jacob's provocation. *We both fell for women who deserve better.* Theo's response. *You think I don't know that?* Evie's reaction. *You deserve her.*

Her.

Someone else.

Someone who wants to be a wife.

Someone who will appreciate what a fantastic husband her best friend is.

Her body tired but her brain somehow wired, Evie rolls onto her stomach to watch the buffered episode of *Love Island,* not caring that Theo will feel some kind of way that she started it without him. She doesn't just want to watch it alone. She needs to. Because since when is this even *their* show? When did that change? Nothing was supposed to change.

Evie starts the episode.

She's snoring before the opening credits roll.

Evie wakes to the scream of a siren, curled around Theo's body. Her arm draped across his torso, one leg splayed over his, what she feels right now is warm and weird. *Weird that it's not weird.* Theo doesn't move. Just holds her, his hand on her thigh as he sleeps through the noise because his body remembers the sounds of the city. She nestles into him because she's semiconscious and she likes it, being held.

Theo holding her.

Her eyes flutter open and the room is dark.

It's dark.

She rolls out of his arms, palming the mattress for her phone.

They overslept.

By a lot.

"*Theodore.*"

He rolls away from the sound of her voice, so she stands and launches a pillow at him. It flies past Theo and connects with the ceramic vase on the end table. It shatters on the floor. Shit. Theo's eyes pop open and he sits up. Blinks, then reaches for his glasses.

"Were you aiming for *me?*"

"Shut up."

She cleans up the mess she made, searching the ceramic pieces for a maker's mark and hoping that its origin is Home-Goods. Nope. DEV is scrawled on the underside of the base. When Dr. Dev Kumar isn't learning how to save lives, he is apparently a master potter. Cool. Great job.

Theo gapes at his phone. "It's *ten?*"

"Yup."

"I set an alarm."

"Me too."

She uses the bathroom. Reads the string of texts from Aunt Mir on the toilet. Evie meant to attend tonight's Shabbat service, so she should feel bad about sleeping through it. Embarrassed. Furious with herself. Anything but what she actually feels when her aunt immediately responds see u tomorrow! to her frantic so sorry!! text.

Relief.

Theo's still on the sofa bed when she reenters the room, sitting upright and reading on his phone, his legs folded like a pretzel. Evie must still be half-asleep delirious because she wants to climb onto his lap and wrap her legs around his waist. She blinks the image away just as he looks up at her and rakes a hand through his hair. "Hungry?"

She isn't.

But she nods, just to get out of this room.

Away from this bed.

She doesn't consider that it might be more dangerous to go outside, to experience New York with Theo at night. Just rebundles. Steals his beanie. Then follows him down Myrtle to Alejandro's, a tapas bar that he used to frequent with dim twinkle lights, live music, and cheap margaritas. It's a mediocre sound setup, feedback crackling the speakers in the middle of a Radiohead medley. Theo holds out his hand, and because bodies are everywhere, she takes it. They weave their way to the bar, where someone who just finished garnishing a margarita looks up, their eyes widening the moment they connect with Theo's.

"Cohen?"

Duties abandoned, the bartender ducks under the bar to embrace him. Evie *knows* she knows them, but can't immediately place this person who has tattoos covering both arms and an impeccable handlebar mustache. Until she recognizes the heart-shaped mole under their left ear, the ear that she once whispered filthy things into.

His eyes shift toward her. "Evie."

Evie needs a drink.

Right now.

She nods a quick hello, then orders a round of tequila shots and pivots to claim an empty high-top table, her heart thrumming in her ears because *what the fuck, what the fuck, what the fuck.* It throws her more than she wants to admit, eye contact with a sloppy hookup. Sex that only happened because she was hurt. Because she wanted to cause hurt in the moment. The next morning, Theo was making eggs when she emerged from Topher's bedroom. *Morning*, he said. So unfazed. Evie wasn't sure what was more mortifying. That she fucked his roommate to hurt him. Or that she fucked his roommate . . . and it *didn't* hurt him.

Theo joins her at the table.

Topher, too, balancing four tequila shots. "I'm taking a fifteen. Second round is on the house."

Cool.

Be cool.

Evie takes a shot.

Swallows the shame of a stupid, near-decade-old mistake while they catch up like adults. Because they are adults. She loosens up after the second shot. Throat warm, Evie leans in, rests her elbows on the table, and learns that the uptight business bro that Topher James once was is no more.

"Alé hired me to do the books while I was applying to be a corporate slut, then tricked me into running the place while he snowbirds in San Juan. It's cool. The old bastard deserves it. And I kind of love it? It's not corporate slut money—"

"Hedge-fund analyst," Theo translates for Evie, his breath tickling her ear.

"—but it pays the bills. Inspiration walks through the door every night. I can *music*."

"Still performing?" Theo asks.

"Writing, mostly. Producing a bit."

"Cool."

"Slippery People is due for a comeback."

Two-Drink Evie snorts. "Slippery People?"

"His band," Theo says.

Topher throws his arm around Theo. "*Our* band."

"Fuck off." Evie laughs, loud. "Theo wasn't in a band."

"Cohen." Topher's eyes are puppy-dog wounded. "She doesn't know about Slippery People?"

"It was *one* open mic."

"An iconic open mic. We made Billy Joel fucking *punk*. People are still talking about it."

"Are you people?"

"I am people."

Evie is just tipsy enough that her jaw drops, her mouth forming a perfect O. Theo shrugs sheepishly, and she tries to imagine it. She isn't listening to the conversation, instead processing information about her best friend that she doesn't already know. Theo in a band. Theo singing. *Since when?* It has no right to hurt as much as it does, this reminder that he had a whole life in New York, that there's this *gap* in their friendship. Evie didn't know New York Theo. Not really. After the Topher Incident, there was a shift. Imperceptible at first. Missed calls. Rescheduling *Survivor*. Insisting to each other that they're fine. *Just busy.* Now she thinks of the college years, the physical (and not-so-physical) distance between them as a blip. But in this moment? Learning about Slippery People?

It feels more like a chasm.

It's not fair. But in college, Evie had a whole life, too.

Without him.

So.

"I should get back," Topher says, disrupting her spiral by drumming his knuckles on the table before taking a step backward. "But really, it's good to see you both. I'm glad it worked out." His smile is genuine as he nods at the ring on her finger, then turns to Theo and claps his back. "Took you long enough."

Topher walks away.

Took you long enough.

Four words have never felt more loaded.

Evie pushes the last tiny glass filled with liquid courage toward Theo. "Slippery People . . . ?"

"Isn't a real thing."

"What did you sing?"

Theo winces, then picks up the shot. "'Piano Man.'"

"No."

"I'm so serious."

"You made 'Piano Man' . . . punk? I wish I was there."

"Me too."

He tilts his head back and Evie waits for the nose wrinkle that always accompanies the burn of alcohol. *Me too.* It's so earnest, it makes her miss a life that was never hers—late nights at Alejandro's, attending Slippery People's one-night-only performance of "Piano Man," experiencing New York with Theo.

Took you long enough.

We both fell for women who deserve better.

Come on.

"Do you ever wonder . . ." Evie doesn't know how to finish the sentence, how to articulate what she's feeling in a way that doesn't cross every boundary that protects her, protects them. Does he ever wonder what? If Evie's natural frequency matches New York, too? If in this city, their relationship would've amplified?

Her cheeks are on fire.

But two shots aren't enough to safeguard her heart from his reply.

"All the time."

Does Theo even know what he's admitting to? No way. If

he ever felt how she once felt, in the past, *a super long time ago* . . . wouldn't she know? Wouldn't she have felt it, too? No. Evie swaps tequila for water before she says (or does!) anything she'll regret, then harasses him about Slippery People until last call and it feels just like waking up in his arms. Warm and weird. Back at Dev's, Theo is asleep the moment his head sinks into a pillow. *Don't be weird.* She lies down and stares at the ceiling. Counts backward from one hundred. Is unable to crash next to him because *she is vibrating,* so she takes a pillow and her phone to the couch.

Puts distance between them.

And then, only then, is she still enough to sleep.

NEW YORK, SPRING BREAK, FRESHMAN YEAR

Evie

She turns nineteen in the sky, on her way to Theo.

It's March. Pisces season. Her first time on a plane.

Yesterday, while texting during *Survivor*, Theo asked her what she wanted for her birthday.

You, she thought.

You.

You.

You.

Twenty-four hours later, Evie's thirty-three thousand feet in the air because she can be. It was impulsive, purchasing a plane ticket without telling Theo. Only because she knew what his reaction would be. *Are you sure you can handle that?* Lately he speaks to her as if she's made of porcelain. She's not. In fact, after a near year working with Dr. Griffith, her gastroenterologist, to figure out what combination of medications seems to best manage her brand of Crohn's with minimal side effects, Evie feels okay.

Finally.

No, her brain corrects. *For now.*

The last time Theo saw her? She was not okay. Still in

physical therapy. Still flaring. Still processing that Crohn's disease is a chronic illness, that *chronic* means *forever*. But now? She feels good enough to be impulsive and it's terrifying and exhilarating, to feel okay enough to want and be able to have, even just for a moment. Evie spent so much of her eighteenth year wanting impossible things. New York. Dance. Cheese. She *loved* cheese. Evie dreamed about baked brie. Yearned to point her toes without hissing in pain. Ached to experience life in New York with her best friend. Next month marks one year since the fall that led to a diagnosis that upended her life and clarified it all at once. Today, Evie has made peace with vegan cheese. Her ankle no longer hisses but whimpers. She's in clinical remission. So when snow fell in New York as her spring break began . . . it felt like a sign to go. Experience snow.

Upon deplaning, Evie learns it's disgusting.

City snow.

She hauls her suitcase onto a crowded E train, toes frozen from stepping in a dirt slush puddle. Someone looks up from the Sunday *Times* crossword puzzle to shoot her a *look* for having the audacity to sit in a seat reserved for people with disabilities. She averts her eyes. Doesn't have the energy to tell him to fuck all the way off. Tears sting the corners of her eyes.

From the cold.

Not from the overwhelm of it all.

Not because she almost shit herself in search of a functioning bathroom at JFK.

Not because a kind grandma-aged woman in a green tracksuit helped her swipe her subway card after *five failed attempts*, then introduced herself as Evelyn. *I'm Evelyn, too,* she said. Grandma Evelyn replied, *Of course you are, hon,* then took her hand and led her to a map. With a chipped lime-green-polished index finger, she traced the line to West Fourth Street.

To Theo.

She follows Grandma Evelyn's instructions, earbuds in but music muted because she's more interested in the sounds of the subway. Rusty brakes scream as they approach a station. Static conductor announcements her ears strain to hear. Conversations among friends, lovers, strangers. Evie wipes a furious tear from her cheek because just a year ago, she was so certain that this cacophony would be hers. Daily.

But then she fell.

Evie doesn't remember hitting the ground, just the sound of her scream.

Knowing it was bad.

Theo carrying her into the emergency room, where she was admitted for a fractured ankle. A nurse entering her curtained-off "room" with vials. So many vials. Resisting. Not understanding the need to draw blood with such an obvious injury. Pep's assurance. *It's just protocol, Sweets.* Theo's hand in hers as the needle pierced her skin.

Evie hates needles.

The bloodwork came back *funky* and that necessitated more bloodwork that kept her in the hospital for two weeks of tests, scans, and a colonoscopy that ultimately led to a diagnosis. Crohn's. A chronic inflammatory bowel disease. It explained so much. Stomachaches so painful that she'd regularly be sent home from school. Pain that her pediatrician attributed to *menses*, even when she explained that these pains were sharp and random and not at all in sync with her cycle. Sleeping in until two every Sunday but always fading in class come Monday ... and believing that was normal because doctors insisted she was *healthy* and wouldn't anyone who spent at least twenty hours a week pushing her body to its limit always be bone-tired?

Evie learned it was not.

Normal.

Losing dance, the stillness that was required of her body to heal, was already painful.

Adding an autoimmune disease on top of it?

Well.

It was so much.

So.

Evie isn't in New York because she couldn't be.

Not physically.

Not financially.

Summer was two surgeries to reconstruct her ankle. Evie opted to start classes at UCLA in the spring. Gave her body, her brain, her *heart* time to heal. Rendered what should've been her first semester of college a monotonous blur of physical therapy and various cocktails of medications to reduce the inflammation in her colon paired with so many supplements because her body has trouble absorbing a lot of critical nutrients. She started seeing Jules, a therapist Dr. Griffith referred her to. Pain ebbed and flowed. Pain that Dr. Griffith and Jules validated. Pain that Evie now understood was not a normal part of being a person but would continue to be *her* normal.

One moment from last fall is burned into her brain.

Theo's voice pressed against her ear, soft and tentative through the phone.

"I've been thinking . . . maybe I'll transfer next semester."

"What?"

"It makes more sense. UCLA. It has an amazing education program. In-state tuition. I'd be there for my mom. We would—"

"Theo. No."

"What?"

"You have to stay."

"Evelyn—"

"I will hate you if you don't stay."

Evie is jolted from the memory as the train pulls into West Fourth Street. She exits the station, then follows her phone to Washington Square Park in search of a face she only knows from photos. Dev Kumar waits for her by the fountain, hands stuffed in his pockets. When their eyes meet, he smiles and she's so relieved she feels like she could cry. *Do not cry.* Evie sent Theo's suitemate and closest college friend a message on Facebook as soon as she booked her flight because while she hates nothing more than asking someone for help, she needed an assist to pull off this surprise. His answer was immediate, gotchu np!, but she didn't trust it until his warm brown eyes met hers.

She never trusts it.

People showing up for her.

"Evie?" Dev asks.

She throws her arms around his neck. "I can't believe I'm meeting you."

He laughs. "Honestly? Same."

Dev drags her suitcase through the slushy park to the dorm on its west side. They chat pre-reqs and *Survivor* and it's easy, small talk with Dev. Theo got him into *Survivor*. She leaves her ID with security and follows Dev through the turnstile, into the elevator, up to his room. *Their room.* It's clean but cluttered, the shared living area, with a small flat-screen television and half-finished puzzles covering the coffee table. Dev unbundles, tossing his puffer and scarf over a kitchen chair, then asks Evie if she wants anything to drink.

"Water or Bud Light?"

Evie laughs. "Water, please."

He pours water from a Brita and nods toward Theo's room. "I'm pretty sure he's in class, but feel free to chill in the meantime."

Her reply is interrupted by his phone ringing. She sees the name on the screen. *Ammi*. Dev retreats to his room, shrugging, like, *You know how moms are*, and then she's alone and once again on the verge of tears because Naomi is somewhere in New York and has no clue that Evie is so close and it's so ridiculous, this primal *want* to understand Dev. Her desire to have a mother who calls too much, to have a mother who calls at all.

She chugs the water.

Swallows her Naomi feelings, then places the *Lost* mug in the sink and kills time excavating Theo's room. Even if she didn't help him select his sheets, she would know which side of the room is his based on the collection of posters hanging above his bed. Billy Joel at MSG and Camp Half-Blood. *The Song of Achilles* lies open on his bed and the sight of it splits her heart in half. Last week, Evie sent a string of incoherent texts about how Madeline Miller ruined her life and now he's already halfway through the book and with this tangible proof that he misses her, too, she feels so relieved and incredibly stupid all at once.

Evie sits on Theo's bed.

Next to the book.

She hasn't seen him in six months, but when he asked her what she wanted for her birthday she knew she needed to go to New York, to Washington Square Park, to his dorm, to his bed. Knew she needed to be wherever he is, *right now*. But now that she's here? Evie hasn't thought up an explanation for *why* apart from the embarrassing truth.

I think I'm in love with you.

Before those words even have the chance to alter their trajectory, Theo stumbles backward into his bedroom attached by the lips to someone else and time slows down into the longest, most mortifying five seconds of her life. He slams the door shut and presses her against it. Her hands cover his ass. His mouth is on her neck. Caro's neck.

It's *Caro.*

Theo's ...

Caro.

"*Fuck.*"

Her voice sends him backward.

Theo blinks, so confused. "Evelyn?"

She stands so fast her ankle hisses. "Oh my God. I'm *so* sorry."

Caro adjusts the hem of her shirt and fills the silence that follows. "Hey! Theo didn't mention you were visiting."

There's no edge to her tone, not a single hint of frustration that she's been cock-blocked or an ounce of jealousy. Caroline Shapiro-Huang has never felt threatened by their friendship. Evie, on the other hand, feels something akin to fury that Theo failed to mention his on-again-off-again situationship with Caro seems to be very much *on* and she wants to scream, to vomit, to ...

"You're ... ?"

"Leaving!"

... get the *fuck* out of here.

Evie dashes past them toward her coat, toward her shoes, toward the door. Lies to Theo's face. *I'm crashing with Mir and Mateo.* Hates that she wants him to say, *Don't go.* Hates even more that he doesn't. He just looks at her like, *Please let this be a horrible dream.* So Evie leaves. Gets as far as across the street and into the park before she curls into herself on a park bench, her head between her knees until the nausea subsides. Then she cries in the snow. *God.* She's such an idiot.

"Hey. Are you okay?" Evie looks up, her swollen eyes meeting a set of concerned, piercing blue ones. There's something familiar about this boy in a buttoned-up peacoat, his shaggy brown hair poking out of his beanie. Evie can't place him, but he recognizes her immediately. "You're Theo's Evie."

"I'm not Theo's anything."

He holds out a glove-covered hand. "Hey, Not Theo's Anything. I'm Topher. His roommate."

"*Oh.*" Evie sniffles as she takes his hand. "Hi, Topher His Roommate. I'm fine. Really."

Topher frowns, then pulls her to her feet. "You're shivering. Come on. Let me buy you a coffee. Or tea. Or whatever your preferred hot beverage is."

"You really don't—"

"I'll use dining dollars. So it's basically free. At least, that's what they want you to think."

"They?"

"The System."

Evie's laugh makes Topher smile . . . and it's cute. *He's* cute. She lets him buy her a chai with dining dollars, then spends the entire day with Topher His Roommate, her phone set to *do not disturb*. Later that night, he takes her to a bar that doesn't card and she dances (well, *sways*) for the first time since she fell. For the first time with a partner who isn't Theo. And when Topher's lips press against hers, she deepens the kiss because she likes that he doesn't know that she's broken and Evie is so desperate to feel something, *anything*, that isn't this persistent yearning for everything and everyone she cannot have. Tomorrow, she'll laugh off the poor timing of her surprise. Maybe spend the day with Theo. But for now, she kisses Topher and lets go of it all. New York. Dance. Cheese.

Naomi.

Theo.

Because Evie is nineteen.

And so done with wanting impossible things.

16

New York makes Theo brave.

Giddy.

A little bit delusional. He wakes to the sound of his alarm, a starfish on the sofa bed. Groggy, eyes still closed, his arms search for Evelyn. As if she's supposed to be next to him. She isn't. He finds her curled up on the futon, cocooned in the duvet, and when he nudges her she hisses at him like a cat. Theo runs to the bodega across the street for coffee and chai and thinks that somewhere in the multiverse, this is his life.

New York is home.

Coffee is across the street.

Evelyn is his wife.

She's curling her hair in the bathroom when he returns with caffeine. She's in a jade satin slip dress with ruching at one side. It's only partially zipped, enough of her back exposed for him to deduce that she's not wearing a bra.

"Zip me?"

"Yeah."

Theo places his coffee on the counter immediately with

this permission to touch her. Feels like he's seventeen and Evelyn's asked him to help with a costume. It's so soft. Her dress. The zipper's jammed, so he works to gently coax the satin to prevent it from snagging. His fingers skim her skin and she jerks away.

"*Shit*, Theodore. You're freezing."

"It's stuck."

Once she stills, he's able to free the zipper with a gentle downward pull before gliding it all the way up slowly, lingering in this moment. Indulging. Because he's in New York with Evelyn and he can't remember the last time he had as much fun as he did while learning that Topher James manages a bar in Bushwick, witnessing Evelyn throw back tequila like water, reminiscing about Slippery People. Last night, Theo felt the end-of-year fog lifting at last. December is always rough. His kids are restless. *Survivor* ends. Holidays are just ... super fucking sad. During the school break, he finds himself trying new hobbies that never stick. Painting. Pottery. Chess. The alternative is sitting with the sadness. He and Evelyn usually deal with the December Blues together. But this past month, he felt like he barely saw her.

At this point he isn't sure who's avoiding who or why they've been avoiding each other. Theo isn't one to read into signs, but bumping into Topher at Alejandro's sure as hell feels like one. His former roommate may have been a catalyst, but Theo never blamed him for the aftermath of Evelyn's surprise visit. Really, Theo had no one to blame but himself for the weeks, months, years of awkwardness that stretched between them because it was easier to be fine, to be busy, to avoid acknowledging how goddamn *gutted* he felt when she emerged from Toph's bedroom.

Now?

Here?

Theo just wants to stop.

Avoiding.

"Thanks."

His eyes meet hers in the mirror.

Eyes that match a dress that is simple and stunning.

All the time.

Even tequila-buzzed Evelyn couldn't get the words out, but Theo knew what she was asking. *He knows her.* And she needed to know that even if she couldn't ask the question, he could answer it. Easily. She pivots so she's facing him, and somewhere in the multiverse he takes her mouth with his, unzips this simple, stunning dress, then drops to his knees, and they skip the bat mitzvah.

Instead, he watches her remove her wedding band.

Fuck.

When did he start thinking of it as *hers?*

"I've been thinking . . . we don't have to pretend here."

"Why have we been pretending at all?"

Evelyn flushes, then shrugs. "I've kind of lost the plot myself. Can we stop? I mean. I suppose in exchange for unreal health insurance you can still be Mr. Evelyn Bloom at school. Though it could probably be considered workplace discrimination that marrying me changed, like, how people treat you at work. But—"

He cuts off her babbling. "Okay."

"Okay?"

Theo nods, then removes his ring. Changes into his suit, pops two Advil with his daily dose of Lexapro, then attends a bat mitzvah both jet-lagged and hungover, an ideal combination for spending the morning in a synagogue. He drifts during the service. Even at his best, he's never able to stay present while listening to prayers in a language that he doesn't understand. Theo's Judaism has always been less a religious practice, more a spiritual one. Evelyn wipes a tear from her cheek as Avia is called to the Torah. Every time the rabbi calls the congregation to stand, she looks over her shoulder.

Confirms that no, Naomi is not here.

Theo isn't surprised.

When it's time to recite the Mourner's Kaddish, Theo stands and recites along. Yitgadal v'yitkadash sh'mei raba. You're technically only supposed to recite kaddish for a parent during the first year of mourning. But Theo hasn't been in a synagogue since Lori died. So as far as he's concerned, he owes it to her. And though he isn't religious, there's something comforting about the ritual. Evelyn reaches for his hand and weaves her fingers through his. Presses their palms together. And then it is over and he's seated and she doesn't let go, not until the ceremony concludes and she's on her feet.

"Let's go."

"Without saying mazel tov?"

Her eyes shift toward the bima, where Avia, Miriam, and Mateo are surrounded by family and friends. "Later."

Having hours of time to kill before the party, Theo and Evelyn get falafel for lunch at Mamoun's and see a movie at the Angelika. She chooses a pretentious independent film about chess that's garnering awards buzz, then sleeps through the entire thing. After her twenty-five-dollar nap, they walk to the venue. The Bowery Hotel. It's a short walk from the theater. Evelyn wears Theo's wool peacoat because it's long and her dress is short. He doesn't mind. He misses everything about New York. Even its weather.

Miriam and Mateo greet guests at the entrance to the ballroom. Mateo is a mop of gray curls, a well-tailored suit, shorter than Miriam in heels. She's dressed in gold sequins, her arms covered in botanical tattoos wrapping around Evelyn in a hug.

"I can't believe you came all this way," Miriam says.

"I wanted to," she says, her smile shy. "It's small. Our family. You know? And Avia is awesome. So."

Mateo chuckles. "Avia *is* awesome."

Polite laughter fills the space before fizzling into awkward silence. Theo hates that Evelyn flew across the country for people who don't seem to have anything to say to her as much as he hates awkward silence.

So he says, "Hi."

Evelyn blinks. "Oh! Aunt Mir, Uncle Mat, this is my . . . do you remember Theo?"

"The plus-one." Theo holds out his hand. "Mazels. It was a beautiful ceremony."

"It was, wasn't it?" Miriam says, then raises her eyebrows at her niece. "Are you two . . . ?"

"Friends."

A wrinkle forms between Miriam's eyebrows. "Oh. I thought . . . Naomi told us you got married?"

"What?"

Mateo snorts, nudging Miriam. "Told you it was bullshit."

"Is Mom coming?"

"Supposedly." Miriam shrugs. "You know how Naomi is. Margot's career always comes first."

Theo frowns.

Career?

Margot is *six*.

Before Evelyn can respond, another middle-aged couple in a cocktail dress and well-fitting suit pull Miriam and Mateo's focus from their niece.

"We'll catch up later," Miriam promises, squeezing Evelyn's shoulder.

"In the meantime, enjoy the open bar," Mateo says.

And then their backs turn and there's nothing to do but be at a bat mitzvah surrounded by strangers. Avia's theme is Broadway at the Bowery. Theo and Evelyn are assigned to the *Mamma Mia!* table, seated with the nieces and nephews from Mateo's side of the family. Lina, Samuel, and Binta, who are hilarious and loud and love to finish one another's sentences. Evelyn flails through the small talk. Refers to herself as a glorified intern. *Fellow*, Theo corrects, yelling over an electropop song that's giving him a migraine. Everything about this night is so opulent and overstimulating. Activities include a photo booth, a VR station, three caricature artists. Evelyn orders a blueberry banana smoothie from a Jamba Juice cart. Theo feels like he's in a movie.

Back at their table, she sips on her smoothie. "I didn't think about this part."

"What?"

"People-ing." Evelyn stirs her straw. "With so many . . . I don't know, family-adjacent people?"

"It's a lot."

"Avia asked me in the smoothie line if I'm friends with her parents. Um. First of all, how dare Disneyland not be a core memory? Second, how old does she think I am?"

Theo laughs.

She lightly shoves his shoulder in faux offense. "Shut up. I just . . . hoped it would feel different. Being here."

"How does it feel?"

Evelyn shrugs. "Honestly? Like a waste of time."

She excuses herself to use the bathroom, leaving him alone. Theo's here to be her best friend, so he stands and approaches

DJ Schmuel because he can't fix her family feelings, but he *can* request a song. And thirty minutes later, when it blasts through the speakers, he can take Evelyn's hand and pull her to the dance floor because one cannot hear "Cupid Shuffle" and not *do* the cupid shuffle. It's just a fact. He's relieved when Avia and her countless friends populate the dance floor. Thrilled that "Cupid Shuffle" is timeless. Elated when Evelyn laughs. Sometimes he thinks he'd be content if that was his only purpose in life, to make her laugh. "Cupid Shuffle" becomes "Dancing Queen" and Evelyn takes his hand, pulls him closer to her, and he feels so helpless, so *hopeless*, as she places his hands on her hips and wraps her arms around his neck.

"I miss this." She flushes, those three words a confession. "Dancing with you."

He stares at her, his heart in his throat because it's not something they talk about.

Dance.

But maybe Evelyn is done avoiding, too.

"Ev—"

"Evelyn!"

Whatever Theo is about to say is cut off and it's so disorienting that she's no longer in his arms. She's wrapped in Naomi, who's dressed in a black Gucci jumpsuit, long pink nails pressing into her back. Theo doesn't take his eyes off Evelyn. Feels the most irrational *rage*, witnessing Naomi embrace her like . . . well, like she's her *mother*.

"I can't believe I heard that you'd be here from Miriam," Naomi says.

"I texted you," Evelyn says.

Naomi's forehead doesn't move when she frowns. "Did you?"

"Maman," says a tiny voice. Margot. Evelyn always insists

that Margot is Gen's doppelgänger, but Theo sees his best friend, too. "Je veux une glace."

"Un moment, mon amour," Naomi says to Margot, then looks at Evelyn. "We're raising her bilingual."

Evelyn's eyebrow twitches. "Oh."

"Good thing, too, because this little star had a callback for a Bonne Maman partnership." Naomi looks down at Margot, who is reaching for her mother's hand. "Mon chéri, this is Evelyn. Your sister."

Margot looks up and offers a small, timid wave with her free hand.

Evelyn isn't a sister to her, but a stranger.

"Hi." Evelyn squats and holds out her hand. Margot places a tiny palm in hers. "Your nails are so pretty."

"Pink is my favorite color."

Evelyn smiles. "Mine too."

"What's your favorite ice cream flavor?" Margot asks.

"Mint chip."

Margot gasps. "No *way*."

Evelyn's giggle is *so much*.

She stands. "This is my friend, Theo."

Theo waves. "Enchanté."

It's a mistake. Margot starts babbling to him in French. Theo doesn't speak French. He nods along and feigns comprehension until Margot spots Jean-Paul at the ice cream station and runs toward her father, allowing Theo to rejoin the adult conversation as Naomi is sharing with Evelyn that they're considering moving back to France. For Margot's education. A waiter walks by with a tray of champagne and Naomi picks up a flute. Immediately stains the rim with hot pink lipstick.

"Jean-Paul is from Toulouse and he had the most *charming* childhood. We want that for Margot."

Evelyn's smile is saccharine. "Of course."

Naomi's lips press together. "Evelyn. I did the best I could for you and Immy. I hope you know that."

"I do."

"Do you?"

"*Yes.*"

Witnessing this exchange, Theo's at a loss. He's used to dealing with parental bullshit, but at least Jacob's is direct. With Naomi, it's not so much what she says, but the way she says it. Her flat, passive-aggressive affect before she pulls Evelyn into another hug, then shifts to embrace Theo. He stiffens at the unsolicited body contact.

"It's wonderful to see you again."

Theo lies, "You too."

"How long are you in town?"

"We fly home tomorrow."

Naomi sighs. "I wish I knew. You could've stayed with us."

"I texted you—"

"But I'm not surprised. I mean, I found out that my first-born is married on *Facebook*." She chuckles, then raises her glass. "Mazel tov, by the way! I'm happy for you. Of course I am." Naomi sips. "You look good, Evelyn." She takes a step backward, her eyes scanning, appraising. "Healthy. Have you been working out?"

Okay.

Nope.

Fuck this.

Theo's rage is entirely rational. "Evelyn always looks good."

Naomi looks taken aback. "I didn't mean—"

"*Maman.*"

"Let me just . . ." Relief is palpable in her expression as she's pulled toward Margot's voice, emitting a tender sigh. "I have to do the toppings. Jean-Paul always messes up the sprinkles-to-whipped-cream ratio."

And then she's at the ice cream station. Evelyn watches Naomi and Margot. Doesn't react. Performs indifference at Margot's giggle as Naomi *boops* whipped cream on her nose. Theo has an intimate relationship with the particular pain of grieving a relationship with someone who's still very much alive. Grieving the hope of it all. It's awful. Theo can't perform indifference.

Instead, he takes her hand. "Let's get out of here."

"I'm sorry." Evelyn kicks off her shoes as soon as they step foot in Dev's empty apartment.

On the counter, there's a note.

ON CALL. ANOTHER OVERNIGHT. BREAKFAST AM?

Evelyn sits on the end of the sofa bed and presses the heels of her hands to her eyes. "I always thought she didn't want to be *a* mother. But . . . now I just don't think she wanted to be *our* mother. Mine or Imogen's. I tried so hard to be good for her, Theo."

"I know."

"And . . . I'm here because a part of me *wanted* to see her. It's so *embarrassing.*" Evelyn wipes the tears from her cheeks. "Knowing something is impossible but still wanting it." She sighs, then tucks her feet up under her. "I'm sorry I dragged you here."

"At least we got to 'Cupid Shuffle'?"

Evelyn snorts.

Theo sits next to her, pressing his thumb to her cheek. "It's not embarrassing to want better from the people who are the only reason we're even on this fucked-up planet. Also? Don't be sorry. I'm not. In addition to cupid shuffling, I got to spend time in my favorite place with my favorite person."

Her smile is small. "You should be here. In New York. Why aren't you?"

Theo isn't sure how to respond to such an infuriating question. *We don't have to pretend here,* she'd said this morning as she slipped Lori's wedding band off her finger. *I don't want to pretend here. Right now?*

Neither does he.

"You're seriously asking me that?"

"I mean. I get why you came home. Obviously. But . . ." Evelyn's voice trails off. Theo's eyes are transfixed on her lips. How glossy they are. "Being here? Seeing *you* here? I guess I just don't understand why you've stayed in LA."

"Don't you?"

It surprises him, the challenge in his voice.

Her brow furrows. "You love New York."

"I do."

He whispers this confession, as if it's not obvious. Silence stretches between them. He could—*should*—fill it with bull-shit excuses. It's what he'd do at home.

But New York makes him brave, so he continues, "It'd be impossible. Leaving again."

"Because of work? You can find another job—"

"God, Evelyn. No. Not leaving my *job*. Leaving *you*."

Her eyes widen.

"Ev—"

But before he can walk those words back, she leans in and

presses her perfect lips against his. Wraps her arms around him and runs her fingers through his curls, her nails scraping against the nape of his neck. She tastes like vanilla. When her teeth graze his bottom lip and bite softly he moans, then braces himself for their brains to catch up to their bodies.

They always do.

But she just smiles against his mouth, then keeps kissing him like he's a goddamn revelation. Theo's palms stay pressed against the mattress. He doesn't dare touch her when she climbs onto his lap and tells himself he still has an ounce of self-control when the reality is he is so far gone and it's so sexy. Evelyn's tongue in his mouth. Evelyn's hands in his hair. Evelyn grinding against him, her dress hiked up to her hips, her mouth lowering to his neck as she reaches for his belt buckle, her fingers teasing him.

She pulls away.

Her eyes shift to his hands, which have sunken into the memory foam. And it's devastating, the furrow of her brow. She bites her swollen lip and lowers her gaze. "I'm . . . I thought. Fuck. You don't want—"

"Evelyn." Theo presses the pad of his thumb under her chin, tilts it up so her eyes meet his. "I want."

"Yeah?"

"Yes."

"Then fucking Christ, Theo. *Touch me.*"

17

"W here?"

"*Theodore.*"

"Where?" he repeats, voice low.

In the stretch of silence that follows, their eye contact doesn't break. Evie wonders if this is another lapse of judgment that they'll spend the next five years not talking about. Just like the first, last, *only* other time she climbed onto her best friend's lap in a moment of weakness. Their hearts beat loud as she searches Theo's expression for any indication that this desire is a fleeting moment. *So what if it is?*

"*Evelyn.*" It's thrilling and terrifying, the desperate way he says her name. "Show me. *Please.*"

Please.

With that one word, his soft plea, she crashes into his lips, takes his hands in hers, and shows him. Starts at her thighs, his touch so light, so tentative, as she guides his fingers up, up, up and under her dress. She keeps one of his hands on her hip as she skims the other across the hem of her seamless, practical nude underwear. Sucks on his lower lip. In response to the pressure of fingers sinking into the flesh of her hip, she teases herself with his hand. Allows only his fingertips to dip under the fabric of her underwear.

"*Ev.*"

She knows it's reckless, letting him touch her like this.

But.

She wants him.

Sitting on his lap, she can feel his erection through the thin layers of fabric that separate them. His body wants her, too. It feels so good. Wanting. Being wanted. Evie releases his hands. Needs her own to remove his suit jacket, to loosen his tie, to work the buttons of his shirt because it's unbearable how many layers are between them. She rises onto her knees to remove his button-up, her execution clumsy. Sort of like the first pass of new choreography. Evie's fingers run through the hair that lightly covers his chest before pressing her palm against his skin to feel his heart's erratic thrum. She always loved learning choreography. The permission it gave them to touch each other without it meaning anything.

Touching Theo doesn't have to mean anything.

Their lips part.

Theo looks up at her as his chest rises and falls in her hand. "If we're . . . If this is . . ." Evie doesn't move. Doesn't speak. Waits for him to say it. Again. *We can't.* He bites his lower lip and even the wrinkle in his brow is so tender. "Tomorrow?" he continues. "I don't want to pretend it didn't happen."

It's the first time he has ever acknowledged it.

The last time.

When she was intoxicated by grief and he tasted like peppermint schnapps.

"Theo—"

"*Please*," he whispers. "It's exhausting. Pretending I don't want you."

Her heart stutters.

You.

You.

You.

Evie wraps her arms around his neck. "I'm exhausted, too."

She hopes that's enough of an answer and is relieved when he claims her mouth with his, kissing her with reckless abandon. Evie has spent so many years downplaying her attraction, convincing herself it's normal for a filthy thought to enter her head if he looks at her a certain way, insisting that this could never happen. But it is. Tomorrow is a tomorrow problem. Tonight? She has Theo.

His hands return to her body, but he keeps the layer of satin between their skin as they roam up her silhouette. Theo is slow with his touch. Intentional. He cups one of her breasts. Brushes her nipple with a thumb. *Such a tease*. Evie can tease, too. She reaches between them and traces the outline of his cock, then bites his lip before breaking the kiss and bringing her hand between her own legs. *God*. Evie is warm. Wet. Out of control. So turned on as Theo watches her touch herself with the same attentive expression that he once gave to learning choreography, then lowers his hands to her hip dips as she settles back onto his lap. She used to be self-conscious of the divot where her hips meet her thighs.

Now?

Evie grinds against him in response, loving that his hands naturally gravitate to this part of her body. Every time their lips touch, she considers it a tragedy that she hasn't spent her whole life kissing Theo Cohen. In the morning, she'll remember every reason why . . . but right now? His tongue silences every logical brain cell, allowing this untenable want to bloom into something dangerous.

He bunches satin in his fists.

A question.

Evie nods against his lips.

An answer.

Theo unzips her dress, and in one fluid motion, it's over her head and on the floor. She shivers, freezing and on fire as he flips her onto her back. She closes her eyes. Anticipates how good Theo will feel on top of her. Is impatient. Where is he? Why is he not on top of her? Frustrated, her eyes flutter open to find him looking at her like he wants to savor every moment of this. Evie's breath catches in her throat as she watches his eyes move down her body with intention, lingering on the swell of her breasts, the music notes on her ribs, the ink on her hip that's only partially exposed.

"A new tattoo?"

"No."

Evie lowers the band of her underwear just enough to reveal a tiny torch etched into her right hipbone. Her second tattoo. An impulsive decision made at eighteen, a week after he boarded a plane to New York. She chose a discreet placement to permanently etch him onto her skin. Theo curses under his breath. Of course he recognizes the symbol from their favorite show.

"Evelyn Bloom, if I had known you had a literal torch for me . . ."

She rolls her eyes. "Don't make it weird."

He laughs.

It's rich and rare.

Possibly her favorite sound in the world.

Looking up at Theo's lamplit face, fixating on a single rogue curl that has fallen over his forehead, she's never felt more exposed. More safe. More sure. Because though she spent money she doesn't have, on a family she barely has, to be in a city that isn't hers, that decision is the only reason Evie is here now.

With Theo.

Under Theo.

"Do you even have any idea how obsessed I am with your tattoos?"

Yes.

She shrugs.

Traces the ink along his left biceps. "Nope."

Then decides she's done. Teasing Theo. Teasing herself. She grabs his wrist and pulls him toward her, the want transcending into a physical, aching need to be close to him. Theo's mouth drifts across her jaw, trailing down her neck and settling on her collarbone as his hand dips back into her underwear.

"*Ev.*" Theo groans the moment his fingers come into contact with her slickness. "*Fuck.*"

She buckles into his hand as his thumb strokes her clit, the pressure perfect. His mouth makes its way down her body while his fingers continue to work. When his tongue rolls across her nipple as two fingers slide inside her she *whimpers . . .* and it doesn't make sense. Evie knows her body. It's not . . . she doesn't just *come.* Evie keeps a miniature vibrator on her at all times. Refuses to feel any kind of shame that her body typically requires its assistance during sex.

So.

How is Theo about to wreck her with a *hand job?*

"God, you're tight," he murmurs against her skin.

Then presses a kiss to the torch on her hip and it's too much. She bites her lip to suppress the *gasp* as she comes undone and her first thought after riding his hand, riding her orgasm, is *More, more, more.* Then, *Why are his pants still on?* She fixes that. Removes his briefs in the process, too. Oops. Theo has a fantastic cock. She strokes the length and revels in the sounds he makes. The sharp *inhale* when she brushes her thumb across the head before guiding him toward her clit.

"*Evelyn.* Are you trying to kill me? I . . ." Theo pulls back, his eyebrows crinkling. ". . . don't have a condom."

"I have an IUD."

His expression shifts. "Oh."

"Also, I'm good," she continues. "My most recent test was at my annual a couple weeks ago, but I haven't hooked up with anyone since before . . ."

Evie isn't sure what's worse. The end of that sentence or the fact that she can't finish it.

"Me either," Theo admits. "And I'm good, too."

"Cool."

"You're so—"

She pulls his mouth back to hers, certain that talking too much is going to ruin this fun, good, terrifying thing. Evie doesn't want to ruin it, instead choosing to cut off his words with a kiss and continue to show him what she wants.

You.

You.

You.

"Fuck me," Evie whispers in his ear after their lips part, her teeth nibbling the lobe. "Theodore. *Please.*"

"*Ev.*" Theo turns his head so their noses touch. "It's not going to be . . ." He pauses. Even naked and flustered, Theo considers his words. "I just. I'm already pretty close."

"Yeah?"

With the exhilarating admission, she rolls against him.

Guides him inside her as she pulls his mouth back to hers and shifts under him. Wrapping her legs around his torso, they find a rhythm. He feels . . . she feels . . . *so much*, being fucked by her best friend, who is always so gentle, so careful. Who is losing control. Who groans into her mouth when he comes. Her nails sink into shoulders slick with sweat, desperate to hold on to something. Not something. *Him.*

And it feels like it was always a matter of time.

This.

Yet Evie didn't see it coming.

After they clean themselves up, she curls into Theo.

He runs a hand through his sex-mussed curls. "I feel like a fucking teenager."

Evie laughs. Almost wishes that they were teenagers again so she could turn back time and choose New York the moment she was able to make a choice like that. Choose him. Not push him toward this city, toward this dream, away from her. But he came back. Confessed that it feels impossible, the idea of leaving her again.

Impossible.

Evie falls asleep in her best friend's arms, letting herself, just once, have this impossible thing.

18

One weekend in New York with Evelyn, and Theo is seventeen again. Obsessed with his best friend. Attempting to play it cool. Agonizing over how to tell her. If he even should. Every messy feeling he's spent the last decade denying was unearthed the moment he pressed his mouth against that fucking tattoo. Now home, they don't talk about what that weekend meant. If it meant anything at all. But at least they don't pretend it didn't happen. In the week since, *casual* has become their new favorite word. Before school, breakfast ends with Theo casually lifting Evelyn onto the kitchen island and fingering her until she comes. Before bed, Evelyn wrings her hair out with a towel after shower sex and laughs. *Who knew we'd be so good at casual, Theodore?*

Casual.

Casual.

Casual.

Theo falls asleep with her in his arms and wakes up alone and tells himself that's enough.

Safe.

What he wants.

It's Martin Luther King Jr. Day, a Monday holiday that allows Theo to sleep in. When he finally rolls out of bed at 8:05, Evelyn is rinsing blueberries at the sink in an oversized T-shirt that barely covers her ass. So casual. Theo is absolutely not hard at the sight. "Morning."

"Hey." Evelyn places the colander down and spins to face him. Leans back and presses the palms of her hands against the quartz countertop. "Breakfast?"

His eyebrows rise. "You're cooking?"

"I'm adding blueberries to my Cheerios."

Theo laughs, then reaches above her to grab two ceramic bowls from the cabinet. "Tell me more."

"I've spent years perfecting the cereal-to-milk ratio."

"Have you?"

She shoves him. "Stop laughing as if soggy cereal isn't—"

Theo cuts Evelyn off with a casual kiss because that's something they do now. Casually. Casual is his desire to always be kissing her. Casual is her soft gasp as he lifts her so she's sitting on the countertop. She laughs against his lips, breaking the kiss as he tries to deepen it and pressing her hands against his chest. "I have to go to the studio."

He groans. "You're working today?"

"I have a project to wrap before Sadie is back from Sundance."

"When's she back?"

"Tomorrow."

"Ev."

"I know." She bites her lip, then smirks. "I need to stop letting my husband distract me."

Theo swallows.

Hard.

Evelyn's eyes sparkle with amusement as they meet his. "Your face, Theodore. Don't worry. I'm going to crush this assignment and we'll be heading toward divorce faster than you can say *irreconcilable differences.*"

"Right." Theo nods, ignoring whatever that word—*divorce*—is making him feel. "What's the project?"

"It's just, like, a two-minute sequence from some kid's show. *Sarabeth & Jack vs. the Universe?*"

"Wait. Seriously?"

"You know it?"

Theo may or may not have shed a tear over a season two arc involving Jack's relationship with his dad. "My students love that show. And the graphic novels."

Evelyn pops a blueberry into her mouth. "Want to come with me?"

"Really?"

She nods. "We can record the session for your class."

"That feels like an NDA violation."

"Definitely. But I don't see the harm if you show it to them after the episode airs? I'm pretty sure you need all the cool points you can get, Mr. Theodore."

She's not wrong.

Evelyn pushes off the counter with her hands to stand, then pours two bowls of Cheerios. Mixes in the blueberries, then adds the milk. Skim for him, almond for her. A blueberry careens past his face every time he tries to distract her and it's all so domestic. They may have stopped wearing rings, but they're still pretending. After breakfast, Evelyn playfully bumps his hip on the way to her bedroom. Returns with pants on. A tragedy. She's dressed like she's about to spend the day at Miss Stella's—black yoga pants that flare out at the ankles, an olive-green tank top over a sports bra, an oversize cream cardigan layered on top. Her hair is half back in one of those claw clips that attempt to impale his feet at least once a week.

She plucks her keys off the counter. "So. Are you coming?"

Theo should lesson plan.

Spend his day off working.

But.

He just wants to be wherever she is. A thirty-minute commute later, Theo enters the Foley stage behind Evelyn, unprepared for the sensory overload when she flips the lights. The space is a cross between a hardware store and a costume shop. He walks on wood, bricks, tile, concrete. Passes various other surfaces—a sandpit, gravel, leaves, carpet. An empty bathtub. Bins of shoes. Rolls of fabric. So many textures. Barrels. Brooms. Hats. A . . . bike? Pots and pans and bowling balls and chairs and a bowl of lemons and—

"I know," she says, reading his mind. "It's organized chaos."

Evelyn leads him to the mixing room, a space that is empty—muted—in comparison, with windows that look into the studio and two side-by-side desks. Hers has a pink electric blanket draped over the chair, two succulents on the desk, a Post-it note that reads, *I'll know what an anthropomorphic chicken sounds like when I hear it*, and photos taped on the wall next to her laptop. Duplicates of a few on their bookshelves at home, like Evelyn in Pep's recording studio. But also some new-to-him photos. A selfie of Evelyn and Gen at the *Ginger* premiere. Another throwback to their dance life, Theo cheesing at the camera and Evelyn cheesing at *him*, both holding a medal he doesn't even remember receiving. His eyes focus on the pink blur in the top right corner of that photo. It almost looks like a smudge. It's pink nail polish. His mom's signature color.

"She was an awful photographer."

Theo laughs. "The actual worst."

"I'm kind of glad now."

"Yeah."

He wonders what Lori would say if she could see them.

Married.

Casually.

Evelyn drops her tote bag on her desk. "You can hang out in here while I'm recording. Video will play on that screen." She points to the monitor set up on the stage before turning on some of the audio equipment and handing Theo a pair of headphones. "You can listen with these. If you want to. It can get repetitive, so I won't be offended if at any point you . . . um. Stop. Listening." Her cheeks bloom pink. "Here."

Theo takes the headphones. "Cool."

"We can set up a tripod in the corner to record a session. Sadie has a phone mount. For TikTok."

"Sadie's on TikTok?"

"No." She shakes her head, then removes the claw clip and twists all her hair into it. Theo is transfixed. Cannot wait until later when he can unclip her hair. "I already blocked and practiced the scene, so hopefully this shouldn't take too long."

Evelyn has told him that when she's on a Foley stage, it almost feels like she's dancing again. It's one thing to hear her say it and another to *see* it. Evelyn dancing again. Her body moving to the rhythm of the scene to hit every note of an action sequence. Her ability to absorb and execute the nuances of each movement. On the screen, Sarabeth and Jack are being chased in a blizzard. In the studio, Evelyn runs in place over lump charcoal. It has the same crackling effect as snow. Her first take as Sarabeth's feet complete, she returns the mixing booth and listens to the playback. It matches. One take. Content, she switches from heavy industrial snow boots to a pair with a lighter tread to be Jack's steps. *Because he's younger, smaller*, she explains. Theo hangs on to her every word, grateful she has to focus on the monitor because he's unable to contain the goofy grin on his face as he listens to each prop pass.

After recording, Evelyn sits on his lap and layers sound on sound on sound.

He unclips the claw.

Plays with her hair, until she passes the headphones back to him.

"It's just a rough cut."

Theo listens. "This is what you do all day?"

Her laughter crackles in his ear. "I wish. No. Most days are either running around in search of a super specific prop or in here, hanging out with Charlie while Sadie records. I'm hoping this"—she gestures at the sound waves on her monitor—"will change that."

"It sounds incredible, Ev."

"Thanks." She beams at him. "I needed this. Today."

"Yeah?"

"I mean, so far the best part about this fellowship has been the benefits."

Theo smirks.

She rolls her eyes. "Your health insurance."

"Sure. My *insurance*."

Evelyn shoves his shoulder, her expression shifting from playful to something serious. "I just. Sometimes I wish I wanted something easy." She scrunches her nose. "Not *easy*. A path with a clear trajectory. I thought . . . losing dance . . . it would've changed things. Changed *me*. Nope. Instead, I fell in love with this weird and wonderful art that is, statistically speaking, a less viable path than professional dancer. It's, like, I'm wired to want impossible things."

"Or just really brave." Theo shrugs when his eyes meet hers, his smile soft. "That's how I see it. You."

"Shut up."

"Let me be earnest."

"Brave? I didn't even apply for this! You did. If I were brave . . ." The way she's looking at him? Theo's brain goes to a dangerous place. "I'm not."

If I were brave . . .

What?

If Theo were brave, he'd ask her to finish that sentence.

No.

If Theo were brave?

He'd say, *We don't have to be an impossible thing.*

He doesn't.

Those words are the opposite of casual.

Casual is letting Evelyn stand, pull him to his feet, and change the subject. She leads him out of the mixing room to give a proper tour of a Foley stage. Demonstrates how various props can be used in various ways. Plays a clip of Sarabeth popping out her retainer and tells him that Sadie used uncooked lasagna to replicate that *pop*. Has strong feelings about which objects make, quote, *the most fantastic squeaks*. Theo learns it's a toss-up between the cranks of a vintage coffee grinder and an Ice-O-Matic, and it feels like a privilege to see the super specific way Evelyn's mouth quirks when she's excited about a sound.

She holds out a pair of snow boots. "Your turn."

On the monitor, she resets the *Sarabeth & Jack* blizzard sequence. Evelyn made it look so easy. It's not easy. There's no music. Your body has to find the beat in silence. Feel the rhythm of a scene and commit it to memory.

Theo tries.

Evelyn fails to stifle her laughter as she records his attempts. He ends the recording, then successfully stifles her laughter with his mouth. And it's fun. Today. Yesterday. His life.

"Home?" she murmurs.

"Yeah?"

Evelyn nods. "I want . . ." Theo breaks the kiss, brushing his lips along her jaw, down her throat, against the sensitive spot where her neck meets her shoulder, and the sigh that she exhales is so soft. Incredibly sexy. "*Theo.*" She rakes the curls at his nape. "I . . . I need to be able to look Sadie and Charlie in the eyes tomorrow. So. You need to take me home. *Now.*"

"Or what?"

"*Theodore.*"

He smirks. "Let's go."

Theo is obsessed with a flustered Evelyn. Could be undone by the way she says his name. As he drives toward Pasadena, he's unable to get her words out of his head. *Take me home.* It's not the home—not the *life*—Theo imagined for himself at eighteen and that once felt like such a loss. Now? He considers that maybe he moved back because of the worst reason, but he stayed for the best one, and today, this moment, Theo is exactly where he's supposed to be.

"Bed?" Evelyn says, asks, demands the moment they're home.

Done.

Theo carries her toward his bedroom as her nails scrape against his skin, mouth moving from his throat up, up, up. "Hey. *Wait.*" Her breath tickles his ear. "My room?"

There's a tentativeness, a question mark, a vulnerability in the question. Theo and Evelyn have been casual all over their apartment—the kitchen, the shower, his bed, *the fucking floor*—but not in her bedroom. It's a boundary they haven't crossed. An unspoken thing. "Yeah?"

She sucks on his earlobe. "*Yes.*"

Evelyn untangles her legs from around his torso, then weaves her fingers through his and pulls him across the invisible line into her room. His pulse spikes. She pushes him onto the bed and crawls onto his lap. "Is this okay?"

Always, she asks.

Theo nods, his thumbs digging into the soft flesh of her thighs as she removes his glasses, places them on her nightstand, then pulls off her tank top before leaning in and kissing his jaw. Evelyn kisses him softly. Grinds against his hardness slowly. As though they have all the time in the world. His hands settle on her hips, thumbs skimming the band of her underwear. Light. Teasing. Her teeth gently graze his bottom lip in response. Learning what her body responds to, how she responds? It's so much. A lifetime of wondering and now he just *knows* and he'll never *not* know what makes his best friend come and this is casual, they are *casual*, but . . .

Is that even what he wants?

Casual?

Evelyn pulls back. "Pause." She dismounts and Theo watches the shape of her stand on her tiptoes and reach for a box, *the* box that has just been chilling on the top shelf of her closet. Theo would be a liar if he denied ever thinking about that box. How comfortably she'd dug through its contents. How casually she'd dangled a butt plug in his face. How inexperienced he felt in comparison.

Evelyn returns to his lap, her cheeks flushed. "We don't have to. Obviously. But I'm . . . well, if you're open to exploring the world of sex toys and light kink? I'm down for that.

Like . . ." She reaches into the box and pulls out a set of hand restraints. "If you wanted to use these? I'd be into it."

"You want to . . . tie me up?"

Evelyn shakes her head, her smile wicked and wonderful. "I want you to tie *me* up."

Fuck.

He's so completely out of his depth. Will he like that? His body is very much interested . . . but his brain is less sure. What does that even mean? If the feral, possessive part of him is so goddamn turned on right now? Theo feels like a teenager once more, bumbling though those awkward first times. Theo knows what to do with his hands, his mouth, his body. He doesn't know what to do with—

"Hey." Evelyn's palms cradle his cheeks. "Talk to me."

"I just. Um. I don't know what I like when it comes to . . ." Theo gestures to the box, not used to being vulnerable when it comes to sex with, well, anyone. ". . . all of this?" He scans its contents. "Is that a feather duster?"

"Yeah." She laughs, reaches into the box for it, and trails it up his forearm. It leaves goose bumps behind. "Personally, I'm a fan of using this *here*." She starts using it on herself. Brushing the feathers lightly, tantalizingly, over her sports bra, across her breasts.

"*Ev.*"

She shrugs.

Drops the feather duster back into the box.

"But I'm more interested in figuring out what *you* like."

Her nipples are hard. Visible through spandex. God, she's a menace. Theo can't speak. Can't breathe. In the beat of silence that follows, her expression shifts. She bites her lip, suddenly self-conscious. "Sorry. I'll stop—"

"Bra. Off."

"Less clothes." She smirks, then actively consents, another layer of fabric falling to the floor. "Got it." Theo flips her onto her back and reaches for the hand restraints, then the feather duster. Secures the restraints around her wrists, then brushes the skin between her breasts. "That *tickles*." She giggles, and that sound alone almost ruins him. "Lighter."

Theo listens. Likes the quiet hitch of her breath when he lightens his touch. With restraints, she can't show him what she wants but must tell him and he likes the filthy words she whispers in his ear, how vocal she is about what turns her on, the way her back arches when he reaches for one of the vibrators. He brushes the pulsing device over her thin cotton panties. Teases her with it until she asks him why the fuck her underwear is still on. It's an excellent question. Theo removes every layer that remains between them and then he's inside her and *fuck* he likes the way she feels under him. How tight she is. Learning that there are so many ways you can use a vibrator.

Mostly, he likes how much she trusts him.

No.

Not likes.

Theo is pretty positive he loves that.

"*Theodore*," she whispers in his ear. "Talk to me. Tell me what you want."

You.

You.

"You." Theo says, then presses his lips to the hollow of her throat. "Always you."

When she comes, her teeth sink into his shoulder and the lightest pressure of her *bite* is what sends him over the edge, too. After, Evelyn curls against him, her fingers lazily playing with his hair, and Theo tells himself that he can do this. Be casual. Act as though he didn't just tie her up and confess how much he wanted her.

You.

Always you.

They spend the rest of the afternoon in Evelyn's bed, trying to marathon *Love Island* but mostly just distracting each other with their hands, their mouths, their toys. With every release, Theo denies the feeling that resurfaced when they were in New York, then again this morning at the Foley studio, and again and again and again in this bed. Attempts to push away that unruly feeling that's growing every day into something more untenable, the feeling that will consume him—*hurt him*—if he isn't careful.

It isn't until the next morning, when she's snoring in his arms, that he's able to not only name it, but allow himself to *feel* this terrifying feeling.

Happy.

Happy.

Happy.

THE SHIVA

Theo

Theo's mom dies the day before his birthday. It's a Monday in May. She's bones. So small in the hospital bed a hospice nurse set up in their living room two weeks ago. Not at all how he wants to remember her. Theo and Jacob wheel the bed to the back patio so Lori can feel the sun one more time. They don't speak. Jacob is furious that Theo took Lori's side when she told them she wanted to stop treatment. Theo is pissed that Jacob wanted to prolong her pain. It's easier to direct their anger at each other than to acknowledge how fucking powerless they are. Evelyn is there, too. She sits between Theo and Jacob. Talks for them. Theo holds his mom's hand, his final words to her two truths and one lie.

I love you.

It's okay.

I'll be okay.

Lori squeezes his hand.

And then she lets go.

Twenty-four hours later, he stands next to Jacob in an ill-fitting suit. Lori made all the necessary arrangements. Chose a casket, an outfit to be buried in, a quote for her grave marker.

She even took care of the catering for the shiva. Booked a restaurant with vegetarian and dairy-free options. As if she knew that Theo and Jacob wouldn't be able to handle it. She was right. Theo doesn't process a single word Rabbi Goldberg says. Just attempts to mimic his father's stoicism during the brief service, then tosses a handful of dirt onto the casket. Buries his mother and turns twenty-three all at once.

Jacob hosts the shiva.

Theo and Evelyn chase their grief with a shot of peppermint schnapps.

"For Lori," she says.

When she briefly leaves his side to use the bathroom, he tosses back a second shot. Then, a third. His nose wrinkles. His mom always added a splash to her hot cocoa during the holidays. 'Tis the season. Alone, the liqueur burns. But it's pretty much the only reason he can handle the relentless condolences extended by friends, colleagues, strangers who introduce themselves as former students, who all say zikhronah livrakha. *May her memory be a blessing.* Right now? Theo's buzz is a blessing. He doesn't feel too much. Barely feels anything at all.

Until his living room becomes claustrophobic and it's impossible to breathe.

He escapes to his bedroom, the peppermint schnapps tucked into his suit jacket pocket like contraband. This isn't supposed to be his life. Just three months ago, he was in his second semester at Teachers College. Seated in a lecture hall and taking notes on education law when she left the voicemail. Theo called back without even listening to it. Lori doesn't leave a voicemail that could be a text. So. He knew. *It's back.* He blacked out. Didn't process anything except those two words. One second he was at his dorm, and the next he was at the admissions office, begging for a leave of absence and ready to withdraw if it wasn't granted. *Please. My mom is dying.* He booked the first flight home. Called Evelyn before he boarded the plane. Without quite meaning to, months had passed since the last time they spoke. Still, she answered on the first ring.

I know.

It's bad. Isn't it?

It's in her lungs, Theodore.

Theo couldn't breathe. *I'm coming home.*

Now he sits on the bed in the room he grew up in and sips the liqueur straight from the bottle as the worst four-word combination in the world changes tense. *My mom is dying.* Theo coughs. *My mom is dead.* Loosens his tie. *My mom is dead.* Can't breathe. *My mom is dead.*

A soft knock pulls him out of the spiral. "Theo?"

Evelyn's voice is just as gentle. She's the only good thing about being home. He missed his best friend so much. Neither has brought up the last four years. Him leaving. Her pushing. *I will hate you if you don't stay.* Spring break and the awkwardness that formed a fissure that became a chasm. Convincing each other afterward that they were fine. Just busy. With school. With life. *We're fine.*

They're not.

Theo stands and opens the door to find her holding a gift box.

Right.

His birthday.

"It's not from me."

Theo processes his name written on an envelope tucked under the bow in his mom's brush calligraphy as Evelyn swaps the gift box for the bottle of peppermint schnapps and tilts it to her lips. It distracts him from the box. Reminds him that he's not up-to-date on her medications and some don't react well with alcohol and—

"It's safe, right?" Theo asks. "Mixing alcohol with your medication?"

"No." She rolls her eyes, then takes another pointed sip. "Seriously? I'm sad as fuck, but I'm not a fucking idiot."

"Sorry I care."

Care isn't a strong enough word.

Her expression softens, then her eyes shift to the box now in his hands. "Open it."

He doesn't want to open the present. He has to open the present. Decides to save the card for later, wanting to read it alone. Inside the box is a crochet blanket in shades of blue and white. Columbia blue. His mom's last gift to Theo before she died is one of, if not *the* most common first gifts after someone is born. He is *just* drunk enough to appreciate the symbolism, the irony, the whatever it is.

"She asked me to finish it." Evelyn points to the spot where her hands took over, his mom's last stitch marked with the tiniest embroidered initials. "I hate weaving in the ends. Lori's lucky I love her more." Her eyes are wet. Shimmery. Beautiful. She reaches toward him to wipe his cheeks. When did Theo start crying? "She's so proud of you."

"Was."

"*Is.*"

His eyes shift toward the door. "I don't want to go back out there."

Outside, Theo must perform grief in a way that is palatable, stoic, strong.

He doesn't want to be strong.

He wants to drink his mom's favorite liqueur without her and be super fucking sad about it.

"Then don't."

"Stay with me?"

Evelyn nods. She's slept over every night for the last two weeks. Says good night to Jacob after dinner, then a few hours later slips back in through the side door and sneaks into Theo's bedroom. Curls herself around his body and holds him until he falls asleep. Theo is certain she's the only reason he's been able to sleep at all. Now her palm stays pressed against his cheek, her touch so tender it hurts.

Theo wants this hurt.

So he turns his mouth toward her hand. Presses his lips to her palm. Allows his grief, his want, the *alcohol* to touch her skin with his lips. Her breath hitches as her fingers curl and her nails drag across his cheek. Theo buzzes from this gentle pressure that he feels even when she pulls away. When her wide eyes meet his, he wonders if she aches for him, too. If it's becoming as unbearable for her as it's always been for him.

"*Theo.*"

His name is a whisper on her lips.

Lips that answer his unspoken question by pressing against his mouth in the softest, most tentative way. His response is not soft. Not at all tentative. Theo deepens the kiss. Their second kiss. Her first time climbing onto his lap as she brushes her tongue across his bottom lip. His first time unbuttoning her blouse and pressing his mouth against her collarbone. In this moment, Theo allows his grief and pain and desire to meld into one fucked-up feeling that fuels this confession, this revelation, this mistake in the making. Evelyn allows him to slip the black silk off her shoulders, then wraps her arms around his neck and pulls his lips back to hers. She tastes like salt, like peppermint—

Like peppermint.

Theo pulls away. He's wanted this for so long. Her. *Evelyn.*

But not now.

Not like *this*.

"I don't . . . You . . . I don't want this. Like. *You*."

I don't want you like this.

Theo's drunk.

His words are jumbled.

All wrong.

"Fuck," she says. "I'm so . . . *Fuck*."

Evelyn stands and Theo just watches her like an actual idiot as she rebuttons her blouse hastily, then finger combs disheveled hair. Her cheeks are on fire. Words are stuck in his throat. *You. You. You.* As soon as she's decent, she slips out of his room and Theo knows in his bones that she's not staying tonight. Already feels the dread, the panic, the fear that he screwed up so massively that she'll never stay again and that he's just supposed to . . . what? Never sleep again? Then learns that half a bottle of peppermint schnapps is just as effective a sleep aid.

He wakes the next morning with a splitting headache and a body pressed against his back. Images of last night swirl in his brain. Evelyn kissing him. Theo stopping it. Her leaving. But. At some point, she came back. Theo is mortified. Relieved. So in love it hurts.

"Hey," she says when he stirs.

Theo presses the heels of his hands to his eyes. "Morning."

"It's over. We got through it."

"Yeah." Theo swallows, then turns so he's facing her. "Ev. Last night—"

"—really sucked. I know." Theo searches Evelyn's expression for any indication that they're talking about the same moment. *Really sucked* would not be among all the phrases he could use to describe what happened between them last night. "What? Do I have drool on my face?"

"No."

Her eyebrows lift. "Did I do something embarrassing? Yesterday?"

"No."

"I totally did." She covers her face with her hands. "What happened under the influence of peppermint schnapps? Actually. No. Don't tell me. Let me live in ignorant bliss."

Theo tries not to freak out. He's so relieved that they stopped, that he stopped them when he did. Before it progressed any further. There are moments from yesterday that are a blur, but everything about kissing Evelyn Bloom is in sharp focus. Does she really not remember? Just the thought makes him nauseous. Theo is never drinking peppermint schnapps again.

"Ev—"

"Don't."

Evelyn's eyebrow twitches as her eyes meet his, her expression confirming what she refuses to acknowledge out loud.

She remembers.

"Theodore," she whispers. "*Please*."

He nods. Assumes she means not *now*. In the moment, it's a relief not to assign words to this one overwhelming feeling when he's goddamn drained from so many competing overwhelming feelings. He has no idea, as she curls against his body and they drift back to sleep, that they will spend the next five years pretending it didn't happen, that so much time will pass that sometimes Theo will wonder if it even happened at all, or if it was just a devastating dream.

19

"Does anyone know what Foley is?"

Hands shoot toward the ceiling.

"My mom was a sound designer on *Spider-Man: Home Away from Home*."

"I follow Foley Dave on TikTok."

"We weren't born yesterday."

"Right." Evie attempts to maintain a neutral expression, convinced that there isn't anything more intimidating than twenty-two fourth graders. There are so many of them. Just one of her. "Follow-up question. Whose parents work in the industry?"

More than half the class. Evie shoots Theo a look. It's Career Week at Foothill Elementary School. When Theo asked Evie to be a guest speaker she thought it might be fun. Well, no. First, she told him that it's some late-stage capitalist bullshit. Career Week? They're *ten*. Then she considered how cool it could be, to be a kid's introduction to this weird and wonderful art form. And she felt inspired. Stayed up until 4:00 a.m. creating a lesson plan that leaned into moments of discovery, the magic that made her fall in love with Foley when she was their age.

So.

It just would've been nice if she knew to cater this presentation to industry nepo babies. Does her expression convey this? Probably not. Theo at his desk, dressed in chinos and an olive cable-knit sweater, is too distracting. How stupid hot he looks in teacher clothes.

Evie needs to pivot.

She plucks a bag of plantain chips from the snack bowl on Theo's desk, takes a seat on the rectangular table at the front of the room, and folds her legs like a pretzel. Pops a chip in her mouth, then points at the kid whose mom works for Marvel.

"Tyler?" Each student is wearing a sticker with their first name, last initial, and pronouns. "Can you explain what Foley is? For anyone who might not know?"

"Sound effects," Tyler says simply.

Annabelle, a kid with chipped pink nail polish and a wrist full of friendship bracelets, raises her hand and adds, "They're sound effects that are recorded live and added during post."

During post.

These children.

"Postproduction," Evie clarifies for the few scrunched expressions of the nonindustry kids, then asks a few follow-up questions that confirm most of Theo's students do, in fact, have a basic understanding of what her job is and how it works. It's impressive. One student, Jeremiah, says it kind of sounds like ADR for the not-dialogue sounds. Evie needs to know how Jeremiah knows what ADR is. She didn't learn the industry term for dubbing until college.

His answer?

"I was in a Disneyland commercial when I was a kid."

"Tell us *one more time*, Jeremiah."

"Mrs. Theodore literally asked!"

"Jeremiah!" Annabelle gasps in unison with Sierra and Kaia, the two other girls at her table.

"That's so patriarchy of you," Sierra says.

Kaia crosses her arms. "Yeah. She has a name, turd breath."

"*Kaia.*" Theo's voice is gentle but stern. Evie knows she's not cut out to work with children because she's trying not to laugh. "You cannot call Jeremiah *turd breath*."

"Can I call him sexist?"

His eyes shift from Kaia to Jeremiah. "If he continues to call Ms. Bloom Mrs. Theodore? Yes."

"Evie works, too," Evie adds.

Jeremiah's cheeks are pink. "Sorry, Ms. Evie."

"We're cool, Jeremiah."

Evie pivots from the original presentation (as it would be insulting to these kids) and jumps straight to the first activity. She asks everyone to split into groups of three. It almost breaks them. "Six groups of three. One group of four," Theo chimes in from behind his desk, preventing the minor catastrophe that nearly occurred because twenty-two isn't divisible by three. Her eyes flicker toward the sound of his voice, then linger while he pushes the sleeves of his sweater up to his elbows.

She blinks.

Directs her attention back to the students. "What *I* love about Foley is that it's a sort of magic trick. This box"—Evie places the prop box on her lap—"is full of household objects that we use to reproduce various sounds. You're going to use them today to create your own sound effects. But first, we're going to start with a quick activity to warm up our ears . . ."

It's a simple exercise.

Everyone will close their eyes.

Evie will make a sound using objects in the box.

Then the kids will write down what they heard and their minds will be blown over and over again when the object that's the source of the sound is revealed. So simple. Evie starts with an easy example to build confidence. Begins by dropping a set of keys onto a tile surface. Six of the seven groups write down variations of *shattering, broken glass,* etcetera. But the seventh group? Milo, Jeremiah, and Tyler? They answer *keys falling on the floor,* ruining the reveal. Evie assumes it's a fluke. Maybe she slightly jingled the keys before dropping them. Or someone in that group has alien ears. Except it happens again. And again.

Umbrella.

Gloves.

Rice on a cookie sheet.

It's the specificity of that last one that sends the classroom into chaos.

"Come *on*," Annabelle groans.

"*Stop cheating,*" Kaia exclaims, on the verge of tears.

Milo frowns. "Sorry we're so good at this game?"

"No one likes a sore loser, Kaia," Jeremiah adds.

Evie runs her hand through her hair. "It isn't a *game.*"

The entire point of the exercise is not to correctly guess, but for them to use their imagination. Before she has a chance to tell them this, the tide turns against her. "It's a *stupid* game!" Evie is useless in this moment. Completely overwhelmed. Out of her depth, she mouths *Help me!* to Theo who is . . . trying not to laugh? Seriously? His eyes shift to his screen and she is going to murder him if he doesn't—

Ooh hoo hoo!

The opening notes of "1985" by Bowling for Soup blast through the speakers.

It sparks a visceral reaction.

"Mr. *Cohen!*"

"Uuuugh!"

"We kind of deserve it . . ."

He cuts the music and there is a moment of sweet, sweet silence.

"What the *f*—" Evie cuts herself off. Why? Would it be the worst thing, really, if Theo doesn't ever let her enter his classroom again? "What was *that?*"

"The worst song in the *entire universe*."

"You've never heard it?"

"Mr. Cohen tortures us with it." Kaia marches up to the dry-erase board. Under today's date is written 13 DAYS SINCE "1985." Kaia erases the 13 and writes 0. "Our record is twenty-four."

"Ah."

Evie processes this information as twenty-two kids rush back to their assigned seats like some sort of reverse musical chairs. Processes that Theo doesn't raise his voice to get his students to quiet down. *He plays Bowling for Soup.*

I love you.

She barely registers the thought; it enters and exits her overstimulated brain so fast. It sounds like a sucker punch, but the feeling lingers listening to Mr. Cohen, who's only capable of being stern for, like, thirty seconds. He has a devastatingly handsome *I'm not mad, I'm disappointed* face. Milo, Jeremiah, and Tyler apologize for ruining the activity. Jeremiah is having a rough day. After everyone pinky-swear promises to be on their best behavior, Evie continues the presentation.

"Okay. Who wants to watch *Survivor*?"

And the enthusiasm of their response?

Well.

She should've just started with this. Evie plays a short, iconic clip featuring one contestant building a spy shack. Challenges each group to re-create the sounds using classroom items. Theo offers an advantage in this week's *Survivor* Friday challenge to the most creative and collaborative teams. The kids get into it. Practice their footsteps. Search for the perfect substitute for leaves and palm fronds. These kids! Evie's so relieved she could cry. Not because this whole endeavor was only a minor shit show, but because she still *cares* about Foley. Loves it, even. Guiding Theo's students to the perfect sounds. Seeing the looks on their faces when it clicks. She must've looked so similar at their age. Evie wants to pocket this feeling and remember it every time she questions why she married her best friend.

This is why.

She approaches Theo at his desk and asks, "'1985'?" His eyes don't shift from the monitor. "You know they think that's the year you were born, right? Milo was like, 'We get it, Mr. Theodore. You're old!' I'm . . ." Her voice trails off because Theo isn't listening. He's lost in whatever he is reading. If his furrowed brow is any indication, likely *Survivor* Reddit. "Theodore?"

He blinks, then looks at her. "Sorry. Hey."

"These kids are terrifying."

"I know."

"I'm kind of obsessed with them?"

"I know."

She leans into the rest of her afternoon as Ms. Evie, the Foley artist, checking in with each group and offering some tips and advice before their performance. Evie notices red and yellow pom-poms sticking out of Annabelle's desk and nudges her trio in that direction. Pom-poms make perfect rustling leaves.

Before she leaves them to it, Annabelle says, "I can't believe you're married to Mr. Cohen."

"Why?"

Sierra lowers her voice. "You're, like, *so* cool."

Evie beams.

Theo's students think she's cool.

It's embarrassing how validating that is.

"I'm *exhausted*." Evie slumps over a freshly Clorox-wiped desk in the now-empty classroom. "You do this every day?"

"That was a good Tuesday."

"Theodore, they shit-talk the way you *uncap a water bottle*."

He laughs as he continues to sanitize the classroom. "They keep me humble."

"You love it."

"Being harassed daily?"

She snorts. "*Teaching*."

"Yeah. I do."

His earnest declaration is disarming. Similar to how his New York declaration was disarming. *Leaving you*. Despite the exhaustion that's seeping into her bones, Evie had a ridiculous amount of fun with Theo's students. Watching him engage with them, she comes to understand that they only drag him because they adore him. Every fist bump and high five? It melted her heart. After Theo finishes wiping down desks, he returns to his own. Evie stands and joins him. Sits on his desk. Wants to distract him. Distract herself. Calculates the likelihood of him fucking her right here. Low. But the windowless supply closet across the hall . . .

She blinks.

Fuck.

Since New York, Evie has been in a state of constant motion. Work. Sex. Sleep. Repeat. She doesn't want to think about how awful her interaction with Naomi felt or what falling asleep in Theo's arms after meant. What it means to want him but not want to be *married to* him. So she doesn't think or feel. Figures if she's always doing something, she doesn't have to feel anything.

Now she sits still.

Theo's eyes meet hers.

And it's impossible not to feel everything.

If Theo isn't going back to New York, if she is impossible to leave . . .

Maybe it's okay.

To feel everything.

I love you.

"Annabelle says I'm too cool to be married to you."

"She's not wrong."

"I know. I hope the kids don't take it too hard."

"What?"

"The divorce."

Evie's tone is light, teasing, as if a bomb didn't just detonate in her brain.

I love you.

You.

You.

You.

Does it even matter? If she loves him? It doesn't resolve their opposing stances on marriage as, like, a concept. It doesn't change the truth that Evie still wants to file for divorce the moment her IATSE application is approved. Love isn't enough to alter the reality that they want different things out of love. She's going to have to let him go. Revert to platonic soulmates. And it's going to hurt. Until then?

She leans forward and kisses him.

It's soft.

Theo pulls back. Just a few millimeters, so their noses touch. He bites his lip. Reaches for her hands and twines their fingers together. Every sound amplifies. The thud of a heartbeat, the whoosh of an exhale, the tenor of his voice. "Ev, I—"

Evie panics.

Cuts him off with her lips, terrified he's about to utter three words that'll change everything, as if everything hasn't already changed.

20

His classroom is a cacophony of sound effects. Theo sits at his desk and watches Evelyn engage with his students, who are now on their best behavior after they've been "1985"-ed. Well. Most are. Milo flutters his eyelashes at Theo. So dramatic. Such a little shit. He shifts his eyes from his students to his monitor, where a new email is bold in his inbox. From . . . Caro?

Subject: Interested? FW: Curriculum Development
Coordinator—Literacy—NYC DOE

Theo blinks.
His watch vibrates. A heart rate notification.
He opens the email.
Reads.

Hello Hello Mr. Cohen!
It's been more than a minute . . . but I saw this listing and
immediately thought of you. Is this not your DREAM job?

I work in the legal department at the DOE currently, so
if you're interested I can totally put in a referral. Let me
know! NY misses you.

x Caro

"Theodore?"

He minimizes the email, his eyes shifting to Evelyn standing over his desk.

Blinks. "Sorry. Hey."

Short pieces of hair are falling out of the bun she secured
with a pencil this morning. *It's giving teacher*, she asserted,
to which he responded, *Please don't say "it's giving" in front of
them.* "These kids are terrifying."

"I know."

"I'm kind of obsessed with them?"

"I know."

Concern wrinkles her brow and she opens her mouth to say
something else, to probably ask him why he looks like he's on
the verge of a panic attack, but then Annabelle calls out, "Ms.
Evie!" and she's pulled back toward his students. Theo reopens
the email and clicks the link to the job listing. It's an incredible
opportunity. A coordinator role under the director of literacy
for the New York City Department of Education? Theo can't
process this. The job. A random email from Caro. Not when
he's Mr. Cohen. So he stands and checks in with how the kids
are doing with the assignment. Before it's time for them to
present, Evelyn plays the video of his Foley attempt.

"So it won't take much to impress me!" she assures his giggling students.

During their performances, Evelyn's nose crinkles a super
specific way when a sound surprises her. It delights his students, who so obviously want to impress her. Theo spends

the rest of the afternoon trying to imagine a world where he moves back to New York. If he's okay with saying goodbye to his life exactly as it is. He's unsure. But if he's so content here, he shouldn't care about the email in his inbox. Right?

Right.

Theo's still ruminating on this after the students leave, as he's wiping down their desks and tidying up for tomorrow.

"I'm exhausted." Evelyn collapses into a clean desk. He feels her eyes on him. It's only a matter of time before she can hear his thoughts and maybe he should just show her the email. Maybe he can work through these complicated feelings with the person who has always been the best at quieting his anxious brain. "You do this every day?"

"That was a good Tuesday."

"Theodore, they shit-talk the way you uncap a water bottle."

"They keep me humble."

"You love it."

"Being harassed daily?"

"Teaching."

His response is immediate. "Yeah. I do."

He does.

Theo loves teaching.

But.

His classroom now smelling like antiseptic lemons, he returns to his desk and sits. Gathers last night's homework as Evelyn walks over and sits *on* his desk. His eyes flicker toward the door, nervous before he remembers the wedding band on his finger. That Foothill Elementary School is the one space where they're still married. So.

"Annabelle says I'm too cool to be married to you."

"She's not wrong."

Evelyn smirks. "I know. I hope the kids don't take it too hard."

"What?"

"The divorce," she says.

His heart stutters at those words, her casual delivery. Then she kisses him and it's a mindfuck. Is this casual? Theo isn't sure he knows the definition anymore. He breaks the kiss after a moment because he's at work and a two-hour-old email is eating him alive. "Ev, I—"

Her mouth is back on his before he can utter the sentence.

Ev, I . . . might have a job opportunity in New York.

Theo should tell her, but it's easier to kiss her. Easier to process this on his own. Later that night, he googles "foley artist nyc" and learns to his delight and relief that there are opportunities in New York. At 2:00 a.m. he submits an application and forwards his résumé to Caro because he'll regret it if he doesn't even try. Continuing education is a highlighted benefit. Theo could go back to grad school. Evelyn could freelance in New York. It surprises him how much he wants it.

Them in New York.

Together.

In a not-at-all casual way.

But right now, Theo and Evelyn are good at casual. If Theo brings up moving to New York? Memories of their last serious New York conversation resurface, dissolving his desire to share this with her, because if he's honest about the conditions required for him to make this move . . . she'll freak out. Shit. *He's* freaking out.

Besides, it's such a long shot.

The job.

Theo can keep it to himself for now and continue to pretend this, them, his feelings are casual.

Until pretending becomes impossible.

All because of "1985." A couple of weeks after he takes her to school with him, a package shows up at their apartment. It's a Saturday afternoon and their only plans are not to put on real clothes today. Evelyn is crocheting on the couch, headphones covering her ears, when Theo tries to hand her the padded envelope.

She sits up, lowering her headphones. "It's for you."

It's not a holiday. It's not his birthday. "Why?"

"Just open it."

He does.

It's a custom chalkboard. ____ DAYS SINCE "1985" is painted across the top, and his entire body spasms, he's laughing so hard. "*Ev.* I repeat. Why?"

"Because! It's my new favorite Theo Fact."

He plants himself next to her on the couch. "Oh?"

Evelyn places her crochet project on the coffee table and wraps her arms around her legs. "Totally. It's, like, I think I must know everything about you . . . and then out of nowhere you play a Bowling for Soup song to get your students to quiet down. Incredible. *You* are incredible and it's just *so cool* to know you so well and still be surprised. You know?"

He stares at it.

This literal sign.

"I know."

Her cheeks flush the way they always do whenever she slips up and says something earnest. "But also? For the reaction." Evelyn drops her arms and shifts closer to him. Her nails left tiny crescent moons imprinted on her knees. "From the kids."

His thumbs brush the crescent moons. "Oh?"

"Yeah."

"Really?" This is how it starts. Teasing. Nonchalant. Then someone will lean in. Usually Evelyn. Theo lets her make the first move because it's sexy, because it's safe, because then he's not the one putting himself out there. But right now? He's the one leaning in, so close her breath tickles. "For *their* reaction."

She brushes the stubble along his jaw and doubles down. "Really."

Kissing Evelyn so often evokes this hot, intense desperation, but this time when their lips touch it feels different. Soft. *This isn't a mistake.* Gentle. *This isn't a mistake.* Tender. *This isn't a mistake.* Evelyn sits on his lap and pulls his T-shirt over his head. Drags her nails down his chest, then presses her mouth to his neck. His hands return to her legs. Start at those near-faded crescent moons before traveling up, up, up her thighs as hers travel down, down, down to the drawstring of his sweatpants. When he covers her hand with his, Evelyn whimpers— fucking *whimpers*—against his throat.

"Theo."

"So impatient."

"Should I stop?"

"No." Theo kisses her perfect swollen lips, then pulls back so their foreheads touch. "Unless. Do you want to stop?"

Evelyn smirks. "I consent, Theodore. Just to be perfectly clear."

"Cool."

Cool?

She laughs against his lips. "Cool."

It's new to Theo. Kissing like they have all the time in the world. Maybe they do. Maybe this can be their life if they're both brave enough to let it be. Because kissing her doesn't feel casual. It feels like a medical emergency. Theo knows what it is to be tangled up in Evelyn Bloom, but never has he felt so out of control of his emotions. He carries her to his bedroom and removes the layers of clothes between them, removes every barrier between them until his heart thrashes against hers. Her lips are on his skin, and his hands cup her breasts, and every movement is slow. Intentional. He didn't know it could be this good. He always knew it would be this good. Theo's unsure how both things can be true. When Evelyn wraps her hand around his length he sighs into her mouth and wishes this could be enough. Theo wants nothing more than to still believe that this is casual, that he's capable of casual with her— that he isn't, hasn't always been, so in love with Evelyn Bloom.

21

"When are you going to admit that you and Theo are finally fucking?"

Evie's eyes snap up from the pottery wheel in front of her, the already precarious lump of clay collapsing in her hands. "*Gen.*"

"Are you not?"

Her nonanswer is the answer.

"I knew it."

Evie ignores her, re-forming the wet clay in her hands before slapping it onto the center of the wheel. They're at Green & Bisque, a pottery studio just around the corner from the bungalow that's no longer theirs. If Miss Stella's was Evie's second home during their adolescence, Green & Bisque was Imogen's. Her sister has braved the 110 on a regular basis, returning to pottery. Evie's positive there must be a closer studio, but she'll never complain that Imogen has found a reason to be in Pasadena more. It's not lost on her that Imogen's pull toward home grows stronger and more frequent as her countdown to Denver begins.

"*Ev.*" Imogen is pulling handles for a set of mugs that she just threw on the wheel *like it's easy.* Her knack for ceramics is undeniable. "How long?"

Evie lifts her foot from the pedal. "Since New York."

"What? But . . . that was *over a month ago.*" Hurt flashes in her eyes. Evie hasn't told her sister, has actively avoided telling her, because of this reaction. With the slightest quiver of Imogen's lower lip, her big-sister brain activates, and she'll do anything to make that expression go away. Imogen knows this. Evie knows that Imogen knows this. Still, she's powerless to it. "I thought you were mad at me."

"Mad at you?"

"About Denver. You sort of disappeared after I told you."

Disappeared?

"What? I've just been busy with work and—"

"Fucking Theo."

"Gen."

Imogen lays out her handles to dry with a shrug, then cleans up her station and heads to the sink to wash her hands as if she didn't just accuse Evie of disappearing so casually. If Evie's hands weren't covered in clay, she'd scroll through her text history and read their near-daily correspondence out loud. Disappeared? Evie doesn't disappear. She stays.

Is staying.

Really, it's everyone else who disappears.

"This makes so much more sense." Imogen dries her hands, then returns to sit at the wheel next to Evie's lopsided bowl. "God. Finally."

"It's casual."

"Is it?"

Another reason Evie has been avoiding this conversation?

Imogen is the only person who can get away with calling bullshit. "It has to be casual."

"Why?"

"I—" Evie swallows. Attempts to regain control of the conversation, control of her emotions. "Because it's Theo."

Imogen rests her hands on her shoulders. Applies gentle pressure. It's something she's done since they were small, whenever Evie's anxiety lifted her shoulders to her ears. "I never need to do this when Theo's around," she says. "Do you even know that? I noticed when I was, like, ten maybe? Ever since, I've been searching for that kind of ease. A best friend. *My* Theo."

This observation?

It's so disarming.

"I still don't want marriage."

"And yet you are married."

"I don't want to *stay* married or *be* married. Theo does. So."

"You've talked about it? You *know* that?"

No.

They haven't talked about it recently, but she remembers their high school debates. Hurling words at him about the institution of marriage and patriarchy, how she never wanted to be bound to anyone with a piece of paper. Using her grandparents as an example. *Look at Pep and Mo. Never married and the healthiest couple we know.* Theo pushing back, so gently. *It's wild enough to choose someone and for them to choose you back . . . but to commit to that choice? To believe in it, despite logic and data and statistics? I don't know, I think that's pretty cool.*

So.

She does know.

"*Ev.*"

Evie doesn't mean for tears to ricochet off wet clay, never means for her little sister to see her cry. "I don't want to do it again."

"Love?"

"Trust."

Hanna only loved her so long as they wanted the same things. Evie believed they did, when all along Hanna thought she just needed time to come around on the idea of marriage, to come around on relocating to Atlanta, to come around on building a life on her terms. At first, the nudges were so gentle, she couldn't see them. Didn't notice the pressure building with each question, every offhand comment.

Isn't, like, half your team remote?

Did you know that Emory has a dedicated Crohn's and Colitis research center?

My parents are getting older, Evie. We could buy a house. Well, at least a condo? It makes sense.

Then Hanna proposed and, for the first time, it occurred to Evie that maybe the woman she loved didn't understand her at all, and she tried to explain, she *tried*.

I love you, Han, but I don't need to marry you.

I want to do life with you, Han, but I can't marry you.

I won't marry you.

Hanna accepted a job offer in Atlanta the following week.

Love wasn't enough for Hanna.

She wasn't enough.

Imogen's expression softens. "Theo isn't Hanna."

"What if it doesn't work out?"

"What if it does?"

"Seriously? Did we even have the same childhood?"

How is Imogen so optimistic? Evie is baffled. Jealous, even. Hanna is the last person Evie trusted, but she wasn't the first. No. The first person she trusted with her entire heart was her mother. Naomi, who told Evie and Imogen that she loved them. Every night before bed. And then, one day, just left.

"No." Imogen's eyes meet hers. "We didn't have the same childhood, because I had *you*."

Oh.

How is Imogen so optimistic?

It's because Evie took the emotional blows, absorbed the pain, and stayed. Of course. Her staying is the reason Imogen can go. She wraps her arms around her sister. Digs her fingers into her shoulder blades, hoping to absorb some of Imogen's bravery, her ability to trust her heart, to trust Sloane, to follow that terrifying feeling into the unknown, completely forgetting that her fingers are covered in clay.

Work is a welcome distraction. An afternoon with Theo's students made Evie brave enough to put a lunch invite on Sadie's calendar for the following week. That day has arrived and, for the first time in over three months, they talk—really *talk*—about this magical and difficult art. Sadie discloses that it took a decade of working multiple jobs until she could afford to Foley full-time. Shares how demoralizing it can be to work in a male-dominated industry. Admits she doesn't get attached to fellows anymore, that she poured her heart into one too many who quit the moment the realities of freelance life hit.

"If you want this, there isn't room for much else. At least, not at first."

Evie nods.

She understands.

Wants to be consumed by this passion.

"Your work on *Ginger*? It's sublime," Sadie continues. Caught so entirely off guard, Evie responds by choking on a grain of rice. "You need to stop asphyxiating every time I compliment your work."

"Sorry," she sputters.

"You're a dancer?"

"Was."

"Our next project is a movie adaptation of *Save the Last Dance: The Musical.*"

She cannot process a single word in that sentence. "Oh."

"Can you learn the solos?"

"Yes."

Her answer is enthusiastic, spoken without hesitation. It's desperate. She *is* desperate.

"It's no wonder Ross took advantage of you." Sadie's expression remains neutral, her lips pressed together in a thin line. "I understand the impulse to be eager. It's how we're conditioned. As women. As people in these so-called *passion* careers. But when someone offers work that's beyond your pay grade . . ." Sadie shoots her a pointed look. ". . . like learning the solos for a big-budget film? *You need to ask follow-up questions.* About overtime. About credit."

Evie's silent.

After a beat, she asks, "Will I get overtime? Credit?"

Sadie's smile lines are triggered. "Yes. If you deliver *Ginger*-quality Foley, you will absolutely be credited. And Next in Foley isn't going to pay you overtime, but I will give you ten percent of my contracted rate as a bonus."

"Yes. I'm in."

"*No.*" Sadie laughs. "This is where you *negotiate.* And ask for this in writing."

Evie's rattled by this entire interaction. *Time.* How many times had Charlie told her to give Sadie time? In this moment, she feels like she's beginning to understand her mentor. Sadie

Silverman either cares too much or not at all. It's an on-off switch. Has Evie proven that she's worth turning on for? She asks Sadie follow-up questions. Negotiates for twenty percent of her rate. Notes this is the first time in her professional life that someone—anyone—is encouraging her to advocate for herself. By the end of lunch, Evie has a project that she won't start working on until Sadie sends her the terms they've agreed on in writing.

Finally, Evie feels like an actual fellow.

Her first thought after she and Sadie part ways for the day? *I can't wait to tell Theo.*

Her life for the next two weeks revolves around rehearsals and prep and somehow, it's now 1:00 a.m. the night before she's due on a Foley stage. Evie can't sleep. She's always been restless the night before a performance because if she allows her brain to shut down, obviously every step will seep out of her skull. It's irrational. Anxiety is irrational. But if she can't sleep, she may as well practice.

She runs the routines again.

And again.

Two high-energy, extremely technical dances. One hip-hop. The other a contemporary choreographed by Sonya Tayeh. She kept her cool during their session, then called Imogen sobbing in the bathroom afterward because *holy shit she just learned choreography from Sonya Tayeh.* When Evie defined herself as a dancer first and a person second, she could've performed these routines in her sleep. Now? Her body needs to be eased into the movements. Now? Her joints ache after three run-throughs. Now?

It's hard.

Over these last two weeks, she's been noting her limits—

learning when to push and when to rest. She's also reminded that Theo is a fantastic masseuse. If he applies just the right amount of pressure to her arch, it's almost as good as an orgasm. And Evie can't deny that it's nice when he interrupts a rehearsal with a blueberry banana protein smoothie, that she hasn't had to worry about meals, that she could focus on the work. Every night, she crashes on the couch, her feet on his lap, and wakes in her bedroom cocooned in her duvet and feels so cared for.

Supported.

Loved.

Evie arches her back, then bends into a forward fold.

Replays her conversation with Imogen. *What if it doesn't work out?*

What if it does?

Her body is screaming at her to rest. But her brain cannot because she wants this to go well so bad. It's not just a chance to prove herself to Sadie—but a credit that she desperately needs to legitimize her career, to validate her union application, to file for divorce. It's the plan. It's always been the plan. So. Even if reverting to platonic soulmates feels impossible right now? She isn't that selfish.

No.

Theo deserves his white picket fence of a life someday, with someone else.

If you want this, there isn't room for much else.

Sadie said that.

Sadie—

A knock on her door interrupts this spiral. Theo pokes his head into her room. "Why are you still awake?"

She removes her earbuds. "Can't sleep. You?"

"*You.*"

Evie wipes sweat from her upper lip. "Sorry."

Theo opens the door all the way and steps into her room. "Ev. You're ready."

"I'm just—"

"You're ready," he repeats. Firm. Steady. "Go shower. Get ready for bed."

"*Bossy*," she teases. "Will you be joining?"

Theo leans against the doorframe. Shrugs. Evie calls his bluff. Pulls her tank top over her head and throws it at him. Slips out of spandex bike shorts. Revels in the way eyes that once would've averted their gaze don't just look but linger. She expects him to follow her into the bathroom. Into the shower. Is way too disappointed when he doesn't. After, she tosses on a vintage Billy Joel concert T-shirt that used to be Lori's. It's soft and stretched out, the shirt Evie always sleeps in before an important day. In bed, she stares at the ceiling. Counts backward from one thousand, so aware that she needs to sleep.

Cannot sleep.

"Ev?" Theo whispers.

"Yeah?"

A moment later, Theo's shadowed silhouette is above her, a mug in his hand. She isn't sure when he started shortening *Evelyn* to *Ev*, why *Ev* became the default, how her heart can have such a wild reaction to one syllable. Evie presses her palms into the mattress and sits up. Leans against the headboard as he sits on the edge of the mattress and holds the mug out to her.

"Chamomile tea."

Evie takes the mug. Has a small sip, then places it on her night table and scoots over to make space. Once Theo is lying next to her, she presses her mouth against his because she's still a little selfish. He responds with a soft, quick kiss.

"*Theodore.*"

"Good night."

She rolls onto her side. "You're such an ass."

"You need to sleep," he whispers against her hair, nestling in and wrapping his arm around her.

"Yeah." She grinds her ass against his crotch. "So. Make me tired."

He groans. "*Ev.*"

"*Theo.*"

"You need to sleep," he repeats, his breath tickling her ear. "So I'm going to hold you until you fall asleep."

"You think that will work?"

"It's always worked for me."

Silence.

Tears prick her eyes.

Evie swallows the emotion in her throat. "It won't work."

"Okay."

"It *won't*," she insists.

Then, obviously, immediately falls asleep in his arms.

SOME CONVENTION CENTER IN ANAHEIM

Senior Year

By the time she's eighteen, Evie excels at downplaying pain, dancing through pain, existing in pain. What choice does she have? She's spent her entire adolescence bouncing from one unhelpful doctor to the next, who all report that her bloodwork is *within normal range* and assure her that if it were serious, she wouldn't be able to perform at the caliber that she does. One doctor refers her to a psychiatrist. Another prescribes naproxen and a muscle relaxant with a gentle *Some of us just have a low pain tolerance.* Evie is a child, so she accepts this. Lives with unpredictable stomachaches. Learns to first locate a toilet whenever she's in a new setting. Pops pain relievers like candy and gets on with life. What else is she supposed to do?

She's a dancer.

An *athlete* who is curled up in the fetal position on her bathroom floor the night before Nationals, unable to sleep due to severe stomach stabbies. It's just stress. Obviously. If something were serious . . . doctors would take her pain seriously. Right?

Stress.

In the morning, she pops three Tylenol and an antinausea medication.

Sees blood in the toilet and is confused.

Her period is never early.

But she doesn't have time to dwell, instead double-, triple-checking that everything is packed. Costume pieces. Hair and makeup products. She adds a handful of tampons into her duffel bag as Lori and Theo pull up in front of the bungalow. An iced chai waits for her in the back seat cup holder. Car still in park, Lori twists and snaps a candid photo of her sipping the chai.

"*Mom,*" Theo groans.

"What? It's Evie's last competition chai."

"She's been like this all morning."

Evie hears the smile in Theo's voice. Earlier this week, Lori's most recent scans came back all-clear. NED. No Evidence of Disease. Still in remission. Theo's anxiety always spirals into overdrive in anticipation of the results. When Lori told them that she's still in the clear, Evie could literally see the tension leave his body. Now, in the passenger seat, her best friend is at ease. Lori puts the car in drive and blasts the White Stripes, a precompetition ritual. Evie hums along to "Seven Nation Army" with Theo for the last time, relieved that the extra pain reliever kicked in, that her pain has subsided enough to hide it.

Her phone vibrates in her lap.

She's stupid enough to hope that it's Naomi. Her mom is currently in Santa Monica, leading some yoga retreat. Naomi, now vegan, took Evie and Imogen to Gracias Madre, a new restaurant in West Hollywood. Evie told herself she would be stone-cold in her resolve to give her mother nothing at this lunch, only to instantly spill her guts and forward the details for Nationals the moment Naomi asked for them.

But it's not Naomi.

It's Pep.

genny being a STAR. can't wait to see u shine too, sweets xx!!

Attached is a photo of Imogen, a blur in motion on a lacrosse field. Inspired by Regina George, her sister channeled her Naomi Rage into a contact sport. Evie sends Pep a heart emoji. After Imogen's game, her grandparents will drive from Tarzana to Anaheim on a Saturday. Pep and Mo attend every lacrosse game. Every dance competition. Naomi might not show up, but her grandparents do, and shouldn't she focus on that?

Evie locks her phone, then presses her cheek against the window, and because there's nothing to see on I-5, she closes her eyes and drifts to sleep.

"Evelyn?" She's woken by the sound of Theo's voice and a gentle hand on her shoulder. "Hey. We're here."

She blinks. "Sorry."

He laughs. "Why are you apologizing?"

Together they enter some convention center in Anaheim, carrying everything they need in their arms. People pass them rolling garment racks, suitcases, makeup cases. Dance Parents are intense. Evie doesn't have that. She has Miss Stella, who embraces her when they enter the conference room that their studio has been assigned as a backstage holding area. She has Caro, her sort-of-friend, Theo's more-than-friend, who pins the band of her bra to her costume, a simple jade leotard with a flowy skirt. She has Pep and Mo and Imogen, who are on their way. And she has Theo, who French braids her hair because Imogen isn't here to.

In return, Evie does Theo's makeup.

Holds his chin in her hand as she applies charcoal on his waterline.

Ignores how stupid beautiful his face is.

Pops another pain reliever.

Theo's eyebrows crinkle. "Are you okay?"

"Period cramps."

"Do you need the heating pad?"

She shakes her head. "We should warm up and run it."

Evie stands and retreats to an empty corner of the conference room to stretch out her limbs. Holds in her wince and releases it as an exhale in forward fold, then sits on the floor. It's fine. She is *fine*. Evie has danced through an entire recital in worse condition. Eleven numbers. Three quick changes. Today, she only has two dances. First, a contemporary number to her favorite Sara Bareilles song, "Gravity." Then a high-octane Broadway tap routine. Just two and then it's over.

"Evelyn?"

She ignores the concern in his voice.

Stands.

Refuses to cry, to ruin her makeup. "Let's run it."

"Ev—"

"I'm fine."

Theo nods, trusting her. At first, she *is* fine. Dance is a salve that mitigates her pain, that reminds her she's strong, that storytelling through movement is her purpose. Confident after the second pass, as if the choreography hasn't been absorbed into their bloodstream, Evie takes some time alone to get into character, to become the girl in the song who's falling for someone she absolutely shouldn't *under any circumstance* fall in love with. Because to dance well is to act, to emote, to evoke a response from the audience.

To *act*.

She lets the song loop on her iPod.

Paces.

Her phone vibrates in her hand.

Naomi.

It's a photo of her in Joshua Tree, along with a message.

HEARTBROKEN to miss u, evelyn. next time???

Next time?

Embarrassment crashes into her rib cage.

But she will *not* fuck up her makeup over Naomi.

"Evie?"

Miss Stella's voice pulls focus. It's time. She drops her phone. Pops one more Tylenol for good luck. Ignores the pain that shoots straight to her gut as she follows Miss Stella down the hall and through the door leading backstage. She doesn't let go of Theo's hand until she must. Swallows the emotion in her throat. *Save it for the stage.* It's time to separate, but first he wraps his arms around her, then brushes his lips against her forehead. Evie doesn't react to this very out-of-character action. She's in character. He's in character.

In.

Character.

"Ready?" she whispers.

Theo nods.

Evie ignores his flushed cheeks as the emcee calls them to the stage. *Dance through.* It's what she always does and it always works. But her stomach cramps return with a vengeance the moment the producer says, *Cue music*, and *fuck* she's behind the piano notes, only a half beat but just enough to feel off even when she's back on track after the first rond de jambe. Evie's not in character. Her body is on autopilot while her brain screams, *You fucked up*, and there isn't anything to do except continue breathing, continue moving, continue dancing. *Focus on Theo.* He's grounding during a moment of stillness, his eye contact a different sort of excruciating. *I love you*, she thinks, and it's not an in-character thought, but a simple truth. She pliés into a split lift, a move that's as second nature as breathing.

Ignores her heart.

Her body.

Her pain.

And when she slips out of Theo's arms and hits the ground?

Evie doesn't even see it coming.

22

Seated in the waiting room of Dr. Keating's office, Theo texts Evelyn.

He needs a distraction from his impending appointment that isn't refreshing his inbox. Yesterday, Theo had his first interview to be a curriculum development coordinator. Some minor lunch drama between Annabelle and Kaia made him ten minutes late to the video call, but Amira Montez, a curriculum development specialist that he'd be working closely with, seemed unfazed by the delay. *We've all been there*, she'd said with a knowing chuckle. It went well. Really well. Learning more about the role from someone who's leading a project to diversify classroom reading, someone who's as passionate about the necessity for phonics-based curriculum as he is? His anxious, conflict-avoidant brain hoped that the role wouldn't resonate, that he and Amira wouldn't click, that it would all feel too bureaucratic.

Nope.

He wants it.

He has to talk to Evelyn.

But first, he's desperate to know how her Foley session went this morning.

How'd it go?

She answers immediately. !!!

Theo grins like an idiot at those three exclamation points on his phone. He types you're amazing without overthinking it and the moment he taps send, a nurse says his name and ushers him down the hall to Room 4. It's his first appointment in an entire year. Once upon a time, he'd catch up with Dr. Keating on a monthly basis. Convince her that he needed x, y, z tests run, only for everything to come back normal. Then he'd go on to make appointments with various specialists. Just to double-check. Doctors frequently misdiagnose.

It seemed so rational at the time.

Theo is healthy, so the appointment is straightforward. Dr. Keating orders a standard CBC, a lipid panel, STI tests, and a colonoscopy.

"Based on your family history," she explains, eyes not lifting from the screen.

As if Theo doesn't know he's at an increased risk, that CDC guidelines suggest first-degree relatives begin screening a decade prior to the age their immediate family member was diagnosed. Lori was thirty-eight. Theo is about to be twenty-eight. Even without a family history, colon cancer has become a leading cause of death in people under fifty. It's what kept him awake last night, the reason his brain and body couldn't settle until he climbed into Evelyn's bed. Evelyn, who has regular colonoscopies because her autoimmune disease puts her at an increased risk for the cancer that killed his mom, too, a fun fact that absolutely does not terrify him. Lexapro does wonders for managing these fears, but he's still unprepared for Dr. Keating to state this one so casually.

Based on your family history.

"Right."

Dr. Keating's eyes meet his, her expression softening. "You have zero concerning symptoms, Theo. It's just a preventative screening. Insurance will cover it because—"

"—of my family history."

"Exactly."

Theo leaves Dr. Keating's office with a referral and his heart in his descending colon as he processes how fucked it is that he's so easily able to get a preventative screening with zero symptoms. His mom had had worrying symptoms that were brushed off for years because she was young and otherwise healthy. Lori died from a cancer that's treatable with early detection *because she was denied early detection* and because she was denied early detection . . . he qualifies for it.

Theo wants to scream at the unfairness of it all.

He blasts "Seven Nation Army" on the drive home, ready to decompress by listening to a *Survivor* podcast and deep cleaning the kitchen. Evelyn's car is parked outside their building. Inside, he finds her curled up on the couch watching *Love Island* and clutching a heating pad.

Pain.

Evelyn is in pain.

"Are you okay?" Theo drops his backpack on the floor on his way to her. Curses under his breath, as if this is somehow his fault for not paying closer attention to the toll taken by two weeks of obsessing over complex choreography. He kneels in front of the couch, eye level with her. "What do you need?"

"To be seventeen again." Evelyn pauses the episode, her eyes meeting his concerned gaze. "The fatigue is fatiguing and I'm just relieved that Sadie gave me the afternoon off, but otherwise? Totally fine. More than fine. Today was *incredible*, Theodore."

His shoulders relax. "Yeah?"

She nods.

Theo sits on the other end of the couch, lifting her legs to place them on his lap, and rubs her feet as she tells him about her day, about the session, about how it felt to dance again. Her socks have tiny avocados on them. As she reaches for the remote to resume the episode after sharing her news, he considers plucking the remote from her hand and blurting out his news. *I am interviewing for a job in New York.* These past two weeks, he justified not telling her because he didn't want his opportunity to distract from hers. But now, on the other side of the session, what's his excuse? He needs to tell her. Word vomit all his messy, complicated feelings and just see where her head is at. Once this episode ends.

After a cliffhanger conclusion, she palms the coffee table for her phone and her face scrunches, confused, at whatever is on the screen.

"Wait. Why are you home so early?"

He's never home before 4:00 p.m. on a school day. "Doctor's appointment."

"Oh."

"Just my annual. I kept putting it off because, well . . ." Theo shows her the referral on his phone, then shrugs. ". . . *because.*"

She sits up.

Reads.

"Are you okay?"

"Not really. No."

"When is your appointment?"

"I haven't made one."

Evelyn scoots closer to him. "Don't fuck around with this. As someone who has had"—she counts on her fingers—"*five,* I promise it's a chill screening. Like. In terms of pain? My

IUD insertion was way worse. *My period cramps are worse.* Granted, my barometer for pain is different, but I swear you don't have anything to be anxious about. Truly. It doesn't hurt."

But this hurts.

"I'm not anxious. I'm pissed."

"What?"

"It's bullshit. No one took my mom's symptoms seriously for years. She dealt with so much pain before her diagnosis. And you! You *literally had to get injured* before anyone took your pain seriously. I'm fine. I have zero concerning symptoms, according to my doctor. But I just get a free colonoscopy?"

Well.

Instead of messy, complicated job feelings, Evelyn's getting messy, complicated health feelings.

Oops.

"Theodore." Evelyn wipes his cheek, then wraps her arms around his neck. He's not sure when he started crying. His nails dig into her shoulders and Theo doesn't know how long they stay like this, how long their hearts smash into each other's before she says, so soft, "This is why you couldn't sleep last night."

"Sorry I blamed you."

"You can sleep through my snoring. I should've known."

Evelyn takes his phone out of his hand and dials the number in the referral email. Doesn't let go of his hand while she makes the appointment. Gives her name and phone number to the scheduling nurse as his emergency contact, smirks at him as she replies *wife* when asked for the nature of their relationship, then adds the date to her calendar. After his colonoscopy is booked, he admits to Evelyn that he didn't process any of the scheduling nurse's instructions.

"Just don't google how to make the prep better. Nothing makes it better."

"Cool."

"I'm serious. Mixers just prolong the *blech*."

"Can't wait," Theo deadpans, then speaks his most anxious brain thought out loud. "What if they find something?"

"Then at least we know," Evelyn says with a simple shrug. "It's always better. Knowing."

We.

We.

We.

Theo presses his lips to her forehead, then stands and makes his way to the kitchen because he still needs a distraction and it still needs a deep cleaning. First, he fills and turns on the electric kettle before scrubbing the sink. Makes herbal tea. Hands a mug to her and he knows he should tell her, but he's already emotionally exhausted from scheduling a colonoscopy and a part of him knows deep in his bones that one way or another everything will change and that freaks him out. It's an excuse. Another terrible one. But his brain screams *Avoid, avoid, avoid* as he scrubs the kitchen until his fingers prune and continues to live in the delusion that a universe exists where he can get the job and keep the woman. As if she's even his to keep. When he returns to the couch, Evelyn's lightly snoring. Theo refreshes his inbox, and the email he's been waiting on has arrived.

"Ev?"

She doesn't stir.

Theo schedules his second interview.

Later, in the middle of the night, she climbs into his bed.

Theo is so sleepily delighted when her ice-cold toes brush against his calf. "Hey."

"Sorry," she whispers.

"Don't be."

He makes space. Evelyn curls around him, the big spoon, her arm draped across his torso. He takes her hand and brings it to his mouth. She sighs. He rolls over. Faces her. Their foreheads touch. Kissing her, Theo cannot imagine a universe in which he moves back to New York without her. He can't believe they wasted so much time pushing, denying, insisting that anything about their relationship is platonic. As if this wasn't inevitable. Them.

She whispers against his mouth, "We aren't supposed to need each other like this."

"Ev." Theo's exhale is a soft chuckle. "When haven't we needed each other like this?"

23

Evie spends the next two weeks tangled up in her three favorite things.

Work.

Dance.

Theo.

She's finishing a cloth pass for a video game project when Sadie gets word from the studio that Evie's mix of *Save the Last Dance: The Musical* has been approved. "The studio will verify your credit, so you can submit your application."

Evie throws her arms around her mentor, then promptly bursts into tears because that's what one does on the precipice of everything one has been working toward becoming a reality. Then, she goes home, to Theo, the first person she wants to tell. He's always the first person she wants to share good news, bad news, any news with.

Because she loves him.

She's always loved him.

Really, it's an exhausting amount of work to *not* love him. *When haven't we needed each other like this?* He whispered those words in the middle of the night and her brain wanted to push back, deny, refute, but her bones knew that he was right. Is right. And maybe some of Imogen's bravery did seep into her marrow, because for the first time, Evie wonders how it would feel—who she would be, could be—if she trusted it.

Him.

Herself.

Evie enters their apartment and drops the stack of mail on the island next to his keys. She hears him at the end of the hall and follows the sound of his voice to find him sitting at his desk with noise-canceling headphones on.

"And the benefits package?" he asks his computer screen, oblivious to her presence in the doorframe. "Could HR forward that along, too?" *Benefits? Is Theo leaving Foothill?* She's confused but not overly concerned. His benefits are great, but soon she'll have union benefits that are also great. "Cool. Great. Yeah, I'll discuss it with my wife and get back to you shortly. Thank you *so* much."

Theo removes his headphones and lets them hang around his neck, entirely unaware that she's leaning against his doorframe, heart exploding in her chest.

My wife.

My wife.

My wife.

Evie Bloom never wanted to be a wife.

But.

"What will you be discussing with your wife?"

"*Shit.*" Theo jumps at the timbre of her voice, then spins around in his chair, scratching the back of his neck. Evie watches his Adam's apple bob before he asks, "How much did you hear?"

"Are you leaving Foothill?"

He bites his lower lip. "Maybe."

"Wow." Evie enters his room and sits on the end of his bed, pressing her palms into the mattress. "Tell me more."

"It's a job in curriculum development. Elementary literacy curriculum, specifically. I'd be working on projects like diversifying reading lists, developing more inclusive curriculums for neurodivergent students, leading focus groups." His mouth quirks, that hint of enthusiasm easing the tension in his shoulders. "I love teaching, I *do*. But I think I could really make a difference in this role? And after six months, they would subsidize my master's. So."

Her eyes widen. "What?"

"Yeah."

Theo leaving teaching is so much to process, but it sounds incredible. Also, who would turn down free grad school in this economy?

"Theodore!" She pulls him in close, her entire body initially vibrating with joy for this man who she loves. Why didn't he tell her? Did he not want to jinx it, to admit how much he wanted it? Evie can understand that. "There's nothing to discuss. Seriously! I—"

"It's in New York, Ev."

"What?"

"The job."

Evie doesn't see it coming.

That's the worst part.

"You've been . . . applying to jobs in New York?"

"Not jobs! Just this one. Caro sent me the listing and—"

"What the fuck?"

She stands. Paces, unsure whether to laugh or cry, because of course. Caro. Every time her guarded heart cracks open for him she's ambushed by *Caroline Shapiro-Huang*. She's seventeen again, Theo rejecting her earnest promposal because Caro beat her to it. She's nineteen and on an airplane to surprise Theo and who is he hooking up with when she arrives? Caro. It's the story of her life. A tragic comedy. Objectively hilarious. *It'd be impossible. Leaving you.* Did Theo say that to her before or after he applied to a fucking job in fucking New York because of fucking Caroline Shapiro-Huang?

"I'm sorry. This is a messed-up way to find out. I didn't think I'd get it," Theo says weakly. "Really, I thought it was a long shot. You've been so busy and we've been good and I didn't want to be a distraction, to make this into a thing if it wasn't going to be a thing."

She's sat on the end of his bed once more, bunching the navy duvet cover in her hands. "When would you start?"

"June. So I can finish out the school year."

"Cool." Evie opens Google on her phone, her mind racing. "Okay. Well. We should probably file the paperwork as soon as possible? I don't know shit about divorce law or how long it will take. Probably something we should've checked before we became, like, legally tethered to each other? But I'm sure you don't want to return to New York, to *Caro*, a married man—"

"Whoa—"

"On average it takes *six months* to finalize a divorce? *Why?*"

"Ev. *Slow down.*" Theo stands. He sits next to her on his bed, so close she can feel his breath on her cheek. Evie scoots away, her rational brain needing the space to think. "I'm so sorry I didn't tell you that I applied, but I would never just accept a job on the other side of the country without talking to you first. It's a cool opportunity, but I'm also super happy here. I don't have to take it."

"Obviously you're taking it."

"Obviously?"

"I'm not a factor. Seriously! The studio just approved my mix for *Save the Last Dance*, so my union application should be approved by June. Honestly, I was so excited to tell you the news. We can file. This is over."

Theo's eyebrows knit together. "Is that what you want? Us to be over?"

"Take me out of the equation. Would you go?"

"Yeah. But—"

"Then you have to go."

He blinks at her, looking so at a loss. "But that's such a *pointless* question."

"Theodore. Take the job. There's nothing to discuss with your wife because *we're not actually married*. You know that, right? This? Us? It isn't real."

Evie stands.

She needs to put more space between them, needs him to retreat.

Instead, Theo reaches for her wrist. "Come on. We both know that's bullshit."

Evie shakes her head. "Still."

Still.

Still.

Still.

It's an accidental admission that emboldens him to press his palm against hers, to weave their fingers together. "Ev. You are part of the equation. Always."

Theo states this so simply, and she isn't sure if there has ever existed a combination of words so tender, so terrifying.

"I don't want to be." Evie pulls her hand out of his and steps back, back, back because she can't believe that this is happening again, her pushing him away for their own good. "You can't stay for me."

"I *can*." Theo takes a deep, measured breath. Closes his eyes, then continues, "But also . . . you could come with me?"

"What?"

Evie remembers when Imogen told her about Denver, moments before plummeting down Big Thunder Mountain. *It was easy. Saying yes.* If she loves Theo, why does every bone in her body scream *no*?

"New York was always our plan? Right?"

Sure. As children. When both their dreams led them there. Now his is within reach there, but she has a new dream, one that's within reach right here. Still, Evie closes her eyes and tries to imagine herself in New York. She can't. It's exhausting to think about moving across the country, finding new doctors after years spent building trust with her current team of physicians, securing an apartment in an elevator building because no way in hell can she deal with endless stairs during flare-ups, living so close to Naomi.

No.

"I can't move to New York. What am I supposed to do there?"

"There are Foley jobs! I did some research. Checked. Before I even applied." Theo runs a hand through his hair, his ears turning pink. *You are part of the equation.* "You could freelance. Or work for a studio. I know it's a competitive industry, but you'll have Next in Foley on your résumé. So—"

"But I'm building a network here. I can't just give that up. To what? Follow a man across the country?"

Theo flinches. "A *man*?"

Evie continues, "Take the job. Why wouldn't you?"

"*Because,* Ev. I—"

"*Don't.*"

Silence.

Theo clenches his jaw.

Exhales.

Then he asks, "What are you so afraid of?"

You.

You.

You.

She crosses her arms and clutches her elbows. "I need a beat."

Then Evie retreats to her room, a part of her hoping that he will follow, but she's mostly just relieved that her tears can free-fall when he doesn't.

NEW YORK, SPRING BREAK, FRESHMAN YEAR

Theo

Theo meets Caro at the basketball court adjacent to the West Fourth Street subway entrance. Pops one, two edibles, then offers them to Caro when she greets him. *Literally, the only perk*, she says, plucking one from the tin with a cheeky grin. When you're the kid of someone who had cancer, the universe provides access to a medical marijuana card. Theo used to be so overwhelmed by so many feelings, but now he just pops a gummy that dials down the intensity, that dulls his anxiety so he can function. He pockets the tin and takes Caro's hand, leading her toward the nearest Duane Reade.

"Snacks?"

Caro nods. "Obviously."

After registering the cost of a bag of chips, they pivot to the dining hall at Theo's dorm, where the snacks are still overpriced, but at least he can use dining dollars. In College Math, that basically means they're free. Content with their haul, they head toward the elevator that will take them up to his room, to his bed. As they're debating the merits of various Lays flavors, the edible hits.

"Classic?" Caro's laugh echoes off the elevator door. "Fuck off."

He leans in, his arm against the cool aluminum. "It's *classic* for a reason, is it not?"

"Okay."

Caro tastes like Sour Patch Kids, like his childhood, like *home*. Caroline Shapiro-Huang is not—has never been—Theo's girlfriend. She set the terms of their situationship in high school. Whispered, *You're not my boyfriend, you know,* in his ear after prom, both naked in the back seat of her Bronco. *Yeah.* He nodded, so relieved. *Cool.* Theo didn't want a girlfriend. Not then. Not now.

It's easier.

Better.

So. Theo and Caro understand what they are to each other. Friends that are tethered together by Pasadena, by the experience of typing *electric razors best* into Google, by undeniably good sex. It's enough. An antidote to the homesickness, the *loneliness.* Her mouth is on his neck as he fumbles with his keys and pushes the door open. His fingers tease the hem of her shirt before gliding under the silk fabric, and every sensation is amplified by the high. When Theo's palms press against her lower back, Caro's lips return to his as she backs him into his room and it's enough. *It is enough*—

"*Fuck.*"

His best friend's voice sends him backward. Theo blinks once, twice at the voice, at her *face*. Evelyn is *here*, dressed in his mom's Billy Joel concert tee and leggings, her hair in a messy bun. Theo must have bought a bad batch of edibles, laced with something else because weed doesn't make anyone hallucinate a goddamn fantasy mid-hookup with someone else.

With Caro.

This is a bad trip.

Please, let this be a bad trip. "Evelyn?"

She's on her feet, grimacing when her bad ankle buckles. "Oh my God. I'm *so* sorry."

How is she here?

In New York.

In his bedroom.

Caro tugs at her shirt, her voice breezy, casual. "Hey! Theo didn't mention you were visiting."

Theo is entirely at a loss. "You're . . . ?"

Evelyn picks up her backpack off the floor and tosses it over her shoulder. "Leaving!"

Then she's gone.

Caro's eyebrows rise as she nods toward the door. "You should probably . . ."

Theo is in motion. "*Ev.* Wait. Don't . . . You just got here?"

"I'm crashing with Mir and Mateo," she says, bending down to tie her sneakers as she exhales an awkward chuckle. "I wanted to surprise you. Obviously, I should've called."

"Can I see you tomorrow?"

Evelyn zips her coat. "Sure."

"Cool."

It's been six months since he's been in the same room as Evelyn Bloom. Since he could touch her. He misses touching her. Theo rakes a hand through curls that are tangled, long overdue for a trim. There's so much to say. He's too stunned to speak. So fucking high. He wants to reach out to her, wrap his arms around her, ask her how she feels, tell her how much he *misses her*, but she's gone before he even remembers to wish her a happy birthday.

Caro's mid−giggle fit when he returns to his room. "Well. That definitely killed *my* boner."

"I'm sorry."

"Why?" She ties her hair up with a neon blue scrunchie. "You're not my boyfriend."

"I know. But—"

"Theo."

"I'm such an asshole."

"No. If you were an asshole, I'd actually be into you. Romantically," Caro teases, as if Theo isn't on the verge of a meltdown. "Theo. I can *see* you spiraling. Calm down. We both know that this isn't . . . that it was never anything more than sex. I mean. We have nothing in common, except for the worst thing to have in common."

"Right."

Caro bro-punches his arm. "We're cool, Cohen. Don't screw this up."

"What?"

"Evie flew across the country to see you."

"I know."

"On her birthday."

Theo drags his hand across his face. "*Fuck.*"

Caro gives him a sympathetic pat on the shoulder as if their tongues weren't just in each other's mouths. Then she exits his room, swiping the half-eaten bag of Sour Patch Kids on her way out. *What the fuck?* Theo's so overwhelmed, so *overcome* by everything that just transpired that all he can do is eat an entire bag of Classic Lays, take a hit from Dev's bong, and fall asleep.

In the morning, he texts Evelyn immediately.

hey

7:30 A.M.

i'm sorry about yesterday
7:31 A.M.

i'm so happy you're here
7:32 A.M.

meet me in the park at nine?
7:32 A.M.

washington square park
7:32 A.M.

just to clarify
7:32 A.M.

there are a lot of parks here
7:32 A.M.

or i can come to you . . . if commuting downtown
again is too much?
7:33 A.M.

God.

He sounds like such a *loser*.

Theo drops his phone and rolls out of bed because he needs coffee and a shower. After, he tosses a hand towel over his shoulder and cracks two eggs into a sizzling frying pan. Waits for Evelyn to text him back. When the door to Topher's room creaks open, Theo cracks two additional eggs. His roommate always emerges from his slumber just in time for eggs. In return, he cleans the kitchen. It's a win-win. His eyes shift toward the door, toward Toph. Except. Not Toph. *Evelyn?*

Evelyn . . . in a Metallica shirt that skims her knees.

Toph's shirt.

"Hey." Her *just woke up* voice is raspy and he feels like such an idiot for believing that this visit meant something more. "Toph and I ran into each other—"

"It's really none of my business."

He attempts a lighthearted tenor, a *no big deal* shrug to mask how much he hates that Evelyn woke up in someone else's clothes, in someone else's bed. Cuts her off because Theo has no right to feel any kind of way about who Evelyn wakes up next to, but that doesn't mean he needs to know how the fuck it happened. Theo returns his focus to the eggs, doesn't want them to burn. He flips the omelet, then pours two cups of coffee.

Evelyn shakes her head. "Oh. No, thanks."

She's refusing coffee? "Are you okay?"

"Yeah. No, I'm . . ." She chuckles, awkwardly. "I'm just currently on this, like, gluten-free, low-FODMAP diet? Sort of . . . still in the process of relearning what I can and can't eat?"

"Oh."

He looks at her. Registers how much thinner she is and is overwhelmed all over again by how much he misses her, by how much he's *missed* because his life is so far away from hers. He's found his footing in New York. It took months. In the beginning, everything about New York was so loud, incredibly overstimulating, way too much. Theo couldn't focus during classes. His anxiety became unmanageable. He only ever felt like himself on *Survivor* Wednesday, while watching his favorite show and texting with his favorite person. By mid-October, the homesickness was suffocating. He called Evelyn after *Survivor* because he missed her voice, because he wanted to mention that he's considering transferring. Coming home.

He remembers the pain in her voice, so soft against his ear.

You have to stay.

I will hate you if you don't stay.

Her words reminded him of a conversation they had after she was discharged from the hospital, in the aftermath of his careless mistake that shattered her dance dreams, and a diagnosis that recalibrated her future entirely. *Obviously, New York is off the table. I can't dance and . . . I have to figure out what the fuck is going on with my body.*

Theo completely understood, was grateful even that he hadn't committed yet. *USC has an excellent teaching program.*

What? Just because I'm not going doesn't mean . . . no. You have to go.

I—

Theodore. You can't stay. New York is your dream. He could hear the panic in her voice, the pain. *You're going. Promise me.*

And because he didn't know how to articulate that *she* was so much a part of that dream, he promised, committed, and went. Then felt like such an asshole during that phone call in October because he was here, and she wasn't, and he was *complaining* about it. So again, he listened to his best friend. Stayed. Called Caro. Became really good at compartmentalizing. Convinced himself, his heart, that it was for the best. If he stayed away from her, he wouldn't have to deal with any of it. Her. These reckless feelings.

Except.

Now he doesn't even know what his best friend can and cannot eat.

"Eggs are cleared." Evelyn nods at the carton on the counter. "Scrambled. Plain."

Theo nods. "I can do that."

"Thanks, Theodore."

His shoulders settle as soon as she says those three sylla-
bles.

Theodore.

Okay.

They're okay.

Theo can be okay.

24

Theo throws back a "Honey I'm Home"-a Paloma like a shot, not a themed cocktail meant to be nursed. Micah and Pranav are hosting a housewarming party at their West Hollywood condo. It's a two-bedroom in an elevator building, with an open floor plan that has plenty of natural light for Micah's plants, furnished with an eclectic mix of contemporary and vintage pieces that somehow all work together. Theo counts the attendees, who range from casual acquaintances to total strangers, then stops at twenty-five and marvels at the fact that over twenty-five people can exist in this space and there's still room to breathe. *How?* He pours another Paloma. Theo sat in traffic for an hour. Alone, because Evelyn needs a beat. It's been a week and he's not sure what pisses him off more—that he didn't tell her sooner or that she reacted just how he knew she would. He stops thinking about it the moment the tequila burns hot in his throat.

"Cohen!" Pranav embraces Theo, positively glowing in homeownership. "You made it!"

"Wouldn't miss it," Theo says, handing him Trader Joe's most expensive bottle of wine. "This space is awesome."

"Is this you forfeiting, Singh?" an unfamiliar voice yells from the living room, where a chessboard is set up, midgame. "Smart move!"

"I will never surrender!" Pranav bellows, then looks at Theo. "Excuse me."

"Garrett's been a grand master since he was, like, ten." Theo's eyes shift to a woman standing at the opposite end of the island, who's scanning the wine selection before ultimately selecting a bottle of red. "Pranav's pretty screwed."

Theo tips his cocktail. "But we love his delusion."

"We sure do." The woman laughs, clinking her wineglass against his. Tattoos cover her left arm, a fine-line botanical sleeve. He'd compliment them, if he were to flirt with her. Or her eyes. They're pretty. Objectively. Clear blue, rimmed with gold charcoal. She's dressed in low-rise jeans and a black tube top, the ends of her brunette bob skimming her shoulders. "I'm Claire."

"I'm married."

Claire smirks. "And I'm a lesbian."

Theo nods.

He needs to cool it with the fruity cocktails.

"Fuck." He runs a hand through his hair, then holds it out. "Theo."

Claire works in ad sales at the same company as Pranav, but her dream is to be a stand-up comedian. She introduces herself not to flirt with Theo, but to tell him that she has a monthly stand-up show at the Elysian and to pass him a card with her Instagram handle and a QR code linking to her performance schedule.

"This isn't a networking event, Claire-Bear," Micah chastises, appearing out of nowhere, then booping her on the nose after he puts down the stack of catering trays. "We talked about this."

"And I hear you!" Claire says, then sips her wine. "I do. But then I merely said *hello* to this man and he needed to inform me of his marital status." Micah's cackle is so loud, it interrupts her defense. "What's for dinner?"

"Chipotle," Micah says, eyes crinkling in the corners. "In all fairness, if I had a face like Theo's, I'd also assume everyone wants to fuck me."

"Fuck off."

Micah boops him. "Nope."

Theo stands to help set up the buffet as if they're still roommates, as if he knows where the cutlery is. He doesn't. So he removes the foil from the trays. Makes himself useful as Claire and Micah continue to roast him and he should've stayed home . . . except being home right now is unbearable.

"Where's Evie?" Micah asks.

"Home." Theo dips a chip in the bowl of guac. "She needs a beat."

Claire's brow furrows. "A beat?"

"Come again?" Micah asks.

"It's my fault." A small floof presses against Theo's calf, sending his gaze down to the twelve-pound menace he misses so much. "Hey, Puck." Puck hisses when Theo bends down, scoops him into his arms, and cradles him like a baby. "I sort of got offered a job in New York . . . and never told her I applied for a job in New York?"

Claire blinks. "Wait. You applied for a job in New York *without telling your wife?*"

The crowd that has circled around Pranav and Garrett

roars. It gives Claire an out, who swipes her wineglass off the counter, mutters, "*Men*," under her breath, then gravitates toward the commotion just as Pranav squeals, "Shit! Am I *winning?*" Theo is curious enough to join, more than happy not to discuss the beat that's taken over his life. But Micah keeps him in the kitchen.

"*Talk.*"

Theo shrugs.

Repeats, "I fucked up."

"Not to *me*, Cohen."

"I can't."

"Because she needs a beat?"

"Yeah."

Theo spills his guts to his former roommate about his current roommate, his best friend, his wife. Tells Micah the truth. *I love her.* States it so plainly, so obviously, and it terrifies him. Hasn't it always? Isn't it, on some level, why he applied for the curriculum coordinator position? He knows Evelyn Bloom enough to anticipate her reaction, that history would repeat, that she'd push him away. Theo *knew*. Yet he applied.

"Okay. So." Micah drums his fingers on the quartz countertop. "Just to be clear. You can't talk to her until *she* wants to talk to you?" Theo tosses back what is left of his drink and considers for the first time how often those four words—*I need a beat*—are wielded to end a conversation, oftentimes before it even begins. "You know that's not cool, right? Disengaging when shit gets real is . . . super unhealthy."

Still, his instinct is to push back. "Ev just needs some space to process. You know?"

Micah shakes his head. "Theo? I'm going to say this as gently as possible, because I love you. Get the fuck out of my house."

"I can't drive."

"I'm requesting an Uber. I'll drop your car off before my lab tomorrow."

"You have a Saturday lab?"

"Go home, Theo. Talk to your wife."

"*Micah.*"

"Karl with a K will be here in five minutes."

An eruption of cheering pulls Micah's focus before Theo can push back, shifting his gaze toward the living room as Pranav jumps to his feet, then onto the couch.

"Checkmate, *bitch.*"

Theo spends the next forty-five minutes in the back seat of Karl with a K's Lexus LS emboldened by two-and-a-half fruity cocktails and Micah Solomon. *You know that's not cool, right? Honestly?* No. Theo has never much thought about how these beats make *him* feel. Six weeks, when she attended a dance intensive in Santa Barbara. Five days, after he admitted to being the reason she got into her fellowship. Four years, following the aftermath of spring break. Well. Evelyn would never call their college years a *beat.* It's not like they ever stopped talking. No. They just got busy.

Busy.

Busy.

Busy.

Bullshit.

Theo fumbles with his keys, standing on the doormat of their apartment. Is he a doormat? Does he ever consider how *anything* makes him feel? *I need a beat.* Evelyn may utter the words, but Theo latches on to them as permission to avoid, to deny, to not feel anything at all. Inside, he flips a light switch, his eyes instantly drawn toward the stack of papers on the kitchen island, thick and held together with a binder clip. In bold are three words that he saw coming.

PETITION TO DIVORCE

Cool.

Theo saw this coming, but it's still a fucking blow to the chest. His whole life, Evelyn Bloom has dictated the terms of their relationship, and it was always enough for him, to just be in her life.

Talk to your wife.

His heart leads him to her room and he knocks, his knuckles rapping the hollow wood twice before he twists the doorknob and lets himself in to find Evelyn wrapped in her electric blanket, watching *Grey's Anatomy* on her laptop. Katherine Heigl is on the screen. Classic *Grey's*. An episode she's likely seen countless times.

"Hey."

"Are you okay?"

Evelyn shrugs. "Honestly, it's been an up-and-down week. Pain-wise."

Same.

Theo pushes that thought away because it's different, their pain. It *is* different. Obviously. She scoots over, makes space for him, and he folds because it's an olive branch, because she's in pain, so his pain can wait. Theo strips his street clothes and climbs into her bed. Wraps his arms around her and *sighs* when she snuggles into him and rests her head on his heart and it hurts. She hurts. He removes his glasses and presses the heels of his hands to his eyes, suddenly feeling overwhelmed. Always, he let Evelyn set the boundaries, let her *take a beat*, let her push him away. Never pushed back because it was easier to leave it be, to bury his feelings, to safeguard his heart. Because isn't to love to lose?

But this hurts, too.

This hurts, too.

"I'm sorry," Evelyn says, pressing her thumb against his cheek. "For my reaction. I didn't see it coming. I'm not sure why. You sort of belong in New York, Theodore? I'm happy for you. I *promise*."

Theo turns his head so their foreheads touch. "Do you want to be with me?"

"I don't want to be married."

"That's not the question."

"I can't move to New York."

"Also not the question."

Her brow furrows. "Have you been drinking?"

"Not really?" Theo frowns. "I had, like, two drinks at Micah and Pranav's. Then took an Uber home because we need to—"

"No." Evelyn pushes him, *literally* pushes him away. "I don't want to do this right now."

"I do."

The weight of those words settles between them.

I.

Do.

"I'm not drunk," Theo continues. His voice is so solid, so *sure*. "We need to talk about us. I *want* to talk about us. I'm done *not* talking about—"

"Theodore. There is no *us*."

"Ev—"

"I got the paperwork started."

"I saw. But—"

"It's a straightforward process, considering we don't have

any assets. It won't be finalized until midsummer at the earliest, which isn't super convenient but—"

"*Stop.*"

Theo doesn't raise his voice. Never yells. But the way her eyes widen at the *snap* in that single syllable? He may as well have screamed. "Just *listen*," he says, softer. Begs. "I never said I'm taking the job. I meant it when I said that you are part of the equation. We don't have to be married for that to be true."

"Why?"

"You're seriously asking me that?"

She nods. Digs in. "Yeah. Why *now?*"

"I don't understand the question."

"Theodore. I can only be rejected so many times."

"Rejected?"

"Prom," she says, counting on her fingers, and Theo's unsure what throws him more, that she's still holding on to prom or the insinuation that maybe, possibly, they have felt the same way about each other since *prom?* Evelyn continues her list. "Spring break . . ." She pauses. Swallows. Then holds out her third finger. Her ring finger. "Lori's—"

"*Evelyn.*"

"You wanted to talk about us."

"One, we were both wasted. Two, *my mom had just died.* I'm . . ." Theo rakes a hand through his curls. "Are you serious right now?" Evelyn shrugs. "I wanted to talk about it. The morning after. *You* acted like it didn't happen, then got back with Hanna."

"*Months* later."

"I know. I'm sorry! We were just . . . my mom . . ." Theo's losing the plot. "I'm sorry. But you have to know I felt the same way. I *feel* the same way. Present tense."

She shakes her head. "It doesn't matter."

"Of course it matters."

"You need to be in New York."

Frustration raises his blood pressure, his watch vibrating against his pulse. "Evelyn. Can you please stop acting like you know what I need? I'm telling you what I need. *You*. Any way I can have you. Every way I can have you. And that terrifies me! It always has, but I don't want to waste any more time pretending that I just love you, that I'm not also hopelessly *in* love with you. I want to be with you. Whatever that means. However you want me." He shifts onto his knees, tilts her chin up with the pad of his thumb so that her eyes meet his. "I don't need New York. Or a job in curriculum development. I. Need. You."

There it is.

Theo's feelings.

Felt out loud . . . and met with silence.

Then, a single word. "No."

25

"What?"

"I'm answering your question," Evie whispers. She lets out a shaky exhale as she pulls away and wraps her arms around her knees to soothe the stomach stabbies that have come and gone all week, that refuse to subside. *Fuck.* She needs them to subside. Needs this minor flare-up to not become a full-blown flare-up. Needs *Theo.* "I don't want to be with you."

Theo covers her knee with his hand, so gentle it hurts. "I love you."

"You won't change my mind about marriage."

"Noted." He presses his lips against her forehead. "I love you."

"I can't leave Dr. Griffith."

His expression softens, then shifts into something so hopeful that Evie immediately knows she's said the wrong thing. "*Ev.* Dr. G loves you, too. I'm sure she'll refer you to the best. We can figure that out first. Choose a neighborhood depending on where the best GI doctor in New York City is based."

"No." She digs her nails into her knees and inhales. "I don't *want* to leave Dr. G. Or any of my doctors. It isn't just doctors . . . it's finding a new infusion center, deciphering new state insurance laws, convincing new phlebotomists that I know where my best veins are and to please use the 25G needle, so I'm not covered in bruises from a bad draw. I know it's invisible, so sometimes it's easy to forget that I'm sick but—"

"Is that what you think?"

Theo looks wounded. Theo, who keeps their kitchen stocked with her favorite foods. Who will carry her around Disneyland based on one super specific eyebrow twitch. Who knows her medication and supplement dosages and when she's running low on something. Who would be at every infusion if they weren't on school days. *It's easy to forget that I'm sick.* It's an unfair accusation and Evie knows it. But. She will not be the reason Theo doesn't accept his dream job.

He needs to go.

She needs to stay.

"No. But . . ." Evie presses on the wound, feeling eighteen all over again. "A move is a life-changing decision *without* an autoimmune disease and I've . . . well, I've been in remission since you moved home. You weren't around when it was bad—"

"I would've been." His voice is strained as he leans in, so close their foreheads touch. So close she dares to press her palm against his chest. "God, Evelyn. You *know* I would've been."

"I know."

It's unintentional, this admission.

"Okay. I'll stay."

Theo says it so simply, makes it *feel* simple.

Staying.

Loving her.

"Theo."

"I want to stay. *I love you.*" Theo attempts to wipe away her tears, cannot catch them fast enough. "Ev. *Trust me.*"

And.

Well.

She *does*.

Evie Bloom trusts Theo Cohen with her whole heart. It's not something she has the best record with. Trust. For the first eighteen years of her life, she trusted doctor after doctor who assured her that she was healthy. She trusted that Naomi's beats would always be temporary. She trusted that Hanna understood that marriage was off the table and still loved her anyway.

Trusting Theo?

It scares the shit out of her because if—*when*—he breaks that trust?

It will break her.

"How can I?" Evie squeezes her eyes shut, knowing the perfect combination of words that will puncture, deepen the wound. "Theo. The last time I trusted you? You literally dropped me."

Theo recoils.

All the air exits his lungs in an audible *whoosh*.

She may as well have slapped him.

"I'm sorry." Instant regret buoys her toward him as soon as she sees the guilt that flashes across his face. It was a fucked-up thing to say, to insinuate that her injury was in any way his fault when she knows—she *knows*—that he still believes that. Evie pinches the bridge of her nose, her stomach gurgling. "I didn't . . . I don't know why I said that. I feel like shit. Can we just talk in the morning? Take a beat?"

Theo stands, expression blank.

"Okay, Naomi."

It's Evie who recoils now. "Fuck you."

"What? Is this not what Naomi did to you? Shut down and disappeared when shit got hard or complicated or real or—"

"*Theo.*" She cuts him off, her nostrils flaring. She only lobbed words that hurt, pushed him away, because *she loves him* and if he's going to get everything he wants, he needs to let her go . . . and he's retaliating with the most painful combination of words *to hurt* and she is already in so much pain. "I can't do this."

"Ev—"

"Get. The fuck. *Out.*"

Theo raises his arms in resignation. "Okay." Then he drags a hand across his face, so exhausted, so sad, so *done* as he backs toward the door. "But, Ev? You can't blame people for leaving when you're the one shoving them out the goddamn door."

Their marriage was always going to end in a no-fault divorce. It's what Evie wants. In the days after their fallout, she takes antinausea medication every night before bed. It's what she wants. Watches *Love Island* alone. It's what she wants. Works overtime. Pushes her body beyond its limits, so she crashes as soon as she gets home. It's what she wants.

Currently, is dedicating an entire therapy session to this assertion. "It's what I want."

"You keep saying that." Jules nods, a floating head on Evie's computer screen. "So. What's keeping you in Pasadena?"

"Work."

"Valid."

"Phoebe." Jules's eyebrows rise, prompting Evie to elaborate. "My car."

"Ah."

"You."

"Me?"

"Yeah. I'd need a new Jules if I moved to New York, wouldn't I?"

"You would."

"*Fuck* that."

Jules's mouth quirks, but then their expression softens. "Evie. Is the idea of building trust with new providers maybe, possibly, triggering some medical trauma stuff for you?"

Evie shrugs.

Rips a hangnail.

Bleeds.

"Maybe," she concedes. "I don't know if I have it in me to start over? I think about it and get so overwhelmed and I just . . . can't. How am I supposed to let go of the first doctors who saw my pain and believed me?"

"I understand that." Jules has ulcerative colitis, so this isn't some false platitude—a huge reason that she trusts Jules is because they *do* understand health stuff. "Navigating the healthcare system while chronically ill is the *worst*." They take notes. Evie fixates on the *clicks* of the keyboard, continuing to pick the skin around her nails as they type. "Did you talk about this with Theo?"

"I did."

"What did he say?"

"*I'll stay.* As if it's that simple!"

Jules blinks. "Isn't it?"

"No."

"Why not?"

"I think, for me . . ." Evie has moved on to fidgeting with the hair elastic on her wrist after adequately destroying the skin around her thumb as she attempts to articulate what she means, looking everywhere but at Jules. "If I had another chance to dance? I would take it. Without hesitation. I wouldn't choose him. So. I can't let him choose *me*."

"His decision isn't yours to make."

"I know."

"Do you?"

"Yes! I just don't want to be a factor in his decision."

"Why not?"

Shit, Jules! Why didn't Evie stick to health stuff, social anxiety, Naomi? Seriously, there's nothing her therapist enjoys more than validating Evie's *Naomi fucked me up* feelings, then sending her links to books written for children with emotionally immature parents. She should pivot to one of these comfortable topics. Instead, she flails in extended silence that makes her want to crawl out of her skin.

"Because it can't be on me," she begins, finally. "When he regrets it."

Jules nods. "So. His decision isn't yours to make . . . but the consequences are on you?"

"Yeah."

"And he'll regret staying?"

"Yeah."

"That's a bold assumption."

"Is it?"

"Is it bold of you to think you know someone better than they know themselves? Yes." Jules blows a raspberry and runs their hand through their longer-on-top pixie cut. "It's also unfair to the other person in the equation . . . and, speaking from personal experience, super fucking annoying."

"Jules!"

"Evie." Jules's voice is softer, a normal volume. "Children of people with the traits of a personality disorder—"

Evie cuts them off. "This is *not* about Naomi."

"Okay."

"Not everything is about Naomi."

"True." Jules shrugs. "But you did grow up anticipating her needs, managing her emotions in order to protect yourself, downplaying your pain . . ."

Evie can hear the ellipsis at the end of Jules's sentence and knows where she's being led, what conclusion she's meant to come to. Is that not what this is? *No.* Is she not anticipating Theo will resent her if he stays? *No.* Is she pushing him toward New York now (again!) because obviously, eventually, he'll leave anyway? *No.*

No.

No?

Exhausted, her eyes shift to the bottom right-hand corner of her screen: 11:59. Evie's never been more relieved to tap out of a session. She snaps and points finger guns at Jules. "I'll totally spend the next week unpacking that!"

Jules snorts. "You will not."

"I will not."

Evie closes her laptop and flops backward onto her bed, somehow feeling worse than she did an hour ago. She's been unpacking this shit with Jules for five years. She knows who her mother is. Has worked so hard not to become—or exist as a reaction to—Naomi.

Okay, Naomi.

The casual cruelty of those two words rattles against her skull.

She didn't mention them to Jules.

Because this isn't about Naomi.

Evie stands. Stretches her limbs before exiting her room. Theo is in the kitchen, slicing an avocado like he's not supposed to be in school. Her stomach is on the floor. It's Monday. And . . . Theo's on spring break this week. She completely forgot and just, like, *therapied* about him for an entire hour.

"*Fuck.*" She passes him on her way to the fridge, unsure what she even wants. "Were you listening?"

"Thin walls."

He doesn't even deny it.

Evie closes the fridge, indecisive and empty-handed. "I have to go to work."

"Cool."

"Cool."

His eyes meet hers. "Are you hungry?"

"No," she lies.

Because it would be unbearable to sit here and let him prepare a meal for her, she swipes her keys off the counter and reaches for the doorknob.

"Ev," Theo says, and that one syllable, her name, is a strained exhale. It stills her, but she doesn't dare turn toward his voice, doesn't dare turn toward him. "I have to make a decision by the end of the week."

God.

He's so stubborn.

"Theodore—"

"I think I'm going to take it."

Oh.

"Obviously you're taking it."

She squeezes her eyes shut. Braces for Theo to push back. He doesn't. So. She's gone, so ready to get out of here, to get to the studio where she can turn off her brain. It doesn't register until she's on the freeway that she's still in her pajamas, so she reroutes to the nearest department store, and the tears that stream down her cheeks as she's thumbing through athleisure are *happy tears* because Theo is accepting the job. His dream job. In New York.

It's fine.

She's *fine*.

It's what she wants.

26

Milo continues to be such a little shit.

"Okay. Seriously. Mr. Theodore, what is *up* with you?"

"Just doing some grading." Theo keeps his voice nonchalant as he continues to mark up spelling quizzes. "*Circuit* really stumped a lot of you."

"Because there's a quiet *u*?" Kaia asks, not looking up from a tattered copy of *The Son of Neptune*.

Tyler groans. "There's a *u*?"

Milo narrows his eyes, undeterred by his deflection. "It's Ms. Evie. Isn't it?"

"Sit down, Milo."

"I *knew* it."

Kaia closes her book. "Did she make you sad?"

"Did *you* make *her* sad?" Annabelle asks, then nudges Sierra with a glittery elbow. Why the fuck is there glitter all over her elbow? "I *told you* something was wrong when Mr. Cohen didn't '1985' us last week!"

Commotion ensues, rendering silent reading over.

"Mr. Theo—"

"*Milo.*" His voice is firm. Sharp. "Sit. Down."

Silence.

Twenty-two sets of eyes stare wide at him. Theo doesn't snap at his students, doesn't snap at anyone *ever*, but he is exhausted. Some days, he worries it's a mistake. Leaving Foothill. Moving back to New York. Accepting a job developing curriculums for kids when he's found so much meaning and purpose working *with* his students. But in this moment? He can't get out of here fast enough.

"I'm sorry." Theo presses his index and middle finger to his forehead in an attempt to dull the early stages of a tension headache. "Can we not talk about Ms. Evie?"

Sierra looks at Kaia, then whispers loud enough for the entire class to hear, "Ms. Evie made him sad."

"We hate her," Annabelle declares.

Sierra's nod is emphatic. "Obviously."

At this swift, *protective* turn, he can't help but laugh. "Don't. *I* don't."

He doesn't.

Theo just misses his best friend.

"You know what I do hate?" Theo asks.

Annabelle gasps. "You can't say that word, Mr. Cohen."

Theo looks at her like *Really?*, then stands and continues, "The average score on this spelling quiz! Let's figure out these words together."

Kaia frowns. "Shouldn't we have ten more minutes to read?"

Theo replicates the *Really?* look, then gives Kaia permission to finish her chapter because he knows the rest of her day will be thrown off if he doesn't. Then he's at the board, writing down the *ui* words that tripped up his students. *Circuit. Anguish. Guilt. Bruise.* Then frowns at the board as if he's just registering these words for the first time, as if he didn't create this spelling test. If his students notice the theme, they don't say anything. For the rest of the afternoon, they're nice to him. It's disconcerting.

At the end of the day, Tyler compliments his shoes on his way out the door.

Theo needs to get himself together.

You literally dropped me.

It's been a month since Evelyn's response to *I love you* broke his brain, since he signed an offer letter in an attempt to ease the pain, the guilt, the *blame* those words reactivated. He relives the memory every night, is seventeen again and back in that conference center in Anaheim, before drifting into a restless sleep. Does she still blame him for the fall that ended her dance career before it began? He does. Blame himself for it. Hate himself for it. And even if she doesn't . . . if Evelyn just panicked and said that precise combination of words to hurt him?

It worked.

Rendered him an asshole.

Okay, Naomi.

Theo made such a mess out of his first attempt at vulnerability. Now he's just doing his best to move through time on autopilot. Stays late to get his grading done, then goes home and cooks dinner for two, leaving the second serving in the fridge. Weekend mornings, he wakes up early and trains for a half marathon that he'll never run because her snoring permeates the walls and it is unbearable. Even *Survivor* is a bummer, watching it together but not *together*. None of this is what he wants, but it's for the best.

Evelyn doesn't trust him.

Because it can't be on me. When he regrets it.

Theo knows those words weren't meant for his ears, but *fuck*, it hurt so much to hear the raw honesty in that confession to her therapist. He couldn't have been clearer about his feelings and *that* was her takeaway? That he'd regret her? In that moment, he didn't know how else to convince her. Didn't want to have to convince her.

So.

He took the job.

Because if she is really, truly incapable of believing him, it's easier to just give in, to be the person that she already believed him to be. Choose New York, the better salary, the life that he imagined for himself at twenty-three. Leave.

It hurts.

He hurts.

But it's for the best.

This, at least, is a pain he can handle.

"Where's Evelyn?"

Those are the first words out of Jacob's mouth when he registers that his son is standing on the front porch, alone, on a Sunday morning. It's a fair question. Evelyn doesn't miss Sunday breakfasts. Theo is the one who opts out. But he's here. Alone. Because Jacob still believes that they're married and someone needs to tell him the truth.

"It's me this week," Theo says, crossing the threshold into his childhood home. "Sorry to disappoint."

Jacob's brow furrows. "Is she okay?"

"Yes?"

"So she made a GI appointment?"

Theo attempts to mask his concern, his obliviousness. "I think so."

"You *think* so?" Jacob's expression renders him fourteen again. Theo's watch vibrates. "This is the third breakfast she's missed. Keeps oversleeping? *Get your wife to a doctor.*"

Theo clenches his fist.

Unclenches it.

Breathe.

Evelyn is probably just avoiding Jacob.

Because of the divorce.

But. He can't *know* that.

Jacob *pffts*, shaking his head as he pulls out his phone and types. It vibrates in his palm moments later, her response immediate—and only when his father's shoulders sag in relief do Theo's mirror his. Jacob slaps the message into Theo's hand then escapes to the kitchen.

> oh! thanks for checking. yeah, dr. g bumped up my infusion a week, then told me to take it easy for the rest of the week. i'm already feeling much better. my fault for being a workaholic, oops! see you next week?
>
> 9:01 A.M.

Theo's pulse thrashes against his throat, so relieved, but also? He's pissed. Mostly at himself for allowing the hurt to cloud his attention, for taking the food left uneaten as stubbornness, for believing Evelyn when she says *I'm fine.* But just as pissed that she concealed her pain from him when he could have been there for her. Health stuff trumps everything. She *knows* that. Does she think she's sparing him? From the worry? Doesn't she understand that he cannot turn that off? Theo could be in the next room, in New York, on the fucking *moon.* No matter how far away she pushes him, he will never stop worrying about her, wanting her, loving her. Theo sinks into the couch, the same couch where he used to watch *Bake Off* with his mom, and swallows his emotions.

He will *not* cry.

Not in front of Jacob.

"So," Jacob says, returning to the living room with two mugs. "You going to tell me what the fuck is going on?"

"Yeah. Um . . ." Theo chugs the coffee. Burns his tongue. "That's why I'm here."

Jacob smirks. "And I thought it was to check in on your old man."

Theo's eyes shift down, settling on a streak in the coffee table where acetone once spilled. Evelyn wanted to paint their nails black before a competition and the bottle tipped over. Took the finish right off. "Evelyn and I started the process of getting divorced."

Jacob sets his mug down. "What did you do?"

"What did *I* do?"

Jacob waits for an explanation and the sooner Theo gives one the sooner he can go. He starts at the beginning and tells his father a version of the truth. He needed their joint income to keep his apartment. Evelyn needed health insurance to take the fellowship. Them? This marriage? It was always meant to be a temporary condition. Transactional.

"We should've just been honest," Theo admits. "We're not married. Not really."

Jacob's eyebrows rise.

Then he *laughs.*

A bent-over, full-belly laugh.

"Like *hell* you're not."

The oven beeps once, twice, three times. Jacob stands, still chuckling as he's called back to the kitchen to retrieve a quiche. Returns with a slice for Theo. He's stunned. Coffee and quiche? Is this trying? Is Jacob . . . trying? Theo cuts into the quiche with his fork.

There are bacon bits in it.

He sets the plate on the coffee table. "Dad. I don't eat meat."

"Still?"

Theo has been a vegetarian for fifteen years. "Still."

"Your loss." Jacob takes a bite. "So. How are you going to fix things with Evelyn?"

"There isn't anything to fix."

"*Bullshit.*"

Theo flinches.

With the harsh snap of Jacob's voice, he's twenty-two. Lori's most recent round of treatment didn't do anything to shrink the tumor in her lung. She wanted to stop with the treatments, just wanted the pain to *stop*. But Jacob wouldn't hear it, not even when Theo begged him to listen. His mom went through one more clinical trial and a final round of radiation before they finally told Jacob *enough*. Lori was steady. *I'm dying.* Theo was firm. *There isn't anything to fix.* Jacob was livid. *Bullshit.* Cracks in their relationship were long apparent, but if he had to pinpoint a moment that severed father and son? It was this one. Theo's choice to accept that some things are impossible to fix.

"Theo." Jacob's voice softens and it's so out of character. "You love her."

A statement, not a question.

"It doesn't matter."

"Bullshit."

"I took a job in New York."

"There it is."

"It's a curriculum development role."

"Last time, it was NYU."

"What does that mean?"

"I need something stronger than this." Jacob retrieves a bottle of Kahlúa from his liquor cabinet. "I'm shit at this. Feelings. Obviously." He pours a generous splash into his mug, then chugs the rest of his tainted coffee. "But I loved your mom. *Love*."

Theo's eyes sting. "I know that."

Love made Jacob selfish.

Possessive.

In so much pain.

"You love Evelyn."

Theo's too worn down to deny it. "She's my best friend."

"Lor was mine. And I'd choose her again and again, even if our story ended the same way." Jacob pushes a hand through his curls, so similar to Theo's own tendency to mess with his hair in frustration. "Because a love like that? It's a goddamn *privilege*. You don't run from it."

"Run?" His voice is strained. "Evelyn told me to go. What am I supposed to do with that?"

"You stay."

"Dad."

"You fight for your wife."

"Do you even hear yourself right now?"

Why is he here? Theo stands and reaches for his jacket. This news could've been a call, a text, an *email*, so why the fuck did he subject himself to this misogynistic bullshit in person? He can't be here another moment. Can't face the whisper of truth in his father's words. It's too much to be not just called out, but clocked by the person who has never understood him.

It isn't until he's at the door that Jacob speaks again. "You're wasting so much time."

"Really?" Laughter bubbles in his throat because if he

doesn't laugh, he will scream. "What kind of parent tells their kid that their dream job is a waste of time?"

"*Mine.*"

One word, the rarest *glimpse* of vulnerability from Jacob Cohen, sucks all the air out of the room. Cuts off his laughter. "Dad—"

"I never said don't follow your dreams . . ."

He hears the ellipsis in his father's voice. "But?"

"But, Theo. Is she not a part of that dream?"

27

Gen?"

Evie is in the passenger seat of Imogen's Ford Maverick, a recent acquisition on her path to becoming a full-fledged (eco-friendly!) mountain lesbian. She was cueing an episode of *Sarabeth & Jack* from the comfort of her couch when Imogen broke into her apartment midafternoon, insisting she pack an overnight bag and request to take a personal day tomorrow. And what was the first thought that entered Evie's brain? *It's* Survivor *Wednesday.* Pathetic. She reached for the backpack on the top shelf of her closet the moment her phone buzzed with Sadie's permission. Ok. Now they've been driving north on the 101 for over an hour. Imogen blasts a pop girlie playlist. Chappell Roan. Sabrina Carpenter. Fletcher. Bops her head and sings along off-key as she drives up the Southern California coastline until Evie cuts the music and demands an answer.

"*Imogen.* Where are we going?"

Her sister's fingers drum on the wheel, eyes fixed forward on the road. "To the most magical place on Earth."

But.

They're driving *away* from Disneyland.

Oh.

"No."

"Yes."

"Imogen."

"Trust the process."

Evie groans, then presses her cheek against the window. She should've asked follow-up questions. She didn't. So, aside from flinging herself out of the truck à la *Lady Bird*, there's nothing she can do but accept her fate. An hour later, after leaving the coastline and weaving through the Santa Ynez Mountains, they arrive in a small mountain village that's straight out of a Hans Christian Andersen book. Solvang. It's impossible not to be charmed by the authentic Danish architecture, the windmills, the people who just . . . *live* here? Naomi used to bring them, her two princesses, to this fairy-tale town for a fairy-tale day. Imogen loved it so much, she begged Pep and Mo to take them back every summer. She still makes this annual pilgrimage. It's a step away from real life, a lo-fi excursion, a certified angst antidote.

Evie should've *Lady Bird*–ed herself.

"I hate you."

"I love you, too."

Imogen pulls into Solvang Inn & Cottages and Evie isn't taken by the thatched-roofed accommodations.

She's not.

They enter the bare-bones cottage and Imogen tosses first her backpack, then herself, onto the one bed they'll share. "I texted Steve." Steve is a local who Imogen befriended years ago during an aforementioned pilgrimage. Midforties. Wears eyeliner. Has a chihuahua tattooed on his biceps. "We're going to the Tiki Lounge tonight."

"Okay."

"It's karaoke night."

"Have fun."

"*Evie.*"

"What?"

"It's been *two months.*" Imogen's nails dig into Evie's shoulders. "I love you, but this mess of your own making? It's so *dumb.* So! We are here to have fun, because we are happy in Solvang! Then? You're going to go home and talk things out with Theo. Because you love him and he loves you and *this*"—Imogen lets go and gestures at the lovesick mess that is Evie Bloom—"is such a bummer to be around."

"So then why are we here?"

"*Because—*"

A knock on their cottage door cuts off Imogen, who's on her feet to answer like she's been waiting for it. Evie is so overcome and overwhelmed to see her grandparents at the threshold. Pep, dressed in an NPR T-shirt, loose linen pants, and hiking boots. Mo, with a sunburned nose and a grown-out beard.

"Hi, Sweets."

Imogen waves dramatically at their grandparents. "Because!"

Wrapped in their familiar embrace, Evie is happy to see them.

She *is.*

But also.

Is this an ambush?

"I can't believe you're here!" As much as she misses Pep and

Mo, she's unable to keep the suspicion out of her voice. How does she get out of whatever this is? Imogen has her cornered. "Sorry. What are you doing here?"

Mo makes a silly face as he ruffles her hair. "We missed you, too, kiddo!"

"Oh, we've been meandering our way back down the coast!" Pep slips her shoes off. Makes herself comfortable on the two-seater couch. "Just came from San Simeon."

"Have you not seen the photos?" Mo frowns. "We send them to the clouds."

"The *cloud*, Mo."

"Is that not what I said?"

Pep rolls her eyes. "Anyhoo, Genny called. Wanted us all to be here together before her big move. So we came!"

Oh.

This . . . is not an ambush?

She feels like such an asshole for her assumption that she goes along with everything Imogen wants to do, which is likely what her sister wanted all along. Imogen Bloom is sort of a master-mind like that. *We are here to have fun, because we are happy in Solvang!* Evie attempts to embrace it. Solvang. Serotonin. It's easy when she's spending time with her grandparents, who are still so stupid in love with each other. Mo surprises Pep with her favorite ice cream, unprompted. Pep reapplies sunscreen to his nose every ninety minutes. Hand in hand, they browse the street stalls and gift shops and this—*this*—is the love that Evie wants. Over thirty years of choosing each other without being tethered by a marriage license. She sips on soda water and picks at crack-ers and grapes on a charcuterie board while listening to their travel tales during a wine tasting that stretches on for hours.

Imogen shares photos of her soon-to-be cabin in the woods.

Everyone Evie loves is in the same place.

Almost.

Still. It's just one day. A fleeting moment. She yearns for a universe where this is their life, where she's a part of a family who stays. She isn't. David left first, before she knew her father enough to even miss him. Naomi left over and over again. Hanna. Pep and Mo sold the bungalow. Imogen is going to Denver. Theo back to New York. Everyone left or is leaving, and she considers what it could feel like.

Leaving, too.

"How's Theo doing?" Mo asks.

Evie swallows wrong, has to cough to clear her throat before she answers. "Good."

"Did you hear his news?" Imogen asks.

Pep's eyebrows rise. "News?"

"Yeah! Theo—" Imogen is cut off by the swift force of Evie's foot connecting with her shin under the table. "Ouch. *Shit*. Did you seriously just *kick me?*"

"*Girls.*" Pep chuckles, her chide so unserious. "Well. Now I *must* know this news!"

Imogen looks to Evie.

Gives her a chance to break this news.

Then blurts, "Theo accepted a job in New York."

Pep's eyes widen as she covers her mouth with her hands. "Evelyn! What?"

Evie's eyes shift from Pep's overzealous expression to Mo, who is staring at the ground. "You already know."

Her grandmother drops the act. "Of course we know."

"Theo comments on our pictures in the clouds."

"*Cloud.*"

Mo waves off the correction, then rests his hand on Evie's shoulder. "Are you okay, Evelyn?"

Imogen shakes her head. "No."

"*Gen.*"

"What! You're not."

Evie snaps a cracker in half. "It's, like, a dream opportunity for him. He has to take it. I told him to."

Pep's expression softens. "It's okay to not be okay."

"You can be happy and sad all at once," Mo says.

"I'm *fine.*"

Pep, Mo, and Imogen each flash their own distinct *no, you're not* expression.

Then they drop it.

At the Tiki Lounge, Imogen duets "My Heart Will Go On" with Steve, who has an ethereal voice that puts her sister's to shame. Pep and Mo sing "Islands in the Stream," so wine-tipsy and adorable that Evie can't *not* giggle. Solvang magic. Imogen signs them up for "Wannabe" and drags Evie to the makeshift stage to do the ridiculous dance that Evie choreographed for a talent show when they were in elementary school. It's fun. Evie leaves the stage laughing. Damn it, Solvang magic! She grabs another soda water from the bar, then returns to the high-top where her grandparents are seated, returns to her phone that's face down but glowing with a notification.

Notifications.

She has five missed calls.

Theo.

Theo.

Theo.

Theo.

Theo.

Something is wrong. Is it Jacob? Theo? She doesn't think, just calls him back, pressing her phone to her ear as her feet carry her outside.

Theo answers on the first ring. *"Ev."*

"What's wrong?"

"Where are you? Are you okay?"

She closes her eyes and exhales. "I'm fine, Theo. I'm in Solvang."

"What?"

"I'm in Solvang with Gen. My grandparents, too."

"Oh." His voice is so soft. His heart is so loud. She wishes she could reach through the phone and press her palm against his chest. "Shit. You could've told me."

"I . . . did I need to?"

"I thought something was wrong."

"Why?"

"It's Wednesday."

Oh.

Her heart is in her throat. "Right."

"But you're good?"

No.

"Yeah."

"I'll let you get back to your family, then."

Theo disconnects the call. The first thing Evie sees on her screen is a Google Alert that spoils the *Survivor* finale—and that is the moment when she loses it on a park bench. Outside the Tiki Lounge. In Solvang. Because Theo hasn't even left yet but he already feels so far away, and it's her fault because she pushes, she checks out, she built a concrete wall around her heart and it's fine, she is fine, it's what she wants. *It is what she wants.* If she keeps telling herself this, it must be true.

"Sweets?"

Evie wipes her eyes, unsure how long she's been out here, and it's all so ridiculous.

Sobbing in Solvang.

Her life.

She hiccups. "I don't know what's wrong with me."

Pep's answer is so simple, so obvious. "You're in love."

Evie is exhausted, so sick of everyone telling her how she feels.

Hates that it's so *obvious* how she feels.

"Am I like Naomi?"

Pep's brow furrows. "What do you mean?"

"Theo said I am."

"People say things they don't mean when they're hurting, Sweets."

"I don't know. I stay. I'm *here*. But sometimes I get so overwhelmed and I just . . . check out? Just like Naomi did. Does. Maybe I am like her. Jules is right. It's always about Naomi. I *am* basic and boring." She wipes snot from her nose and exhales a sharp laugh. "I threw the accident in Theo's face. My fall. Made him think I blamed him for it. I don't know why. No, I do. I think it really messed me up? Not because I lost dance or because of my diagnosis." Evie lets out another shuddering breath. "You know what one of my first thoughts was on the way to the hospital? *Mom will come home.*"

Evie has never said those words out loud before.

"Oh, Sweets."

"She didn't. Or, well, she didn't stay. Obviously." Months after Evie was discharged, when she broke down over this at Theo's house, it was Lori who held her hand, who told her the purple tulips next to her hospital bed were from Naomi. Her mom did make an appearance, dropped off those flowers while Evie was asleep. Didn't stay because seeing her daughter in a hospital bed, hooked up to so many machines? Learning that all this time Evie had an undiagnosed IBD? It was all too much for Naomi. Too much for *her*. "So. How am I supposed to trust him, anyone, when she didn't stay for me? My *mom*."

"Listen to me, Evelyn." The furrow deepens, her grandmother's expression turned sad and serious. "Naomi's decisions have nothing to do with you. Some people are just not capable of being a parent. Okay? Her loss was our gain. David's loss, too, though I suppose that one's on me. Him being raised by a workaholic and all. You and Genny were my chance to do better, and you have to know your grandfather and I think the world of you. We love you."

Evie blinks back fresh tears. "I'm sorry."

Pep rubs her back. "What on earth are you sorry for?" Evie wordlessly gestures at the mess that is herself and earns a soft chuckle, then her grandmother holds her closer. "There's nowhere I'd rather be."

"I think I love him."

"You think?"

"I can't leave LA."

"Why not?"

"Well. I can't exactly bring my doctors with me, and I spiral into panic at just the *thought* of finding new ones. I don't want to. So."

Pep nods. "I understand that. But Ev? Your care team will still be here if New York isn't the right fit. Or maybe they won't! Maybe Jules will switch practices and no longer take your insurance. Maybe Dr. G's research will take her elsewhere. There is no guarantee that staying means keeping them forever. But you trust them, right? So, if there's a part of you that *does* want to go, trust them to set you up with excellent care, no matter where life takes you."

Pep's point is a fair one. Evie hasn't considered this and will surely spiral over her care team leaving *her* before falling asleep tonight. Cool. Awesome. "It's not just that. I sort of have a great thing going here with Sadie?"

"New York isn't exactly lacking in opportunity."

Evie blinks. "Are you, Peppy Bloom, suggesting I put my career on the backburner and move across the country for some man?"

"Theo isn't just *some man*." Pep *tsks*, swatting her shoulder. "Stay! Go! Either way . . . it's okay to try to make it work, to hold on instead of push."

"Even if the end result is the same?"

"You don't know that, Sweets."

"I *do*."

"How?"

"I don't want to be married to him."

"No?"

"I won't be reduced to a wife."

Pep is quiet for a moment. Leans back on the bench. "Is that how you see it?"

"Is that not how *you* see it?"

"Evelyn. Sweets. No. Not at all."

"You and Mo are the strongest couple I know, and you're not married."

Pep chuckles. "Mo and I both had that already, and we didn't want to go through the hoopla again. That was our decision, but it doesn't mean we don't believe in marriage. More importantly, it doesn't mean that you shouldn't." She tilts her head, considering. "Of course, it's also okay if that is how you feel. Is that a deal-breaker for Theo?"

She sniffles. "He says no, but—"

"Evelyn," Pep cuts her off. "I'm sorry, but I'm even more confused. What is the problem?"

Silence.

Evie faintly hears Imogen butchering "Shake It Off" and everything in her wants to run back inside, toward her sister, away from these feelings, but she forces herself to stay still, to listen to the thrashing of her heart, to listen to herself. Theo loves her and she loves him, too, and marriage isn't a deal-breaker for him so . . . what is the problem?

Is she the problem?

"Me." She brushes her knuckles across her cheeks. "When I saw you and Mo, I thought you were ambushing me. I didn't mean to ambush myself."

"Oh, Sweets." Pep stands and holds out her hand, lips up-turned in a wry smile. "This was always an ambush."

STELLA HOFFMAN'S DANCE ACADEMY, SUMMER AFTER FRESHMAN YEAR OF COLLEGE

Evie

Evie is the first to arrive at Miss Stella's. It's a hot Monday in mid-July, the first week of a monthlong dance camp. She opens the studio with a key that no longer belongs to her, a key she never returned, to warm up before the kids arrive. Sitting alone in an empty studio that was once synonymous with home, she slips on her jazz shoes, then stands and stares at her reflection in the mirrored wall, a focused determination furrowing her brow.

Evie inhales.

Rests her palms on the maple wood barre.

And dares to go on relevé.

Fuck.

She winces, falling out and folding forward to relieve the pain. Evie squeezes her eyes shut. Fifteen months since she fell . . . and the simplest exercise still hurts.

Is this just her life now?

Will everything she loves always hurt?

Evie used to love dance camp. Attending it as a tiny dancer.

Working as a student teacher alongside Theo. When Miss Stella called her mid-infusion and asked if she'd be home for the summer and willing to teach? Her heart fluttered from the potential and she took the job without hesitation.

Evie needed the money.

Wanted a reason to be at the studio.

Assumed Theo would be here, too.

"Evie?" Caro's voice draws Evie's eyes up to her mouth, a mouth that is chewing a wad of pink gum, a mouth that has been on Theo's mouth. "I can lead warm-ups today if you need—"

"No."

Does Caro deserve the *snap* in Evie's voice?

Yes.

Caro pops her gum. "'Kay."

"I've got it."

Evie once lived for these last four weeks of summer. Now? It's going to be unbearable teaching with a fucked-up ankle, with no future in dance, with *Caro*. Not Theo. He took some internship in New York. Subletted an apartment somewhere. Since spring break (or, as Imogen calls it, the Topher Incident), their communication has been extra exclamation points. Excessive apologies for delayed responses. Super off. Neither addressed it. Both kept showing up for *Survivor* Wednesday, and the texts in between became sparser and sparser, but it was fine. Evie was certain dance camp and Afters and time together in real life would be a reset. She never considered that he wouldn't come home.

It's fine.

They're fine.

"Morning, girls!"

Miss Stella waltzes into the studio carrying coffees for

herself and Caro and a chai for Evie. Stella Hoffman is still as gorgeous and graceful as she was when Evie became her student over a decade ago; her only sign of aging is the stripe of gray in her platinum-blond ponytail. Evie was once obsessed with Miss Stella's hair, her nails, her lipstick. Now? She can acknowledge that her slight fixation on her dance teacher in elementary school was so baby gay.

It quickly faded.

Her crush.

Evie became a dancer and didn't have time for crushes.

Miss Stella's eyes shimmer when they meet hers. "It's good to see you in the studio again."

Evie beams. "It's better to *be* here."

"I missed it, too," Caro adds, as if she misses it in the same way.

Caro chose not to dance.

Evie had dance taken from her.

She ignores the comment as she ties her tap shoes, then pops two Tylenol as tiny dancers in tights and tutus filter into the studio in friendship clusters, all between the ages of six and ten. They greet Evie and Caro with enthusiasm, wrapping their arms around their waists. *I missed you, Miss Evie!* Sophia Rose, one of her former students, exclaims with her cheek pressed against her torso. Evie leads warm-ups while Caro sets up the arts and crafts station, then teaches the first thirty-two counts of choreography to a routine that the dancers will perform for their parents at the end of the summer. Attempts to mask the pain that spikes her heart rate whenever she overextends her bad ankle. Fails to hide the fatigue that builds over the course of the morning session. Dance camp is more babysitting than dance, so she thought she could handle it and is unprepared for the physical toll.

By lunch, she's ready to nap.

For the rest of the week.

Miss Stella notices.

"Ev."

"I'm fine."

Her eyes narrow. "Go home. Caro and I can handle the afternoon session."

Evie wants to scream.

She is too tired to scream.

Stella adjusts her schedule without fuss. Slashes her hours from full-time to part-time. Morning sessions Monday, Wednesday, and Friday. Afternoon sessions Tuesday and Thursday. Doesn't slash her pay and Evie's stomach flips, embarrassed because a naïve part of her believed if she just rehabbed her ankle, if she just managed her Crohn's symptoms into remission . . . maybe, *maybe* she wouldn't have to let go of this.

Dance.

She wipes her tearstained cheeks in the bathroom after her last session of the week concludes.

Feels so stupid.

Misses Theo so much.

Evie composes herself, then opens the bathroom door and Caro is just *there*, like a jump scare.

"*Shit*, Caro."

"Sorry, I just—"

Evie pushes past Caro and exits the studio. Caro follows her, two beats behind, then slides into the passenger seat of Phoebe.

"Question."

No. Evie doesn't have the energy to deal with Caroline

Shapiro-Huang. Every time she looks at Caro, she's transported back to Theo's dorm and feels like an idiot because whatever confusing feelings brought her there . . . weren't reciprocated. Obviously. Embarrassment still courses through her veins and touches every text, insisting that if she just adds one more ! at the end of a sentence, everything will be fine.

Everything is not fine.

Evie rests her forehead against the top of the steering wheel.

"I'm going to ask this as gently as possible." Caro lets out her ponytail just to bunch it all into a messy topknot. "What is your problem with me?"

"I don't . . . Caro, I don't have a problem with you."

Caro snorts, then flips the vanity mirror and applies vanilla lip balm. "Your energy this week is super hostile."

"It's—" She cuts herself off before she says *not*, swallows the defensiveness that's so Naomi. Besides, hostile is generous. She's been a bitch. "I'm sorry. It's not . . ." Evie's voice trails off as she gestures at her ankle, at her poor excuse.

"It's never been serious or, like, romantic."

Evie blinks. "What?"

"Theo."

"Okay."

"He's too obsessed with you."

"Caro."

She laughs. "It's good! *Seriously*. I never wanted something serious and he never wanted serious with me." She gets out of the car. "My sex life is none of your business, but I just wanted you to know that . . . Theo is no longer the person I call when I need a platonic fuck buddy. He hasn't been that person, well, since spring break."

"*Caro.*"

"I just . . . I get how it looked."

"It's not like that."

Caro's expression hardens with Evie's double down. "Well. You should probably tell him that."

"Tell him what? It's not like that for either of us."

"Evie." Caro shakes her head and it's so infuriating, the thought that Caro knows Theo better than she does. The reality that she might. "Theo will waste his entire life waiting for you if you let him."

"It's not like that," Evie repeats, but her voice is softer now, less sure.

"He adds mushrooms to his eggs now."

"What?"

"Topher's allergic."

Caro leaves it at that, slamming the passenger door shut without saying goodbye. Evie puts the car in reverse and gets out of the studio parking lot before she chokes on her tears, on Caro's words. *Theo will waste his entire life waiting for you if you let him.* Evie told him to go to New York. Pushed him to stay. *I will hate you if you don't stay.* Now she wonders if she only pushed because she knew that he would come back. Or thought. Because she's his best friend. Because he loves her, too.

Too.

Does he?

Did he?

Does it even matter?

Summers were supposed to still be theirs, but Theo didn't come home.

Not for dance.

Not for her.

I will hate you if you don't stay.

Evie pulls into a street spot in front of the bungalow. Puts the car in park and manages to throw the door open just in time to hurl onto the street. Then she presses his name on her phone and it rings and rings and rings, and it's for the best that it goes to voicemail. What would she even say? *I'm obsessed with you, too. I think it was some fucked-up test. Insisting that you should stay. I didn't want . . . I fucked up.* No. She hangs up. Cuts the line.

Evie pushed Theo away.

Theo stayed away.

Is it not for the best that she pushed before he left?

28

"Hey, Theodore."

Theo is reading Kaia's final book report on the Heroes of Olympus (the entire five-book series, because how could Kaia possibly choose just one?) when Evelyn returns to the apartment after she didn't come home and he had a not-so-mild panic attack *because* she didn't come home. He acknowledges her presence in the apartment but keeps his eyes on the book report, unable to focus on the words but too mortified to look at her. Evelyn's overnight bag lands on linoleum with a thud a moment before she slides into the seat across from him.

"I'm sorry." She nudges his foot with her toes. "I didn't mean to scare you."

"I know."

"I hate Solvang."

"I know."

"*Theo.*"

It's the pain in Evelyn's voice, her inability to exhale the second syllable that sends his eyes upward. She's bone-tired.

Puffy eyes. So beautiful. *Home.* His heart slams against his chest cavity. When she didn't come back to the apartment last night, didn't come home for *Survivor*, didn't answer his first *five calls* he . . . well. He freaked out. One more unanswered call and he would've driven to every emergency room within a thirty-mile radius until he found her. *I didn't mean to scare you.* It's not Evleyn's fault that everything about her *terrifies* him.

Loving her.

Losing her.

She breaks eye contact first, standing to pull two pints from Afters out of the freezer. Scoops the ice cream into ceramic bowls thrown by Imogen. Ube brownie for him. Dairy-free mint chip for her. Theo watches the flex of her biceps as she scoops and swallows the emotion lodged in his throat as she sets the bowls in front of them, then slides back into her seat. They eat their ice cream in silence. Evelyn always takes a too-big scoop. Always licks it on the spoon like an ice cream cone and Theo is transfixed by her tongue. Wants it on his skin. In his mouth.

Wants her.

After Afters, she nudges his foot with her toes once more. "Can we talk?"

"Maybe I still need a beat."

The metal spoon clatters against ceramic. "Okay. That's fair."

Theo is just as surprised by his response.

By his anger, and his ability to say no to her.

Evelyn stands and sets their dirty bowls into the sink. "Well. I'll let you get back to it."

He nods. It's supposed to feel good—setting a boundary, turning those words back on her, being a person with a semblance of dignity. But Theo just feels like shit. He drags a hand through his curls and is on his feet the moment he hears the soft *click* of Evelyn's bedroom door closing behind her. It swings open, that door, before Theo can even knock, and Evelyn crashes into him.

Their chests rise and fall in tandem.

Theo's brain screams, *Go, leave, push.*

His heart whispers, *This is home, stay, pull.*

In the end, his impulsive lips just crash into hers. Evelyn sighs into his mouth, weaving her fingers into his hair and rocking her hips against his. *I love you.* He cups her cheeks, his thumbs brushing away her tears. *I love you.* Kisses her hello, goodbye, everything in between. *I love you.* Evelyn's hands leave his hair as she backs him against the wall. He tastes her tears as her fingers trails past his chest, down his torso, toward his zipper—

"Ev."

Theo pulls away.

Fuck.

What are they *doing?*

Her eyes widen. "Sorry! I . . ." Her lower lip wobbles. She bites down. Steadies it. "I fucked up."

"Ev—"

"I fucked up," she repeats. "Again. Naomi—"

"You're not Naomi," Theo interrupts, cheeks hot with shame. "That was a messed-up thing to say."

"You didn't drop me. *That* was a messed-up thing to say."

"It's the truth."

"*No.*" Evelyn shakes her head. "I've never told you just how out of it I was that day. I was in so much pain and I performed anyway, because so many doctors convinced me that I was healthy, that the pain was all in my head. You didn't drop me,

I *fell*. I fell because of what I now know was a *massive* flare-up of my then-undiagnosed autoimmune disease."

"Evelyn."

"I don't blame you."

"*I* blame me."

Theo's bones remember that day.

Her fall.

Being two beats behind.

"Listen." Evelyn presses her palms into his cheeks, forcing his eyes to meet hers. "I meant what I said to Jacob. You have never let me fall. Well . . ." Her nose scrunches. "*Dance* Theo never has. *Pickleball* Theo on the other hand . . ."

"Whoa! *You* slammed into *me*."

"Debatable," she teases. "Regardless? I have never blamed you. Okay?"

Evelyn holds his gaze and her expression is so fierce, so *serious*.

Theo is still unsure how to forgive himself for being two beats behind.

But he can believe her.

"Okay."

"I think—" She exhales a shaky laugh, then lets go of him and stretches the sleeves of her sweatshirt to cover her hands before pressing them to her cheeks, allowing fabric to absorb her tears. "I freaked out and I knew it would hurt. Blaming you. I think Naomi fucked me up."

"*Ev*—"

"Jules clocked me weeks ago. I *do* shove you out the door. Then I get pissed when you listen and stay away. It's not okay. I'm so sorry. You scare me, Theodore. I want impossible things with you. Forever kind of things. But my definition of forever doesn't match yours and I don't know what to do with that because—"

His mouth meets hers, cuts off this declaration like a coward. *I want impossible things with you.* Evelyn is still holding tight to marriage being this deal-breaker, but Theo doesn't give a fuck about what he thought he wanted when he was a child. He grew up. He should tell her this. Instead, he memorizes the shape of her mouth, its taste, this *feeling*, before he agrees with her, their definitions don't match, and it's going to hurt.

"It's not supposed to be this hard," she whispers against his mouth.

"It's not."

Loving Evelyn Bloom has always been as effortless, as necessary, as breathing.

But if he loses her?

If their story ends like Jacob and Lori's?

How will Theo breathe?

"I love you, too," she says. "Obviously."

Obviously.

That one word forms a fissure in his resolve. Evelyn reaches toward him, her thumbs brushing away his tears. Theo isn't sure when he started crying. *Fuck.* She removes his glasses. He resists his impulse to smash the heels of his hands to his eyes to stanch the emotion.

"I signed start paperwork."

"I know. You're going."

He nods. "And you're staying."

"For now."

Evelyn's eyes meet his, shimmering and hopeful, but Theo is so used to his best friend pushing, to her giving him an out, that he isn't sure what to do with this information. *For now.*

He won't allow his heart to latch on to it. Pasadena is home. Her future is here. It's better for him to go.

To let her stay.

Understanding flickers in Evelyn's eyes. Then she's in his arms, burrowing her face into his shoulder, and this hurts, too. Theo isn't sure how long they stand in stillness, holding each other.

"Pep is going to be furious," she says against his throat.

"Jacob, too."

She shakes her head. "Did everyone see it?"

"Obviously."

Evelyn's lips brush against his pulse. "For what it's worth, you were a fantastic husband."

"You weren't a terrible wife."

Her smirk is sad as Theo presses his lips to her forehead, protecting his heart and breaking it all at once.

29

Evie spends the next two weeks falling asleep alone and waking up next to Theo. Her restless heart wakes her in the middle of the night and thrums his name until she's on her feet. It doesn't settle, her heart, until she slips under the duvet and curls her body around his, the big spoon, just like she would when they were kids. *I love you, too. Obviously.* When sunlight filters in from his east-facing window and her eyelids flutter open, the first thing she registers is her hand in his. How even in their sleep, their fingers twine together. Usually, she slips her hand out of his, slips out of his bed before he wakes. This morning, she chooses to stay, to hold on for as long as possible.

Because in a few short hours, Theo will board a flight to New York.

And Evie is staying.

Why is she staying?

"Morning."

Theo's laugh was once her favorite sound in the world. Now? It's the sleepy rasp of his morning voice. Evie wants to bottle that sound, already so jealous of whoever gets to hear it next.

"Hey."

"I miss you."

Evie squeezes his hand, then lets go. "Do you need a ride to the airport?"

"I'll Uber."

"You sure?"

"*Ev.*" She feels the *ache* of that one syllable in her bones. "I need to actually get on the plane."

"I know." She sighs, then slips out of his bed. "I miss you, too."

It isn't until Evie gets out of bed and closes the door behind her that she realizes: tonight, even if her half-asleep feet carry her to Theo's bed, tomorrow she'll wake up alone. Next week, it will be Mindy Singh's room, Pranav's sister who just earned a Ph.D. in rocket science and works at the NASA Jet Propulsion Laboratory. Because of course Theo found a subletter, so Evie wouldn't have to stress over her living situation, at least in the short term. They've spent the days before the inevitable good-bye packing up the boxes that will meet him in Bushwick and unpacking two decades of missed opportunities, what-ifs, and unbearable angst. *Obviously.* Evie conceded while wrapping the framed photos of them that he asked to keep that it's easier to push than be left. Theo confessed while boxing up his kitchen gadgets that it was easier to go than to fall. *As if I even had a choice.* It's hard. Boxing up his life. Their life. But these feelings will fade.

Eventually, she'll have her best friend back.

Obviously.

Evie cries in the shower, then gets ready for work. Isn't sure how her tear ducts are still operational. Asks herself again why she is staying. Pep and Mo are gone. Imogen is leaving. What is still here? Work? Doctors? Her pulse thrashes in her throat. *Go. Go. Go.* One step at a time, her feet carry her to Theo's room. But it's empty. She didn't even hear the door close behind him and her heart twinges with understanding, imagining his quiet exit. *I need to actually get on the plane.*

He's gone.

Theo left.

She wipes her cheeks.

Then, because Evelyn Bloom is someone who stays, she pulls herself together and goes to work.

She's rummaging through a bin of shoes in search of boots with a block heel when Sadie says her name. Her assignment today is a step pass for *Mr. Knightley*, a miniseries based on *Emma* adapted by a team of men. Why? A perfect *Emma* adaptation already exists. A film that made Imogen, a lesbian, declare, *I think I'm a ho for Johnny Flynn now?* But alas, some network executives decided that this is what society needs right now. Jane Austen, from a male point of view.

"Sorry. One sec," Evie says, assuming they're behind schedule. "Have you seen the broken-in Clarks?"

"No. Ev—"

"Shit. I'm—"

"*Evelyn Bloom.*" Evie drops the shoes and spins around when Sadie Silverman full-names her like ... like a *parent.* "Can we talk for a second? In the mixing booth?"

Evie's eyebrow twitches. "Did I do something wrong?"

"No."

Without further commentary, Sadie pivots and walks toward the booth. Evie follows behind, a little bit flustered and a whole lot confused because her mentor doesn't just *pause* a session when they're on a schedule. Inside the booth, Charlie is waiting, holding a cake-size chocolate chip cookie, *It's a girl!* written in pink icing.

Sadie breaks. "*Charlie*. What the fuck?"

Charlie shrugs sheepishly. "It was the only vegan option left."

Evie still isn't sure what's happening, but the fact that Charlie Crosby has paid enough attention to her to know her dietary restrictions is enough to have her on the verge of tears. Sadie turns toward her, laughing so hard tears *do* stream down her cheeks. She takes a measured breath to compose herself, then says, "Your union application was approved, Evie. Congratulations!"

Charlie smiles at her. "Great work, kid."

"Oh."

Evie blinks, then bursts into tears. Because she's in the union thanks to supportive mentors who she only has because of her best friend, who applied to a fellowship on her behalf, *then married her* so she could accept it. Evie worked her ass off for this. Earned it. But Theo's belief in her got her into the room and it sucks that this moment isn't theirs to celebrate. Sadie's and Charlie's expressions morph from pride to tender concern when she wipes snot from her nose.

"What is happening?" Charlie asks.

Fuck.

She sniffles. "I'm sorry."

"Don't apologize." Sadie rubs her back. It's humiliating. "What's wrong? Is it the cake?"

"No." Evie hiccups, shaking her head. "Charlie, the cake is perfect. Thank you. This is so nice. Why are you being so nice to me?" She swipes at her swollen eyes. "I just . . . there's someone I want to call right now, so bad, and I can't and it's my fault."

"Ah."

"Breakups suck," Charlie says.

"It's . . . more of a divorce."

Sadie's inhale is so sharp, she sputters, "Divorce? But . . . you are a fetus?"

"I'm twenty-eight."

"A fetus!"

"It's not . . . I did it for you."

"Come again?"

Evie exhales. "So, um, this is a full-time fellowship. Obviously." She runs her fingers through her hair, nails scraping her skull. Continues, "In order to accept this opportunity, I had to quit my job. Which, oh my God, I was so happy to do! But the fellowship doesn't come with benefits. Like, health benefits. I'm sick. Crohn's? It's an inflammatory bowel disease and it's under control right now, with minor flares here and there. I'm rambling. Basically, I can't *not* have health insurance, so I married my best friend for his health insurance. So I could take the fellowship? Which . . . America! Still, it seemed like a good plan. Except, I fell in love with him. No. I've always been in love with him?"

Silence.

Sadie and Charlie look at each other. Then at Evie, who's mortified and positive that her mentors did not wake up this morning and think a cookie cake would induce a teary trauma dump. Sadie's eyebrows pinch together. "*What?*"

"I'm sorry, this is so unprofessional—"

"If you apologize *one more time*." She crosses the booth, reaching for latte à la Sadie on her desk. Pops the lid and rips a sugar packet in half. "Just so I understand. You got married for . . . a fellowship?"

"Yeah."

Charlie snorts. "No one can say that you're not dedicated to your craft, kid."

Sadie is not amused. "You. Out."

Charlie raises his arms in defense. "I'm gone."

Sadie sits and massages her temples, something that Evie's used to witnessing in the context of a tight deadline. Her eyes settle on the gray hairs that streak Sadie's temple. Are they becoming more prominent in real time? No. That's impossible. "First of all," she begins, "I'm sorry. I had no idea . . . I didn't think. But I'm furious that you were put in that position."

Evie shrugs. "This is an ableist industry."

"It's not an excuse." Sadie squeezes her eyes shut. "Fuck, my *head.*" Evie produces a bottle of Tylenol from the top drawer of her desk. Sadie pops two. "Thanks. Okay, help me understand. If you love the person who you're married to . . . what happened?"

She attempts to explain, but every excuse feels like just that. An excuse.

I don't want to be married.

I can't move to New York.

I want this more.

She instead opts for a factual approach. "He left. But it's not . . . I told him to go? Because his dream job is in New York and mine is here and—"

"*Evie.*" Charlie cuts her off and she has no clue when he reappeared but here he is, leaning against the doorframe, arms crossed. "You love him?"

"I do." She nods, then gestures at the studio, remembering some of the first words Sadie spoke to her once she saw Evie's passion. *If you want this, there isn't room for much else.* "But I love this, too."

Charlie presses his lips together, understanding etched in the wrinkle between his eyebrows. "Well. Speaking as someone who has a few years on you, this . . ." Charlie mimics her, gesturing toward the Foley stage. "It's just a job."

"And it doesn't love you back," Sadie adds, and Evie's eyes

shift to her mentor, whose expression can only be deciphered as *I think I fucked up.* "The work. I spent thirty years married to this career—putting my ambition, *the work*, first—and it's been wonderful and fulfilling and lonely. I believed there couldn't be room for much else, and it did get me to where I am now." Sadie's eyes shift to Charlie. "Lately, I wonder if the journey didn't have to be so lonely."

"I—" Evie blinks, so disarmed by Sadie's vulnerability. "I don't know what to do with this."

"What do you want to do?"

Sadie and Charlie leave her with this question because they have a schedule to adhere to and need to set up the stage for their afternoon session. Evie sits with their words, the gentlest of nudges. *What do you want to do?*

Her heart hammers in her chest.

Go.

Go.

Go.

She hesitates for only a moment before she's at her desk and hacking into Theo's airline accounts to find his flight info. (What? It's not her fault that Theo has had the same three passwords since high school.) She pulls up the flight on her phone. The only seat left on the plane is a middle seat next to *Theo's* seat and that must be a sign. She wants it to be a sign. Evie screenshots the seating chart and texts Imogen.

> i . . . think i'm about to book the last
> seat on theo's flight to ny??
> 10:42 A.M.

Imogen Bloom

!!!

10:42 A.M.

I AM SCREAMING

10:42 A.M.

THAT IS ROMANTIC AS FUCK

10:42 A.M.

FINALLY

10:42 A.M.

The next text is a photo of her sister Meredith Grey ugly-crying.

She laughs, then secures the ticket, exhilarated and terrified all at once. Sadie and Charlie pause on maneuvering a car door the moment she steps onto the stage and says, "I'm going to New York."

Charlie's eyes crinkle in the corners. "When?"

"In . . ." Evie glances at her watch. "Three hours?"

"Shit." Sadie snorts. "What have I *done?*"

"You've gone soft, Sadie." Charlie laughs. "Go on, kid. We'll call this a sick day."

"*Day,*" Sadie emphasizes, pressing her fingers to her temple. "Rest of the week, tops. Not *months.*"

"Oh my God, I'm coming back!" Evie insists. Charlie's eyebrows rise, like, *Sure.* But Evie isn't done learning from Sadie Silverman and Charlie Crosby. "Seriously! You're stuck with me for the rest of the fellowship. At least."

Sadie laughs, then wraps her arms around Evie in a hug.

Evie holds on.

She wants to hold on to the people who matter to her.

"We know people in New York, kid," Charlie says. "Just saying."

Sadie releases her first, shoving Evie out the door because

she has a bag to pack and a flight to catch and the next hour is hurried steps and tossed clothes and her erratic heartbeat. *I love you, too. Obviously.*

Obviously.

Obviously.

Evie settles into the back seat of her Uber in disbelief that she's going to New York. Of course she's going to New York. Evie listens to Billy Joel on her way to the airport as the ETA ticks up, up, up. Friday traffic. She arrives at the terminal twenty minutes before boarding closes and begs to cut the security line. Tears are fine. Her "I Can't Wait" card is even more effective. Thank *fuck* for that accommodation. She has time to use the bathroom, the combination of stress and physical exertion resulting in an emergency situation. Bodies. They're so fun. Evie arrives at her gate just as its final boarding call is uttered over the PA system.

She scans her ticket and enters the Jetway.

Whispers, "Goodbye for now."

It *is* for now. Evie will come home to finish her fellowship. But after? Will her heart still be tethered here or pulled to New York? Who knows? She supposes it depends how this airplane ambush goes. Either way, she doesn't want to waste another second pushing away the person she loves or denying that these last eight months pretending to be Theo Cohen's wife haven't changed everything. Evelyn Bloom is—has always been—someone who stays.

But for the first time in her life, she wants to know who she could be if she left.

30

Not even Billy Joel soothes Theo's flight anxiety as he attempts to settle in his aisle seat while boarding continues. It's impossible. His knee bounces, so restless. An elder in the window seat reading a Nora Roberts book offers him a cocktail of Xanax and melatonin. He politely declines, then puts headphones on, presses shuffle, and closes his eyes as the opening piano notes of "Vienna" play. The same piano notes that are tattooed across Evelyn's ribs. Theo skips the song. He couldn't even say goodbye to her. He chose to slip out of their apartment while she was in the shower like a coward because when he was close to her, everything in his body screamed *stay*.

But it was time to go.

To let go.

Letting go has been a process that began in the classroom. In his final weeks at Foothill Elementary, Theo thought about begging for his job back on a near-daily basis. He loves teaching. Loves how connected he feels to his mom in the classroom. Theo didn't consider what it'd feel like to lose that until it was almost gone. Instead of sitting with those feelings, he kept busy. Allowed his students to each choose a book from his library to keep and left the rest to be inherited by the teacher who takes over this space. Asked Juniper to take Maude, the guinea pig who will outlive them all. Consoled Kaia, who cried on the last day of school. Milo, too. And rallied to push his field trip proposal through. It took a few grant applications, a "generous donation" (i.e., a portion of his signing bonus), and some opinionated parents . . . but in the end, he got a fourth- and fifth-grade field trip to the Griffith Observatory on next year's calendar.

So eventually, his kids will see the stars.

Theo shifts in his seat, drumming his fingers against his thigh as the final boarding call is announced. It's a full flight. Allegedly. But the aisle is clear and the middle seat between him and the grandparent with a drugstore in their purse is still empty. A small victory. His phone vibrates with a text from Jacob.

Let me know when you land. Or if you get your head out of your ass and deplane. I can pick you up. Don't fucking waste $80 on an Uber.—Dad
2:02 P.M.

Texting. It's something that Theo and his father do now. Sporadically. Letting go of his anger toward Jacob is a work in progress, but he's trying. Both father and son are trying. Instead of sprinting past Jacob on his Sunday runs, Theo rings the doorbell and steps inside his childhood home. Sips on coffee and asks questions. Evelyn is right. Jacob will talk. Theo learns more about a man who internalized so much shame for the things that brought him joy, a man who let grief swallow him whole and would still choose it—his mom, the inevitable grief—over and over again. He's still unsure that Jacob Cohen will ever fully understand him, but Theo can try to better understand his father who is still here, while he is still here.

He's typing a response when "1985" starts playing in his ears.

Ooh hoo hoo!

And suddenly, Theo cannot breathe. *Because of a Bowling for Soup song.* ___ DAYS SINCE "1985." He left the sign in his classroom that's no longer his classroom because Evelyn told him to go, and it used to be easier to listen, to let her push, to tell himself it's better this way. Is it better this way? *I love you, too. Obviously.* The woman he's in love with loves him, too, and he's on a plane that is about to fly three thousand miles away from her because . . . he's scared of losing her?

Is this not losing her?

His library is on shuffle.

So when the next song is "Seven Nation Army," Theo is on his feet. Most days, he isn't sure what he believes about life, about love, about the point of their temporary time on this fucked-up planet. But every so often, he swears Lori sends him a sign. And right now? His mom is screaming at him.

Go.

Go.

Go.

Theo needs to get off this plane.

Right now.

He reaches for his carry-on in the overhead bin, then speed walks down the aisle, cursing under his breath because why did he choose a seat in the back of the plane? *Who chooses the back?* He has to get out of this metal tin before they close the door. He can't leave without saying goodbye. He can't leave without—

Fuck.

Theo's so focused on the LED EXIT sign that he doesn't register the body approaching until he crashes into it.

"Theodore?"

"Ev?"

He blinks.

Presses his two index fingers to his pulse because there's a fifty percent chance that he's having a stroke. There's no way she's here, dressed in leggings and his NYU sweatshirt that he swore he packed and yet she's wearing it. Her hair is in a messy bun. Sweat coats her upper lip. She's so beautiful. Evelyn reaches out to him, covers his heart with her hand until he can breathe again.

He hears the smile in her voice when she asks, "Where are you going?"

"I—" Theo exhales, still at a loss. "To you."

You.

You.

You.

Evelyn beams at him before standing on her tiptoes and pressing her lips to his and he still isn't quite sure what is happening. If this is a fever dream or if he's dead or—

Someone clears their throat. "Sir? Ma'am?" They break apart to make eye contact with a flustered flight attendant. "We're preparing for takeoff. You, um, really need to take a seat. And keep it PG."

Evelyn's cheeks heat. "Sorry."

Theo laughs. "Where are you?"

She smiles. "42B."

The empty seat next to his.

Evelyn follows him to the back of the plane, and his heart settles because *she is here*. Theo stores her bag in the overhead compartment and slides into the middle seat just as the cabin crew begins their safety spiel. Evelyn gets some major side-eye from their window seat companion, who scolds her for, quote, *almost giving this sweet boy a heart attack!*, then offers them both an edible. The plane smells like sour cream and on-ion chips. The child sitting behind Theo kicks him relentlessly after their parents tell them the iPad needs to go away until after takeoff.

"This was more cinematic in my head," Evelyn confesses.

Theo's still in disbelief. "You're here."

"You almost *weren't*." She shoves his shoulder, then twines their fingers together. They're freezing. Her fingers. Evelyn smirks. "God. That would've been . . . so *us*."

His laughter cannot be contained. Neither can his stu-pid smile. Now in motion, the aircraft heads toward the runway, toward the sky, toward New York. Theo has so many questions. Evelyn Bloom is someone who stays, but she is here, next to him, clutching his hand and there's so much he wants to say. He doesn't know whether to begin with his head or his heart.

Then she rests her head on his shoulder and whispers, "Hey."

And Theo chooses his heart. "I love you."

"I love you, too." Evelyn laughs. "Obviously."

Obviously.

"You're *here*," he repeats.

She lifts her head.

Their eyes meet.

Hers sparkle in amusement. "Yeah."

"What does this mean?"

"Hmm?"

"Sorry." He winces, unsure if the question came off as guarded, or like pressure, when really he just needs to know if he should pull a parachute on these feelings or if it's safe to free-fall. "I just . . . your fellowship . . ." Theo is great at forming a coherent sentence right now.

"Well." She squeezes his hand. "There are three months left. I'm going to finish it. I'm not done learning from Sadie and Charlie. I still love the work we do. But after . . . I was thinking it could be cool to check out the Foley scene in New York? Maybe set up some consultations with new providers? See how it feels to be there? With you? If . . . that's still something you'd be into?"

His heart explodes as his brow furrows. "I don't want you to leave for me—"

"I'm not."

"Ev."

"It'd be for *me*."

"But—"

"Theodore." Her voice is firm. Solid. "Stop. I love you. I love waking up next to you. I love your morning voice. I love that you treat *blueberry Cheerios* like a five-star breakfast. I love choosing photos to display in our home . . ." Her voice trails off in a giggle, followed by a goddamn adorable nose scrunch. "I love saying *our home*."

Theo is free-falling.

"I never wanted to be married to anyone," Evelyn continues. "Ever. Honestly? I still don't know if I want to stay married. But I want to be with you. Whatever that means, however that looks? I want to figure it out together. I've always stayed because it was safe, because then I could tell myself that it was everyone else who had left me . . . as if I wasn't also making a choice. I'm trying out New York for us, but also for myself. And whatever happens? It's worth the risk. We are worth the risk."

"Yeah?"

She nods. "No more beats."

Theo brings her hand to his lips. "I'm very into all of this. Obviously."

"Obviously."

Because they're on an airplane (the best worst thing ever in this moment), Evelyn rests her head back on his shoulder. He offers her an earbud, and they listen to a *Survivor* podcast as the wheels lift and they ascend into the sky. Someday it will hurt. Theo knows this in his bones. All the time in the world still won't be enough. But he can choose happiness in the meantime. They *deserve* happiness. Theo doesn't want to waste another second not loving Evelyn Bloom. He's about to say this, to match her declaration with his own, but she's already snoring, drooling, on his shoulder. *I love you.*

You.

You.

You.

He chuckles softly. He'll just have to tell her when she wakes up, as soon as they land, on the subway, before they fall asleep tonight, the moment they wake up tomorrow morning. Again and again and again. Now, as they take flight and careen into the unknown with their hands and hearts intertwined, Theo just presses his lips gently against the top of her head, so happy, so terrified, so *content* to allow both things to be true.

ONE YEAR LATER

Evie

"You'll never believe what we heard on our walk." Evie enters their apartment like a hurricane, a leash wrapped around her wrist. Rupert, a nine-year-old mutt with cavalier ears and the squishiest, most perfect face, dashes over to Theo the moment Evie frees him, in the hope of scoring some kitchen scraps. "A *cerulean warbler*."

"Oh?"

"It was majestic, Theodore." She inhales the scent of home-made tomato sauce. "God, that smells incredible."

"Lasagna is in the oven." Theo brushes his lips *hello* against hers. "What's a cerulean warbler sound like?"

She smiles. "I'm so glad you asked."

Evie plays him the sound and is still somewhat in disbe-lief that she moved all the way to New York City and became *a bird person*. It's less about the birds and more about their songs. More about the fact that a cerulean warbler is part of the soundscape of the city, a layer that she never could've un-covered if she didn't live here. How inspiration is everywhere. Evie collects new sounds every time she steps outside. Mimics a random person's gait every time she walks her dog. Becomes a better Foley artist.

"What did you think, Roo?" Theo squats to greet him with plain pasta he set aside. "Was it majestic?"

Evie rolls her eyes. "Pretty sure Rupert's definition of *majestic* is Penelope's butthole."

Penelope is the miniature schnauzer who lives next door.

"Evelyn! So judgmental." Theo's laughter fills their five-hundred-square-foot apartment as he stands and washes his hands. "This is why I'm the favorite."

"Right. It has nothing at all to do with the pasta."

"Nope."

Evie kisses the smirk right off his face. Rupert (who will also respond to Roo, Dude, and Short King) made eye contact with Theo when they came across a fostering booth at the Union Square farmers market. Then he just trotted over to Evie and Theo like he belonged to them. It was love at first sight. *We're taking him home, Theodore.* She swore it would be a foster situation, to test out how it felt to have a dog. *Temporary.* After a month, they signed the adoption papers, and just like that, oops, they had a dog!

Rupert zoomies around the apartment before collapsing onto the pile of blankets that he prefers to his bed.

It melts her heart.

Evie washes her hands in the bathroom sink, then unzips and shrugs off her track jacket. She reenters their living space in just a sports bra and leggings and their apartment doesn't just *smell* incredible. The table is set with the ceramic dishware. A bottle of red wine is uncorked. Fancy bread is on the table. In a *basket.*

"What—?"

"Happy anniversary, Ev."

"We said we weren't doing anything!"

"It's just lasagna."

"How much did that bread cost?"

"Don't ask."

"Theodore."

"Sit."

"Bossy," she teases.

Theo tosses a towel over his shoulder. It's so sexy. She's so hungry, so she sits without any additional fuss. It's been exactly one year since her husband became her boyfriend. One year since she boarded a plane to New York and chose herself. A year later, nine months after she completed her fellowship and moved in with Theo, they are still married, technically, in the legal sense. Evie's in a union . . . but she doesn't make enough income as a Foley artist to qualify for the health benefits. Yet. It's a cute excuse to not sign the papers. In their day-to-day New York life? They're dating. When she introduces him to her New York friends, he's her boyfriend. For a whole calendar year, Theo Cohen has been her boyfriend. And her boyfriend was always going to splurge on the bougie bread today. She knew that. They recap their days while they eat. Evie loves the soundscape of this city, but it's these quiet nights at home that are her favorite. After dinner, she changes into cotton shorts and one of his sweatshirts, then settles onto their couch to choose a movie—as if they are going to actually *watch a movie*—and Evie could be content to end every day like this for the rest of her life.

She wants every day to end like this.

With him.

For the rest of her life. That is why Evie tore their home apart after he left for work this morning, in search of two gold bands that she's now clutching on to for dear life, hidden in the pocket of her sweatshirt. His sweatshirt. Theo was always going to splurge on the bougie bread today, and she was always planning to upstage the bougie bread.

"So." Kitchen cleaned to his satisfaction, Theo settles onto the couch next to her. "What're we watching?"

"Oh." She shrugs, then climbs onto Theo's lap and kisses her way from his jaw to his earlobe. "Was I supposed to pick a movie? My bad." Her lips meet his and he sighs into her mouth and it feels so good, so *safe*. Had she known that this is love, that it's supposed to feel safe? Evie might've let herself fall so much sooner. As her fingers weave their way into his hair, she pulls back so their foreheads touch. "Hey."

"Hi."

"I love you."

"I love you, too."

"I love being your girlfriend."

His palms press against her thighs, fingers skimming the hem of her shorts. "Yeah?"

She nods. "But . . . I think I miss being your wife?"

Theo groans. "*Ev.* Is this a roleplay thing? Because—"

"I'm serious!" Her laughter bounces off the walls as she drops one hand to her pocket to reach for their rings and she's sort of in disbelief that something once so terrifying now just feels right. "I know we're still . . . that we never signed the papers to change, um, the legal status of us." Evie's doing great. This so romantic. "We're married. I guess what I mean is . . . I want to *be* married."

Theo cocks his head, his expression so intense. "I'm not going anywhere, Ev."

"I know." She presses her palm against his chest, like she has so many times before and will do so many times again.

Evie doesn't want their marriage to be real because she's scared of losing him. She simply wants it. Marriage. What once terrified her now just feels safe and steady and right—because *Theo* feels safe and steady and right. And really, hasn't it always been real? "I *know*. Okay? You're it for me. And boyfriend is cute, but husband? Hot."

"So it *is* a sex thing."

She smacks his shoulder. "Can you just answer the question?"

"Did you ask me a question?"

"Oh my God, Theodore. I want to be your wife. Do you want that, too?"

"Do I want that, too?" Theo looks at her in stunned disbelief for one more moment before breaking out in the goofiest grin as he takes the rings from her palm. It's the exact smile he flashed her as children when she called him Theodore for the first time, as teens when Miss Stella declared them dance partners, as one year ago today when she boarded a plane and reenacted the most cliché rom-com ending for them. Then her best friend, her favorite person, slides Lori's wedding band onto Evie's finger like it's back where it belongs now, always, forever, before his lips crash into hers and he whispers his answer—just one word, their word—into her mouth.

"Obviously."

Acknowledgments

Romance is a soft place to land for so many, and I am so honored to be launching into this genre with *Friends with Benefits*. With this story, my aim was to infuse all the angst and tenderness I love about romance into a tale of two twenty-somethings navigating an economy and healthcare system that make it so hard to be a financially secure person. If those themes resonate with you, I am angry for you. We deserve better. Evie and Theo's journey toward accepting the love that they deserve was such a joy to write and there are so many people I want to thank who had a hand in bringing this book into the world.

To my agent, Taylor Haggerty. You've championed this story since the moment I tacked it onto the end of an unrelated email as a one-line pitch. Your endless enthusiasm while I navigate this new career era has made the transition so effortless. I am forever thankful to have found a true partner in you. Jasmine Brown, thank you so much for all you do behind the scenes, including but not limited to listening to all my *Vanderpump Rules* takes. And to the entire Root Literary family, thank you for empowering authors and being absolute rock stars.

To my editor, Randi Kramer: I had such a blast working with you to make Evie and Theo's story sparkle. You immediately got them (and got *me*) and under your brilliant editorial eye, *Friends with Benefits* truly became the story I set out to tell. There aren't adequate words to thank you, so I will simply say, *thank you*.

To the entire team at Celadon Books, it's been a dream working with you. To Ryan Doherty and Faith Tomlin, thank you for the guidance and enthusiastic support every step of the way. To Deb Futter, Rachel Chou, Emily Walters, Elizabeth Hubbard, Morgan Mitchell, Vincent Stanley, and Michelle McMillian—thank you for all you do behind the scenes to turn a Word document into a tangible, beautiful book. To Cassie Gutman, copy editor extraordinaire who got all my *Survivor* references. To Kimberly Glyder and Chloé Dorgan for designing and illustrating, respectively, a cover that dreams are made of. To my marketing and publicity team, Jaime Noven, Liza Buell, Gregg Fleischman, Rebecca Ritchey, Emma Paige West, Isabella Narvaez, and Emily Radell, thank you for ensuring *Friends with Benefits* finds its perfect readers. It takes a village, and I'm so grateful to be working with some of the best in the business.

To the sales reps who work tirelessly to get our stories onto shelves.

To every bookseller, librarian, and reviewer who takes our stories from the shelves and places them into the hands of readers.

To Katie Waters, for indulging my fascination with and all my questions about Foley. Thank you so much for responding when I slid into your DMs—this book is so much better because of the fun tidbits and answers you provided about your art.

To Kelsey Rodkey, Rachel Lynn Solomon, Auriane Desombre, and Carlyn Greenwald for their unwavering friendship through the highs and lows that come along with publishing. I am forever in awe of you all and still cannot believe that my closest friends are also my favorite authors. How lucky am I?

To Jodi LaFountain, for being central in all the best memories I have about dance. I so wish you were here to see this and that I could've sent you a copy.

To *my* Grandma Peppy, who was the coolest person I knew and whose memory is embedded in everything I do.

To the doctors who didn't dismiss my pain.

To Noah, for always showing up.

To Vanessa, for being the best sister and my favorite person. I'm so proud of all that you've done and continue to do.

To Mom and Dad, for your unconditional love and support.

To Sam, for the health insurance (and a million big and little things that make doing life with you my favorite thing in the world). I love you.

About the Author

Marisa Kanter is the author of modern love stories for both teens and adults. Born and raised in the suburbs of Boston, Marisa followed her obsession with books to New York City, where she worked in publishing for a number of years. She currently lives in Los Angeles with her husband, where she writes by day and crochets her wardrobe by night. *Friends with Benefits* is her debut adult novel.

CELADON
BOOKS

Founded in 2017, Celadon Books, a division of
Macmillan Publishers, publishes a highly curated list
of twenty to twenty-five new titles a year. The list of
both fiction and nonfiction is eclectic and focuses
on publishing commercial and literary books and
discovering and nurturing talent.